"I'd better stand or else I'll end up on your lap."

———— ❧ ————

"I wouldn't mind, love," Nicholas crooned, patting the tops of his thighs and earning a perturbed glare.

Even so, Briar was too intent on her goal and stood, settling her cool, delicate hands on his face. The simple touch of her fingertips, soft and uncertain, stirred a low flame of arousal.

"I thought your rule was 'no hands.'"

"Hush. I am immersing myself in the full experience," she whispered as if afraid of breaking the spell. "Besides, it was my rule for you, not for me. Now close your eyes, if you please."

He complied, half humoring her and half curious to see if she would balk and shy away. Yet she lingered, her warm, clean fragrance filling his nostrils and making him think of fresh bed linens, sun-kissed and wind-beaten into a decadent suppleness. He wanted to lie down with that scent, tumble with it, bury himself inside of it. And all this was before he felt the sweet rush of her breath over his lips.

By Vivienne Lorret

The Misadventures in Matchmaking Series
HOW TO FORGET A DUKE
TEN KISSES TO SCANDAL

The Season's Original Series
"The Duke's Christmas Wish"
(in ALL I WANT FOR CHRISTMAS IS A DUKE and
A CHRISTMAS TO REMEMBER)
THE DEBUTANTE IS MINE
THIS EARL IS ON FIRE
WHEN A MARQUESS LOVES A WOMAN
JUST ANOTHER VISCOUNT IN LOVE (novella)

The Rakes of Fallow Hall Series
THE ELUSIVE LORD EVERHART
THE DEVILISH MR. DANVERS
THE MADDENING LORD MONTWOOD

The Wallflower Wedding Series
TEMPTING MR. WEATHERSTONE (novella)
DARING MISS DANVERS
WINNING MISS WAKEFIELD
FINDING MISS MCFARLAND

Ten Kisses to Scandal

Misadventures in Matchmaking

VIVIENNE LORRET

AVONBOOKS

An Imprint of HarperCollinsPublishers

Rom

This is a work of fiction. Names, characters, places, and incidents are products of the author's imagination or are used fictitiously and are not to be construed as real. Any resemblance to actual events, locales, organizations, or persons, living or dead, is entirely coincidental.

TEN KISSES TO SCANDAL. Copyright © 2019 by Vivienne Lorret. All rights reserved. Printed in the United States of America. No part of this book may be used or reproduced in any manner whatsoever without written permission except in the case of brief quotations embodied in critical articles and reviews. For information, address HarperCollins Publishers, 195 Broadway, New York, NY 10007.

First Avon Books mass market printing: January 2019

Print Edition ISBN: 978-0-06-268550-6
Digital Edition ISBN: 978-0-06-268551-3

Cover illustration by Jon Paul Ferrara
Design by Amy Halperin

Avon, Avon & logo, and Avon Books & logo are registered trademarks of HarperCollins Publishers in the United States of America and other countries.

HarperCollins is a registered trademark of HarperCollins Publishers in the United States of America and other countries.

FIRST EDITION

19 20 21 22 23   QGM   10 9 8 7 6 5 4 3 2 1

For my sisters
We have a special bond, forged by more than blood but by our history. We even have our own lexicon of knowing looks, certain laughs, and single words that can tell an entire story. We've misunderstood and plagued each other, but we've also found solace in shared tears, memories, and long talks. And in every moment, there has always been love.

Acknowledgments

This book would not have been possible without the support of some truly wonderful people.

Thank you to the readers, for giving my books a chance and for inviting the characters to spend time with you. I feel blessed and honored to have found a place in your e-readers and on your shelves.

Thank you to my editor, Nicole, for all your hard work and especially for adding smiley faces and "lol"s in the margins just when I need them most. And to my agent, Stefanie, for being my sounding board and support team whenever the need arises.

And thank you to Lisa Filipe for your insight, words of wisdom, and eternal love for Jack Marlowe.

Ten Kisses
to Scandal

Chapter 1

"There could be no harm in a scheme, a mere passive scheme. It was no more than a wish."

JANE AUSTEN, *Emma*

Autumn, 1825

Today was the day.

Briar Bourne knew it the instant her feet slipped into the cool confines of her lucky ivory slippers and a zing of breathless exhilaration scurried through her.

In a matter of an hour, she would have single-handedly launched the family business into greatness. The *ton* would soon be buzzing with excitement, beating a parasol-armed path to the doors of the Bourne Matrimonial Agency. And all because Briar was about to secure the most elusive bachelor in London as their premier client.

But first, she needed to look like a capable and confident woman of the world, and not a debutante sneaking out of her family's rented townhouse.

One could never underestimate the power of the proper attire. The right garments could alter the course of one's life, turn a beggar into a shop clerk, a servant into the lady of the house, or—in Briar's case—an underestimated youngest sister into a genuine matchmaker.

Since the agency opened two weeks ago, Uncle Ernest,

Ainsley, and Jacinda were the only ones with the important occupations. They interviewed the applicants, discovered their interests and beliefs, their hopes and dreams of happily-ever-after.

Briar's tasks, on the other hand, were essentially useless. She served tea and filed papers like any trained monkey. She didn't even have her own office. At least, not yet.

That was the reason for her predawn errand. She was determined to prove that she could sling Cupid's arrow as well as anyone else. Perhaps even better.

After all, Uncle Ernest spent his time wooing nearly every woman he interviewed. Because of him, they had to establish a rule at the agency—*never fall in love with the client.*

As for Ainsley, she was far too pragmatic. All of her facts about the clients were on paper, comparing one list to another. She was blind to the soulful yearning in the eyes of the few people who'd dared to cross their threshold.

And Jacinda was far too skeptical. She investigated every client to ensure they were telling the truth, and not hiding dark secrets that could potentially destroy a marriage and family. But not everyone was like their father.

The problem with her family was that they were so caught up in their own agendas they didn't realize that a vital component was missing from the agency— *excitement.*

Wasn't falling in love supposed to be the most thrilling of all experiences in one's life? It should be celebrated with wine, showered with rose petals, and glorified with cascades on harp strings.

Briar flung herself back onto the bed with a sigh, arms wide, imagining it. She would be the best matchmaker in all of London—no, all of *England*. Perhaps even the world!

"They simply cannot understand how difficult it is to have such a wild, romantic heart beneath my breast without any opportunity to unleash it," Briar said to the book propped up on the pillow beside her.

The red leather tome of *Emma*—the second volume of three—had been a gift from Mother before her untimely death ten years ago. Mother had adored the story of Miss Emma Woodhouse and her matchmaking endeavors, often wishing that she'd had someone so clever to look out for her. Instead, she'd suffered years of betrayal.

In the end, the heartbreak and agony had been too much to bear. And because of that, the Bourne family set out to make the right sort of matches for people based on love, trust, and respect, and to keep others from suffering her fate.

"I am determined to do my part as well," Briar said, pressing a kiss to the cover before she stood and fastened a fawn cloak over her shoulders. At the door, she looked back once more and grinned. "Wish me luck."

In the ashen light of early morning, she quietly wended down the marble stairs, the soles of her slippers issuing the softest of whispers. Then, crossing the foyer, she stole outside into the thick autumn air, careful to leave the door on the latch. By the time she rushed down the whitewashed steps and onto the pavement, she was vibrating with excitement.

She'd swallowed ten thousand stars, whole, and they were shimmering inside her. Never mind the frothy layer of fog hovering inches above their street in St. James's. She was a light. A force. Nothing could stop her.

The disembodied *clip clop* of horse hooves and the telltale crunch of stone beneath iron wheels told her that there were, indeed, a few carriages about at this early hour. She only hoped one of them was a hackney cab.

Though, in truth, she'd never hailed one before. They'd

arrived in London only a few weeks ago, and before that she'd spent her life in a small Hampshire village. She was twenty years old but had yet to experience much of life's delights. Mostly because her sisters were under the delusion that they had to protect her from the rest of the world. They claimed she was too romantic, too purehearted—as if those were *inferior* characteristics.

Briar scoffed. She would show them.

And honestly, how difficult could it be to hire a cab?

In the next few moments, however, she realized it wasn't as simple as she'd thought. With the fog as thick as cotton batting, she was more likely to hail a foul-smelling, offal-brimmed scavenger cart by mistake. Of the two carriages that had passed by, neither had been for hire, but were owned by those who preferred to keep the shades drawn.

Briar had overheard whispers about those kinds of people, the ones intent on gambling and carousing until dawn. She wasn't entirely certain what manner of activity was involved in *carousing* but, since the word was always spoken in low behind-the-fan susurrations, she was sure it was decidedly scandalous.

The very thought caused a frisson of wanton fascination to skitter through her. Whatever it was, she wanted to experience it at least once in her life. After all, in order to become a successful matchmaker, she needed a full understanding of . . . well, *everything*.

Hearing the deafening jangle of rigging and a shouted *gee—o* echo off the surrounding stone façades, Briar knew this was her chance. And suddenly, a pair of grizzled horses broke through the fog, their heads bent low as they hurried around the corner. Lifting her arm in a quick gesture, she hailed the blue-coated hackney driver.

This was happening just as she had planned! Soon,

she thought with a grin, *she* would be the one the *ton* hired to help the Fates along.

Yet, as she waited, she watched in puzzlement as the driver came to an abrupt halt across the street in front of Sterling's, an elite gaming hell.

She lowered her arm. Strange, but she'd watched others make the same gesture and it usually brought the driver directly to them. Hmm . . . she wondered if there was a trick to it. A flick of the wrist. A waggle of fingers, perhaps.

Whatever it was, she was determined to learn it. Once this morning's venture was successful, surely she would need to perform many errands for the agency. *Briar Bourne—matchmaker of the* ton's *elite*.

With very little traffic to impede her progress, and not a single other hackney cab in sight, she lifted her skirts to rush across the cobblestones. Yet, spying the rank foulness in the gutter, she realized that her lucky slippers weren't designed for haste. And since the last thing she would ever do was meet a future client in soiled attire, she slowed her progress.

"My good sir," she called out, but the jarvey did not answer. His head was turned in the opposite direction, his attention caught by something toward the pavement on the other side. Repeating herself, she added a forceful push of authority to her usual breathy voice.

"Aw shove off, why don't—" He stopped the instant he saw her, jaw slackening. Quickly doffing his weathered hat, he pressed it against the center of his chest and blinked. Brows arching high, a slow smile revealed a few stained, narrow teeth between the gaps. "Beg pardon, miss, sometimes I think without speakin'."

Briar believed he meant to say it the other way around. But by the age of sixteen she'd learned that drawing attention to such a slip tended to tongue-tie a man even more, so she did not mention it. Though, realizing that her hood had dipped to her shoulders, she lifted it over her pale blond hair as she continued. It would do her no favors for someone to see her without a chaperone. "I should like to hire your cab, if you please."

"Blast me, but the gent already tossed up his coin," he said with obvious regret and a jerk of his head to the other side of the carriage.

Oh. Apparently, one had to be quick with the coin to hail a hackney. She would remember that for the future. As for now, however, she fully intended to see if the "gent" might be willing to relinquish his claim over this one.

Wasn't that precisely what a resolute matchmaker would do in this situation?

Offering a nod to the driver, she walked around the carriage toward the footpath, minding the hazards of horse dung. The copious quantity was likely due to the near constant flow of eventide traffic that stopped in front of the gaming hell.

Even now at this early hour, another carriage—a fine, glossy black with gilded coronets on the corners and wheels trimmed in red—lined up behind this one. A wealthy patron, to be sure. If only the Bourne Matrimonial Agency had such problems.

Soon, she thought.

Stepping onto the pavement, she was ready to address the gent. But Briar stumbled to a halt instead. Now, she understood why the hackney driver was stalled in this spot.

His fare was otherwise engaged. Or more to the point, he was in the throes of . . . of kissing.

At least, she presumed it was kissing. Though, to her, it appeared as if the raven-haired man was slowly devouring the plump brunette in his arms with open-mouthed bites of her lips, feeding on the sounds of her moans. His hands—and rather large, ungloved hands, at that—molded over the woman's curves as if he were mapping every inch of her terrain. But a cartographer, he was not.

Since they were in front of the gaming hell—where Briar had overheard mention of private rooms for their clientele—she believed he was another type of man altogether. *A rake*.

Cheeks scorching, she turned away, her breath coming up short. She closed her eyes to . . . to *what*? To allow the couple privacy? To pretend she hadn't seen their passionate interlude? She wasn't sure. The truth was, she could still see those hands in her mind, long-fingered and dusted with dark hair near the wrists, and she couldn't help but wonder what they were doing now.

All she had to do was look, of course. It wasn't as if her sisters were there to clap a hand over her eyes as they had done countless times before. But wait . . . By turning away, Briar had just done the same *dratted* thing to herself!

Irritated by her own unconscious act, she faced the pair of lovers again.

But that was a mistake. Her presence had not gone unnoticed. The man was now watching Briar, and *while* he was still feasting on the woman.

Briar should look away this time, surely. Shouldn't she? It was rude to stare, after all. It should not matter that his eyes were captivatingly dark, his irises the color of polished ebony wood, rich, exotic, and filled with a lifetime of experiences she could not even fathom.

Still, she should definitely look away. And she would, most assuredly. As soon as *he* stopped looking at her.

The fringe of his black lashes lowered as his gaze roamed the length of her, following the parted fabric of her cloak to the azure blue sash tied beneath her breasts and down the pleats of cream-colored muslin. A rush of heat traveled through her, taking the same path with the flickering burn of a candleflame.

Once he reached the tips of her slippers peeking out from beneath her ruffled hem, she expelled a tight breath, feeling as though she'd endured a trial by fire.

But he wasn't finished.

His gaze reversed direction. Unhurried and thorough, he gave a sense that he could see through her skirts well enough to trace the scalloped pattern embroidered along her stockings. Her pulse followed, leaping in staggered places like fireflies winking in the night. And when his gaze locked on hers, something heavy and taut shifted in the pit of her stomach, tilting.

She pressed a hand over her midriff, and warmth simmered in his erudite expression as if he knew precisely what was happening beneath her skin. Better than she knew herself.

His lean, angular cheek lifted enough to reveal a fissure, bracketing one side of his mouth. *Indeed,* that smirk said. *I could teach you all sorts of things—wondrously wicked things.*

She wanted to be appalled by him. Outraged. Yet, she was trapped between mortification and being wholly mystified. After all, she'd never had a front row seat to debauchery before. It was quite fascinating. Oh and scandalous, of course.

"Oy, see here!" the driver called down. "This ain't no private, *at-your-leisure* coach, sir. I've got another fare waitin' if you ain't leavin'."

Briar startled, a fresh wave of embarrassment flooding her cheeks. Thankfully, her hood concealed her rapt countenance from the driver of the hackney, leaving the rakish man watching her as the only witness to her inexcusable ogling.

"Yes, as . . . as a m-matter of fact," she stammered, her tongue oddly thick, "I require the use of this carriage. Clearly, you are not in need of it. Quite yet."

The man arched a brow, the crease beside his mouth deepening as he broke the kiss, but not before settling a crimson hood over his companion's head, securing her anonymity. In turn, the woman fell silent, averting her face toward the waiting carriage. Reaching into his pocket, he then passed a handkerchief over his damp, arrogantly cocked lips before he gave it to the woman.

Straightening, he was much taller than Briar first imagined, his lean frame outlined seamlessly in the fit of his clothes—a black evening coat with brushed lapels, a gray silk waistcoat, and snow-white cravat with a smear of scarlet lip rouge near the angled ridge of his jaw. He was older, too, her senior by at least ten or twelve years.

The sharp precision of his features and the emphatic wealth of his aquiline nose kept him from being handsome, at least by any classical standards. And yet, he was arresting and fascinating in a way she didn't comprehend.

But she wished she did. Such an understanding, she was sure, would only aid her in her ultimate plan. It could be argued that one could not make matches for perfect strangers when one possessed only a rudimentary knowledge of her own nature.

"From my perspective," he said to Briar, "you did not seem in a great frenzy to depart."

The sonorous timbre of his voice tunneled through her in a series of low vibrations, one after the other. Against her midriff, her hand curled over the muslin. Yet she wasn't certain if she meant to quell this foreign sensation or to savor it.

"Well, I was," she said crisply, not appreciating the intimation that she'd enjoyed watching his amorous exploits. When those ebony eyes glinted with amused disbelief, she realized that she'd spoken in the past tense and quickly amended with, "I *am* still."

She even went so far as to take a step toward the door. But he did the same, a challenge in the arch of a single brow. Unfortunately, he was on the correct side, and his companion stood in Briar's path.

"That may be true. However, I'm afraid she requires this particular carriage and cannot share it. She is, without question, in a rush."

"No more than I—"

Before Briar could finish, he opened the door and guided the woman up the folding step and into the dark interior with such efficient expertise it might have been his occupation. Or perhaps, he was so accustomed to sending women away at dawn that the gesture came to him by rote.

Ignoring Briar's outraged gasp, he closed the door succinctly. Then, stepping around her, he tossed another coin up to the jarvey. "The lady will give you directions."

Without argument, hesitation, or even a by-your-leave to Briar, the driver snapped the reins and set off.

"I saw him first." The inane, immature statement tumbled forth before Briar could take hold of her annoyance. *Drat!* She hated being treated like a child and yet here she was sounding like one. But she despised unfairness in any guise and being the victim of it tended to bring out her less-than-favorable characteristics.

The rogue's unrepentant gaze raked down the length of her once more, making her conscious of the fact that she'd set her hands on her hips, her cloak parting like a display curtain in a shop window. Instantly, she huffed and lowered her arms, letting him know that she was not offering up her wares. No, indeed!

"Yes. But I *paid* him first, love. Besides, I do not imagine you would have any difficulty procuring another hack. No doubt you are quite accustomed to obtaining whatever you wish by way of your feminine wiles."

"My . . . my *wiles*? How dare you, sir! I practice no such arts. When I procure another cab, it will be from pure determination and nothing else."

He clucked his tongue in an outrageously familiar manner while his hand absently brushed leftover flecks of pearlescent powder from his lapel. "We are strangers and as such, there is no cause to deceive the other. You've clearly adorned your entire person in artifices that would gain admiration. After all, you could have worn a black cloak that would have made you less conspicuous on these streets. Yet you chose one that would highlight the golden color of your tresses, and the peaches and cream of your cheeks."

"You know nothing of the sort," she snapped, seething.

The fact that the thought had crossed her mind— though briefly—was completely irrelevant. Besides, black made her look far too pale. She simply had not wanted to meet a potential new client while resembling an ashen-faced ghoul.

"Even your sash is the same cornflower blue as your eyes. And the rouge on your lips is designed to capture a man's undivided attention."

Rouge! She'd been accused of being many things— naive, dramatic, and overly romantic, just to name a few—but never in need of *enhancement*.

Affronted, she lifted her hand, swiped her kid glove across her mouth, then thrust out her arm showing her unblemished fingers. "Sir, you have insulted my honor."

He dared to look surprised with a quick lift of his dark brows, his eyes narrowing in scrutiny as he stroked a hand over the shadow of stubble along the razor edge of his jaw. Then, apparently finding the entire episode amusing, his lips quirked. "Shall it be pistols or swords at dawn, love? I imagine you're a fair shot with a pistol. Why, I can see murder in those fetching eyes right now."

"Make light if you wish, but this is not the moment to underestimate me. Had I such a weapon, you would be clutching your heart this instant and dropping to your knees. Fortunately for you, I do not have time for murder this morning."

She pivoted on her heel and faced the street, hoping another hackney would emerge through the veil.

"Do you always take offense when a man pays you a compliment?"

"From a man such as you, it was most unwelcome."

Behind her, he answered in a low, husky laugh that tunneled through her in a decadent rush of warm tingles, effectively proving her a liar.

She'd never encountered anyone like him, so bold and flirtatious, inciting her blushes as well as her ire as no true gentleman would have done. Her family had always endeavored to keep her in the company of those who understood the rules of propriety and lived by them. Yet this man was unfettered by such restraints. And the strangest part of it all was her own reaction to him.

She was speaking her mind as she never would have done *if* he were a gentleman. In polite society, she embodied decorum and affability in every word and gesture. But here, cocooned in fog on the pavement in front of a gaming hell, she was rather shocked by her own impudence.

"And what do you know of me?"

She answered without hesitation. "I've heard that those with sinful natures prefer the cover of darkness. Frankly, I'm surprised you are about at this time of day. Shouldn't all rogues and roués be abed by sunrise?"

"Only the fortunate ones," he said in an even lower tone that altered the meaning of her statement, turning it decidedly risqué. "Men such as I, however, never sleep. It's just a constant parade of sin all day long."

Part of her—and she would reprimand herself for this later—wondered what a *parade of sin* might look like. With such limited knowledge, her imagination didn't even know where to begin. The notion was intriguing to say the least.

But Briar had no time for murder *or* for random titillation.

A carriage approached and she lifted her arm automatically. But instead of seeing a cab for hire, a noisy landau lumbered past, shades drawn.

Another spear of disappointment pricked her. She needed to hurry or she could miss her opportunity, and all her careful planning would come to naught.

Where was a hackney when she needed one?

The answer was obvious. *Her* hackney was a good distance away, and all because this man had appropriated the one that had rightfully been hers.

She whirled around to face the culprit. "I shouldn't be surprised that you never sleep, considering your tawdry public exhibition. It shocked me to the very core of my being."

"It wasn't *shock* you were feeling in your"—he leaned in, his voice dropping to a seductive murmur—"*core*, but something else altogether, love."

His sinful gaze gleamed at her. This close, his irises were not simply a dark ebony, but woven with slim striations of amber that gave them a lustrous sheen. Being snared by them, her skin grew taut, prickling with gooseflesh down her arms.

"You really shouldn't say such things," she admonished on a breath, a wayward pulse fluttering at her throat.

She felt her nostrils flare as she caught the cloying odor of a woman's perfume rising from his black wool greatcoat—something dreadful with hyacinth and gardenia. But there was another fragrance, too—something richer, deeper, and entirely masculine. The musky aroma reminded her of leather boots warming by the fire, and of autumn leaves baked in the sunshine. An unexpectedly appealing combination.

"Gee—o!"

The call broke through the haze surrounding Briar, bringing her focus back to her purpose. Intent on one goal, she whirled around. She didn't even bother to bid farewell to the stranger. It wasn't likely she would ever see him again, regardless.

Slipping her fingers into the special pocket of her cloak, Briar grasped a coin. She held it aloft like a trophy as she stepped onto the street . . . and directly into a pile of horse dung. There was no denying that terrible, warm *squish*.

No! This couldn't be happening. Not now.

And yet, it was. Lifting the hem of her skirt, she saw that her slipper had made a perfect impression in the brown-green muck. An involuntary whimper escaped her but she quickly shook herself free of dread. There was still hope, after all. If she managed to raise her foot at the correct angle, then she might be able to save her lucky slipper.

Distracted by her task, she didn't realize the yellow carriage bearing down on her had no intention of stopping.

NICHOLAS DIDN'T have a chance to call out a warning. One minute, he was enjoying a morning's flirtation after a lackluster tryst, and the next he was dashing into the street, hellbent for leather.

He caught her just in time. Roping an arm around the young woman's slender waist, he hauled her against him and stumbled back to the pavement before they were both flattened by the hackney.

"You little fool!" His heart battered against the cage of his ribs where the wall of his chest met the delicate wings of her shoulder blades. Still in the grip of icy panic, he couldn't even take pleasure in the soft curves fitting perfectly against him. Instead, he had the urge to shake her until her teeth rattled. "Are you in such a bloody rush that you would risk your life to hail a cab?"

"I wouldn't be in a *bloody rush* if you hadn't appropriated the only one! I must get to the . . . Oh, look what you've made me do to my slipper."

Her lithe body jerked forward as if she expected him to release her so that she could run into the street. Again. *Unbelievable.* "You're worried about a shoe?"

Tightening his grip, he drew her further back onto the footpath. Not wanting to give in to the temptation to throttle her, he bid her to hold on to the lamppost, then released her.

"It isn't just any ordinary *shoe*." She pointed toward the pale slipper left behind in the street, the heel arching aloft while the toe was inches deep in shite. "That is one half of a pair of lucky slippers, so be careful how you extract it."

Nicholas had not been accustomed to taking orders for many years now. And if it wasn't for the sweet, airy sound of her voice—holding no more of an edge than a toasted meringue —he might have left the shoe in the gutter.

He was no hero, after all. He was a rake. And rakes did not rescue damsels in distress or their wayward apparel. At least not until this moment, apparently.

Scrubbing a hand over his face, he expelled a tight breath and tromped into the street.

"Whenever I wear them, something momentous happens," she continued, her tone lilting with encouragement.

"Like the day a duchess became the patroness of my sisters and me. The day I arrived in London. And even last week when the clerk in the confectionary shop put four ginger comfits in my parcel when I'd only had coin enough for two. And just now, they saved me from a dangerous encounter with a carriage."

Nicholas headed back to her, soiled shoe in hand. "I believe I was the one who pulled you to safety. Not the slippers."

"Yes, but if I hadn't been wearing them, then you wouldn't have needed to save me. Therefore, they are lucky." Glancing down, her wispy brows furrowed and she tsked. "And now you've ruined them with your willy-nilly extraction."

"Willy . . . nilly? I could just as easily toss it back into the street and see how you fare on your own." He turned, making a show of doing just that.

She hopped forward and seized his arm with both of her dainty gloved hands. "There's no call for barbarism. I was only pointing out that if you'd paid attention to the weave of fabric, then it wouldn't be caked with so much . . . so much . . ." She pursed those harlot red lips as if searching for a proper word.

"Horse shite?" he supplied, believing there was no reason to put a coat of varnish over it.

"Yes, *that.*" Pink tinged the crests of her cheeks as she held out her hand for her shoe.

Instead of giving it back, however, he reached into his pocket, prepared to set matters aright.

"If you're looking for your handkerchief, I believe you lent it to the woman you were devouring a few moments ago."

Hmm . . . yes. He'd already forgotten about her. Which was the point of random encounters, he supposed. After attending a masquerade last night, he'd forgone the company of his usual paramours in favor of the anonymous woman in scarlet, hoping the novelty would break him out of his ennui.

It had not.

Of course, it wasn't the woman's fault. She'd been comely enough, lively, even if too clingy for his tastes. She'd kept inviting him to spend the day with her, intimating a desire to become a permanent fixture in his life. Though, like he'd told her, he had no need for a mistress because he was heading to the country in a day or two. Rendezvous were solely for pleasure, not attachment. So he'd done his best to send her off with a fond memory, even if he'd been left unsatisfied.

He patted his empty pocket. "It would have been ungentlemanly of me to leave a task only half-done. Though the farewell I was bidding my companion seemed to hold *your* undivided attention."

She sniffed, straightening her shoulders. "It is rare in polite society to witness an act of cannibalism. I was merely astonished by the spectacle."

He laughed, knowing she was deluding herself. From the first glance, she'd been just as intrigued by him as he'd been by her. And his own reason wasn't because of her flawless beauty, for he'd been with many such women. What struck him was the openness in her rapt expression, as if the world were bright and new and every part of it fascinating.

In his circle, everyone was guarded and jaded. Usually for good reason. They tupped to pass the time, filling empty hours. They gambled fortunes on bad cards, hoping to feel something of the thrill they'd once had, long ago. When that didn't work, they tried other ventures—traveling and whatnot. Yet it would all end the same. None of those in his circle could ever capture the guileless animation in this young woman's countenance.

As for her, if she found comfort in self-deception, then he would not deny her. After all, in a moment from now, he would never see this fresh-faced miss again. And all the better for her.

"In regard to your shoe," he said with a glance over his shoulder toward the glossy black carriage that waited, "I believe my driver can assist us. A splash of whisky from his flask, a quick wipe of a tack cloth, and it will be good as new."

She snatched the slipper out of his grasp and glared at him. "That has been your carriage all this time?"

"Of course, how else would I find my way home after a night of debauchery?"

"You are about to discover that answer," she said with resolute calm.

Before he could ask what she meant, she hopped away from him, holding her skirts in one hand and her shoe in the other. Then she reached out and took hold of the door. "I am appropriating your carriage, sir."

"Indeed? And how do you expect to do that without my permission? I'm afraid Adams is rather loyal to me."

She pointed her soiled shoe at him. "You owe me recompense."

A peculiar thrill sprinted through him. He wasn't certain if the quickening of his blood was a warning to steer clear of this young woman and her absurd sense of logic, or an inducement to stay the course. However, since the previous hours had afforded him nothing by way of genuine entertainment, he chose the latter. A few more minutes in her company could hardly damage a devout rake's sensibilities, after all.

"You heard the lady, Adams."

She extended her arm, wiggling her fingers impatiently. "And I'm going to need that flask as well."

Amused, Nicholas obliged her and closed the carriage

door. Then he launched his frame up into the driver's seat, hip to hip with Adams.

Under the brim of a coachman's hat, brown eyes squinted in disapproval.

"Don't look at me like that," Nicholas said. "It's clear as the nose on my face that she's out of her element here, gadding about the degenerate streets in the early hours like a country lass. She's far too young and likely to get herself into trouble."

"And perhaps for that reason we should see her home, my lord."

Nicholas grinned. "But where would be the fun in that?"

Chapter 2

"And then, he saved her life. Did you ever hear of
that?— A water party; and by some accident she
was falling overboard. He caught her."

JANE AUSTEN, *Emma*

"I'm ever so sorry, Miss Bourne, but his lordship just
left."

No. Briar shook her head, the quick, desperate motion
causing the narrow alleyway and the freckled coffee shop
maid to blur out of focus.

Then again, another cause might have been the few
sips from the driver's flask on the way here. "Becky, I
cannot be too late. My entire existence is depending upon
this morning. Lord Hulworth is the one bachelor who
will entice the *ton*. My success depends on him."

"Like I told you, his lordship comes here *early* every
Monday for his breakfast takeaway pot. But don't fret, for
it's only a week, after all."

To Briar, that was no consolation. "Do you know
what could happen in seven whole days? He might drop
dead from a heart seizure—he is five and thirty, you
know—or worse, he might decide to find a bride without
our assistance."

Becky knew all about the Bourne Matrimonial Agency.
Until a month ago, she'd been living on a tenant farm at

Uncle Ernest's estate in Hampshire. But when he'd let the place to start the agency, Becky had packed her things and taken a chance on a new life in London, too. And better still, with her job in this shop, she'd introduced Briar to the wonders of sipping chocolate.

She laid a comforting hand on Briar's shoulder. "Fear not, for I took that calling card you gave me and tied it with a string to his parcel. It won't be any time at all before he's reading your name and wondering all about the Miss Bourne it belongs to. He'll be knocking on your door for calling hours tomorrow, mark my words."

"I shall wish upon an eyelash that it comes true." Briar heaved out a sigh, wavering a bit on the uneven cobblestones beneath her feet. She was thankful that when the driver had helped her down from the carriage he'd told her he would take her home after her errand. "At least the day is not lost, however. I still have chocolate to look forward to."

It was a wonder what this shop could do with a humble bean. Dried and crushed into a silky powder, the cocoa was combined with pepper and cinnamon, almonds and aniseed, then formed into cakes. Mixed in a copper pot with sugar and milk, the rich brew was whipped by the cook into a frenzy that resulted in a thick viscous drink with mountains of divine froth rising to the top.

"I'm afraid I have bad news," Becky said warily. "Lord Hulworth had the last cup."

Briar blinked. She was speechless for a full minute, waiting for Becky to crack a smile and say she was teasing. But she never did.

"No chocolate? If it's a matter of preparation, I'm willing to wait." Briar knew that it took a long time for the cocoa to blend with the milk. It was a most delicate and delicious process.

"Mr. Studgers got into a row at the market for the high price. Said he refused to buy any more until they were reasonable again."

"Surely you have some in a tin that I could purchase and have Mrs. Darden make at home." She fumbled with the coin purse tucked inside her cloak.

"Lord Hulworth took the last cake, too."

Briar winced, the statement effectively cutting her hopes twofold. Not only had her lucky slippers let her down, but this? At once, she understood what Caesar had felt the moment of Brutus's attack. *Et tu, chocolate?*

"Here, now. I can't have you despairing. Let me check the pot one more time." Becky held up her index finger and disappeared through the door.

Then moments later, like Cleopatra coming forth on a golden chariot, she came back carrying a small dish, brimming with beautiful pale whipped heaven.

"Oh, my dear Becky, you are an angel. I don't think I could have lived through this day without you." Briar took the offered dish, lifting the simple crockery in both hands like a chalice as she drew in the sweet essence.

The maid laughed. "That's the very last of it, miss, and not enough for a proper cup. But I must get back or Mr. Studgers will start shouting my name to the rafters."

Briar bid farewell and turned away. Then, just as she was about to take her first sip, the heel of her slipper caught on a cobblestone.

She teetered. And before her lips could form a gasp, her reason for living spilled down the front of her dress.

❦

HAVING DESCENDED from the driver's perch, Nicholas moved fast across the cobblestones. He slipped a hand beneath the young woman's elbow to keep her from stumbling, and snatched the dish in midair. "It doesn't appear to be your morning, love."

She didn't respond. Her gaze was fixed on the front of her dress, her delicate hands frozen and curled slightly in the empty air, as a distressed whimper escaped her.

"No need to fret. Surely it will come out in the wash."

Other than a slow shake of her head, she still did not move.

Nicholas wondered if the resolute, yet patently naive, young woman had finally reached her limit. "See here. There is no need for these histrionics. It was only foam. In fact, there's still a spot of chocolate at the bottom."

"But . . . but the froth is the best part."

She lifted her face, her cornflower blue eyes distant and dim, causing something oddly chivalrous to tunnel through him.

"I'll get you another cup."

Again, she shook her head, the delightful curve of her lips turning the wrong direction. "That was the last of it. There's no more, and likely not for days. Perhaps weeks. A lifetime, really, if you think of how much could happen, and worse, how much could stay the same. And I was ready for a change. It was supposed to happen today."

His mouth quirked as he held back a grin at her dramatic soliloquy. The funny thing was, he suspected she wasn't acting but sincerely forlorn over the loss of the chocolate.

Slipping an arm around her, he guided her sluggish steps toward the waiting carriage. "Come on, love. Let's take you home. You need to start this day again on the right footing."

"It won't do any good. My lucky slippers are ruined. I even sacrificed my gloves and one of my best stockings, trying to scrub the stain away."

"Did you now?" He set his hands in the dip of her

waist, nearly spanning the distance with his splayed fingers, and lifted her without effort into the carriage. Though, as her face drifted past his and her lips parted on a breath, he caught the unmistakable scent of whisky.

She fell back against the red velvet squabs and pointed the toe of her soiled slipper at him, her skirts rising to display a trim ankle and a lovely portion of tapered calf as well. "See?"

"I do, indeed." He also saw the flask on the floor beside a discarded pile of embroidered ivory silk—her stocking, he presumed. Reaching for the former, he shook it and found it empty. "By any chance, did you have a little nip on your way here?"

"Well, I was . . . curious. I've never even been near spirits. Since it isn't one of Uncle Ernest's vices, we don't keep any at the house. Terrible stuff the first swallow, and the second wasn't much improved."

"And the third?"

She offered a hapless shrug, carefully not meeting his gaze, her cheeks tinged a sleepy pink. "After that, it didn't seem to matter. *Wh-what* are you doing?"

"I'm climbing inside my own carriage," he said, narrating his movements as he proceeded to settle the bulk of his frame on the bench across from her. "Closing the door. Rapping my knuckles to let Adams know we are ready to return to Sterling's, where—I presume—your residence awaits nearby?"

Nodding, she demurely arranged her skirts. She looked delightfully disheveled, blond curls mussed, cloak draped crookedly over one shoulder, and the toes of her slippers peeking out from beneath her skirts. "Surely you could sit in the driver's box. I presume that is how you came to be here."

"It's less conspicuous at this time of morning, and less crowded than the perch."

He lowered the shades, and in the shadowy confines, her eyes turned watchful.

"Just so you understand, I'm not like her—your friend from earlier."

"Then you're in luck. Wide-eyed young maidens, fresh from the country and looking to marry, are not to my taste."

"For your information I have been in London for over a month, and if I were inclined to marry—which I am not—I would choose a man closer to my own age." She waved a dismissive hand in the air between them, lifting her winged brows. "What would be the point of marrying you if I were to become a widow in five years, left to raise our children alone and manage the household on a pittance after your greedy relatives strip the accounts? After that, how could I afford a governess? Tutors? University? I'd be forced to dismiss servants I'd grown attached to. The house would fall into disrepair. There would be no one across from me at dinner. No one to sit beside me when I embroider, gently scolding me to wear my reading glasses, and tucking a lock of silver hair behind my ear. And no one to lend me his arm when I can no longer manage the stairs on my own."

Nicholas felt his jaw drop. He'd just witnessed an entire life—*his* life, apparently—flash out of existence in a matter of twenty seconds. "Just to be clear, how old do you think I am?"

"I hope not to insult you by marking you older than you are, but my first estimation was two and thirty. Though I suppose you could simply be a weathered thirty."

His decrepit bones shifted on the seat. "I am *four* and thirty."

"Oh, I am so very sorry," she said with the quiet gloom of someone visiting a deathbed.

"No need to worry. Once Adams hands me my cane, I'm sure to make it out of the carriage."

Across from him, she tilted her chin to her shoulder and bit her full bottom lip as if to suppress a smile.

"And just how young are you, love?" he asked. "Young enough that you must sneak out of your home for whatever rendezvous you'd had planned this morning."

She stiffened but wavered on the bench as the rumbling carriage took a corner. "It is bad form to ask a grown woman her age, and this was no mere rendezvous, but a vital errand."

"I'd wager a five-pound note that you are not more than twenty, love."

"Please stop calling me *love*. Such an endearment should be reserved for the one who claims your heart, and a man who engages in lascivious activity in the center of town likely doesn't know the meaning."

"And you do, I suppose?"

"Every woman understands what love should be in its purest, most wholesome form."

He could not help but smirk at her idealistic view. Love was far from pure and wholesome. It was a barb, rough edged, razor sharp, and designed to cut all the way to the marrow, leaving only jagged scars behind. "You're full of grand illusions. By your age, I'd received a healthy dose of reality that knocked sense into me."

"With a father who abandoned my sisters and me, and a mother who died of a broken heart, I've had plenty of reality, thank you very much," she said, some of her words slurring together. "But I refuse to let it embitter me. A true abiding love—or even just the expectation of it—is the only reason to wake up each morning. Well, unless there's chocolate."

He studied her with renewed interest. It wasn't until she'd mentioned her parents that he saw the mark of loss in her eyes, a sadness that lingered in the deeper blue ring that surrounded her pupils. Yet when she spoke of love that darkness receded, those petal-blue orbs brightened and filled with hope. "I doubt you've ever been in love."

She glanced down to her lap and plucked at the saturated muslin. Then, when her gaze darted back to him and she saw that he was watching her, she let her hands fall and expelled a sweet, liquor-scented sigh. "Is it terribly obvious?"

Her expression was so open and torn that it was impossible to lie to her. He nodded.

"*Bother*. How am I supposed to prove myself a competent matchmaker if I can't even convince a practitioner of hedonism that I know what I'm doing?"

"Did you say . . . *matchmaker*?"

"It is the family business." She gave an absent flick of her wrist, as if it were an everyday occurrence for a seemingly well-born young woman to admit to having an occupation. "Likely, you read about the Bourne Matrimonial Agency in the society pages, announcing our recent premier. There was even a cartoon, but it was a rather unflattering caricature of Uncle Ernest. Why, his nose isn't nearly that big. Certainly not as large as yours."

"Very few are," he said dryly, having forgotten for a moment how ancient—and clearly monstrous—he was.

"Oh, I didn't mean . . . Well, that is to say . . . The rest of your face appears to support it well enough."

"Through a great feat of engineering."

Again, she tucked her chin, trying not to smile, but her lips refused her bidding this time and curled upward like unfurling rose petals. Even so, he found that he could not feel cross with her. In the past thirty-four years, he'd grown used to such observations. But whatever he lacked in prettiness of feature, he compensated for with other endowments and talents.

Skills which, he reminded himself, he would not use to seduce a marriage-minded young woman.

Still, he was entranced by her. He reasoned that the core of it stemmed from her youthful vibrancy. Through her, he glimpsed what life was like for someone who didn't drag bitterness around like a shackle and ball.

His own youth had been less than idyllic after his father had died, and his mother had shifted the sole focus of her life to rearing Nicholas's older brother. But that was nothing compared to what had happened later, when he'd discovered that one brief moment of carelessness could change a man forever.

This young woman across from him was even more naive than he'd been. Even though she was no more than a stranger, the notion that she could suffer a similar fate knotted his stomach.

He reclined back to ease the sensation. "Tell me more about the family business."

He still wasn't sure he believed her. Women working in a matchmaking business and with society's approval? Highly unlikely. Yet he was too intrigued by the narrator to question the validity.

"As I mentioned, we only just opened our doors. Since the Season won't begin for a few months, we haven't had many clients—a handful of widows from the peerage and daughters of landed gentry. Our patroness is attempting to lure in a duke from a family she knows, but I'm not certain she will be successful. And oddly enough, we have a number of older gentlemen looking for young wives, which I don't understand at all. I asked Uncle Ernest why they wouldn't prefer women their own age, but he refused to answer." Her expression turned thoughtful as she rested her head against the squabs and after a moment she shrugged. "If you can believe it, most of our male applicants are even older than you."

"Can such a thing be possible? Tell me, did they enter your establishment while garbed in their burial shrouds?"

Ignoring his sarcasm, she continued. "We are open three days each week. Ainsley and Jacinda—my sisters," she explained, "meet with the clients, make notes, and set up introductions. And what am I doing while they are performing the tasks of genuine matchmakers, hmm?" She splayed a hand over her chest, her brows lifting for an instant before her features flattened on a huff. "I'm serving tea and filing papers like a trained monkey. That is why this morning's errand was so important. I was going to procure London's most elusive bachelor as a client."

"If this gentleman is so *elusive*, how did you know exactly where he would be? Or is this a secret matchmaker talent?"

"By way of the UBB—the *Urgent Bachelor Bulletin*. Every debutante subscribes for all the latest information on the most eligible gentlemen."

Her countenance was as stone-faced as a cardsharp. And for an instant, he wondered if such a publication existed.

She must have read the uncertainty in his expression because next she cast him a coolly sardonic smirk. "From gossip, of course. I have a friend who is one of the serving wenches at the coffee house. She informed me that this particular gentleman fends for himself on his cook's day off, dropping by each week for his breakfast pot takeaway. And I was going to use this to my advantage."

Nicholas sobered, an uneasy ripple breaking his merriment. He didn't know what foolish lengths she would go to in order to achieve her goal. From what he'd already witnessed from this idealistic young woman, he had to ask. "How precisely?"

"Before you ruined everything by appropriating my cab, I'd planned to happen upon him as if by accident, smile, and say something serendipitous about our meeting. Then, after a few pleasantries, I would have explained that I am a woman of business who knows exactly how to give him the most happiness imaginable, and bring him to the very summit of fulfillment by finding him the perfect m—"

He cursed. "And before you could have finished, he would have found the nearest alley wall and lifted your skirts, taking you for a prostitute," he said, incredulous. "You should thank your *lucky slippers* that I stopped you from making the worst mistake of your life. Have you no notion of what a man would think if a woman approached him and started talking about bringing him to the *summit of fulfillment*? It wouldn't be matchmaking, I can assure you."

She blushed even as her eyes narrowed. "Not every man has the same lecherous view of the world as you do. There are some who are good and kind and are not fixated on . . . on fornicating in the streets of London." She gasped. Then a low mewl of distress escaped her as she slumped forward, burying her face in her hands. "Just listen to what you've made me say. I've never used the word *fornicate* in my entire life, and here I am speaking it to a completely corrupt stranger. I don't know what's come over me."

"Perhaps it was the flask of whisky you drank."

She bobbed her head in something of a nod, her words coming out muffled. "Terrible stuff."

"There is another part of your plan that you failed to think of—women aren't allowed in coffee houses, at least not the gently bred sort. Men gather there, and at their clubs, to speak freely without being restricted by social niceties, saying the things that would corrupt a young woman such as yourself. Things that truly would shock you to your core."

"Precisely," she said, lifting her face to his, her expression steadfast. "All the things I need to know in order to make matches for these men. How else would I find their perfect counterparts without knowing their inner desires?"

That uneasy ripple turned into a shudder. "I know many of those men and more than I care to—certainly enough to understand that there is no counterpart for some. And for that, we should all be grateful."

"I'm not a nitwit." She scoffed. "I'm speaking of decent men, ones who journey to coffee houses to recite poetry and speak of their political aspirations, among other things. And, even though I heartily disagree, I'm well aware of the rules against allowing women admittance. But women have every right to hear the inner workings of a man's mind, and to express themselves in a public forum. What better way for the two sexes to learn about each other?"

"I could name a dozen off the top of my head."

"Truly?" She stopped breathing and leaned forward, fascination glowing like a beacon around her.

He shook his head, adamant. "Do not even finish that thought. You are too green, your perspective limited by the fact that you've seen nothing of the world. And you know nothing of men."

"Then tell me everything there is to know about men."

She was so guileless and trusting. *Far too trusting.* And those eyes of hers, filled with such unfettered curiosity, roused more than mere lust in his blood. But something fierce and primal.

He had no intention of answering her, but *damn it all* if he wasn't tempted to show her.

Yet he would not turn into the very type of man he'd just warned her against. He might be a rake, but he was not a libertine. There was a difference.

Nicholas lived by his own code of honor. He established rules beforehand—no attachments, interference, or manipulations of any sort—and his companions understood this. He never set out to wound or blindside anyone. For then he would be no better than his brother had been.

Feeling the carriage shift into a slow rocking rhythm, he tore his gaze away from temptation. Slipping two fingers beneath the shade, he saw the gray stone façade of Sterling's. The fog had lifted, and the pallid light of morning revealed the broken bottles, cigar and cheroot stubs, and all manner of papers strewn over the pavement. And, for just an instant, he had a wayward desire to keep her from seeing the ugliness of it.

He nearly laughed. An hour in her company and some of her romantic notions had already started to infiltrate his thoughts. It would be better, for both of them, if he never forgot the man he'd become.

Once they stopped, he let the shade fall back in place and rapped his knuckles against the panel, signaling Adams to bring the step. "Shall I escort you to your door, ensuring you don't fall into some other sort of mischief along the way?"

She blanched and darted a quick peek through the shade. "Bother. This morning didn't go as I'd expected it to at all. I was supposed to arrive with a wonderful announcement. Laughter and dancing in the foyer. Perhaps even . . . a shower of rose petals over my head." She expelled the most forlorn sigh he'd ever heard. Then she set a heavy hand on the door like a defeated soldier returning home from a lost battle. "Of course, you know, this entire debacle will have to be our secret."

"I don't even know your name, love." And she didn't know his either, which was all the more important.

She offered him a wan smile before she stepped out of the carriage. "That's right. Perhaps there was a little luck left in my slippers after all."

Chapter 3

"... she would gladly have submitted to feel yet more mistaken—more in error—more disgraced by mis-judgment, than she actually was, could the effects of her blunders have been confined to herself."

JANE AUSTEN, *Emma*

'London
Spring, 1826

"You cannot tell a soul, not even your mother. Actually . . . especially not your mother, for she would lose all faith in me." Briar darted a fretful glance through the fronds of a potted palm. Lady Waldenfield's candlelit ballroom was practically brimming with guests for this evening's musicale. All the more reason to remain in this stuffy corner behind a wide column.

The secluded spot was essential for the moment. She refused to reveal her matchmaking debacle where someone might overhear.

Beside her, Temperance Prescott shifted impatiently, her topknot of dark golden curls swaying with the motion. "For someone who claimed to be unable to hold in this news any longer, you sure have been taking your time telling it. Briar, I am about to burst."

"Oh, very well." Briar looked into her dearest friend's

tea-colored irises, hoping to hear that it wasn't as bad as it seemed. "As you know, today I introduced my very first clients to each other."

The agency had been open for nine months now, and she'd finally been given an opportunity to become a genuine matchmaker. However . . . not everything had gone to plan.

"Did you hire that harpist I recommended?"

"Yes."

"And lined the garden path with rose petals?"

"Yes." Briar held back a groan. She'd done everything to make it perfect. "Temperance, you're not making this any easier."

"Sorry, I won't interrupt anymore." Reaching up with her gloved hand, she pantomimed turning a key to her lips and tossed it over her shoulder.

"I won't mention the particulars for privacy reasons, but I will say that one was a widow, looking for a younger man, and the other was a younger man, looking for an older woman."

"Scandalous! Ah, sorry. I must have used the wrong key before." Temperance repeated the locking gesture, this time pretending to slide the new key down her décolletage.

Briar glanced through the palm fronds again, stalling more than hiding. "I was shocked as well, of course, but still determined not to let it block the path of true love. I gave the applications careful consideration and discovered that they had quite a bit in common as well. Naturally, I thought they were perfect for each other."

Temperance made a point of unlocking her lips. "Well, what happened? Did they fall madly in love?"

"There was a *degree* of love involved, yes. But that was due to the fact that they were already acquainted. In fact, they might have been"—Briar winced—"related."

"Hmm . . . how related, exactly? Cousins?"

Briar shook her head, her stomach rolling over. "Closer than cousins. Much closer, unfortunately. But in my own defense, the lady had used a *nom de guerre* when filling out her application, so there was no way to know."

Well, that wasn't entirely true. If Briar hadn't been so eager to make her first match, she might have taken the time to perform a cursory investigation. And then this entire debacle could have been avoided.

Temperance pressed her white-gloved fingertips to her mouth as if she were mulling over the complexities of existence. Then, in the next instant, her cheeks lifted, the almond shape of her eyes turning into crescent moons. Her shoulders began to shake. "Tell me that you did not introduce a mother to her son."

Briar wobbled her head in a humiliated nod. The episode had been completely awful. She could still hear their shocked voices ringing in her head.

"Sebastian?"

". . . Mother?"

Dreadful. Briar had been waiting a veritable lifetime for this opportunity, only to have the worst outcome imaginable. "You're supposed to tell me that it won't make too much of a splash in the rumor pond."

Eyes watering with barely suppressed amusement, Temperance issued a brief snort, and then giggles erupted.

Bother.

Worst of all, her sisters would never let her forget this.

Ainsley had coolly regarded the situation. Then, without speaking directly to Briar, had accused Jacinda of *allowing* this to happen. As if Briar wasn't even capable of making her own mistakes.

Jacinda, too deliriously happy after her recent wedding to the Duke of Rydstrom, hadn't chastised her, but simply stated that the Bourne Matrimonial Agency could recover from this. However, there had been a measure of doubt in her eyes and in the placating pat on Briar's shoulder.

"Well . . ." Temperance hemmed. Half a head taller than Briar, she peered over the long fronds near the top, toward the guests shuffling through rows of fiddleback chairs in preparation for the musicale. "It is possible that the ones who are whispering behind their fans and glancing back this way are only admiring the curtains."

Briar sagged against the column and stared at the empty dark corner. "I've ruined my family's business. The agency will fail. We'll lose the patronage of the Duchess of Holliford, who's been so kind to us all these years. Then Uncle Ernest, Ainsley, and I will become homeless, turning into the poor relations that Jacinda and Rydstrom must support."

"Nonsense," Temperance said with a cluck of her tongue. "Even if a rumor starts today, there will likely be a new one to replace it tomorrow. I should know because my cousin, Nicholas, has been at the center of so many that I've lost count."

Having been close friends with Temperance these past months, Briar had heard about many of *Cousin Nicholas*'s scandalous exploits. He was an unrepentant rascal, to be sure.

Still the news did not cheer her. "But with your cousin away, we have no guarantee that a new rumor will start with the required expedience."

"Fret not, for we received a missive last week with the news that he and my brother will be returning any day. In the meantime, there is always Lord Hulworth— unmarried and as elusive as ever, whetting the *ton*'s appetite for matrimony. You could still make a match for him."

"True. But it would be so much easier to marry him off if I could meet him first." Yet after that fateful morning last fall, she'd given up the notion of a solitary, chance encounter. Considering the fact that her actions had shocked the rogue who'd *lent* her his carriage, she'd come to realize that she could have suffered a worse fate.

Lesson learned, and she'd swallowed it like bitter medicine. "I'm beginning to think that Lord Hulworth is more myth than man."

"If your family would permit you to attend something other than two of the most mundane events per week, perhaps you might meet him."

It was true. Ever since Jacinda's accident and temporary amnesia earlier this spring, Ainsley had become excessively overprotective. Frankly, Briar was surprised she'd been trusted with her very own clients at all.

And just look how swimmingly *that* had gone. Drat!

"Regardless," Temperance continued, "I have the utmost confidence that you will be the one who finds him a bride. You were born to be a matchmaker, far more than anyone else I've ever met."

Briar nodded. She could not let today's episode stop the Fates from working through her.

"Furthermore, without you, I will be rudderless in a sea of men with no one to direct me away from the wrong sort. My future husband may very well be taking his seat right this instant. And you are going to help me find him."

Temperance's declaration was just the boost Briar needed.

Yet as they stepped out from behind the column, several heads turned. Whispers began. A slow hum of laughter mingled with the discordant notes of the quartet warming up for the program.

Briar's confidence slipped like a garterless stocking. "Where is your cousin when we need him?"

WHEN HIS carriage came to an abrupt halt, Nicholas peered out the window to find a chaos of coaches clogging the lamplit street. After endless months at his country estate, the one thing he did not miss was London traffic during the height of the Season.

"Looks to be a row between drivers up ahead, my lord," Adams called down, his voice rising with the excitement of a cockfight den. "The barouche just tore the landau's livery coat."

In other words, the resolution was going to take a while.

Nicholas stirred on the velvet seat, too restless to wait it out. He was ready to shake the country dust from his boots and immerse himself in a much-needed night of hedonistic pursuits.

"I'll walk from here, Adams." The *hell* was near enough. "But I'll wager a crown on the landau."

Adams grinned, greedily chafing his hands together. "Make it two. I've got a grand feeling about the barouche."

Nicholas touched a finger to the brim of his top hat in agreement, then set off. Alighting from the vehicles around him, society matrons and their protégés were dressed in finery and feathers, scurrying over the cobblestones to the pavement. Apparently, there was an assembly in Waldenfield's house on the corner, every window lit, every room likely packed full of society's darlings.

"Lord Edgemont, as I live and breathe."

Nicholas jolted to a halt, staring hard at the brunette moving away from the crowd entering the house and walking toward him. The first time he saw her, she'd merely been an anonymous woman in scarlet.

More than anything, he wished that their association had ended the morning he'd sent her away in a hackney in front of Sterling's. Unfortunately, it hadn't.

She grinned slyly at him. "Once again, the Fates have put me in your path."

He gritted his teeth, pretending to be unaffected here on the street with so many people milling about. To stem the curiosity of those already sliding glances in his direction, he even moved closer to bow over her hand. Only his voice, dark with warning, revealed the anger brewing inside him. "The *Furies* would be a closer match."

If only they'd never met. For then he might have avoided all the pain his family had endured these past months. But how was he to know he would see her again within a fortnight of their hapless tryst, and discover that she was not who she'd pretended to be?

She was not a young widow as she'd told him. No, *Miss Smithson* was actually an unmarried debutante. And when he'd had the misfortune of introducing her to his unworldly cousin, she'd played the part of an innocent like a finely trained actress. Of course, Nicholas—and doubtless others—knew better. His cousin, however, did not. Daniel had been smitten at first sight.

"Oh, come now, I thought we left all that animosity behind us when you paid my father an exorbitant sum to make certain I did not marry your cousin." She laughed, the sound as brittle as ice breaking over a pond after a hard freeze.

"You never intended to marry *Daniel*."

Unaffected, she smoothed the cascade of dark brown ringlets away from her cheek. "Can you blame me? Marriage to a vicar's son would hardly have been an improvement from the match my father intended. And a young woman in her fourth Season must think of herself. Should she resign herself to an odious marriage to an old man? Or should she take matters into her own hands and find a husband who shares her particular appetites?"

"Or perhaps she should have listened when the gentleman she sought out explained—and from the very first moment—that he had no intention of marrying. Now or ever."

She heaved a resigned sigh. "We could have been happy together, Nicholas."

He did not bother to argue the erroneous declaration. Instead, he glanced over his shoulder to see that the line of guests had all ascended the stairs. Even the carriages were starting to wend their way through the street. Absently, he wondered if the landau won the fight, or if it was the barouche.

"It appears to be time to bid adieu, Miss Smithson." He turned, gesturing for her to proceed toward the stairs.

"Tut. Tut. It's Lady Comstock now, as you are well aware." She flashed the emerald on her left hand. Then her lips pursed sourly as she twisted it on her gloved finger. "But tell me, how is poor Daniel? From what I hear, he has become a recluse, pining over a love he cannot forget. I must say, it is quite flattering to know that I ruined him for any other woman."

Nicholas refused to validate that statement, or to reveal the turmoil Daniel had suffered from the day she'd left. He'd fallen into a state of melancholy from which he had yet to recover. "Once he finds a bride, you will be nothing more than an unfortunate event in his past."

"Well, if he's anything like his sister, it will take him years. It's so sad, really. With you sequestered in the country for most of this Season, I've heard Temperance had to resort to employing an agency to find a husband."

His teeth grated together as she walked beside him.

"Now that I've returned, I will ensure that both of my cousins are married by the end of the Season."

He hadn't the first clue on how he would achieve his goal. All he knew was that he would stop at nothing to see his cousins settled at last.

"The Earl of Edgemont, perusing the marriage mart? What fun! But be careful that you do not incite the interest of debutantes looking to marry you instead. They can be rather scheming, or so I've heard."

"I'm certain none could hold a candle to you, Lady Comstock."

At the base of the stairs, he inclined his head in farewell.

"One never knows. There are some very clever girls amongst our set." She curtsied, eyes glinting like a serpent's before the strike. "Perhaps one of them might find a way to drag London's most irredeemable rake to the altar."

This was far from the worst threat he'd ever received, but it sent a cold chill all the way to the soles of his feet, nonetheless.

Chapter 4

"She knew the limitations of her own powers too well to attempt more than she could perform with credit . . ."

JANE AUSTEN, *Emma*

Briar slipped quietly out of the gallery in the middle of Haydn's *Surprise*. The trills of the oboe blended too well with the titters of haughty laughter for her tastes. She'd had enough of sideways glances, too.

No one in that room, aside from Temperance, knew how much pressure Briar had put on herself to make the perfect match. Since it had been her first one, Ainsley had offered to assist her, which was an insult in and of itself. She may as well have said, *You're not up to snuff, dearest. Why don't you fetch another pot of tea from the kitchens, instead?*

Abhorring the thought, Briar shut the door to the retiring room and leaned against it, shutting out the jarring roar of instruments. Then closing her eyes, she chanted a mantra. "I am more than the bringer of oolong. More than the presenter of scones. More than the carrier of—"

"If you say *cakes*, I'm going to start eating my gloves. I'm famished as it is."

Briar's eyes flew open to see a petite brunette saunter around the corner and into the antechamber. "Forgive me. I didn't realize there would be anyone else in here."

"I arrived late." The young woman flitted her fingers in the air as if the matter were of little consequence. In the mirror, she cast an appraising glance at Briar, her green gaze squinting. "Say, I know you, do I not?"

The faint scent of hyacinth and gardenia tickled Briar's nose as she drew a step closer. There was something vaguely familiar about the woman, but she could not place her. "If you are one of my uncle's clients, then perhaps we are acquainted. Have you applied to the Bourne Matrimonial Agency?"

The woman laughed instantly, the high tittering sound rising to the coffered ceiling. "*No.* This is too rich! Surely you're not one of the *helpful nieces* I heard rumor about a few moments ago—the ones who tried to marry off an old woman to her own son?"

Briar bristled but did not cower behind a lie. "That was my own error. Neither my uncle nor sisters had a part in it. At the time, I did not realize that the lady was already . . . acquainted with the gentleman."

"I'd say."

"This solitary occurrence does not reflect on the agency's ability to make proper matches, in the least." Briar huffed, a rant flowing past her lips before she could stop it. "My uncle's establishment is highly revered by much of society, including the estimable Duchess of Holliford. As a matter of fact, she is our patroness. We even live in one of her own houses, in a premier, undeniably respectable part of St. James's . . . if you overlook Sterling's gaming hell across the street, and um . . ."

Briar pressed her lips together. She realized she wasn't presenting a very good case in her own favor when the woman's eyes widened in the mirror.

Slowly, she turned to face Briar with decided scrutiny. The woman drew in a breath as if she had remembered how they were acquainted, but she did not share it. Instead, a peculiar glint of avarice lit her expression, like a person standing in a confectionary shop, deciding whether or not to purchase one comfit, or all of them.

"A premier location for success, to be sure. Doubtless, hundreds of potential clients travel by your door each day," she said, then tsked. "Which makes your blunder all the more tragic."

Briar's hackles rose and she crossed her arms beneath her breasts. "We will recover."

"Of course you will. I meant no offense," she said, not unkindly. "However, unless you do something daring, and quickly, this unfortunate event will be cemented in society's collective viewpoints. They will be jeering about the Bourne Matrimonial Agency for years."

"We take pride in our matches, believing that every person deserves to find their perfect counterpart. And we have an excellent record of success."

"That's splendid, then. But tell me, have you made any matches among the nobility?"

"A duke, in fact." Never mind that the agency's only duke had married her sister. It still counted as a mark in the success column.

"Any others?"

Briar swallowed. "Not at present."

Their one viscount client, in addition to a handful of barons, had all rescinded their subscriptions. Sadly, some people believed that Uncle Ernest had started the business solely to marry off his nieces. Which wasn't true in the slightest. They never fell in love with their clients.

Well . . . except for Jacinda. And occasionally Uncle Ernest.

"That's what it will take to get you out of this pickle, you know. You'll need to marry off someone high in the ranks. Someone who titillates the imaginations of every debutante and on-the-shelf spinster. Someone whose name is frequently in the newspaper's society page. For then your agency's name would be right beside it." Sconce light gleamed in the emerald depths of her eyes, making them almost hypnotic. "I can tell by the look of you that your first inclination is to make a hasty match so the *ton* will forget today's error. Perhaps you even have a country squire in mind, and the daughter of a clerk. Veritable paragons of virtue."

Dimly, Briar nodded. Strangely enough that was precisely what she'd planned.

"But what attention would you gain from such an uninspiring union? Nothing at all," the woman continued, raising her finger to stir the air as if she held a wand. "Ah, but if you found a bride for an obscenely wealthy nobleman, then no one would stop talking about the match for years to come. Your matrimonial agency would be legendary."

Briar let out a breath, shaking free of the spell. While it was a compelling notion, there was one glaring flaw in her idea. "Unless you have a duke in your pocket, the point is moot."

"Would an earl do?"

Briar's attention was caught, snared on a sudden rush of expectation. "Just to be clear, you know an earl who is eager to sign up for a subscription?"

"Even better. I'll pay you . . . *hmm* . . . fifty pounds if you find him a bride."

"*Fi*—that's quite a lot of money." Briar's income barely kept her in gloves and ribbons. In fact, she'd dipped into her £200 dowry to hire the harpist to play lovely music for today's dreadful event.

"True, but it would be worth every penny if you succeeded."

Suspicion prickled along Briar's spine. "If he's such a wealthy earl, then why hasn't anyone snatched him up yet? Is there something wrong with him?"

"Not at all. He's very fine, indeed. Handsome. Clever. A bit of a rake—irredeemable, some might say—but nothing too terrible."

As the daughter of a philandering father, rakish tendencies were something she could not overlook. She would rather the agency fall into ruin before she made a match for a man like that and risk having someone suffer the same fate as her mother. "Sorry, but we only make matches for suitable applicants with redeeming qualities."

Briar turned to leave, her fingers curling around the smooth brass knob.

"When it comes to his family, he's loyal to a fault," she said quickly, her words clipped, tense. "And his love for them is unshakable."

Love and *loyalty* were Briar's weak spots. Such characteristics covered up all manner of sins. In her mind, if a man was loyal to his family and truly loved them, he would never betray them.

She released the knob. "Yes, I could find a bride for a man like that. But only if he wanted to be married."

The woman took a step forward. "Don't you find that the most worthwhile of men tend to be elusive . . . until they are wooed toward the idea of marriage?"

Again, Briar found herself nodding. "But he would have to be faithful."

"Why marry otherwise?" She shrugged, the ghost of a grin on her lips. "Once you find someone he cannot resist, she'll bring him to heel."

"You make it sound quite simple, but how will I know what he finds irresistible? How can anyone truly know?"

"That, my dear, is where the true test of your abilities will come into play." She strummed her fingertips together and began to pace, plotting along the way. "The way I see it, this particular earl doesn't spend enough time in polite society, mingling with the marriage minded.

However, if someone from a matchmaking agency were to let it slip that he was looking for a bride, then he would be beleaguered by invitations to balls and parties. Dozens of husband-hunting mamas would find their way to him. He wouldn't be able to go to his clubs without fathers bartering off their simpering daughters for a profitable alliance. Doubtless, he would see it as pure torture." She laughed and clasped her hands together as if she'd caught a gold sovereign. "It would be positively perfect."

"By your description, matchmaking sounds like unleashing a pride of lionesses on a single gladiator."

"What is the Season if not a blood sport? Most debutantes are escorted to this London coliseum by their parents, instructed to make a fine match or else an odious one will be made for them." She paused, issuing a taut exhale through the seam of her lips before her hands curled into fists as she lowered them. "But you, Miss Bourne, could fight for them—be the claws and teeth that bring this earl to his knees. That is, *if* you keep the doors of your uncle's agency open by inciting interest instead of ridicule."

Briar frowned, not terribly keen on the analogy or the violent imagery it conjured. And yet . . . there was something intriguing about seeing herself as a warrior. *A warrior of the heart.* "Still, it hardly seems like something to which the earl would agree, and there is no assurance he would marry one of these debutantes."

"Ah, but if he does, then you will have proven your abilities. The *ton* will never doubt you or the agency again. And don't forget the £50 prize." She shrugged. "If you're up for it, that is."

Briar felt the sudden zing of challenge course through her in a rush of pins and needles. Thinking about the experience she could gain—not to mention the respect of her sisters and perhaps even an office of her own—the proposal was too tempting to pass up. "How much time will I have to find him a match?"

"Let's say you have till the end of the Season."

"But it's nearly May. That would only give me a month."

She pursed her lips. "True, and there is always the potential of a house party in the summer. Very well, we'll make it August." She held out her hand.

Briar hesitated to take it. "But I don't even know your name. How are we to settle up?"

"I'm Genevieve . . . *Price*, but that's just between us. I'm a friend of the family, you might say. So it wouldn't be prudent to speak of our arrangement." Receiving a nod of agreement, she continued, her lips curling slowly upward at the corners. "As for settling up, I already know where to find you, don't I?"

Indeed. Briar's profession and blunder were all they had talked about. "I suppose I only need to know now the gentleman's name."

"Are you acquainted with the Earl of Edgemont, by chance?"

Briar stifled a triumphant smile. Yes, the name was *quite* familiar. She'd heard it nearly every day since meeting Temperance. Only, her friend referred to the earl as *Cousin Nicholas*.

And if Temperance was so fond of her cousin, it surely wouldn't be that difficult to find him a bride. "I am not, but I shall make it a point to become so."

Briar shook the woman's hand. This was going to be as simple as sinking an arrow into a target from just two paces away.

Chapter 5

"She was disgustingly, was suspiciously reserved."

JANE AUSTEN, *Emma*

Briar threw off the coverlet the following morning, brimming with an eagerness she hadn't felt since they'd first arrived in London.

Today was most assuredly the day. Proof of that was the missive she'd received from Temperance this morning, announcing her cousin and brother had arrived and inviting Briar to meet them at her earliest convenience.

Padding barefooted across the crisp weave of the bedchamber rug, she withdrew a box from her wardrobe. Then, with great reverence—and an imagined chorus of angels—she lifted the lid.

And there they were . . . her lucky slippers.

After last year's debacle, she'd taken them to the cobbler to have them recovered in a pretty azure blue with silver threading. Since then, she'd carefully tucked them away, hoping that when she needed them, their luck would be overflowing.

Dressed in a bib-front white muslin dress with blue netting, she pinned her pale hair up into a twist and glanced at the book on her bedside table. "What do you think, Mother? Do I look like a determined matchmaker today, one capable of finding a bride for a rake?"

Mother agreed, of course.

Blowing a kiss to the red leather tome, she swept out of the room, heading in the direction of the offices. In the corridor, she met up with their maid, carrying a basket of linens.

"Good morning, Ginny."

Ever cheerful, she smiled back, her copper penny eyes bright. "A fine one, to be sure. Mrs. Darden has a fresh batch of scones waiting in the kitchen."

Among the pleasures in the world—at least the ones Briar had experienced—Mrs. Darden's scones ran a very close second to a good cup of chocolate. Pair them together and you could actually feel the rebirth of your soul.

"Is there a pot of chocolate, by chance?"

If ever a day deserved to begin with chocolate, it was today.

"Sorry, miss, just tea. Mrs. Darden said you'd had your heart set on chocolate but bid me to tell you that there were no cakes in the larder. The price has been too high at the market of late. And with so few clients . . ." Ginny let her words trail off.

Yesterday's matchmaking blunder hovered like a storm cloud overhead. Briar felt an eerie twinge in the soles of her feet. She glanced down at her lucky slippers and contemplated changing them for another pair.

Then again, not having chocolate was surely just a matter of mischance. "Well, I'd best be off. I have an urgent matter of business to attend."

"Of course, miss. Are you making a new match today?"

"Yes, indeed! I'm going to marry a rake." A jolt buzzed up from her instep all the way to the top of her head and back down again. The sensation stopped her so fast that she nearly tripped on the runner, a peculiar tingling sprinting through her limbs.

She tried again. "What I meant to say is that I'm

going to marry off a rake—to find a bride for him—not to become the bride." A nervous hiccup escaped as she forced out a laugh.

Without another word, Briar left Ginny to her task and hoped the peculiar sensation would stay far behind as well.

Down one set of stairs, she headed toward the offices of the Bourne Matrimonial Agency. These were actually small parlors that had been allocated for business. On one side of the hall was Uncle Ernest's, and on the other, a pair of sitting rooms —one for Ainsley and one for Jacinda.

To this day, Briar had never been given an office. And since there was not a third sitting room that adjoined the two, it was also clear that they never anticipated Briar becoming a matchmaker at all. *How wonderful it will be to finally prove them wrong.*

It came as little surprise to see Ainsley already at work, head bent over a stack of papers, her teacup and scone nudged off to the side of her slender writing desk. She lifted her head in a cursory brown-eyed glance, absently brushing wisps of chestnut hair from her cheek. "You're awake early."

"And good morning to you, too."

"It's just that no one usually sees your face until half past ten. Did you have trouble sleeping?" Ainsley's voice was edged with needless worry like a mother hen clucking over her young.

Part in parcel with having older siblings was that they tended to be overprotective.

"If it was the noise coming from Sterling's again," Ainsley continued before Briar could answer, "then I'll march over there this instant and have a word with that oaf."

"No need to bother Mr. Sterling this week. Unless, of

course, you simply desire to see him in his shirtsleeves again. Then I'd be happy to accompany you."

During their last visit to complain about the filth on the pavement in front of his establishment and the papers that had blown onto their own doorstep, Mr. Sterling had just finished a boxing match in the ring upstairs when he'd come down to greet them. Perspiration had dampened his hair, curling against his temples, and made his shirtsleeves cling to his broad, muscular torso. He was quite the specimen.

At least, Ainsley seemed to think so. She'd gone completely still, ogling him, open-mouthed for a full minute before she started to harp on him about the rubbish.

Briar grinned when she saw the barest spots of color bloom on her sister's cheeks. "Come to think of it, I did have a very restless night."

"He should never have greeted us in such an unsavory state," Ainsley grumbled, but with a slight catch in her breath.

At the escritoire, Briar helped herself to tea, nipping sugar from the cone. Looking over her shoulder, she saw Ainsley staring distractedly toward the door, and she couldn't help goading her just a bit. "Well, you did demand to see him straightaway. Do you think he removes his shirtsleeves when he boxes, or just his cravat and waistcoat?"

Ainsley straightened in the chair and quickly resumed reading the letters. "I wouldn't rightly know. It isn't something I waste my time pondering when I have more crucial matters at hand—like keeping the agency afloat. Six of these letters are from clients who wish to withdraw their subscriptions."

Briar felt a knot of guilt rise up her throat. Nevertheless, she did not appreciate that Ainsley's verbiage made it seem as if the burden were her own to bear, not Briar's.

"Since it was my blunder that cost us a handful of sub-scriptions, then I should be the one to make amends. It would help immeasurably if I could attend a few more events."

Ainsley didn't even glance in her direction. "Jacinda and Rydstrom have already accepted the invitations for this week. There's no reason to send another person from the family."

Briar swallowed her sip of tea and set her cup in the saucer, a glimmer of hope shimmering on the surface. "Then next week, Uncle Ernest and I will accept. After all, Jacinda is newly married. Surely she doesn't want to spend so many evenings at balls and parties when she could be alone with her husband."

"Jacinda is a duchess now. Her attendance at these events is the only thing that gives us any credence at the moment."

And there it was, the undertone of blame. Yet, since yesterday, Ainsley hadn't directly accused her for the blunder, as Briar wished she would have done. If Ainsley had raised her voice or even shouted, at least then Briar would know that she was seen as an equal.

"I didn't know they were related," Briar said quietly, awash in frustration and guilt.

Ainsley lifted her head, her dark features set in stone, her voice cool. "If you would have vetted their infor-mation instead of becoming enamored with the idea of finding a match, then it never would have happened. And we wouldn't be the laughingstock of London."

For an instant Briar went still, her breath catching in her lungs. As strange as it was, she was thrilled that her sister might actually argue with her.

But then, Ainsley slowly expelled a breath, her unerr-ing gaze alighting on the red leather book propped on a table along the far wall. The third volume of *Emma*, the one that mother had said showed Miss Woodhouse's wisdom.

Ainsley's features softened. "Never mind all that. I know it was your first time."

"I won't fall apart, you know. We can have a row just like you and Jacinda do," Briar said, disappointed.

"That's silly. It would be like arguing with—"

Ainsley stopped, leaving the rest unsaid as she pretended a sudden need to clear her throat. She affected a cough as well, but her dramatic skills had always been lacking. So she completed her performance by taking a sip of tea.

But Briar knew what Ainsley had been about to say. She'd heard it often enough throughout her life—that she was Mother's exact copy, both in appearance and mannerisms. The same woman who'd been so fragile and brokenhearted after Father abandoned them that she'd given up on life. Who'd sat for days in her room listless and staring out the window, until her heart had beat for the last time.

And that was all they could see when they looked at Briar.

"Someday, you'll realize that I am not her." Briar was much stronger, and soon she would prove it.

"Good morning," Jacinda said, gliding into the room, her auburn coiffure mussed, cheeks rosy, calamine blue eyes bright as she stifled a yawn behind her hand. "I had the devil of a time waking up this morning."

"Really, Jacinda. Must you use such language?" Ainsley glanced pointedly at Briar as if she were standing there dressed in nappies.

Jacinda wrinkled her nose. "The minister says *devil* each Sunday."

"Oh, how my innocent ears doth bleed. No more, dear

sister, I beg of you," Briar intoned, pressing the back of her hand to her forehead and expelling a dramatic sigh. She aimed a rueful look toward Ainsley.

Lowering her slender frame onto an upholstered chair, Jacinda laughed, the unreserved sound breaking through the palpable tension in the room. "Crispin is below stairs, seeing if he can cajole a few scones out of Mrs. Darden. We'd just finished breakfasting before we left not a quarter hour ago and he is hungry again, if you can believe it. That man certainly has an appetite."

Jacinda's grin turned sleepy and gradually color climbed to her cheeks until even her ears were rosy.

Ainsley cleared her throat and returned to the pile of correspondences. "We were just speaking of the Throckmeyer Ball and the Huntington dinner. You are still planning to attend, are you not?"

"Because if you would rather spend time alone with your husband, I would be more than happy to take your place," Briar interjected.

"Since Crispin is acquainted with Huntington we can hardly refuse. However—" Jacinda was interrupted by Ainsley's forced cough. The two sisters exchanged a glance and Jacinda nodded before continuing. "Actually, I'm looking forward to the ball as well. Miss Throckmeyer was on Rydstrom's list of potential matches, and it would be good to show him how fortunate he is to have me instead."

Briar felt as if her cup of cheer had sprung a leak. "I'm sure he already knows."

"Perhaps, though it never hurts to remind him."

"Briar, you have the Duchess of Holliford's dinner on Wednesday," Ainsley reminded. "We need you to be our representative. After all, we must keep our patroness happy, and you know how fond of you she is. Why, she'd even thought of having you marry her nephew."

Thankfully that had not come to pass. Briar had nothing in common with Clyde Ableforth, who was far more interested in studying insects than in anything romantic. And if it hadn't been for Jacinda's intervention, Briar might have found herself married to a complete bore. Instead, the Bourne sisters—well, mostly Jacinda—had found Mr. Ableforth's perfect match. The duchess had been so grateful that she'd taken them under her wing and assisted in opening the agency.

"I'm sure she would understand if I were absent this one week. After all, she knows how important it is for us to make successful matches. And I am tired of only being the person who serves tea to our clients. I can provide a great deal more."

"Of course, you can," Jacinda said at once.

"*After* you've learned to take matters a little more seriously, instead of being caught up in the romance of it."

"But we are matchmakers," Briar said, including herself. "In the very least, shouldn't we start off being a bit in love with what we do? Feel a rush of possibility whenever we meet a new client?"

"The same way Uncle Ernest falls in love with someone new at least three times a week?" Ainsley arched a brow in derision.

Briar could see she was getting nowhere. She loved her sisters, and most of the time they got along swimmingly. They shared the close-knit bond of children who had survived the worst pain imaginable. But when it came to business, they still treated her as if she were a child.

The only way to change her sisters' minds about what they saw when they looked at her was to show them she was just as capable as they were. "I promised to pay a call on Miss Prescott this morning. I should only be gone a short while, and will return before our doors open for business."

"Uncle Ernest is still on his morning walk through the park, so there isn't anyone to escort you."

Briar fought the urge to roll her eyes at Ainsley. "I can hire a cab for the short drive."

At least, she presumed she could if ever given the chance.

"No need for a cab. You can share the carriage with Crispin," Jacinda said.

And just in case it wasn't patently clear that they saw her as a child, Ainsley added, "There is no need to hasten back, for I doubt we'll have any new clients today. Enjoy the day with your friend."

⤐⥰

NICHOLAS HAD stayed out far too late, seeking the diversions of his usual London haunts. And this morning his head throbbed with every barefooted step as he padded downstairs.

He'd been determined to forget the things he'd done and the repercussions that followed. Yet no amount of liquor, hazard, cockfights, or women had soothed the restlessness abrading his raw nerves. Nor had it banished the guilt that plagued him.

His encounter with Miss Smithson—or rather, Lady Comstock—had ensured it.

Cinching the silver cord of his banyan around his waist, he sought out Aunt Lavinia and his cousin, Temperance, who'd been out when he'd first arrived last night. He needed to warn them that the months he'd spent in the country with Daniel had been for naught.

Daniel was still in a state of melancholy over the sudden end of his betrothal. Nicholas had only himself to blame. However, he kept that unfortunate truth—along with a host of other sins—from his family. It wasn't that he was trying to deceive them, but more so to protect them.

As the wife and children of a clergyman, his aunt and cousins were less worldly than most. Until three years ago, and for Temperance's first Season, they'd never even been to London. They had lived in a small vicarage in Lincolnshire, where his uncle was buried.

Nicholas remembered visiting them often, and with great fondness. He'd been more like an elder brother to Daniel and Temperance than a mere cousin. His aunt possessed all the gentle affection that had always been absent in his mother. They were the only true family he had. And because of those reasons, along with scores of others, he could never tell them what he had done.

If they ever found out, they would surely cut Nicholas out of their lives. Therefore, he needed to find a way to make amends for having destroyed Daniel's hopes, his faith in other people, and his will to live after his heart had been shattered.

Passing through the breakfast room and the morning parlor, Nicholas did not find Aunt Lavinia or Temperance, so he moved toward the garden terrace.

The smooth stone tiles were warm beneath his feet, the air balmy and perfumed inside the walled garden. But he winced the instant he stepped out from beneath the shade of the ivy-shrouded arbor, blinded by needle-tipped rays of sunlight. Shielding his eyes, he shrank back into the shadows.

From there, he saw Temperance amidst the flowers, her bright magenta dress standing out in sharp contrast to the delicate pastel blossoms around her.

Wiping a blond lock from her brow, her gaze shifted to him and she beamed broadly. "Cousin! Early this morning I'd heard a rumor among the servants that you had returned."

Abandoning her cuttings, she scuttled up the short

series of stairs to kiss his proffered cheek. Only a few inches shorter than his six feet, she was nearly able to look him in the eye as he gave her a wink. "This is the one time that any rumor regarding me has been correct."

She withheld her disputing laugh, but her pale brown eyes danced with merriment. "Of course. I should never believe otherwise."

Her willingness to pretend helped to ease his conscience marginally. Out of all the members of his family, Temperance might very well be his favorite.

Setting a hand at her elbow, he escorted her to an ornate wrought iron table situated beneath a fluted awning. There, he noticed a tea tray waiting with five cups and saucers. "Expecting callers, Teense?"

"Mother hates it when you use that moniker, you know. She thinks you're having a go at my expense."

With a sideways glance, he caught the shadow of worry breeze across her features. "It's only because I remember the day you were born, just a tiny, bawling, fuzzy-headed chick."

She scoffed. "That hardly applies any longer."

"To me, you'll always be that teensy wonder of creation," he said fondly, pushing in her chair. From over her shoulder, he saw a blush tinge the apples of her cheeks, a dimple peering out beside her small grin. Taking his own seat, he gestured to the empty cups waiting in a cluster. "So now tell me about the horde of gentlemen callers you are expecting this morning. Should I be prepared to throttle each one of them?"

"I am expecting a call, but not of the male variety. I've invited my friend to discuss a matter of business."

He smiled and snagged a scone from the tray, breaking it apart to expose the pale airy interior, the scent of lemon filling his nostrils. "Would this be the elusive *Miss*

B you always mention in your letters?" he asked around a mouthful, then looked at the pastry with wonder. "This is delicious. Since when did my cook learn how to make a scone that didn't resemble a *stone* in both flavor and appearance?"

"They are divine, are they not? Mother simply cannot live without them. They are from Mrs. Darden, my friend's cook."

He savored the last morsel and raised his brows. "Is this Mrs. Darden a persuadable type of creature? Perhaps she'd be willing to work for me."

"Mother already tried. Regrettably, Mrs. Darden is entirely faithful to the Bourne family."

A wayward tingle shot up his spine as he reached for another scone, the name sparking a hazy memory. "*Bourne.* I know that name from somewhere, do I not?"

"I should hope so. Your steward has been sending payments to the Bourne Matrimonial Agency for my subscription ever since this Season began. My friend is . . ."

Another vibration scurried over his flesh. The hair at his nape stood on end. He had read the nearly illegible name in his accounts without thinking much about it. Hearing it spoken, on the other hand, sent him reeling with remembrance of a fresh-faced young woman with cornflower blue eyes, lips as red as a harlot's, and spouting the utter conviction that she was destined to be a . . . a . . . *What* was it exactly?

He could almost hear the sound of her voice now, so light and airy it might have been composed of the center of this scone.

". . . a matchmaker," Temperance supplied.

"Now I remember." And he did, all of it. Right down to Adams's empty whisky flask and her soiled stocking lying on the floor of his carriage.

In fact, he believed he still had that stocking upstairs,

tucked away in his bureau. Which was unlike him. He never held on to items of clothing from his paramours, as that would have only encouraged them to cling. Though, since his carriage companion had never been with him in a biblical sense, he'd made an exception, planning to return it to her after a short visit to north Hampshire.

Of course, that visit had turned into a lengthy stay because of an unfortunate encounter with Miss Smithson.

The memory was a bitter one that he wished he could forget.

He'd been enjoying an afternoon jaunt about the countryside with Daniel and Temperance when they'd spotted a coach on the side of the road and stopped to offer assistance. Nicholas hadn't even recognized her. If he had, he never would have agreed to Daniel's suggestion that she wait for repairs at Blacklowe Manor. It wasn't until dinner that evening, when a pair of green eyes had glinted knowingly at him across the table, that he'd remembered.

All at once his mind had flashed to the color of scarlet, to eyes lined with kohl and lips painted with rouge. He'd recognized her but, as it had turned out, too late.

For the following days in Hampshire, she'd cast a spell over Daniel by way of secret letters and clandestine meetings. By the time Nicholas learned of this, Daniel had already been determined to marry her. And she had eagerly, cunningly accepted.

From that point on, she'd dined with the family every night and had spent each day keeping Daniel entranced by her charms. Nicholas did his best to warn him, but his cousin was deaf to every word.

There had been only two options left—either reveal the intimate details of their acquaintance, or tie her hands so she could no longer put her claws in Daniel.

Since admitting to having carnal relations with an unmarried debutante would bring the expectation of marriage down on his own head, he'd opted for the latter option.

Temperance sighed, her cup clacking against the saucer. "I wanted her to meet Daniel. But then his valet informed us that he was still abed and does not plan on rising anytime soon. He didn't even ask for a breakfast tray, but Mother sent one all the same. I'm sure she's outside his door now making a fuss. I'd hoped that after that terrible, jilting woman was out of his life, he would have returned as the dear brother I once knew."

"Retiring to my estate hadn't worked as I thought it would have done."

So Nicholas had returned to London, believing that it might be better for Daniel to be in society instead of removed from it. In his own experience, to get over one woman, all a man needed to do was replace her with another. By the dozens.

The only problem was that Daniel wasn't like Nicholas. He didn't want dozens of women—he still wanted the same one who'd never intended to marry him in the first place.

"Surely he didn't stay abed at your country estate."

"No, there was too much work to be done. The farms are running dry this year and I needed every available man to dig irrigation trenches."

"Ah. So that is why your skin is nut brown. It gives you the rather swarthy appearance of a pirate."

He grinned back at her, taking the cup of tea that she poured for him. "Been spending much time with pirates in my absence?"

"If only. From what I understand, they mistake sea cows for mermaids, and it's just that type of visual impairment I'm hoping for in a husband."

"Teense," he chided softly.

"Look at me, Nicholas. I'm four and twenty, taller than most gentlemen, and doomed for the shelf. And I'm not even sure *it* will have me. In the past four Seasons, I've only been asked to dance eight times, and that includes once from you and twice from my brother. I spend most of my time blending into the wallpaper. That was the reason Mother and I enlisted the help of the Bourne Matrimonial Agency. At this point, a matchmaker is my only hope. Fortunately, Briar understands me."

"Briar?" His cup stalled, his body teeming with awareness. Could that be *her* name?

Temperance nodded. "We met when Mother first filled out my application. Briar served me tea in the parlor and we started chatting about . . . oh, dozens of things, including these scones. And it was as if we'd been friends for years. Since then, we've been inseparable. We've even joined an archery club. Though, perhaps, I shouldn't have revealed that so casually. Her family doesn't know about the club. They're quite protective of her. So you won't mention it, will you?"

From what he recalled about her reckless naivety, her family's desire to protect her was well-founded. "You and your friend could always shoot at targets here in the garden for your amusement."

"It's far more than a mere diversion for Briar. She takes archery as seriously as she does matchmaking, and that's saying quite a lot. But when you meet her you will understand."

"Is this your way of asking me to have a shave and change my clothes?"

"Well, you'll want to look somewhat respectable when she arrives." She took a hasty sip from her cup. "I thought, perhaps, she could find Daniel a bride who will help him forget Miss Smithson."

Nicholas scratched the sharp stubble along his jaw, admiring Temperance's cleverness. With all that had transpired these past months, he hadn't paid much attention to the fact that she had subscribed to a matrimonial agency. But now, he wondered if such a plan wouldn't be just the thing for both his cousins.

Chapter 6

"Wickedness is always wickedness, but folly is not always folly."

JANE AUSTEN, *Emma*

"It was kind of your cousin to set up targets for us in his garden," Briar said with a glance over her shoulder to the doors leading to the house.

The archway was still empty, just as it had been the last dozen times she'd looked. As of yet, she had not met Lord Edgemont and impatience was starting to rattle her nerves. After the conversation with her sisters this morning, she didn't want to wait a moment longer to prove herself their equal.

"Nicholas would deny it with his dying breath, but he is soft at heart and tends to dote on me exceedingly. I've become quite spoiled, so you'd best find a husband for me who tends toward generosity."

Briar laughed, the insight into his character like music to her ears. The bowstring twanged and she could feel the vibration against her cheek as she sent an arrow slicing through the stagnant air. As expected, it hit the blackened center of the coiled straw target.

Temperance fired her shot, too, but frightened a gray squirrel up in the tree where the arrow landed. She called out a quick "sorry" to the creature. "Though, after you told me of your morning, I imagine it feels good to expend some violent aggression."

"Indeed, it does."

"If you were my sister, I should treat you just as you are—remarkably fascinating and worldly."

"Worldly?" Briar laughed again, but this time with incredulity. "Most farthings have seen more of the world than I."

"Yes, well *I* know that, but even so, you possess a certain air that hints at another life altogether. I can't quite explain it. But it's as if, at any moment, you might tell me that you plan to run away with a gentleman who'll sweep you off to the Mediterranean and bathe you in diamonds."

Briar batted her lashes playfully. "How scandalous! Oh, but they would be sapphires, of course, for he wants to find a jewel to match my eyes."

"And that is precisely the reason we became friends from the very start. Until I met you, I never would have conjured such an outlandish scenario. Though now I can picture it so clearly that I can taste olive-scented air on my tongue. You have a gift for inflicting everyone you meet with wild, romantic notions."

"I wish you would tell that to the cartoonist who drew that unflattering caricature in the *Post* this morning. Now all of London knows of my error." She took out her displeasure on the next arrow, and summarily struck the target squarely in the center. Yet she felt little satisfaction. "If only our most embarrassing mistakes were private events."

Temperance agreed with a commiserating sigh as her next shot pierced the ground three paces away. "It will all be forgotten soon. After all, this was your only misstep since the agency opened."

That wasn't entirely true. But Briar had never confessed her other near-disaster—the day she'd tried to meet Lord Hulworth but ended up sharing a carriage with a rogue instead.

And she never would tell a single soul, not even her dearest friend.

Thankfully, the rogue had been the only witness to her folly and she would never see him again. After all, a man like that would hardly grace the doorstep of the agency looking to marry. Or attend the very respectable dinners at the Duchess of Holliford's.

A peculiar shiver swept over her again, starting at the soles of her feet and ending at the tips of her fingers as she pulled back the bowstring. For an instant, the memory of those dark sinful eyes swept to the forefront of her mind.

Though truth be told, he was never too far from her thoughts. In fact, whenever she glanced out the windows of the agency toward Sterling's, she looked for a glossy black carriage with red spoke wheels and wondered if, perhaps, he'd ever thought of her.

It was silly, she supposed. He was certainly not a romantic figure, by any means. And yet, on that one morning, she'd had more of an adventure than she'd ever experienced in her life.

A frustrated growl from Temperance brought Briar back to the walled garden, the scented air thick as nectar.

"I think there is something wrong with my arrows. They look fine on the outside, but inside their cores must be all twisted."

"I'm sure that's it," Briar agreed for her friend's sake and offered a handful of her own. "Try some of these instead."

Temperance studied the new arrows carefully as she returned to the matter at hand. "I do wish Daniel would have come out of his rooms when you arrived. Since Mother can pester anyone into submission, there's still hope, I suppose. Though, now that I think on it, perhaps we shouldn't remind him about your family business for now. I don't want him to think that we're plotting to marry him off."

"Even if that's exactly why you asked me here?"

"Well, you are the only matchmaker I would trust with my own brother's happiness. And do you know what else, I think you should make a match for my cousin as well."

Briar inhaled sharply, then coughed.

Temperance whacked her between the shoulder blades. "Are you quite well? I hope you didn't swallow an insect, for it would ruin your appetite for tea."

Briar shook her head, knowing it wasn't an insect. The sour flavor on her tongue tasted far too similar to guilt. She hadn't yet told Temperance about the challenge she'd accepted from Genevieve Price.

"You want me to make a match for your cousin?" Briar croaked.

"I think Nicholas is lonely. There's been something off about him since last year. Of course, I could be wrong and he's merely worried about Daniel. But all the same, I should like to see him happy. Would you consider it?"

"Well, yes, certainly. But there's something I need to tell you."

Temperance held up a finger. "Hold that thought, for I am eager for the two of you to meet. I'd better go and see what's keeping him. Surely, meeting with his steward couldn't take this long. Though if I had to guess, I'd say he was rooting around in the kitchens for more of Mrs. Darden's scones. He was quite mad for them when he tasted them earlier."

"Then I'm glad that I brought more with me—not lemon, but orange and ginger with a jar of fig preserves."

Temperance set down her bow and put a hand over her midriff. "Tell me not to look in the kitchens for my cousin, for I fear I will eat the scones myself."

"Just think of them as a necessary indulgence. Don't they say that idle hands are the devil's workshop? Well, if we keep a scone in each hand, then we are working toward our own salvation."

"I absolutely adore the way you think." Temperance walked up the terrace steps and called over her shoulder before she disappeared into the house, "Shoot some of my arrows, will you? If Daniel does come out into the garden, I want to have something to boast about, and hope that he doesn't see the havoc I've wreaked on the shrubs in the distance."

Left alone, Briar resumed her task, methodically shooting the arrows in her own quiver, each of them striking in the center circle of Temperance's target. She mulled over how she would tell her friend about the challenge she'd accepted.

Distracted by her thoughts, she felt an odd prickling down the back of her neck, as if someone were watching her. Likely it was Temperance, returning to tell Briar that she'd succumbed to the temptation of the scones. Yet with a glance over her shoulder, she saw that she was wrong. It wasn't her friend at all.

She gasped, her eyes going as round as saucers. A man stood there, tall and dark, and . . . oh-so-familiar. *"You."*

It was the stranger from that day!

Forgetting that she had a loaded bow, she let the shot escape. The arrow sailed aloft, landing in the rhododendrons near the edge of the terrace.

Leaning casually against the archway, his long legs crossed at the ankle, the rogue merely raised a black eyebrow at the rustling leaves but did not stir from his spot. Clearly, he was used to sudden attacks—random arrows, women's kisses in public, debutantes bent on appropriating his carriage . . .

"I seem to recall once believing that you would have been a fair shot with a pistol, when some lout accused you of wearing rouge on your lips. Now I realize I'd been wrong. I was at greater risk of death by arrow."

"Depending on your proximity, of course." She was breathless with disbelief, and perhaps from the deep timbre of his voice as well. The lush, wicked sound burrowed into the pit of her stomach the same way it had before, like a cat clawing a cozy spot on a coverlet for a long nap. "But what are you doing here?"

Strangely, it seemed that no time had passed since their last meeting. Though, clearly it had, for his appearance was somewhat altered, his skin a little brown, his face thinner, and there was an overall sense of exhaustion that she had not noticed before. Still there was no mistaking the unforgiving angles of his cheeks and jaw, the wealth of his nose, those erudite ebony eyes, *and* her unaccountable fascination with his countenance.

"I'm merely enjoying the beauty of the garden, and a serendipitous reunion with an old acquaintance." He pushed away from the door and ambled across the terrace toward her.

She felt a blush creep to her cheeks in a wave of tingling heat. It had been foolish to share a carriage with a man who'd showed no qualms over engaging in salacious activity on the pavement outside of Sterling's. There was no telling what other thrilling activities such an irredeemable rake was capable of . . .

Her thoughts trailed off as the most disturbing realization occurred to her. "Surely you're not—you couldn't be—*Cousin Nicholas*?"

He sketched a bow. "The very one."

No. When she'd accepted the challenge, Briar had been sure Temperance's cousin would possess *some* redeeming qualities. But this man?

Bother. How could she ever convince such a man to marry? And more importantly, how could she find a sane woman willing to marry such a man?

It seemed that her slippers had lost every drop of luck, after all.

"Come here, Briar," he said with unabashed, toe-curling naughtiness, a sinful gleam in his dark eyes. Then he opened his arms. "Give your long-lost cousin a kiss."

Chapter 7

"One half of the world cannot understand the pleasures of the other."

JANE AUSTEN, *Emma*

"You and I are hardly cousins. And it is *Miss Bourne* to you." She offered a haughty sniff. Then, tucking a wisp of corn silk hair behind her ear, she turned away to select an arrow from the quiver, leaving Nicholas peculiarly disappointed.

Where was the unforgettable young woman he'd met last year who would have had far more things to say? Who wouldn't have hesitated to level him with her opinions, either on his conduct or his countenance? Who would have conjured a ludicrous scenario out of thin air, convinced of its possibility?

He hated to think that something or *someone* had altered that wholly vivacious, charming, and unabashedly ingenuous carriage appropriator, and turned her into a standard society debutante—pretty but far too bland.

"Well then, Miss Bourne, it is a pleasure to make your acquaintance. Though it may shock you to realize that I once met a young woman who bore a striking resemblance to you. Ranted on and on about a pair of lucky slippers, if I recall."

She went still. Staring straight ahead, her hand gripped

the string, elbow cocked. "You haven't mentioned that to anyone else, have you?"

"And risk having Aunt Lavinia hear that I'd had a tipsy and unchaperoned debutante in my carriage? I'd never hear the end of it."

Briar expelled a breath and sent the arrow flying. It struck the straw target soundly, and she didn't hesitate to slip another arrow from the quiver and continue.

"We'd have been forced into marriage," she said in a stage whisper, facing an audience of manicured shrubs. "Likely have our third child by the time Mrs. Prescott stopped mentioning the scandal at family dinners. Our oldest son would be constantly warned against following the example of his father's debauched past. Our daughter would be an angel but spoiled beyond offering any true guidance. And our youngest son, though still in the cradle, would have your dark eyes, but everyone would know he was going to be a trial on his mother's nerves."

And there she is.

He grinned, feeling an uncanny tingle of pleasure to know that London had not changed her after all. Nevertheless . . . "While I admire your ability to invent these outlandish scenarios, I do wish they'd find a target other than my own head."

"It cannot be helped," she said without the barest apology and sent another arrow flying. "I've given my imagination free rein to invent at will. I know that, someday, it will come up with some brilliant idea that will make me an excellent matchmaker."

Had there actually been a time when she'd suppressed her imagination? Highly doubtful. "The last time we met, you were not yet a matchmaker."

"Correction—I was very much. It's just that I was the only one who knew it."

"And now?"

She hesitated, the plump flesh of her bottom lip curling inward as she issued an uncertain hum. "I have a potential opportunity to change my circumstance."

So that hadn't changed either. Which was odd, because she'd been so determined to make her mark on the unmarried population of London.

He studied her with renewed curiosity, noticing every alteration. As opposed to that dim, foggy morning, sunlight made her complexion glow, the apples of her cheeks tinged with a lovely carnation pink. Her hair seemed more lustrous, too, a pale golden silk, curling at her nape and brow. Her lips were still a velvety rose-petal red, and absently, he wondered how many suitors she had at the moment.

Then he shook himself free of the errant thought. It did not matter, of course, for he would never be one of them.

She drew back the bowstring, her movements graceful, the toned sinew of her slender arm on display beneath short capped sleeves. When they'd met before, she hadn't offered so much lovely skin for him to admire. If she had, he might not have been able to put her out of his mind. Because now he was imagining how those arms would feel wrapped around his neck, those high, pert breasts crushed against his chest.

The tips of his fingers tingled with the desire to skim them down from sleeve to wrist. Though instead of giving in to his baser impulse, he merely allowed his gaze to take the journey, admiring every delectable inch of her.

Dimly, he noted that she was nearly out of arrows. Moving beside her, he took up the abandoned quiver from the ground, and slung it over his shoulder, offering her one.

She looked down at it and pressed her lips together

once more. So full of indecision today. He wondered what was occupying her thoughts.

"A *potential opportunity* suggests that you have not yet decided to seize it. Perhaps you're not ready to become a matchmaker." He quirked a grin, wanting to rile her, and was rewarded by a flash in those cornflower blue eyes.

With her gloved hand, she reached out and took hold of the shaft. Strangely, he felt the tug within him as she pulled it from his grasp.

"It is in my blood. Of course, I am ready and perfectly capable of taking on any challenge."

"Not according to the gossip column in the *Post*."

She swallowed, her voice strained. "How do you know it was me? Any one of us at the agency could have made that error."

"Not entirely reassuring news to your clients." He chuckled.

"That should not matter to you. Unless . . ." She gasped, whirling to face him, winged brows lifted in hope. "Are you already thinking of applying to our agency?"

He didn't know what she meant by *already*, but he chose not to ask. "I do not want a bride. Though if I did, I would find one on my own from the slew of women eager for my hand."

"Arrogance is not an attractive quality."

"It is only *arrogance* if I believed the prize they sought was this ancient rhinoceros." He turned his head to offer the best angle of his nose. "But the sentiment has more to do with my wealth and titles—I even have extra to pass along to my heirs. A trial really."

She slid him a rueful glance before angling toward the target and setting the nock to the bowstring. "Dear me! Not a title *and* a fortune! How utterly dreadful for you. Pray tell, why haven't you married one of those women?"

"As a general rule, I should like to trust the person who would run my household, rear my children, and inherit all my worldly goods. But in my experience, women are a rather untrustworthy lot."

And he was being kind, considering his history with the *Miss Smithsons* of the world.

Releasing another arrow, she stared distractedly toward the target as if lost in thought. "It is a commendable characteristic for a man to think of his future children's well-being."

"I was merely speaking in hypotheticals."

"Yes, of course. It is a language I understand quite well." She pivoted slightly, tilting her head to scrutinize his countenance, a mysterious light glinting in the depths of her eyes. "But it wouldn't hurt for you to think about marriage and children. After all, you haven't many years ahead of you."

If it wasn't for her sugar-coated smile, he might have thought she was serious and thinking of him as a potential client. Yet, since he knew how she enjoyed wild flights of fancy, he smirked back at her. The only marriages he was interested in were those of his cousins, or more pressingly, Daniel's.

"So, tell me, how did a born matchmaker become such an excellent marksman? Training for Cupid's army?"

"Lessons. Practice. Years of pent-up frustration. There are few activities deemed suitable for a debutante's life. And even fewer if you have an overprotective family. It wasn't until my uncle introduced my sisters and me to the Duchess of Holliford that our social education was refined." Stripping another arrow from his grasp, she proceeded to use it like a tutor's pointer over a study list on an imaginary blackboard. "Should a gentleman require entertainment—but of a blander variety than you are used to, no doubt—I can also play piano and sing. If he has a taste for art, I could paint a watercolor, embroider a tapestry, or cover a screen. I have practiced with a dancing master. Learned how to pour tea with a graceful turn of the wrist. And can converse on several topics bound to keep a dinner partner enthralled."

"Quite a list of accomplishments."

She inclined her head regally, playfully holding the arrow like a scepter.

"But still, nothing that would qualify you as a matchmaker."

At once, she squinted at him, her deep golden lashes crowding together. "Don't you have a parade of sin to attend, somewhere else, and far away from me?"

"The jugglers were tired, so I sent them home," he said with a grin, enjoying this little reunion of theirs.

Even so, it wouldn't be long before they were interrupted. It was time to get to the main reason why he'd waited to find Briar alone this morning—to help him find a wife for Daniel.

The way Nicholas saw things, he needed someone with inside information. Someone who had a proverbial finger on the pulse of the marriage mart. Not only that, but someone who had a close tie to the family—Briar's friendship with Temperance, for instance—was more likely to desire a solid union. And he would be hard pressed to find anyone more motivated than Briar.

All in all, she was the best option for expedience, lack of experience aside. "However, in regard to your accomplishments, I noticed that you did not list your chosen profession as one of them."

"I haven't had much practice, that's all. Nevertheless, I have studied under the incomparable tutelage of Miss Emma Woodhouse and I'm eager to use the knowledge I've gained."

He felt the flesh of his brow pucker in confusion.

"I've heard that name before, but I cannot quite place where."

Briar shifted and looked down toward a knobby elm root protruding from the clipped grass. The silver threaded toe of her slipper peeked out from beneath the hem of her skirts and struck softly, as if in a tentative test of its foundation. "Perhaps through Temperance, for I know she has read all three volumes of *Emma* as well."

"Wait a moment. Are you speaking of a character in a romantic novel?" A laugh rumbled out of him, unexpected and hearty.

Her incredulous gaze whipped up to spear his. "It is the matchmaker's bible, after all."

"You cannot learn all your skills through a work of fiction and expect to impact those who live outside the pages."

"And what do *you* know about making matches? Aren't you more interested in avoiding them?"

"I know a great deal about attraction—not merely physical, but what draws people together elementally."

"Oh, yes, the *spark*!" She nodded encouragingly, eyes bright. "That's what happens when the Fates bring people together."

He shook his head. "Sparks are blinding and fleeting. It's best to avoid those at all costs. What you need is someone to teach you how to observe men and women. How they see each other. How to discover what they are truly saying when they fill out their applications. After all, you said yourself that you took *lessons* to become skilled. Why should this be any different?"

"Are you offering to become my tutor?" This time *she* laughed and lowered her bow.

"I'm certainly more skilled than a character in a book. And by the time I've taught you a fair amount, you'll have produced so many matches that no one will think about yesterday's embarrassing incident." As the words left him, he was surprised that they sounded as if he was, indeed, volunteering.

When, precisely, had he made that decision?

And yet . . . it wasn't a terrible idea. Perhaps by offering his own knowledge, he might guarantee a good, solid match for Daniel. Someone who could wipe away the memory of Miss Smithson once and for all.

Her amusement faded and she grew quiet for a moment, considering. "And you would just . . . give this information to me freely?"

"Nothing worth having comes without a price, love. Think of the fate of poor Prometheus when he gave fire to man. He was punished by Zeus every day for the rest of his life, chained up, his liver a ready feast for an eagle."

"Lucky for you, I know how to make fire, and I have no desire for your liver or any other part of you."

He held up a finger. "Ah, but you do *desire* to make matches. For that, you'll need my instruction."

"Tell me, Lord Edgemont—"

"Nicholas."

She expelled a huff and continued. "Tell me, *my lord*, if you already know so much about men and women, then why are you interested in helping me? Surely, you could find a match for both of your cousins without my assistance."

"The truth of the matter is that you have far more access to debutantes, and I should prefer to keep it that way. Once a titled gentleman with a fortune begins making appearances at too many polite societal events, the eager swarm of husband hunters follows."

He could not imagine a worse fate.

She tilted her head in scrutiny, her lips curving in a slow, beguiling grin. "And even though you profess a disinterest in marriage, you're still taking steps to ensure the nuptial bliss of your family. When it comes to them, you're quite tenderhearted, aren't you? And here I thought you wouldn't have any redeeming qualities."

"How very kind of you to notice," he said dryly.

"I am in earnest," she declared and proceeded to tick items off with her fingers as if she were making a list. "Thus far, you've demonstrated a selfless regard for your family's contentment. You've been chivalrous, at least once, when you rescued a debutante without interfering with her person. Always a plus. You've professed to having a fortune and innumerable titles. And you even care for the children you do not yet have. Unless . . . of course, you *do* have illegitimate offspring."

"I do not have any bastards. I've made certain of that, though I don't see how—"

"*How* do you make sure of it?"

For an instant, her question interrupted his train of thought. He wasn't prepared for the full potency of her undivided attention, or how it quickened his pulse. Gazing at her eager countenance, he was tempted to tell her everything she wanted to know.

Then reason took over, warning him that one question from her would likely lead to another. And besides, she did not need to know that he always used French letters and never spent his seed inside any of his paramours. Or that, after previous experience, he'd learned never to take the chance. No, indeed. He did not want to have that conversation with anyone.

Instead, he redirected, his eyes narrowing with suspicion. "Pray, why were you listing my more favorable attributes just now?"

"Because I'm going to find you a bride." She shrugged her shoulders as if the matter were of little consequence.

Ah. Another one of her scenarios. "As I said before,

if I wanted a bride, I would have one. You've essentially promised me air to breathe when it isn't even yours to control."

"It would be if I were smothering you with your own cravat." She smiled sweetly, her dark humor adding another element to her overall appeal.

A ghost of warning whispered in his ear to be careful of such thoughts. Naive debutantes were not on a rake's menu.

"Besides," she continued, "finding a bride for you will be excellent practice."

"Only in failure."

"You say that now, but just wait until you meet her. She'll be completely irresistible."

The jangling of that ghost caused a shiver to coarse through him. "There isn't such a creature."

Reaching out, she pulled a forgotten arrow from his grasp, the shaft leaving a trail of tingles over his palm. "The challenge you're presenting only gives me additional incentive to find her."

"Additional?"

She looked down, her finger grazing the feather's edge. "Well, I don't suppose I would be violating any privacies by telling you—and I'll have to tell Temperance anyway—so, I'll just come straight out with it." She drew in a deep breath and squared her shoulders. "I've accepted a challenge to find a bride for the most irredeemable rake in London, which happens to be you. There. All settled."

Nicholas stared at her, stunned. It wasn't often that he was taken by surprise, and yet Briar Bourne had a knack for it.

"It's best to have everything in the open, since we're in the midst of striking a bargain," she continued. "And we are striking a bargain, are we not? Your lessons for my assistance in matching your cousin, *and* I'll throw in a bride for you absolutely free of charge."

His head was spinning. "So then, you knew who I was when you accepted this challenge?"

"I had no idea that you were . . . well, *you*. An oversight on my part. All I knew at the time was your name. And since the *Earl of Edgemont* is Temperance's cousin, I believed you couldn't have been all bad."

"Oh, but I am, love," he warned, and watched her gaze dip to his mouth. When her cheeks colored, he felt the warmth of it rush through his veins. "By the by, how much did this *challenger* promise to pay you?"

She sniffed. "It was about far more than money. So if you're thinking of buying your way out of this, it won't work. I'm quite determined."

He had been thinking of doing just that. "If it isn't about money then what do you stand to gain?"

"Put simply, if I do not succeed in this, then I will serve tea and file applications until the day I become so crippled with age that I can barely shuffle down the hall. My hands will curl into knobby claws, shaking from all the years of careful pouring. Of course, I would surely expire by the time I reached your age, just a winnowed husk of the person I might have been." She sighed. "So you can clearly see that I have nothing left to lose."

He didn't know whether to laugh or to beat his forehead against the brick wall between his and Lord Penrose's garden. "Somewhere along the way, I've given you the impression I'm apt to change my mind at any given moment. That isn't true. So I'll say this plainly . . . I. Do. Not. Want. A. Bride."

She grinned patiently as if he were a child. "Love isn't something you can predict."

No doubt she was under the delusion that love was a

wondrous thing. He would let her discover the truth on her own. "Why don't you focus all that determination on making matches for my cousins, hmm?"

"Oh, I will. I promise not to rest until I find each of you your ideal counterparts. It isn't in me to give up." She twirled the arrow between her fingers. "When do we start? Right this instant?"

"Now wait," he said, holding up his hand, "we have yet to come to an agreement. You've just added a new element to our bargain and the scales are tipping largely in your favor. After all, you'll still keep Temperance's subscription, which I've already been funding, and you're about to gain another client with Daniel. But secretly, I cannot have his name listed in your registry. If he ever discovered that I hired someone to find him a bride, I'm sure that would only lengthen the duration of his melancholy. He is of a romantic nature— a concept, I'm certain, that is familiar to you. He would only be happy by believing he met his bride by happenstance."

She agreed with a resolute nod. "He will never know otherwise."

"So this leaves us to barter over the price of my tutelage." Turning possibilities in his mind, he grazed his knuckles across the edge of his jawline.

He wasn't aware of the gesture until he watched her gaze follow, her pupils slowly expanding, turning to spills of inky black surrounded by a ring of blue. She likely had no idea that her simple glance revealed a certain degree of interest, an innocent curiosity. Doubtless, if he mentioned how the rake in him had learned to notice such things, she would blush and stammer. She might even balk and abandon her ludicrous challenge.

And suddenly, the kernel of an idea formed.

Perhaps there was a way to dissuade her from her futile attempts to find him a bride, torturing him with endless scenarios about happiness and felicity in marriage. There was only so much a man could take.

"The way I see it," he continued, "providing you with my accumulated knowledge is the most valuable asset. Therefore, I deserve something more tangible in return. After all, I have years of experience, love. Thousands of things I could teach you. So, for every lesson, I should like a kiss as payment."

Her gaze dipped to his mouth once more. "Wh-why would you want a . . . kiss from me? You've already stated that you have an endless list of women vying for you."

"A little token for my troubles. Besides, I recall how fascinating you were as a voyeur, and I'm curious about how you would be as a participant."

She pointed at him with the arrow, her cheeks a brighter pink. "You're a wicked man."

"True. Though, I could have asked for something else. A kiss isn't much, especially from someone as determined as you. And you'll be the one receiving the accolades from making the matches. Not to mention, the respect of your sisters, and future clients for years to come." He stepped closer, drawing the pad of his thumb over his bottom lip, her gaze flitting downward once more. "Of course, you could always give up on that challenge, instead."

Her breath caught, her nostrils flaring like a perfumer drawing in a scent. Still, she held her ground and pressed her lips together as if to guard them. "I'm not about to give you a *thousand* kisses. Think of the scandal, and neither of us could afford the consequences. I'm just about to start living, I don't want it ripped away from me."

"And yet, you are tempted. I can see it in the way your eyes have turned to the darker blue of a summer sky every time you glance at my mouth."

"I only did that to see if someone as ancient as you still had teeth."

He grinned, feeling a tug low in his gut that was in direct opposition to his intention. Instead of using the kiss as a means to shock her, he was starting to warm to the idea. "I'm offering everything you want and for just a small price."

"Drat you, horrible man. You're making it impossible for me to refuse."

He chuckled, and didn't bother to point out that she hadn't even attempted to barter with something else. "Then say, 'Yes, Nicholas.'"

Hearing the voices of his aunt and Temperance, he looked over his shoulder to the empty terrace doorway. They would arrive at any moment.

Eyes wide, she glanced to the open doors and back to him. "Surely you wouldn't . . . kiss me here? Now?"

No, but he wanted to. Suddenly he was feeling exhilarated, more alive than he had in months. Perhaps even years. "I only want your answer. But the offer will not stand once my aunt and cousin have joined us."

Briar was breathing fast, her eyes darting from the doors to his face, to his mouth. She wet her lips. And then at the last possible instant, she whispered the words he wanted to hear.

"Yes, Nicholas."

Chapter 8

"Human nature is so well disposed towards those who are in interesting situations . . ."

JANE AUSTEN, *Emma*

That evening, Briar was grateful for the distraction of the Duchess of Holliford's dinner party. She didn't want to spend another moment thinking of her bargain with Lord Edgemont.

It should have eased her thoughts of uncertainty when he'd left on an errand before taking tea that afternoon. But it hadn't. Instead, her mind had become preoccupied, conjuring one scenario after another about what it might be like to . . . submit her payments. All of them had left her shamefully breathless. And as a woman whose sole interest was in finding wholesome, respectable matches for her clients, she should not be this curious about kissing a rake.

Tucking those thoughts inside her bonnet as she handed it to the duchess's maid, Briar stepped into the parlor.

The Duchess of Holliford's residence in Mayfair was like a second home to Briar. Many members of the *ton* vied for an invitation to the weekly dinners, but the Bourne family always had a place at the table. Briar and her sisters were like the daughters—or more aptly, granddaughters—that the duchess never had.

Greeting her with unabashed fondness, Briar dipped

into a curtsy that brought her to eye level with the diminutive figure before her. "How lovely you look this evening, Your Grace. I dare say, that dark teal shawl quite matches the lustrous color of your eyes."

Beneath an elegant nest of dove-gray hair, the Duchess of Holliford looked sideways at Briar, a faint vellum-creased smile bracketing her pursed mouth. "Tush, girl. You're beginning to sound like that flattering uncle of yours. Where is Eggleston, by the by? Surely he didn't send you alone?"

"No. He is here with me," Briar said, pressing a kiss to the proffered lilac-scented cheek. "However, as we disembarked from our carriage, we met with another of your guests—Mrs. Richards, I believe—who dropped her handkerchief. Supposedly by accident Uncle Ernest bid me to go in without him while he rescued the fallen silk and accompanied her up the stairs."

The duchess drew in a patient breath and lifted her eyes to the ceiling. "The viscount is never in want of admirers."

"Very true," Briar agreed as her uncle appeared across the room.

When they'd first arrived in London, she'd thought his appeal came from the fact that he'd aged so well, with waves of silver-sand hair, lapis blue eyes, and only the slightest paunch to his lean physique. Yet lately she'd come to realize that it wasn't his handsomeness or charming mannerisms. Women were drawn to him because the years of his life and the trials he'd born had never darkened his soul. He treated each new love as if it were the very first and the very last.

Already she knew that her uncle would stay awake this night, writing a sonnet to Mrs. Richards. He truly loved women, whether he was wooing them or simply in their company. And no matter what transpired between him and his latest loves—the details of which Briar did not want to even imagine—they would always part as friends. Or rather as what he called *affectionate friends*.

Briar supposed that was the best of ways to end a love affair. With an amicable separation, neither party would have to endure any crippling heartache, and only suffer from the occasional sigh of fond remembrance as Uncle Ernest often did.

"Your uncle should use the resources of the agency to find himself a wife, lest he steal any more hearts."

Briar grinned. "But if you ask him, he'll tell you that he finds the perfect wife at least three times a week. Even so, he isn't allowed to fall in love with the client. None of us are."

"Ah, but your sister did, and all turned out well in the end."

"Yes, but with her amnesia, she couldn't remember that she wasn't supposed to. And besides, the *ton* was quick to forgive the new Duchess of Rydstrom." It was unfortunate that Briar's misstep hadn't yielded a similar consequence.

"I see you fretting, my dear, but do not worry. I forbid anyone this evening from speaking of the slight oversight at the agency."

If Briar had been a dog, she would have had her ears down and her tail between her legs. As a woman, her shoulders wanted to slump forward in shame. But she refused to give in to the impulse. What was the use in overthinking a mistake she'd already made? She would rather look past it and contemplate the future.

"What's this I hear? Women discussing business? Scandalous!" a low voice said from behind her, the sonorous timbre all too familiar.

Briar was stunned into utter stillness. It wasn't possible. A man like Nicholas would never be permitted to set a single roguish toe into the ever-proper Duchess of Holliford's residence.

Eyes wide, Briar slowly turned. And there he was, indeed, moving into their circle and bending to kiss the duchess's papery cheek. The same cheek she'd kissed a moment ago.

What was he doing here? And, more importantly, *why*?

Her pulse quickened with indefensible awareness, their bargain storming to the forefront of her mind.

"Unconventional, perhaps, but hardly scandalous," the duchess said, patting his arm fondly. "Though it is rather serendipitous that Miss Bourne and I should be discussing her uncle's matrimonial agency in the same instant you happened our way."

Nicholas grinned rakishly—though a man such as he likely had no other way of grinning—and inclined his head toward Briar, his gaze skimming over her flushed cheeks. "You must forgive my godmother, for she occasionally confuses the definition of serendipity with contrivance. She waved me over when she spotted me at the door."

Godmother? Briar eyed him with suspicion. He'd conveniently neglected to mention an association with the duchess when Briar had mentioned Her Grace earlier.

"Pay him no heed, Miss Bourne, but allow me to present to you my godson, the Earl of Edgemont."

"My lord." Briar dipped into a curtsy by rote, pretending she didn't know him at all. Then again, she didn't. Not really . . . and yet, she'd said yes. *Yes, Nicholas.*

"Miss Bourne, a pleasure indeed." Reaching out, he took her hand and pressed a kiss to her gloved fingertips. Wayward tingles waltzed down her limbs, beneath her skin.

"He has just returned from his estate in the country, and can you guess the recipient of the first social call he paid?" The duchess splayed her small hands over the brooch pinned to the gathers of her paisley shawl, her tone warm and eyes bright with pleasure. "Such a pleasant visit. We chatted for more than an hour before I had to shoo him out the doors and adjust the plans for dinner."

So that was the errand he'd had in mind when he'd left his house. But surely, he couldn't mean to collect on their bargain this very night. They hadn't even discussed the particulars. And though she was filled with a reprehensible amount of curiosity, she was also suffering from a degree of shyness.

"And can you guess the topic that most enthralled him, my dear?" the duchess asked.

Briar shook her head, her heart rising to her throat, certain that her shocking bargain was all over her face. *Yes, Nicholas* might as well be written in India ink across her forehead. "I cannot."

"My godson was thoroughly intrigued by the Bourne Matrimonial Agency, wanting to know how it began, and about my own involvement after you helped to find my nephew a wife. I told him everything I could. Of course, he claims his interest stems from his cousin's subscription. Oh, and I believe you are well acquainted with Miss Prescott, are you not?" At Briar's nod, the duchess went on. "Yes. Yes. I'm sure you would have met Lord Edgemont eventually. Though I am glad to take my part in it. After all, once a man starts speaking the word *matrimony* freely, then he might very well be thinking of it for himself."

"I do not understand why everyone I meet lately wants to marry me off, armed with Cupid's arrows and wicked propositions." He had the gall to wink at Briar.

Vexed, she inhaled so quickly that she choked on her own saliva. Oh, but she wished it had been an insect instead—one large enough that a physician would be summoned to extract it. She would be sent home then and given orders of complete mouth rest for the next few days. *Wicked proposition,* indeed!

Still coughing, she watched as the duchess lifted her hand to call a tray-toting servant over.

Nicholas slipped his handkerchief from inside his superfine black coat. Then, presenting the folded linen square between his fingers, he leaned in to whisper, "Are you quite well, Miss Bourne? I should hate to cancel such a promising evening due to the pretense of a cold. However, if you aren't feeling as determined as you were earlier, you need only say the word."

"If I were infected with the plague," she croaked, temper simmering, "I should be more than happy to give it to you."

"If yellow fever or the black death came in such an enticing package, all of humanity would surely perish. Even I would welcome it with open arms."

He stepped apart from her then, his wicked words leaving her warm and wobbly kneed. If she'd had any lingering doubts about how irredeemable he actually was . . . well, she didn't now.

"Here, my dear. What you require is a glass of wine to truly fortify you," the duchess interjected, handing Briar a goblet from the tray. "I have the best of surprises for this evening. I had the footmen reassemble the entire dining room out on the terrace. What fun! In lieu of a formal dinner, we'll be eating like bohemians. Is there a better way to welcome a warm evening than dining by torchlight?" Briar did not have the chance to answer before the duchess turned to her godson. "Would you mind being Miss Bourne's escort, Lord Edgemont?"

"Not at all. Would you do me the honor, Miss Bourne?" Nicholas proffered his arm. And when his devilish gaze slanted to her, it was almost as if she could read his thoughts. *Say, "Yes, Nicholas."*

Briar might very well have to kill him instead of kiss him.

NICHOLAS NEVER imagined that a *bohemian* dinner would feel so confining.

Here he was, out on the terrace with a warm breeze stirring the smoke rising from the torches, and he couldn't find a bit of air. Of course, the reason likely stemmed from the fact that the woman beside him had been using it all up with her incessant rambling about her *pretty* daughter, who was presently at Almack's under the chaperonage of her elder brother.

He shifted in his chair, restless. He'd known that the instant he set foot into polite society, the ravening horde of husband hunters would sniff him out.

In the past hour, Nicholas had learned more about Lady Baftig's family than he'd ever known about his own. *We used to summer in Bath until it fell out of fashion . . . With seven children, it is important to have ample opportunities for enjoyment . . . Matilda has always been ever-so-patient with the little ones . . . Do you come from a large family, my lord?*

"No," he answered succinctly and caught Briar smirking from her seat near the middle of the table. Oh, she was enjoying this a bit too much.

She'd been pretending to be absorbed in conversation with the gentleman beside her, offering occasional nods and interested lifts of her brows. But her gaze had been distant, her focus often straying to this end of the table.

Nicholas had to give her credit, however. She was good at avoiding direct eye contact. He would not be able to accuse her of watching him, certainly not in the same way he was watching her. Yet it was clear that she was more interested in his conversation than in her own.

His arrival had taken her by surprise this evening. Clearly, she hadn't known about the connection between the duchess and himself, but seeing her eyes widen and her cheeks flush had given him a peculiar thrill of satisfaction, and he was glad that he'd decided to accept his godmother's invitation.

Though, he'd never intended to come. It wasn't until Aunt Lavinia introduced him to Briar—at least, as far as his aunt knew—that he'd excused himself from joining them for tea, claiming an errand. In truth, he'd required a diversion.

The instant Briar had agreed to their bargain, it was all he could think of. And the prospect of listening to his aunt's hopeful yearnings that Daniel would soon emerge from his melancholy only made Nicholas feel as if the walls of his townhouse were closing in on him.

Restless, he'd gone out and, without preconceived plotting, he'd ridden his horse here. The reason he'd called on his godmother hadn't even occurred to him until she'd started chattering about her protégés, the Bourne sisters. Then it became clear.

He'd likely heard mention of them countless times before, but over the years he'd learned to turn a deaf ear to talk of unmarried young women. Today, however, he'd hung on every word. Absorbed every detail, including the fact that the youngest attended dinners here each week. And since the bargain he'd made with Briar still lacked form or rules, he felt there was no better opportunity to set things in place than tonight.

A fresh rush of impatience tore through him at the thought. He wanted to barter with her. Exchange quip for quip. Make her blush. He was eager for dinner to end but it was taking an eon. He'd go mad if his godmother didn't ring the deuced bell beside her plate and end his—

The bell tinkled in that instant, and Nicholas expelled a tense breath.

At the opposite end of the table, the Duchess of Holliford rose from her chair, which did nothing to alter her petite stature. "Being that we are all out of doors, I see no reason why the men and women should separate. Let us continue to enjoy each other's company in the night air and adjourn for cards later."

Murmurs followed, some of discontent but others of scandalized excitement. A few glances slid his direction as if this small alteration was breaking all of society's rules and he was the cause of it.

With a grin, he lifted his glass in a salute to the party and drained the contents.

A regiment of footmen moved as one to pull out the women's chairs as the head butler carried a cigar tray around the table for the men. Briar rose and, without a backward glance, moved toward the opposite end of the terrace where his godmother stood. He wondered if she believed that standing beside the duchess would keep him from seeking her out.

Nicholas grinned at her naivety.

Rising from his own chair, he made his way to them, noting that their hushed conversation came to an abrupt halt. "I see I have caught the pair of you deep in a discussion unsuitable for my ears. For shame."

His godmother tapped him with her fan when he clucked his tongue, amusement crinkling the flesh surrounding her sharp eyes. "Outrageous accusation, dear boy. We were merely speaking of marriage."

"A topic which is surely dear to your heart, by now, my lord," Briar said smugly. "After all, you did spend the majority of dinner conversing with Lady Baftig, who—from what I gather—is quite eager to make a match for her daughter."

"And during the whole of it, I was wishing someone would take pity and smother me with my own cravat."

He shared a glance with Briar, watching as she hid a grin behind her cup of cloudy lemonade. Her breath fogged the glass when she whispered, "The night is still young."

Indeed it was, and he was tired of waiting for it to begin.

He'd spent a restless day thinking about how their bargain would unfold. And now, anticipation charged through his blood like a firestorm, turning his usual cool temperament hot and tense, which might be alarming if he thought for a moment it was about more than simply satisfying his curiosity. But that's all this was.

"What was that, dear—something about the night air?" his godmother asked, spreading the fan beside her ear and tilting her head to listen closely.

Briar swallowed and lowered her cup, shifting her slippers on the terrace stones. "It is very still."

"Mmm . . . yes. Perfect for brewing romance." His godmother smiled, a mysterious glint in her eyes that had the effect of tightening the corded muscles between his shoulders in warning. But then she turned her attention to a fair-haired young woman and gentleman standing near the stone archway leading to the garden, and he relaxed. "I expect an announcement of Lord Aselton and Miss Carrigan's betrothal any day now. Perhaps this very evening."

"Is that so?" Dubious, he glanced again at the pair. Miss Carrigan's stiff spine seemed comprised of glass and on the verge of shattering at any moment, while Lord Aselton's jaw might fracture from the force of clenching his teeth. "I'm afraid you will be waiting a long while for that event, *if* it ever happens at all."

The little duchess pursed her lips and tsked. "But of

course it will, for I have it under good authority—Oh, there is Mrs. Carrigan, hailing me from the fountain now, so I must leave the matter to Miss Bourne. She will explain how well suited they are, and then you will see that we are right."

"Before you go," Nicholas said, seizing this perfect opportunity, "I wonder if I might have your permission to speak with Miss Bourne privately—about that matter regarding my cousin?"

Torchlight revealed rows of fine lines deepening on her brow beneath finger curls of dove-gray hair. She drew in a hesitant breath. "With your reputation, I should not allow it at all. However"—she glanced at Briar and back to him—"since Miss Bourne's character is always above reproach, I see no harm in it, as long as you keep to the open rooms. And not for long."

The duchess descended the stairs toward the garden, and beside him, Briar stiffened, her easy manner replaced by narrow-eyed wariness. "Is it truly your design to speak of making matches for your cousins?"

"Of course, just as it will be each time we meet. My sole focus for the remainder of the Season is to ensure their happiness, *and*"—he added with a weighted pause, his gaze brushing her rose-petal mouth—"to honor our bargain. I will teach you what I know and in turn . . ."

Her lips parted, a deep breath leaving her in a rush. "Surely not here."

If she'd asked to amend their agreement earlier, or even to withdraw from it altogether, he would have done so. A gentleman might still offer her another chance to rethink her choice. Unfortunately for Miss Bourne, he was no gentleman.

"If you are nervous, then the best remedy is to hurdle this first disbursement and realize that it is just a diversion. For both of us."

"*Diversion.*" She huffed. "And I'm not nervous. Far from it. I should like to be done with it in short order. However, we haven't even discussed matters, I'm not about to continue unless we establish the full agreement—quantity, stipulations, rules."

Though still quite green, she was a force to be reckoned with. She knew herself and would not let anyone take advantage. And Nicholas found his appreciation of her growing moment by moment. "We are like-minded. I believe in stating the parameters of any arrangement upfront as well."

She nodded succinctly. "If your part is to offer knowledge about what draws men and women together, then the sensible thing would be for me to witness it firsthand, at social events and such. The way I see it, there are no more than twenty worthwhile events left in the Season. And if I were able to attend half of them it would be a miracle."

"Very well. Ten, it is. And I shall ensure that you receive invitations to events that are so innocuous that your family need never worry."

She slid him a skeptical glance. "And how will *you* manage that?"

Little did she know, but he still had a number of boring friends. They weren't all cardsharps and libertines. "All that should concern you is our agreed-upon method of payment. Now, what of your stipulations?"

"Well," she hemmed, trying to take a stalling sip only to find her cup empty. She sighed and lowered her hand. "I think I should be the one who proceeds first in these encounters."

"As every woman should—a principal I live by as well," he said matter-of-factly. But she must have caught a hint of wickedness in his tone because she eyed him shrewdly. In turn, he lifted his brows in a semblance of innocence.

"I do have one rule," she said, raising a finger, her tone and expression as severe as a scolding governess. "No hands involved. I've already born witness to what yours are capable of. This is strictly a mouth-to-mouth arrangement. That way there won't be anything untoward."

He crossed his heart. "I only have two rules. Don't fall in love with me, and don't ever believe I will change my mind about marriage."

"The first is hardly a rule at all since it is an impossibility. As for the second . . . we shall see."

"No, *we* shall not." He growled with warning, but it was difficult to keep his expression stern when she laughed. The warm effervescent sound sparkled around her like bubbles lifting on a summer breeze. He caught himself holding his breath. Fully enthralled, he listened and heard a bright little hiccup at the end before she simply grinned, torchlight dancing in her eyes.

"You're making me quite impatient," he said, his voice rough. "So, with those matters settled, it is time to adjourn to one of the open rooms."

"But . . ." Her gaze drifted to his lips before she pressed hers together. "What about my lesson? That is part of our bargain, is it not?"

"For someone who claims to be *far from nervous*, you certainly have a knack for hesitation." Nicholas flicked a hurried glance to the reserved couple still standing near the garden entrance. "Your presumption that Miss Carrigan and Lord Aselton are romantically attached is completely wrong. Unless they are forced by circumstance, marriage is not in their future. It is clear they cannot stand each other."

"Impossible. I've spoken with them on many occasions and found them both excellent conversationalists, ever so polite. Why, it's nearly as if they can finish each other's sentences."

"And have you never been polite, all the while gritting your teeth?"

She slid him a wry glance and bared her clenched teeth in something of a smile.

He knew very well that she was goading him but chose not to call her out on her lie. "Take your dinner partner, for instance. Lord Beechum was certainly a prattler. Do you happen to remember straightening your shoulders and curling your hands into fists?"

"Well, no, I . . ." Then Briar looked past the terrace to witness Miss Carrigan doing that very thing. "Hmm."

"And do you notice anything about the way I am standing right this instant?"

Her gaze raked over him, from the top of his head to his shoes. The return was slower, her head tilted in such thorough scrutiny that he felt overdressed, the fine wool of his trousers abrading his skin, a heated shiver making every hair stand on end.

"You do have a look of intolerance about you. Your shoulders and jaw are taut and one of your feet is pointed toward the door as if you are ready to bolt at any moment." She glanced to the couple. "Lord Aselton is doing that as well. In fact, both of their feet are pointed in opposite directions, and now Miss Carrigan's arms are crossed. They look eager to escape each other." Then she turned back to Nicholas, a furrow puckering the flesh above her pretty nose. "Are you eager to escape me as well?"

If only that were true. "Look again. Are my hands open or closed? Am I angled toward you or away?"

She perused his form again, killing him slowly, tapping her gloved finger against the corner of her mouth. "It might sound peculiar, but you're poised as if ready to waltz with me—shoulders bending slightly forward, your palms open as if to pull me close, arranging me into the cage of your form."

"Very good, Miss Bourne. And not peculiar at all, especially if you take note of our closer proximity to the door."

Her mouth opened on a silent gasp. "Have you been herding me all this time?"

"You should give yourself more credit than a sheep." He slipped her cup from her grasp and proffered his arm.

She took it without hesitation, her fingers curling over his sleeve. "I feel as if every eye is on us."

"If they are watching, they will think that I'm escorting you to the parlor. And I told my godmother that we would remain in plain sight all the while to ensure your reputation."

Briar issued an airy laugh, her lips curving in a smile as they walked inside and down the corridor. "So we are going to talk, after all. Do you know, for a moment, I actually thought you intended to—*Wait,* this is the music room."

"Is it?" He closed the door behind them, his pulse quickening in greedy anticipation.

She stopped on the edge of the rug, still as a lamppost. "We aren't in full view of anyone."

"If they opened the door, we would be." He made a mental note for a lesson in her future, regarding how men tend to become quite literal when it suits them.

"But then we would be discovered."

"Very true." Crossing the room, he sank casually onto the blue sofa as she quietly railed at him, the flickering torches beyond the window bathing her in lush golden color.

"And my reputation would be in tatters. My family's business would falter out of existence. We would be cast out of London. I would grow old in the country, my entire existence depending upon the infrequent visits of my sister Jacinda, her husband, and their future children.

And because all of this was my doing, I wouldn't even have the honor of being their favorite aunt. Instead, the children would clamber into Ainsley's arms, pelting her with their soft puppy kisses and telling her stories of their exciting adventures."

"All the more reason to be discrete, and to make haste," he said in a casual tone, belying the impatience teeming through his veins. "Come away from the door, Briar, and kiss me."

Chapter 9

"Can you trust me with such flatterers?"

JANE AUSTEN, *Emma*

Come away from the door, Briar, and kiss me.

The sinful timbre of his voice tumbled through her, stealing her breath. Her curiosity reached an anxious simmer, brewing hot and frantic beneath her skin.

In contrast, *he* was draped casually over the sofa as if he hadn't a care in the world. As if there wasn't an ounce of anticipation in him, or even a smidge of nervousness.

And speaking of nerves, hers were now making themselves known in tiny shivers that skated over her limbs, drawing her flesh tight. Was she truly about to kiss a rake?

A man like him possessed heaps upon heaps of experience, whereas she had . . . well . . . a bit less. She shifted her feet on the rug.

Why, oh why, had she made it a stipulation that she would be the one to begin their encounters? "Aren't you going to stand or something?"

"No hands, remember? I wouldn't want to risk your teetering on tiptoe just to reach my lips."

"Yes, of course," she said with a shrug as if that very thing happened to her all the time.

"Shall I put my arms like so?" He linked his hands

behind his head, arms bent at the elbow. With his tai-
lored jacket rising and his satin waistcoat in taut hori-
zontal furrows across his chest, he was the very portrait
of a man in unfettered repose. A man comfortable
within the confines of his own skin. And with his long
legs extended and crossed at the ankles, his trousers fit
over every muscle, snug and . . . enticing.

Even for one unused to observing a man in such a
relaxed arrangement of limbs, she could appreciate that
he was well formed. Very well formed, indeed.

She didn't know why the observation caused her pulse
to race, or why her throat was suddenly dry as parch-
ment. Nevertheless, she took her first step.

Dimly, she wondered if this was how prisoners felt
when approaching the gallows.

"I'm hardly your gaoler," he said with a growl.

She felt her cheeks grow even hotter. "I hadn't meant
to say that aloud. I am fully aware that I agreed to our
bargain, and I plan to honor it forthwith."

He arched a brow at her measured progress. "I think
you've forgotten that *forthwith* means *straightaway*, love."

"Surely you cannot be that impatient. I shouldn't be
surprised if you'd been kissing another woman on the
pavement outside Her Grace's townhouse."

He did not answer, but watched her draw near, his
focus on every blink, every swallow. And when she finally
stopped beside the sofa, he watched as she wet her lips.

Her pulse quickened, one on either side of her throat.
The two points were like galloping horses on a hunt, one
named *Nerves* and the other *Anticipation*. And she wasn't
sure which one was outpacing the other. Was she more
eager to kiss him, or more worried that—like her first real
attempt at matchmaking—she would make a blunder of
the entire event?

In her mind, she could almost hear the blare of the hunting horn, telling her it was now or never.

Stealing a glance at his broad mouth, she wondered how to proceed—charging head on with a shout of *tallyho*? Or something stealthier, slower, like a huntress stalking her prey?

Briar furtively met his gaze as if he might supply the answer. Yet when she saw those alert ebony eyes—darker and more intense than she'd ever seen them before—she suddenly realized that she was not the hunter in this scenario at all. She was the doe emerging from the forest. And all along, he'd been waiting for her to come into the clearing.

She wet her lips again, *Nerves* taking the lead over *Anticipation*.

Slowly, she lowered her head, the soft crunch of taffeta sounding her descent. Scant inches from his face, she hesitated one last time, drawing in the fragrance of his skin. The lush dark scent of warm leather and mulled spices and the earthy aroma of the port he'd drunk on the terrace worked like a tonic to put her at ease.

Her eyes drifted closed and, unerringly, her lips found his.

The shock of first contact trampled through her—the subtle heat and firm pressure of his lips. The pliant give of her own. The silken glide of her right nostril against his. The prickle of his stubble against her chin.

He inhaled sharply, stealing breath from her mouth, making it his own. And suddenly the entire experience seemed far more intimate than even she had imagined— and her imagination had always been rather good.

She drew back almost instantly. But bolting upright caused her head to spin and she wobbled slightly. "I suppose you were right about teetering on tiptoe after all. I . . . I do not believe I'm wearing the proper shoes for kissing."

He shifted off the sofa and stood up without even brushing against her skirts. Then he began to prowl about the room as if trapped in a triangular cage walled by the piano, harp, and sofa.

He hissed. "Have you ever kissed a man before?"

"Well, of course, I have—"

"Other than your uncle or someone you're related to?" She snapped her mouth shut on the rest of her reply.

He stopped in front of her, glaring at her eyes. Then her lips. He raked a hand through his hair, and he set about prowling again. "You should have told me."

"I don't see what it could matter," she said on a huff, feeling ungainly and gauche.

"Do you think I wanted to be your first? You should have had that with a boy down the lane, fumbling along together in innocent exploration when you were still in a pinafore."

"There was no boy down the lane."

"An infatuation with your tutor? Music teacher? Blond-haired stable boy? No one?" He seemed to read her answer in the stiffness of her posture and the way she was now gritting her teeth. "*Bollocks.* At your age, you should have imagined yourself in love at least once."

Well, she hadn't been in love, not even a little bit. That was her big secret—a matchmaker who'd never been in love.

Briar had always been shielded by her sisters and there was part of her that had never wanted to displease them, so she'd never taken risks. Well, aside from one fateful day last year. Though, perhaps the fact that she hadn't had those experiences—like kissing a boy from down the lane—was one of the reasons her sisters could never see her as an equal. And the crux of her inability to make matches.

The ever-impulsive Jacinda would have done so, and Briar knew for a fact that Ainsley had kissed a man because she'd been betrothed at one time. But Briar hadn't kissed anyone.

Not until now. And she could still taste him. Still feel the warm press of his lips, her own pulsing with this awareness and feeling plump as ripe berries.

"Surely you're not worried that I'm going to fall in love with you simply because you're the only man I've kissed?" She added a stage-whispered *ha*, for good measure. "Rest assured, this wasn't an experience I'm likely to dream about. I'd have had more enjoyment from kissing the back of my own hand. So I'll hardly start pressing kisses to my pillow while imagining your face and whispering your name. And I'm certainly not going to carry this moment with me, to think back on and sigh, over the course of my life."

Oh alright, she would think back on it and sigh, but only on occasion. And she would scold herself for it each time.

"Bloody romantic debutantes. Any man with sense would avoid the lot of you," he grumbled.

Was he planning to *avoid* her, then?

"Now wait a moment. You're not cancelling our bargain, not after all I just went through. Why, the pulse at my throat nearly broke the skin. I might have been scarred by this entire ordeal and left to wear unfashionably high collars for the rest of my life." She stiffened, hurt that he clearly had not experienced the same sensations that had riffled through her. "If all this is because I need to kiss more than one man, then I shall remedy the situation by kissing a slew of them. Younger men of course, classically handsome, and not so critical."

"Don't be a fool." He hesitated, his irritated—somewhat feral—gaze settling on her lips again. "This was . . . unexpected, and I don't particularly like being caught unawares."

"Oh, I see. You can dole out surprises—like proposing kisses for lessons—but you refuse to be the recipient?" She hiked her chin, prepared to walk out the door this instant. Feminine pride was on the line, after all.

He studied her, his expression thoughtful. "A valid point. Though I expect complete honesty from this moment hence. In addition, if there is ever a time that you suspect your regard has grown beyond the bounds of our bargain, you must tell me at once."

She laughed at his arrogance and the preposterous notion. "Oh, and you must do the same as well. If you ever have even the slightest inkling that you are falling in love with me, you must confess it at once. I will not be responsible for breaking a rogue's heart."

But he did not smile in return. Instead, his expression was set in stone. "In the spirit of disclosure, I will tell you that I have no heart to break. You would do well to remember that. Always."

Was it her imagination, or did a shadow of pain glance across his hard-set features?

No heart to break? Well, to her way of thinking, that simply wasn't possible. Unless . . . his heart had already been broken and never mended. She couldn't help but wonder about the woman he might have loved once.

Before she could ask, he approached and expelled a port-scented breath, his hard expression softening by degree. His tone was warmer, too, coaxing and soothing away the initial bruising to her ego. "We could stop here and part ways, but that would not change what has occurred. With everything in the open—*I trust*—I see no reason why we shouldn't continue our bargain. If you feel differently, however, you need only say the word."

Briar found herself ensnared by the gentle caress of

his eyes, the barest tinge of uncertainty lingering in those ebony depths. And there was something else there as well, flaring to life the instant he glanced down at her lips. Whatever it was caused a ripple of sensation to wash through her, and her stomach clenched sweetly. All at once, she was thinking of what it would be like to kiss him again. Heat climbed to her cheeks on an admission she dared not speak aloud.

"I agree that we should continue. The benefits to us both are undeniable." Obviously, she'd done something incorrectly and would need further study.

He moved a step closer as if he intended to proceed that instant, but voices in the corridor stopped him.

She gasped, her anxious gaze darting to the door. "Oh dear."

Quick and capable—as if this sort of thing happened all the time—Nicholas calmly took her hand and drew her to the piano, pulling out the bench for her. When she sat, he leaned over her and lifted the fall board, his arms surrounding her in a cage of delicious toe-curling heat, the scent of warmed leather filling her every breath. It was only with the pressure of his chest against her back that she could feel the heavy thudding of his heart that matched her own.

Then his lips grazed the sensitive shell of her ear as he whispered, "Play something, love."

Play? She could hardly think. Her body was too busy vibrating with tingles, heart racing too fast to count the beats.

By rote, she placed her fingertips on the cool ivory, making up a melody until she could remember the notes of one she'd studied.

At the door, he turned the knob with careful discretion. Then, leaving it ajar, he strode to the far corner and opened the camouflaged servant's entrance. Pausing there, he cast her a conspiratorial wink and inclined his head before he disappeared.

A peculiar sort of lightness swept through her in trilling notes. So *that* was what it was like to kiss a rake.

Chapter 10

"The muffin last night—if it had been handed round once, I think it would have been enough."

JANE AUSTEN, *Emma*

Briar opened the closet door and carefully slipped the canceled subscriptions back into the files, silently shushing the crinkly pieces of paper. She didn't want to get caught. Using the agency's resources to further her own pursuits wasn't completely aboveboard. Although, since sneaking a list of client names to Nicholas for his cousin would eventually have a positive effect on the agency, she refused to feel too guilty.

As for her other indiscretion—kissing a rake in her patroness's music room last night—well, she tried not to think about it.

But honestly, *not* thinking about something as startling as that kiss, would have been like not paying attention to a rain shower that suddenly turned into a storm of chocolate, the streets covered in whipped froth.

There simply was no way to ignore it, *or* to forget how he'd reacted.

Clearly, Briar had been an abominable flop at kissing. Nevertheless, giving up was not in her nature. After all, she hadn't been able to hit the target with her first arrow. Like anything else, she supposed that kissing required practice.

Kissing practice with Nicholas . . . hmm. The instant the thought entered her mind, her face grew hot, her lips tingling—

And that was how Ainsley found her, standing half in and half out of the closet and pressed against the glazed trim to cool her cheeks.

"An odd place to daydream," Ainsley said, lifting her brow, a glimmer of amusement in her brown eyes.

Briar straightened, shoulders back. "I wasn't. I was merely . . ." But nothing came to her. Her mind went blank. Oh, how she wished she had Jacinda's knack for making up falsehoods on the spot. *Bother.* "What is that in your hand, another canceled subscription?"

"No. Or, at least, not this time." Ainsley abstained from further comment or mention of how many they'd received in the past two days. Instead, she handed over the missive.

Seeing that it was from Temperance, Briar opened it at once. "I've been invited to tea today."

Perfect! While she was there, she could hand the list to Nicholas instead of sending it by post.

However, Ainsley had another idea. "I don't know if I like the idea of your going. I heard from Uncle Ernest that Lord Edgemont has returned to town. It was one thing for you to visit your friend at his lordship's townhouse while he was away, but now . . ."

"Surely you don't believe he intends to ravish me in front of his aunt and cousins? Unless you think that is implied in the missive. Here, let me read it again." Briar huffed, making a show of turning the page frontways and backways. "No. Just as I suspected, I've only been invited for tea, not debauchery."

"It was only a concern for your well—" Ainsley stopped abruptly, her lips thinning as she expelled a frustrated breath through her nostrils. "Since he is the

Duchess of Holliford's godson, I suppose the association was inevitable. Though, in the past, Her Grace has made little mention of their relationship due to his reputation, which is enough for me to warn you to be on your guard."

She truly wanted to preach to her sister about trust and having faith that Briar would never fall for the charms of a renowned rake. But . . . having already kissed him, the foundation of her pulpit wasn't terribly sturdy. So instead, she offered a hasty nod.

"Very well, then," Ainsley said with a begrudging frown tucked into the corners of her mouth. "Jacinda is taking the carriage to Mayfair. So if you want to go, you'd best make haste."

THAT AFTERNOON, Daniel stormed into Nicholas's study, a blue silk banyan knotted around his waist and a half-crumpled letter in his fist.

"A summons, cousin? You sent me a summons when you could have simply walked to my chamber instead?" He slammed the paper down onto the desk, his mussed brown hair falling over his brow, making him look the part of the tragic hero.

Nicholas rose from the wingback chair in no mood for Daniel's continued melancholy. Leaning forward, he pressed his fingertips to the dark walnut surface, towering over his cousin by half a head. "The last time I knocked on your door, your valet informed me that you were still abed. At a *quarter of one* in the afternoon. You must begin to join the rest of the family and stop behaving as if your life has ended."

"Genevieve married another man. My life *has* ended!" Daniel sank onto the nearest chair, his arms draping limply over the rests. "You don't know what it's like to have your world completely upended."

He didn't? Nicholas recalled once having his life torn completely to shreds in a single moment but, apparently, his cousin did not. All the better for *him*, he supposed.

Oblivious to the bitter memories he'd conjured, Daniel continued to wallow, sighing at length. "You just don't feel things as deeply as I do. So, you can never imagine what it's like to wake up every day with part of your soul missing."

Nicholas gritted his teeth, biting down on the response that Miss Smithson—*Genevieve*—had only been using Daniel from the very beginning. But that knowledge would do his cousin little good. He simply needed to move on and find a woman worthy of him. "Nevertheless, it has been a year and—"

"No," Daniel interrupted, staring blankly at the ceiling. "It has only been seven months and four days since she left."

Nicholas growled. After months—though it had seemed like years—of letting his cousin brood in the country, it was painfully clear that a laissez-faire approach to Daniel's ongoing misery hadn't worked. Today the incessant wallowing was doing more than weighing Nicholas down with guilt, it was grating on his last nerve.

Though, if he were honest with himself, he'd been in a foul temper since he'd left the Duchess of Holliford's residence last night. He'd spent the evening pacing the halls of his townhouse, unsettled, riled, and irritated beyond measure at little Miss Briar Bourne.

She should have told him she'd never been kissed. But because she hadn't, what he'd intended to be an amusement—a mere *diversion*—had gone awry from the start.

He'd known it the instant her mouth descended on

his and a keen jolt riffled through him, as if he'd been struck by a bolt of lightning. Every breath of air had left his body. Every nerve ending tingled. Every hair stood on end. And he'd had the inexplicable sense that he was wholly out of his depth. *Him*—a man who possessed more carnal knowledge about women in his little finger than most men experienced in their lives.

So he'd done what any sane man would have done. He'd railed at her for neglecting to reveal this secret, fully prepared to end their agreement and make do without her assistance.

Then he'd made the mistake of looking at her lips and—*damn it all*—he'd wanted more. He'd felt a tense current vibrating through him as if he were a lightning rod craving the next thunderstorm. In fact, he still felt that way today, charged with static as if he'd shuffled across the rug in his stockinged feet a thousand times since last night.

Like a fool, he'd even asked Teense to invite Briar to join them for tea today, wanting her to meet Daniel and begin the process of finding him a wife.

Irritatingly, ever since Briar's acceptance had arrived this morning, he'd become a damnable clock-watcher, waiting for the bells to chime four.

"You're coming to tea today," he said tersely and shoved a hand through the air toward the door. "Go. Get cleaned up. Your sister has invited a friend."

"I'll take tea in my rooms."

Nicholas speared his cousin with a dark glare. "That is your choice, of course. But if you don't come to tea today and partake in this one small dose of society, then I will host a ball in your honor next week, and tie you to a column in the center of the ballroom so that you cannot escape."

Daniel sat up and stared agape at him as if he were

seeing a stranger. Then, with a moan of despair, he stood and trudged out of the study.

Nicholas made a mental note to have plenty of rope on hand by next week.

Then, before returning to his ledgers, he caught himself glancing at the clock. Again.

Chapter 11

"A disagreeable truth would be palatable through her lips . . ."

<small>JANE AUSTEN, *Emma*</small>

"Miss Bourne is here, my lord."

Nicholas checked the mantel clock and felt the tug of a frown at his brow. *Half past two.* "Have my aunt and cousin returned from their shopping excursion?"

"No, my lord."

"Forgive me," Briar said, skirting around the butler's back. She entered the room in a flurry of pale pink, from the ribbon on her straw bonnet to the toes of her slippers peering out from beneath a rose-embroidered hem. Accented with white piping along her bodice, sleeves, and sash, she looked like a baker's confection. "I realize I'm frightfully early, but I was at the mercy of my sister's carriage. I promise I won't be a bother until Temperance arrives. You could even stuff me in a cupboard until then if you like. Out of sight, out of mind."

She dusted her hands together as if it were a simple matter. But Nicholas suspected that tucking Briar out of sight was akin to having a plate full of decadent little cakes perched on his desk, and the only thing to keep him from devouring them all was a frilly pink cloche.

He shifted in the wingback chair, conscious of a surge of lust as he imagined her sitting on his blotter. "Delham, would you be so kind as to tell the kitchens that Miss Prescott's guest has arrived and to send up a small tray."

"No, Mr. Delham, I assure you that isn't necessary. I don't want to be any bother. So I'll tour the gallery and leave Lord Edgemont to continue scribbling in his ledger."

The butler hesitated, looking from Briar and back to Nicholas.

Nicholas expelled a breath. "I'll escort Miss Bourne to the gallery."

"Very good, my lord," the butler said with a bow, leaving the door ajar when he exited.

Briar huffed and—casual as you please—lifted her arms above her head to remove the pins from her hat. "Honestly, I don't want to be any bother. All this fuss because my family refuses to allow me to hail my own cab."

"At least that they've realized."

"Oh, I haven't gone on another dawn jaunt. After I had come home and the . . . um . . . flask had lost its potency, I realized just how dangerous it might have been."

"Good." Nicholas had wondered if she'd heeded his warning. He'd even had Adams wait outside of Sterling's for nearly a fortnight at dawn in case Briar—that once-nameless young woman —had decided to be reckless again.

Then, after Adams had pointed out how foolish it was, considering they weren't actually acquainted and never likely to be, Nicholas had decided to leave London for north Hampshire. An ill-fated family visit, as it turned out. And during the whole of the ordeal that followed, he couldn't count the number of times he'd wished he would have stayed here instead.

Taking a step toward his desk, Briar's rosy lips tilted wryly. "Which reminds me. Do you happen to know what became of my stocking and gloves? Though, truly I'm only concerned about the stocking because I still have the other, though it has lived a lonely existence at the bottom of my wardrobe. Of course, I had to replace my gloves straightaway, and I've kept them pristine all this time. See? My lucky gloves."

She flashed the white kid leather, fastened with a pearl button just beneath her delicate wrist bones. Above them, her arms were bare all the way up to the banded sleeves above her elbows, exposing two tempting lengths of creamy skin. He had the peculiar desire to sink his teeth into her, not hard, but just enough to leave an imprint in her flesh. As if he wanted to mark her.

"Given up on slippers, have you?" Unable to control the impulse, he reached out and tugged playfully on her fingertips.

"In a sense. My slippers have been acting rather peculiar," she said, her voice becoming even breathier than usual as she slipped free of his grasp. And as her cheeks colored, she averted her gaze down, adjusting the seam of her glove. Then she frowned and splayed her hand in front of him once more. "If that is a spot of ink, I'm going to be cross with you."

Sure enough, there was a dark smear near the tip of her ring finger. With a glance down at his hands, he saw that his thumb was the culprit.

She grumbled, flicked the pearl fastening free, and began to yank it off, finger by finger. "Is it your aim to leave a mark on everything that brings me a bit of luck? *Bother.* Do you think your valet could remove the stain before I depart? I should hate to always leave your company with fewer clothes than when I arrived."

Nicholas grinned. "What a *dreadful* burden that would be for me as well."

"It was not meant as a flirtation. I'm thoroughly vexed with you."

"I know, love. Give them here, head upstairs to the

gallery, and I'll see you in a few minutes." And damn it all if he wasn't already looking forward to it.

Even before he consulted his valet, Nicholas already knew there was no hope for india ink on brushed kid leather. So, in the end, he sent Winston on an errand to replace the pair with an exact replica. Since society believed it was an egregious error for a man to buy a woman an article of clothing, he decided to keep the matter between himself and his valet. With any *luck*—as Briar would say—Winston would return before his aunt and cousin arrived, and no one would be the wiser.

Shortly thereafter, Nicholas found Briar scrutinizing a portrait of his grandsire in the long paneled room. He stood still for a moment, caught by the sight of her there. The golden light that spilled in through the tall windows caressed her with familiarity, knowing every curve and every line. The shadows knew her as well, nuzzling every dip and hollow. She looked perfectly at ease here, and Nicholas felt a strange sort of jealousy that his townhouse had grown accustomed to her all these months while he had been away.

"If I squint, I can see the family resemblance," she said without turning toward him, speaking as if she'd known he was there all along and they'd been in the middle of a conversation.

He walked toward her, his footfalls echoing up to the gilded cornices on the ceiling and back down. "Is that the secret, then? For I've never seen it."

"It does surprise me, however, that your ancestors have all been very blond, blue-eyed, and with handsomely soft features."

Handsomely soft. Ah yes, he kept forgetting what a monstrous countenance he had, to her way of thinking. "What you meant to say is that there isn't a big nose among the lot of them."

"There is that, of course. You are far more"—she tapped her fingertip against her lips as if contemplating her choice of word—"chiseled than they are. Where you have been carved from granite, they have been molded from clay."

"And now I have the face of an ancient stone?"

"*Are* there rocks as old as you?" She turned toward him, feigned innocence in the upward arch of her brows and the slow curl of her lips. Then her grin stalled. "I was only making a small observation, hoping to understand a riddle that has plagued me since our first meeting."

"From my recollection, you professed to knowing everything about me. So what conundrum has the structure of my *chiseled* countenance offered?"

Twin spots of color stained her cheeks carnation pink. "I meant no insult. To be honest, I've been contemplating your potential application—should you ever change your mind about becoming a client—and I'm not sure what I would put down as your description."

"Is that so?" he asked, making no secret that he didn't believe her.

Turning to walk to the next portrait, Briar linked her hands behind her back and nervously thrummed her fingertips together as she continued. "You couldn't guess how often our female clients request tall, blond, and handsome—as well as tall, dark, and handsome. But who is to say what attributes are attractive from one person to the next? Some may find beauty in a pair of eyes and completely ignore a lack of chin." She nodded in the direction of his grandsire. "My sister Jacinda always talks about the breadth of her husband's shoulders, while I've heard him whisper comments about her ears. And they are just ordinary shoulders and ears to me." She shrugged and cleared her throat. "And then there is you."

"Yes, the *riddle*," he murmured. "But I'll offer you a bit of wisdom that you can share with your female clicnts the next time they request a handsome husband. Tell them that unattractive men make better bed partners."

On a gasp, she whirled on him. "I would never supply that information to a client. And besides, that statement is as ludicrous as it is unseemly."

"It makes perfect sense, if you think about it. Unattractive men have to try harder to earn a woman's affections. They don't have the luxury of having swooning maidens falling at their feet or even randy milkmaids offering a wink." He tugged impatiently at the sleeves of his coat, feeling confined in the garment. "So perhaps such a man might do a fair amount of reading ancient texts on pleasure. Or he might buy inordinate amounts of jewelry to pay courtesans to share their secrets. Until one day, the courtesans start sending him baubles and trinkets in the hopes that he would call on them."

Briar blinked up at him in open curiosity as if he'd just imparted the oracle of the sphynx, then squinted in confusion. "But how would *you* know this? Is it something gentlemen speak of in coffee houses and clubs?"

Now it was Nicholas's turn to be puzzled. "Are you truly asking how I've come by this information?"

Without hesitation, she nodded.

He raised both brows in disbelief. "Wasn't it last year that you proclaimed me the founder of the rhinoceros club?"

Then, as if she was only now understanding the true context of their conversation, her pink blush turned a deep rose. "First of all, I may have noted the proportions of your features, but I never said your countenance was disagreeable. At all. Second, if your outrageous tale was a poorly disguised effort for a compliment, then you should be ashamed of yourself." She tsked at him for good measure. "And third, teasing me, under the guise of dispensing a lesson, is not part of our bargain."

Huh. Well that was an unexpected revelation. The downward trajectory of the fractious mood he'd been in all day stopped abruptly, and slowly began a course in the opposite direction.

"Come with me." Feeling a grin tug at his lips, he slipped a hand beneath her elbow and walked toward the end of the gallery. "See this portrait of the ungainly child atop a pony and looking as if his head might topple off his shoulders from the weight of his most prominent feature? That was me at eleven years old. And that one there is me at eighteen. Beanpole thin, ungainly, and little more than a nose sitting atop a pair of shoulders."

She stared from the two hideous portraits and then to him, homing in on his most prominent feature. "The portrait artist made it much larger than it is."

"Actually, the opposite is true." He chuckled. "My mother paid him to make this outcrop of granite appear smaller. It wasn't until I was four and twenty that the rest of me started to fill in around it. A young man who looks like that has to work very hard to gain a woman's attention and to keep it."

Something he knew firsthand.

"That young man and I have a bit in common. We both know what it's like to be underestimated. And we both sacrificed pride to hire a tutor to teach us the things we could not learn on our own—though, of course, our currency is slightly different," she amended quickly, shyly averting her gaze.

"Slightly."

"And perhaps that young man, upon meeting a rather persistent matchmaker, might have agreed to—"

"I am not going to become one of your clients."

"I suppose I cannot force you. Nevertheless, I am still determined to discover the characteristics you find irresistible in a woman. Then someday, I'll introduce you to her and you'll feel all the more foolish when you change your mind about marriage. But never fear, I promise not to gloat too much as I throw rice at your wedding." She grinned, unashamedly badgering him.

The problem was, he didn't mind it. Disturbing realization, indeed.

Shaking himself free of it, he gestured to the archway of a small sitting room. "That was your lesson for today. Now come along and we'll continue our discussion on *currency*."

Her breath hitched, drawing his attention. But she averted her face and he could not tell if she was eager with anticipation or full of dread. Then she expelled a sigh, and seemingly all her cheer with it. "Very well."

He frowned. Her obvious reluctance was not her own fault, but his. He'd been a poor tutor for her first attempt, and then he'd made it worse by chiding her. He was determined to be a better taskmaster this time. "Contrary to what you might believe, kissing should be enjoyable, not a trip to the gallows. You should start by pleasing yourself. Do whatever you have in mind. Explore."

"Explore," she repeated with a nod as if taking notes for an examination.

As he led her to a pair of straight-backed chairs near the window of the small chintz-papered room, it was difficult not to grin at the way she pursed her lips in concentration. He'd never given a kiss so much thought before, not even his first.

He'd been about seven or eight—before his nose had altered to its current magnitude—and lying on the ground after falling out of the vicar's tree. The youngest daughter, a girl of twelve, had rushed out of the house to see if he'd died. Kneeling beside him, she'd leaned over to check if he was breathing and that was when Nicholas lifted his head and kissed her. And liking it so much, he'd kissed her again.

A youth's rite of passage, he supposed, and one that Briar had never done. She'd been sheltered and protected. There was something about her that made him want to do the same. And yet . . . there was also something about her that made him want to do wicked things with her. For hours.

But he wouldn't, he reminded himself.

She sat and situated her skirts, frowning at his mouth as if it were a mathematical equation he'd asked her to solve. With that level of calculation, he could already imagine her planning to put her tightly closed lips to his and simply press harder, longer. Then, they would both be disappointed in the end.

No, that would not do. If nothing else, he would teach her how to enjoy kissing—one of life's simplest pleasures.

"Better yet," he added. "Pretend that the other person's mouth is something you crave with your entire being."

She perked up at this, her countenance bright and intrigued. "Like chocolate?"

"Yes." He watched her tilt her head to study him, her gaze roving from brow to chin and lingering on his mouth. An un-tutor-like rush of anticipation warmed his blood. "Now, imagine that you've just heard the news that the dry climate this year has inhibited the production of cocoa beans. West Africa cannot export any more for a very long time. And worse, just before you walked into the room, I drank the last cup of chocolate in England."

Her irritated gaze flicked up to his. "You would do that, wouldn't you?"

"Perhaps," he said, his lips giving way to a grin. "Though, if you're lucky, you might capture a fleeting trace of it."

"And you accused me of conjuring dire scenarios," she grumbled, scooting forward to the edge of her chair in a susurration of pink silk.

Drawing in a breath, she leaned closer, then stopped. "This isn't going to work. You're far too tall. Perhaps if you slouched a bit?" But when she looked down to where her knees were between his sprawled thighs, she quickly shook her head, her cheeks coloring again. "I'd better stand or else I'll end up on your lap."

"I wouldn't mind, love," he crooned. Patting the tops of his thighs, he earned a perturbed glare.

Too intent on her goal to tease him now, she stood and settled her cool, delicate hands on his face. The simple touch of her fingertips, soft and uncertain, stirred a low flame of arousal.

"I thought your rule was 'no hands.'"

"Hush. I am immersing myself in the full experience," she whispered as if afraid of breaking the spell. "Besides, it was my rule for you, not for me. Now close your eyes, if you please."

He complied, half humoring her and half curious to see if she would balk and shy away. Yet she lingered. Her warm, clean fragrance filled his nostrils, making him think of fresh bed linens, sun-kissed and wind-beaten into a decadent suppleness. He wanted to lie down with that scent, tumble with it, bury himself inside of it. And all this was before he felt the sweet rush of her breath over his lips.

He held still. It seemed an eternity before the barest contact. More whisper than kiss. A featherlight back and forth sweep without the slightest bit of pressure.

"See here. That isn't a proper kiss," he rasped, disgruntled and more than half aroused.

"Hush." Her chide was a soft caress, the dark golden fan of her lashes resting against her cheek. "Such a disagreeable cup of chocolate. I told you before that the froth is the best part."

His pulse quickened beneath the heat of his cravat. As she continued, he wondered if any cup of chocolate ever felt this eager to be consumed. Willingly, he gave himself over to this intoxicating game of pretend, his breaths mingling with hers like steam rising from his depths, drawing her ever closer.

If this was just the froth, then he wondered what it would be like if she delved to the bottom of the cup.

Skimming her fingertips along his jaw, she shifted closer, her legs nudging his further apart, her skirts bunched between them. He was determined to keep his responses in tandem with hers, brush for brush, press for press. Yet the urge to take hold of her hips, to haul her closer was so strong that his hands ached. Every joint yearned to grip the curve of her flesh. So, he gripped the sides of the chair instead, knuckles straining against taut flesh. And since he was a good and patient tutor, his pupil rewarded him with a firmer press of her lips.

The same galvanic jolt that struck him last night riffled through him again. But this was stronger than before, every nerve ending exposed and raw.

Her upper lip nuzzled between his, the lower parting in a small sip of a kiss. A surprised *hmm* rose from her throat, as if she'd made a new, unexpected discovery. Then she repeated the action, drawing on his flesh in small seeking suctions, and a shudder swept through him, setting off a series of heady pulses that settled low and heavy at the base of his cock.

He gripped the chair tighter as she grew bolder, testing alternate angles. Willingly, he gave his lips over to her study, feeding them to her in whatever manner she would have them. And he felt as if she'd just invented a way of kissing that he'd never encountered before—Briar Bourne's patented *cup of chocolate* kiss.

He'd seduced countless women, finding ways to drive them mad with wanting. Giving pleasure was a matter of principle as much as it provided him a sense of power and control. He'd been blindsided once by a woman who'd used seduction to manipulate him, and he'd vowed long ago that it would not happen again.

Never in a thousand lifetimes would he have predicted that sweet Briar Bourne's untried kisses would have this effect on him.

Again, he wanted to lift his hands, hold her, curl his fingers over the nape of her neck, plunder her mouth until she was trembling and sprawled across his lap. But she was trusting him in this moment, comfortable.

This is such fun, her kiss told him. *You should have told me sooner.*

I'm just as surprised as you are, love, his own kiss answered.

Another warning jangled at the back of his mind. They would be expected downstairs for tea soon. He opened his mouth to say as much. When he did, the tip of her tongue slipped over the edge of his bottom lip and a quick rush of sweet breath shuddered out of her mouth.

Thoroughly absorbed in her task, she only hesitated for the barest instant before her small hands cupped his jaw and she pulled him closer to lick the seam of his lips for another taste.

Her throat vibrated on a soft hungry purr, and he felt the grip on his control—and on the chair—relax. He didn't want this to end, and his pleasure-drugged mind agreed, turning with possibilities. A simple word to Delham could ensure that his aunt and cousins did not know that Miss Bourne had arrived. He could say she'd sent her regrets and could not attend. And as for Nicholas, he would be only too happy to spend the remainder of the afternoon and evening locked in his rooms, kissing her. And whatever else she might enjoy.

He lifted his hands and settled them over hers. "Briar, love, would you like to see my bedchamber?"

It took two more tastes before she lifted her gaze, her eyes a dark, hazy summer-sky blue, her lips a damp rose-petal red. Then she blinked down at him. "You're attempting to scandalize me again, aren't you?"

"Perhaps," he said, pressing a kiss into both of her palms, drawing in the fragrance of her skin. "Or perhaps I'm being a gentleman and offering to make you more comfortable while we . . . sip chocolate together."

Face flushed, she slipped her hands free and smoothed them down her skirts. "Trying to use chocolate against me is positively reprehensible. It is fortunate that I know you're only teasing."

"Yes, you know me so well," he said wryly.

"I took your advice and imagined the chocolate from the coffee house, though without having the satisfaction of drinking it . . ." As she spoke, she fidgeted with her sash and moved to the door only to stall partway there, her gaze fixed on the clock in the corner. "Half past three? Surely, that cannot be correct."

"Delham winds the clocks each day," he said, distracted by her words . . . *without having the satisfaction of drinking it.* Did she mean to say that she was unsatisfied with that kiss?

"But that would mean we were"—she pressed her lips together—"touring the gallery for a terribly long while."

Rising, he turned away to put the chairs in place, surreptitiously adjusting the fall of his trousers. There was no need to show her just how much she'd affected him. And yet, he was still her tutor and so he could not let her walk away without providing some insight. "That's what happens when it's done properly."

Except, for her, apparently it hadn't been as *satisfying* as a cup of chocolate.

When he turned back around, her eager, hopeful face greeted him. "You mean I'm actually . . . *not* an abysmal failure?"

"You could add this to the list of your accomplishments."

"Oh, Nicholas. I'm so happy that I could . . . well, I could kiss you again." She laughed. "Lucky for you, we don't have the time."

Yes. Lucky me

Chapter 12

"A young lady who faints, must be recovered; questions must be answered, and surprizes be explained."

JANE AUSTEN, *Emma*

Briar looked at the flushed face staring back at her in the oval mirror above the washstand. *"Holy froth!"*

She didn't know kissing would feel like that. Her insides had turned warm and liquid, pulsing. Time dissolved away. She'd lost track of where she was, her every sense focused on him. She'd even forgotten her own name for a while. In fact, her head was still spinning, the contents nothing more than a happy puddle of gray mush.

No cup of chocolate had ever done that to her.

It had been on the tip of her tongue to tell Nicholas how exceptional kissing him was, but then it occurred to her that he might stop his lessons altogether. Doubtless, he'd believe that she could mistake this euphoria for love.

His angry reaction to their kiss at the Duchess of Holliford's had proven how serious he took the matter. He did not want there to be any feelings between them at all. To Nicholas, these kissing sessions were merely a matter of currency. Nothing more. Therefore, Briar had to keep this newfound discovery to herself.

Plan firmly in place, she emerged from the retiring

room. She'd done her best with a cool, damp cloth to hide the heated flush from her cheeks and the plumpness of her lips. After all, she couldn't very well descend the stairs with Nicholas on her arm and look as if she'd spent the past hour kissing him. Even if that was exactly what she'd done.

Nicholas was waiting for her around the corner, his tall frame leaning against a pilaster that lined either side of the doorway to the ballroom. A wry smirk bracketed one corner of his unexpectedly delicious mouth.

"What do you think?" she asked, tilting her face up for his examination. "Have I done a fair job of hiding the havoc your whiskers wreaked on my skin?"

Reaching out, he hooked one finger underneath her chin and brushed his thumb over her mouth, his eyes the color of raw cocoa, soft and silken. "Your lips still look a bit bee stung, but I don't suppose there's any help for that. You were quite thorough, after all."

The feel of his hand on her—the sureness of his touch, the light, tingling pressure of his thumb as it swept back and forth kept her brain thoroughly scrambled. At this rate, she may never recover her wits. She even had this uncanny desire to touch the tip of her tongue to his flesh, to taste this part of him, too.

Somehow, she managed to step back and waggle her finger, heart hammering all the while. "Remember the rule."

"Ah yes. You must guard yourself against the persuasive power of my hands," he teased, clearly not realizing the seriousness of the matter. "And as for your little rule breakers. Here."

He reached over to the green marble console nestled against the wall and picked up a pair of pristine white lady's gloves. There weren't even any creases in the kid leather.

"Surely you don't expect me to believe that these are mine."

When she didn't take them from him, he took her hands, boldly gliding his fingers over hers during the exchange. "What can I say? Winston is a veritable wizard with ink stains."

Her chiding gaze flicked up to his and the bracket beside his mouth deepened. Such an unrepentant rogue. What was she going to do with him, argue?

She might have done just that if not for the unmistakable chatter of Mrs. Prescott drifting up the stairs as she ordered footmen to retrieve her packages and to fetch her maid.

Briar glanced uncertainly at Nicholas. "Are you sure they won't know that we've been . . ."

"Touring the gallery?" He winked but gave her a nod of assuredness before leading her to the stairs.

It wasn't until Briar's hand moved to her skirts to lift them out of the way that she felt the sharp edge of something in her cleverly hidden pocket. Reaching inside, she withdrew a folded page. "I nearly forgot to give you this list for Daniel, what with all the . . . distractions and . . ."—her face heated once more at the sight of his wicked grin—"Oh, just take it."

His hand closed reflexively as she thrust the note into his palm. He looked down at it and then back at her, his expression inquisitive as if he didn't know what to make of her. "You've made a list already?"

"I don't know how good it will be, but it's a start. Without having met your cousin firsthand, I had to rely on stories from Temperance to get a good sense of his character, interests, and beliefs. Beside each name, there is a section dedicated to the shops and parks they frequent, for any potential *chance* encounter. Should you find them agreeable, that is." When he tucked the paper into his own pocket without making a comment, Briar shifted nervously, wondering if she'd done it completely wrong and this wasn't what he'd wanted at all. "Though I'm sure Temperance could arrange to have each of them over, if that is more convenient. And I will have more names for you if these aren't suitable. You see, these came from a file of our former—"

"It's perfect," he said quietly, his tone warm and affectionate as if they were sharing something even more intimate than a kiss. "I shall make good use of your diligent efforts. Unfortunately, I'm sure Delham has informed my aunt that you are here, so I do not have time to thank you properly."

As if to ensure she understood the inference, his gaze brushed her lips in a caress that seemed to touch her all the same. She drew in a breath to steady her fluttering pulse and turned toward the stairs. Then with one hand on the rail and the other on her skirts, she walked down beside him.

Brown paper parcels and ribbon-tied hatboxes cluttered the foyer floor at the bottom of the curved staircase. Lavinia Prescott's matronly figure stepped out of view as she followed a pair of footmen down the hall, calling out a plea to be careful with the Belgian lace for it was the whitest she could find in all of four shops.

Then Temperance sauntered into view, her arms lifted, hands fussing with the pins from her straw bonnet. She looked up with a ready smile. "Oh, there you are, Briar. I hope you haven't been here overlong. Mother and I had to stop and speak to Lady Penrose and you know how she tends to drone on about her spaniel. Expecting a litter any day, apparently. Say, are those new gloves?"

Briar slid a chiding glance to Nicholas. "Yes, they are, in fact. Do you like them?"

Temperance studied them with hawkeyed scrutiny,

turning Briar's hand this way and that. "They are very similar to your other pair."

"Indeed, except for one unlucky ink stain."

Temperance clucked her tongue. "Nothing vexes me more than discovering a spot of ink."

Briar was pulled alongside her friend, arms linked as they walked toward the back of the house. A glance over her shoulder proved that Nicholas was not far behind. "I was quite cross with the culprit."

He glanced down to her lips. "Gave him a thorough tongue-lashing, did you?"

Briar faced forward, an instant rush of heat flooding her cheeks. The man was positively incorrigible!

"Don't be silly, Nicholas," Temperance added with a laugh. "Of course Briar was speaking of a pen and not a person. One does not give a dressing down to a writing implement. Although, I have been known to scold the corner of the escritoire in Mother's rooms on more than one occasion."

Through the open door leading to the garden, a full service of tea waited on the terrace, the table draped with lavender linen and scattered with violets—Temperance's favorite flowers.

"What a splendid table you've set," Briar said to her friend.

"Fully inspired by you and the lovely tea trays you always put together for me. I wanted it to be a grand occasion now that everyone is home again. And I'll have you know that I even stopped by for your favorite ginger comfits, which I'm sure one of the maids is putting on a plate this instant. Oh, what's this doing here?" At the table, she lifted the lid of a slender claw-footed copper pot, and peered inside. "Why, it's chocolate. How strange. When I asked the cook earlier, she said we didn't have any in the larder. This is a stroke of luck for you, Briar. Nicholas, I should hate to tell you but my friend is embarrassingly fond of chocolate. At parties, she has been known to stalk the footman carrying the chocolate tray."

Nicholas stood beneath the shade of the ivy-clustered arbor, shadows softening the angles of his face as twin ebony spheres glinted warmly at her. "Is that so?"

Briar's lips tingled at the low timbre of his voice. She could not stop imagining what it was like to have her mouth on his, the sultry essence of his skin permeating every breath, the flavor of him clinging to her tongue.

No wonder that woman Briar had witnessed in his arms during their first meeting hadn't been aware of an audience.

Briar felt a sudden frown tug at the flesh of her brow. Instead of the unabashed fascination she usually felt when recalling the episode, the oddest prickle of irritation abraded the memory. "I imagine scores upon scores of women have exhibited a far greater fondness for it. I could hardly call my own *embarrassing.*"

Temperance laughed. "If that is true, then why are you blushing?"

"It is a warm day," Briar said quickly, pressing her hands to her cheeks, the sharp scent of new leather filling her nostrils. A sudden suspicion occurred to her and she wondered if, perhaps, Nicholas's valet had been sent on an errand for gloves *and* for chocolate. "Although I am curious if your cook makes chocolate as good as the coffee house where my friend is employed, my lord."

He lifted his shoulders in a careless shrug. "The proof, as they say, is in the froth."

"Well, if that is true," Temperance interjected with a skeptical sideways glance, "then this *they* you speak of are an odd lot. Froth, indeed. Pay no attention to my cousin, Briar. After returning from his country estate, his ability to converse is clearly in need of—*Daniel*! You decided to join us, after all."

Briar's gaze followed her friend's dash across the stones.

Temperance flung her arms around a young man her same height, offsetting his balance enough to stir the layers of fine brown hair draped over his broad forehead like ruffled feathers. A fan of lashes crowded together in a swift cringe, then gradually softened with patience as he patted her shoulders in return. "I said I would consider it, didn't I?"

"Yes, but that is usually your way of shooing me out of your chamber." Drawing back, Temperance looked almost giddy as she tugged her brother across the stones. "Daniel, I should like you to meet my dearest friend, Briar Bourne."

Briar inclined her head and offered a smile.

Daniel Prescott was handsome, by classical standards, with a pale complexion and none of his cousin's hard angular features. He was lean of build but somehow soft around the edges. *Approachable*—that was how they would describe him at the agency.

Looking into those solemn, wide-set amber eyes, she felt the unmistakable certainty that he needed a bride. And she was going to find him one. "It is a true pleasure. I've heard so much about you from Temperance that I already feel as though we are old friends."

"I . . ." He opened his mouth, but closed it again, casting an uncertain look to his sister as if wondering if she had revealed *everything*, including how he'd been jilted by his betrothed. Which, of course, she had. However, Briar did not want to invite such a pall to their party this afternoon.

Making a hasty amendment, she added, "She said you are something of a poet. Coincidentally, my very own uncle fancies himself a sonneteer. You would not imagine how many words rhyme with *rose*. I think he has discovered them all and even invented a few new ones when the others have failed him."

She added a lighthearted laugh meant to put him at ease, and saw his shoulders relax on an exhale.

"I'm certain my random scribblings are not nearly as fine as Temperance likely suggested." A shy blush ruddied his cheeks.

Briar could not imagine Nicholas ever blushing. Though if he did, it would be difficult to tell with his darker complexion, tanned from his months in the out doors at his country estate.

"There you are, Daniel, and what a magnificent surprise." Lavinia Prescott came through the doorway with a happy chirrup, splaying a hand over her heart, her eyes glinting with moisture as she beamed at her children. "Temperance, I knew he would come around. Yes, indeed. I feel like planning a dinner to celebrate. The Burkharts are hosting a soiree this evening, but I'm sure the Pomphreys are free, and *oh*! I just heard that Lord and Lady Baftig have a charming daughter."

Daniel shifted on the stones, shoulders tense, fists clenched. Briar glanced down to see that one of his feet was pointed toward the house and, in that instant, she knew this was all too much for him. He was hoping to escape.

"I often find when I've lingered over a beautiful tea on a hot afternoon, I'm usually too satisfied to think of dinner and want nothing more than to spend the rest of the day with family," Briar said, ambling over to the table. "Then again, the Bournes are something of an odd lot and tend to forgo formal dinners for cold suppers in the library."

Nicholas held out a chair for her, gifting her with a flash of a smile. Quick though disarming. "Daniel and

I enjoyed cold suppers often in the country as well. Few things are more enjoyable on a warm evening than an informal meal and the relaxed conversation one can only have with family and old friends."

Mrs. Prescott's hopeful gaze was fixed on Daniel as she took her seat. "But wouldn't it be grand to have a full party here in the garden? And we could dine alfresco. After hearing that the Duchess of Holliford had her dining room reassembled out of doors, positively everyone wants to do the same. There is even talk of the Throckmeyer's hosting a ball in their gardens. Now, I ask you, what could be better than fresh air, dancing, and dozens of pretty smiles?" She smiled encouragingly at everyone at the table. "After all, I cannot find spouses for my children if they linger indoors. Why even Nicholas might choose to marry again."

"Again?" Briar blurted without thinking.

Every bit of warmth swiftly vanished from Nicholas's countenance. He offered a tight, nearly imperceptible nod, but said nothing.

Her throat went dry. She flicked a glance to Temperance to confirm this.

In turn, her friend, who didn't seem at all shocked by this news until she caught Briar's eye, suddenly lowered her teacup with a clatter. "That's right. You know, I'd completely forgotten that our Nicholas was married ages ago."

Briar couldn't fathom how something so monumental could slip Temperance's mind. And Nicholas hadn't said a word either, and by the unyielding set of his jaw, it didn't appear like he planned to now.

Mrs. Prescott sighed distractedly as she spooned clotted cream onto her scone. "Hmm . . . yes, a marriage shortly followed by such a tragedy for our family. And you were so young, nephew. Barely twenty as I recall, when you became a widower *and* lost your brother in that same carriage accident. Dear, sweet James, he was always off to market to bring home some treat for his Catharine. And then there was Marceline, always going with him and wanting to surprise you as well."

Briar absorbed this news, needing to learn as much as she could. They didn't elaborate, however, and every scenario she could conjure only made her sad.

"I'm truly sorry for your loss, my lord," she said quietly. Oh, how she wished she could reach across the table and squeeze his hand for comfort.

A muscle ticked along Nicholas's jaw. "As my aunt said, it was long ago."

Was that the reason he didn't want to marry, because his heart had been torn apart when his wife had died? For a man to marry so young, he must have been madly in love with her. Madly in love with *Marceline*.

Though it was strange, Briar didn't recall seeing a portrait of her upstairs.

"Which is precisely why it is time to marry again," his aunt said. "Set an example for your cousins."

Briar agreed, wholeheartedly, but this was not the time to speak of marriage. She would surprise him with the perfect candidate at the perfect time. And one day, he would thank her.

Now, however, the tension around the table was a tad too palpable, so she altered the topic once more. "Did you mention you were planning to visit your modiste's shop today, Temperance?"

"Indeed, and you must see my new gown. The apricot organdy is simply divine. I plan to debut it at Almack's next week. Though I wish you could attend."

"That would be lovely, for I've always wanted to go. I have a blue ballgown with tiers of ruffles that I've been saving just in case."

"I might be persuaded to attend Almack's. I've always

had luck in their card room," Daniel said, and a hush fell over the table. Cups paused, breaths caught, gazes flitted.

Temperance broke the quiet with a cheerful clap. "Perhaps you'll even ask me to dance. After all, you're one of the few who doesn't mind how tall I am."

"As long as *you* don't mind if I'm a bit clumsy and out of practice. Perhaps even"—he cleared his throat—"Miss Bourne would be just as forgiving?"

"I would, of course," she said immediately, then added a trace of regret to her tone. "But the Duchess of Holliford always has dinner on Wednesdays, and I am obligated to attend."

"I'm sure Her Grace could do without you for one evening," Mrs. Prescott said, with a hopeful glance to Nicholas.

He inclined his head. "I'll pay a call tomorrow."

"You're very kind, but I'm afraid it wouldn't matter, regardless. You see, I haven't been granted a voucher."

"If you wish to go to Almack's, then I'll make certain of it," Nicholas said, his low promise quickening her heart.

"I should like that very much, my lord."

Chapter 13

"I would much rather have been merry than wise."

JANE AUSTEN, *Emma*

"Quite honestly, Edgemont, it would be difficult to approve an invitation for *any* young woman of no fortune," Lady Elston said as they stood in her garden amidst tall stalks of purple irises. She paused from snipping to brush wayward strands of glossy brown hair from her cheek, and issued a bleak sigh. "However, with the recent lack of credibility Miss Bourne's uncle possesses in society, it might very well be impossible."

Nicholas was tired of hearing these words. He'd nearly exhausted all of his resources, and even tried calling in a few outstanding wagers to procure a voucher for Briar. But the patronesses of Almack's were sticklers for who made it on their list.

"Almack's is a bloody dancing establishment."

He couldn't believe the trouble he was having, or the fact that he'd reached the point of asking a former lover for a favor. And they had not ended on the best of terms. Lady Elston—*Elise* as he used to know her—was his last hope because she had the ear of the Countess Lieven, whose approval would open countless doors for Briar.

"Just tell me what I have to do, or whom I have to bribe," he continued, his tone razor-edged and willful.

"From what I've heard, the place could use a bit of extra coin for the uneven floors and horrid refreshments."

Elise stiffened, her gray gaze as cool and stormy as the clouds crowding overhead. "The venue has declined, that is true, but it is still very much revered among high society. They only admit the crème de la crème of gentlemen, and young ladies of good breeding. There is no other place where one can guarantee that one is dancing with an up-standing marriage prospect."

He could think of one—the Bourne Matrimonial Agency. In fact, it seemed a far more agreeable option than enduring an evening of dreamy-eyed, desperate-to-marry debutantes. His opinion, however, would not grant him the invitation he required. And he'd already been to two of the other patron-esses only to come away with a polite rejection.

"Does your refusal to speak with your friend, the countess, have something to do with our history?"

"Frankly, it is only because of my fond recollections that I permitted you this audience. That, and my utter cu-riosity," she said, eying him shrewdly as she laid another cutting in her basket. "I have never known you to put your-self at the mercy of a woman's decision. And yet here you are, at mine. So I have to wonder why you are going to such great lengths for Miss Bourne. Is it possible that this young woman has managed to capture your fancy?"

"I am not here on my own behalf. My aunt and cousin wished for me to make the arrangements," he said briskly, wanting to put an end to any far-fetched notions Elise might have.

"I always did admire your love for family. We have that in common. I even thought for a time that trait would bring you to heel and cause you to propose to me. Though, I believe you knew that, and it was the reason our affair came to an end."

He didn't insult her by denying it. "I was fond of our time together."

"And I was in *love* with you," she said ruefully. "Yes, I know you made it clear from the beginning that you weren't interested in marriage. Part of me always wondered if you harbored an undying love for your first wife . . ." She paused, waiting for him to give her something of an answer. But when he kept his expression well guarded, she clucked her tongue. "Oh, Nicholas, what am I to do with you? You still hold a tender place in my heart. And strangely enough, I want you to be happy."

At last, he felt he was getting somewhere, and he gave her a grin, his tone warm and intimate. "You could remedy that straightaway with a voucher for my cousin's friend."

She laughed quietly and shook her head. "I was speaking of marriage. I want you to fall in love and have a family. Have you never considered it?"

His stomach rolled, memories leaving a bitter taste on the back of his tongue.

"Certainly. For my cousins," he clarified, enunciating every syllable.

"You're impossible." She tsked again and resumed snipping stems. "I heard a rumor about you recently. I was with the countess having tea when someone said that the Bourne Matrimonial Agency had been challenged to find you a bride."

"And just *who* mentioned this gossip—someone from that family?"

"Would I bother to tell you if I thought it was merely their ploy to gain more clients? You're still so untrusting . . ."

It wasn't until a cold, tense breath escaped his lungs in a rush that he realized how much the answer mattered. When he'd struck this bargain with Briar, he'd relied on her to keep it between them. That had been a leap of faith he normally did not take—trusting someone else not to use him for their own personal gain—but he'd taken the risk, with Daniel in the forefront of his mind.

Nicholas was relieved to know that he hadn't been wrong. Still, he wondered who challenged Briar in the first place. It had to have been someone who knew him. Someone who wanted to turn his life into a circus. Unfortunately, he knew far too many people who might do that very thing. The men he gambled with were always plotting new wagers to win. It wouldn't be the first time Nicholas was the object.

Elise waved the clippers in the air. "Oh, I cannot recall who it was at the moment. And of course, considering our history, I instantly dismissed the rumor as being false. Although, *if* it were true"—she paused, cunning gray eyes glinting as she scrutinized him—"then perhaps the countess would be interested in watching how the challenge unfolds. And Miss Bourne could very well become a sought-after guest at all the best parties."

He gritted his teeth. If he confirmed the rumor or gave it any credence whatsoever, then his life would be thrown into chaos. It took only the smallest kernel of an idea to incite a riot from the *ton*'s most ruthless species—those rapacious husband-hunting mamas and their progeny. He wouldn't be surprised if his own friends would open a book at White's betting on the conclusion. Then again, perhaps they already had.

And yet, if he didn't confirm it right here and now, he would disappoint Teense, his aunt, and possibly Daniel. But worst of all, Briar Bourne would never be received at Almack's.

Damn it all, he thought, raking a hand through his hair. This bargain might very well kill him.

❦

"HAVE ANY letters arrived for me, Uncle?" Briar breezed into his office and stood between the two large bronze urns, filled with peacock plumes, that flanked his desk.

Uncle Ernest grinned, his lapis-blue eyes glinting in the hazy morning light that sifted in through the slender window. The scribblings of his latest sonnet were on the page in front of him. "Are you expecting a love letter?"

"Contrary to what you might believe, there are other types of correspondences." She laughed, but inside she felt a trifle crestfallen.

Nicholas had said he would acquire a voucher for her to attend Almack's, and he'd sounded so certain, so resolute, that she hadn't doubted him. But today was Monday, and she still hadn't heard from him.

Regardless of her reservations, she truly had wanted to attend.

She'd even given herself leave to imagine dozens of possible scenarios involving how Wednesday would proceed. She'd planned to use her new skills at reading shoulders and feet to find matches for at least three different couples. Rumors would have spread—as they often did—and shortly thereafter she would have been named the premier matchmaker in all of London.

However, that hope seemed lost now.

"But are those more eagerly received than an outpouring of a heart's desire? I think not." As if to offer proof, he lifted an unsent letter from the tray on the corner of his desk, the red wax stamped with an overly embellished *E*, the final whorl adorned with an arrow tip

Briar expelled a sigh that was both fond and accepting of her uncle's nature. "And who is your latest love?"

"You should know, for you were with me in the park yesterday when our paths first crossed and Mrs. Townley's parasol slipped out of her grasp. My poor heart still hasn't recovered from the sight of those green eyes."

At least for the next two days.

"Why have you never married, uncle?"

He tapped the folded corner of the letter against the surface of the desk. "I'm still searching for my muse—the one woman whose whisper can breathe life into my soul, again and again. For a short while I think I have found her. Then, sadly, it fades. Ah, perhaps I will never find my one and only, but the hunt is rather enjoyable."

One and only? While the former appealed to the romantic in her, the latter caused her inner matchmaker a slight pang of anxiety.

She immediately thought of Nicholas. "But say, for instance, you had met her once, and something tragic happened to tear you apart. Do you think it possible to find another, and to be equally as happy, if not more?"

Before he could answer, Ainsley appeared at the door, her expression harried. "Uncle, if I may have your assistance."

"Do we have a client, dear?"

"It's the *count*," Ainsley said, rolling her eyes to the plaster molding on the ceiling.

Briar followed them out into the corridor. "I'll get a tray from the kitchens."

"Mrs. Darden already has the tray."

Briar bristled. Through the open door, she could see their beloved family cook, rushing to pour the tea, locks of grizzled hair escaping her ruffled cap. "Isn't that what I'm here for?"

"Not now, Briar." And then Ainsley turned her back and went into her office, closing the door partway.

The Comte de Bardot's pinched voice began railing

immediately, his words thickly accented. "I have paid for my, as you say, sup-scrcept-see-on for many months now, and yet I still have no wife!"

"*Monsieur le Comte,*" Ainsley said. "I have introduced you to every female client we have who matches your criteria, but you have found fault with each of them."

"*Mais oui,* because you have only given me wallflowers when I would rather have a centerpiece on my arm."

The conversation paused, no doubt while her sister was trying to maintain her composure. And it must have been difficult because Uncle Ernest chimed in when he usually avoided confrontation. "Of course, your application is at the top of our list. The very top, indeed. In fact, I saw it just this morning and you can rest assured that we will continue to . . ."

Mrs. Darden hustled out of the room, smoothing the plain-front apron over her rounded form, and then closed the door succinctly. "The count's in a fine temper this morning."

Briar fumed, annoyance pinching down her spine like overly tight corset lacings. She could very well have delivered the tea tray, and possibly found a way to calm the count's temper. He was always at ease with her, if not a bit too familiar at times. "Now Ainsley is taking away my only occupation."

"It's only when *he's* here," Mrs. Darden said, drawing Briar down the corridor. "The way that count looks at you . . . why I'd like to take a rolling pin and knock him upside the head. Thankfully your uncle is there, or else I might've put one on the tray all the same."

"What do I care that he has roving eyes?"

"Because a man with roving eyes often has roving hands, that's why." Mrs. Darden tutted fondly. "No need to fret over this. There's too much love between you and your sisters to let squabbles get in the way. Especially not after all you've been through together, losing your mother the way you did, each of you so young."

"And they—well, Ainsley more than Jacinda—treat me like I'm still that ten-year-old girl, as if time stopped for me."

Mrs. Darden paused near the top of the stairs, glancing down at the runner. "It's just that you look so much like your mother. I imagine it's difficult not to think about her. Each of us remember how she slipped away and there was nothing we could do to stop it."

Briar had surmised this long ago, but hearing it spoken aloud didn't help matters. "Well, keeping me from experiencing life isn't going to bring her back either."

A rush of guilt clogged her throat the moment the words spilled out.

She missed her mother terribly, the pain of her loss even keener because no one liked to talk about her when Briar was in the room. Any reminiscence was cut short and usually accompanied pained glances, abrupt avoidances, and long awkward silences.

They didn't speak of Father either, and most certainly never mentioned his other family—the one that had destroyed Mother when she'd learned of it. And Briar had often wondered about him and her half siblings, always having wanted to meet them. Yet, she didn't even know how many other children he had. Every inquiry she made was forever redirected, as if it was an enormous secret and her family thought her too frail of heart to learn the whole truth.

"They only mean to protect you because they love you."

In Briar's opinion, there was no room for secrets or silence in love. Every topic should be open for discussion.

Mrs. Darden sniffed and gave Briar's hand a pat. "If it helps to hear it, that tray was never meant for the count.

It just so happens that I was on my way up to give it to you because we've another guest in the parlor. But then the count just barged in, all bluster and strife. So if you're so eager to serve tea, there's a polished tray waiting in the kitchen." She gave her hand a final squeeze before bustling off, finishing her conversation over her shoulder. "I believe she said her name is Mrs. Teasdale. Peculiar woman, that one. Said she'd come here to do her knitting. Regardless, I'm needed upstairs to help Ginny with the linens."

Briar went downstairs, a sense of futility driving her irritation. She was a grown woman, capable of handling herself. The problem was, no one believed her. This only made her all the more determined to prove that she could interview clients and make matches for them, too.

Below stairs in the kitchen, she poured fresh water into a white glazed pot, her ire still simmering as she went about putting together a tray.

While Mrs. Darden usually left them plain, with only the essential items—pot, cup and saucer, scone—Briar liked to add more. Even when she was angry, apparently, for she draped the silver tray with a square of blue gingham without thinking. Then with a huff, she artfully arranged a selection of scones and preserves.

After all, if she were coming to a matchmaking agency and nervous about taking such a monumental leap, would a sadly adorned tray put her at ease? And would it assure her that the agency planned to find her the best possible match?

No and definitely not. At the very least, the tea tray should tell their clients that the agency would go to the ends of the earth and back again because love had no limits.

She surveyed her handiwork and felt marginally better. Tapping her fingertip against her lip, she realized there was still something missing—more color. Spotting an orange-and-clove pomander on the windowsill, she placed it in a sweetmeat glass and tucked a few sprigs of rosemary around it.

She smiled, pleased with her efforts and no longer fuming as she made her way upstairs to their potential client.

In the yellow-wallpapered room, an older woman looked down at her knitting, the top of her head crowned with a twist of butterscotch brown hair, the severe part in the middle displaying a liberal stripe of gray strands.

"What lovely knitting," Briar said as she set the tray on the low oval table. "I'm Miss Bourne and it's a pleasure to make your acquaintance."

The woman only glanced up from her knitting, the air punctuated by the harried click-clacking of needles. "You can call me Mrs. Teasdale. I decided to keep my third husband's name. He was a better man than the fourth, to be sure."

A startled laugh escaped Briar, believing it a joke. But when she realized the woman was serious, she cleared her throat and busied herself with pouring a cup of tea. "Are you looking to marry . . . um . . . again?"

"I've given it some thought, yes. I've never had luck with the number four, so I should like to make it five. Do you have any candidates for an old crone like me? Without any of that nonsense I read about in the newspaper, of course."

Ah yes, Briar's blunder was never too far away. She wondered if she would ever escape it. "Sugar?"

Mrs. Teasdale paid no attention to the request but continued knitting. "When a person gets to be my age, she wants a man with experience etched clearly on his face. Plenty of lines around the eyes and mouth to let me know he's lived. A good-humored sort with a lust for life. And a lust for other things, too." She looked up with a grin, a peach glow in her cheeks as she cast a wink to Briar. "Rakes have always been my downfall. One wicked laugh and my knees are clotted cream on a hot scone."

"You married a rake?" Briar perked up at this, and suddenly found Mrs. Teasdale the most interesting person in the world. "How, precisely?"

"We fell in love, of course. There's no other way to catch a rake."

So there was no special secret? Briar was afraid of that.

"I managed to reform One—my first husband," she continued with a smug waggle of her brow. "Made him think it was his own idea. Ah, but Three and Four were dreadful failures. Number two was highborn, a titled gentleman and all, but a bit of a temper. But as odds go, one out of four isn't too bad. Though, I'd prefer two out of five."

Apparently, marriage was a game of chance for Mrs. Teasdale. And perhaps she was right. Briar found herself instantly fond of the frank-speaking woman, and wanted to sit and listen to her for hours. Likely, she'd get an earful about all the things people didn't speak about around debutantes. "If you'd like to continue knitting, I could take your application in here."

"Before we do, let me ask . . ." She lowered her needles and squinted at Briar. "Have you ever had a client who filled out an application for her own son?"

"Mothers come in with their daughters all the time." The *all the time* was stretching the truth like taffy since they didn't have many clients of late. "After all, who would know how to achieve your son's happiness better than you?"

At this, Mrs. Teasdale stopped her knitting and scrutinized Briar with a tilt of her head. "I like you, Miss

Bourne, but you're a bit young for my son. You're not the eldest Miss Bourne, are you?"

"No. That would be my sister Ainsley," Briar said absently. She didn't want to bring her sister in on this just yet, if at all. "Is your son looking for a wife?"

"At two and thirty, I should think so." Mrs. Teasdale scoffed and went back to her knitting.

Hmm . . . Briar always thought of Temperance whenever a new gentleman became a client. "And is he a particularly tall fellow, by chance?"

"Tall and handsome as a devil, like his father." She beamed, then issued an impatient sigh. "I came here today because I have a need for grandchildren and he's my only chance for them. At my fiftieth birthday last week, I decided that I was through waiting."

Briar paused, uncertain if Mrs. Teasdale had all her faculties in order, or if she was a few pastries shy of a baker's dozen. Though, with the current lack of new applicants, she supposed beggars could not be choosers. "Just so I have this correct, you would like a husband for yourself and a bride for your son."

Two potential subscriptions for the agency! Briar could hear the accolades now . . .

"And grandchildren, don't forget."

Briar cleared her throat. "Well, the Bourne Matrimonial Agency cannot guarantee those."

"Oh, my son will do fine on his own. Just needs a little nudge in the right direction." For effect, Mrs. Teasdale poked the air with one long needle and snickered. "Do you think his bride would like a stocking cap, too?"

Briar looked down at the slender length of scarlet yarn, the bottom edge pooling on the floor. How that creation would become a stocking cap was a complete mystery.

"Without a doubt," she said, rising from the chair.

"I'm just going to pop out for a minute and I'll be back to fill out your application."

"I'm not going anywhere, dear."

In the corridor, Briar closed her eyes, flung her arms wide, and breathed in a deep victorious breath. She was a matchmaker reborn like the phoenix rising from the ashes of disgrace.

Glancing down at her attire, she took careful note of everything she was wearing. Yellow muslin with a border of blue flowers at the hem, and a new blue ribbon in her hair. Since she'd worn the dress many times before without much luck, she knew it had to be the ribbon.

Her lucky blue ribbon, which would be perfect to wear with her ballgown. *If* she ever received a voucher from Almack's.

Around the corner, she saw her uncle dabbing a handkerchief over his brow, his gaze toward the stairs where heavy-footed stomping and a string of angry French words gradually receded. Then the door slammed—the Comte de Bardot's signature exit.

Uncle Ernest expelled a sigh, then caught a glimpse of her and smiled. "You're a sight for sore eyes."

"Are yours aching from having to stare at the count's abominable wig?"

"There is that," he said, tucking his handkerchief into the pocket of his superfine blue coat as they walked together into his office. "Then there are so many other things that it would be impossible to list them all."

"Uncle, by any chance, do you have additional paper in your desk, so that I might have a stack for applications?"

"Do we have a client waiting in our parlor?"

"We do," Briar said, biting her lip. "But could you not mention it to Ainsley or Jacinda? I want to—no, I *need* to have this chance. Please, Uncle?"

"Very well." He nodded, seldom able to resist pleas

from any of his nieces. Briar may or may not have used this knowledge to her advantage a time or two.

She kissed his cheek. "You're my absolute favorite uncle."

Just then, Mrs. Darden came upstairs, holding a salver in one hand and a mending box in the other. The woman was a marvel at performing multiple tasks at once. Out of breath, she barely dipped into a curtsy before handing the salver off to Uncle Ernest, then disappeared around the corner.

"It seems there is a missive for you, m' dear."

Quickly turning it over, Briar looked at the seal and saw that it was from Nicholas.

Indeed, this was her lucky ribbon after all.

Chapter 14

"Fine dancing, I believe, like virtue, must be its own reward."

JANE AUSTEN, *Emma*

Nicholas had been right about the risks of confirming the rumor regarding the challenge issued to Briar.

Not a day had passed before a wager was on the books at White's debating his marriage by year's end. Those who knew him best had put their coin on the impossibility of such an event. Yet there were still a few who doubted the protestations from his own lips. This needled him, much like a thistle barb camouflaged in his trouser leg, catching and digging into his flesh.

There were other nuisances, as well. Invitations to afternoon teas, garden parties, stuffy dinners, enough to suffocate any man. With every penned refusal, he made sure to mention the fact that he had no intention of actually marrying, regardless of rumors.

Regrettably, it made no impact.

He kept telling himself he'd done it to ensure that Daniel would enter society once more, and to please Teense by having her friend here this evening. Yet there was one small voice in the back of his mind, telling him that he was a fool if he believed he'd done it for anyone other than Briar Bourne.

Well, he wasn't a fool, and Nicholas was determined to prove that voice wrong by any means necessary.

By the time he arrived at Almack's on Wednesday evening, the party was well underway, a veritable oven of bodies twirling around on the floor and pressed against the wall. The combined stench of sweat and perfume rivaled that of a brothel.

Ruddy-cheeked men in black coats and cinched, snowy cravats mopped their brows with handkerchiefs. Women kept their fans fluttering, creating the only breeze to stave off the sweltering evening air.

"I shouldn't have come," Daniel said from beside him. Beneath a sheen of perspiration, his face turned to a pale celadon green as if he were going to cast up his accounts at any moment. The same way he'd looked when Temperance had invited a *friend*—coincidentally from Briar's list—to dinner the other evening.

And just like then, tonight, he'd changed his mind about attending three different times, lamenting that he wasn't up to the task of making merry. In the end, and in no temper to coddle him, Nicholas ladled out a heavy serving of guilt by telling him how disappointed Temperance would be if he broke his promise.

"We are here, so better make the best of it," Nicholas growled. "Now, find your sister."

Nicholas had sent Temperance and his aunt in a separate carriage, knowing that they'd intended to escort Miss Bourne. At the very least, he wasn't going to make Briar miss her long-awaited evening.

He scanned the periphery of the room, where wallflowers and his cousin were known to linger. Surely if he could spot Temperance then he'd find Briar as well. But when there was no sign of either, a cold frisson of worry skated down his spine as he eyed the rows of shiny-faced debutantes gathering between potted palms and columns.

"I . . . I can't. This is all too soon," Daniel said, stepping in front of him, his Adam's apple bobbing above the edge of his cravat, his eyes so wide they looked like pennies in spills of milk.

"What about your promise to dance with Temperance?"

"I'm sure she'll understand. She's always been a good sort. And what's one dance?"

To a young woman who'd confessed to having few partners other than her own family, one dance was quite a lot. Nicholas gritted his teeth. "You also asked Miss Bourne to dance. Now turn around and look for your sister."

Daniel's head wobbled in a nod and he drew in a deep breath before facing the crowd. "You're right. I just need to push onward for a few hours. This is about Temperance's enjoyment and Miss Bourne's, not mine. And if I make a complete and utter fool of myself, then I should only hope that I expire from heat exhaustion, there on the ballroom floor."

Nicholas told himself to be patient. After all, his cousin wouldn't be in this mess if not for him.

Guilt gnawed at him every day. The only cure was to find Daniel a bride, to make him forget about Miss Smithson, but the process was taking too long. Daniel was shy and awkward and broken and Nicholas wanted to fix him. Now. He didn't want to wait.

Sometimes he wondered if confessing all of it would ease the burden for both of them, like sloughing off dead skin after a burn. Yet there was too great a chance that Daniel would never forgive him, and that their bond would be severed forever. Doubtless, such cruel honesty would only bring pain, and Nicholas didn't want to cause any more of that. So he would keep trying to wait through the process.

Unfortunately, patience had never been one of his own

virtues. Then again, he wasn't partial to virtues of any sort.

"Ah. There is my mother," Daniel offered, gesturing toward one of the curved balconies above the dancers. She was pointing the tip of her fan toward the ballroom floor, beaming with pride.

At first glance, Nicholas hadn't even seen Temperance among the dancers. But there she was, looking lovely in the new apricot gown she'd showed off earlier this evening, her partner a good two inches taller. As the music came to an end, only then did he see Briar emerge from behind a rotund gentleman, who'd completely eclipsed her from Nicholas's view. And considering how breathtaking she was beneath the glow of the chandeliers, that was a criminal offense. Briar should never be hidden.

As the gentlemen escorted her and his cousin to the side, Nicholas moved forward, his eyes never leaving them. He took a moment to admire his pupil in a sheath of summer blue that molded over the curves of her body as if the garment had been handstitched over her bare skin.

Most women were struggling with the humidity, shifting restlessly, surreptitiously tugging on their stays and ruffling their skirts to cool themselves. But Briar seemed to embrace the heat, cheeks flushed, skin aglow. She moved with unhurried grace, her steps like a dance of their own, accentuated by the smooth glide of the pearl-handled fan in her grasp. And even though he was steps away, he could have sworn he caught the scent of fresh linens baked in sunlight.

As their escorts left, Briar turned her head to Temperance and those cheeks lifted, her eyes bright as they shared a laugh. Then her gaze drifted over the crowd, clearly searching, and suddenly alighted on him. When their eyes met, a jolt burned through him, hot and expectant.

Dangerous, he thought, knowing that there were likely dozens of people observing him right this instant.

Arm in arm with Temperance, chatting merrily, she gradually made her way to him and Daniel. "Are you certain part of my face hasn't melted off? When you warned me of his bad breath, I did not think you meant *rancid.* Clearly, he has eaten something that died most cruelly."

"And is haunting us!" Temperance laughed and stopped in front of them. "Good evening, brother and cousin. I see you have finally arrived."

"It's always the same with gentlemen, isn't it?" Briar asked Temperance with a conspiratorial smirk. "They take an age to choose what they will wear, fussing over their cravats and such, whereas women can just don any old gown and be ready in a snap."

"It seems our secret is out, Nicholas," Daniel said with a shy grin that chased away the taut lines of dread that were there only an instant ago.

Nicholas understood the reason, all too clearly. Briar had such an ease about her that it was impossible not to be drawn in by it. "So true, and all that careful planning is for naught because we are seldom admired for our efforts."

Briar laughed. "Forgive me, for I meant to say how dashing you both look."

"A clear ploy to ensnare a dancing partner. What say you, Daniel, shall we give in to their bold manipulations?" Nicholas asked, forgetting that he'd never intended to dance with Briar, not tonight or ever.

"I'm afraid we must."

"Oh, but you are too late," Temperance chimed in, jingling her wrist at her brother, where a tiny booklet hung from a shiny silver bracelet. "Our cards are quite full."

Briar concurred, untying the ribbon of her own card and passing it to Nicholas. "It is true. Temperance and

I have come up with a system for this evening. When a gentleman asks for a dance, whichever one of us it is invites him to escort our friend first and promises to hold a place for him for the following dance."

Nicholas absently perused the names and frowned. "Who is this *Lord M.M.*? You cannot give one gentleman three dances."

"The letters stand for *matchmaking*," Briar said on a whisper, leaning close enough that he caught the sweet essence rising from her skin. And all at once he was transported back to the sitting room off the gallery, with her lips coasting over his, her scent filling his every breath as she slowly consumed him.

He'd been unable to think of anything else for the past five bloody days. Which was precisely the reason he'd come up with a solution—*lesson number three*. He knew he would be cured the instant she completed her next task.

Temperance spoke, pointing to the card and breaking him away from the sudden dark turn of his musings. "Briar is ever so clever, is she not? We dance with our shared partners, then talk about their finer points and see if they hold any potential. However, I am willing to forgo my dance with *Lord M.M.* and give it to my dear brother, should he ever ask, that is." But Temperance did not give Daniel the opportunity to utter the request. She simply linked arms with him and began to walk toward the floor.

Daniel looked over his shoulder and shrugged.

"I guess he's dancing whether he likes it or not," Nicholas said as he returned Briar's card. Before he was even aware of doing it, rakish impulse took over and he glided his thumb along the underside of her wrist.

Briar did not lift her gaze to him, but her cheeks colored slightly. "I never should have doubted you, my lord. You declared that you would arrange an evening at Almack's and you have done just that."

"That is a lesson learned for you, for if I say I will do something, then it will happen." Then for good measure, he added, "And if I say that I will *not* do something—like remarry, for example—then I will not."

She tapped his sleeve with a graceful flick of her pearl-handled fan. "Don't be so disagreeable on such a promising evening. I know that I cannot force you to alter your opinion. Only someone you find wholly irresistible could do that. But be warned, I plan to keep careful watch over where your feet are pointed."

"Then you will be disappointed, for my feet will remain angled toward the door all evening."

"That cannot be true. With only the best of society permitted entrance, I'm sure to have wonderful luck in finding your potential bride this evening. I've already imagined the entire scenario."

"Is this one like the others, ending with my death and my relatives scavenging through my belongings?"

"Only after a long and happy life. So, you can wipe that frown off your face. Oh, and by the by, your widow simply *adored* you," she said with an unrepentant smirk. "Never fear, you left her surrounded in the cherished comfort of your seven children."

"Seven?" A startled cough escaped him before he remembered that there were inquisitive ears about. "Isn't that a bit generous?"

"Twenty-eight grandchildren as well. And no, I think the number is quite low for a man like you."

He was strangely offended. "I do have other pursuits, I'll have you know. I'd hardly confine my wife to—" His words cut off midsentence as he glared down at her dancing eyes. *Damn it all to hell.*

"See? You're already talking about marriage. Just

wait until I tell Temperance. She'll be so pleased!" Briar laughed and tapped him once more on the sleeve. "And that is a lesson learned for you. If a matchmaker says she will find you the perfect counterpart, she will do just that."

"You're not a matchmaker yet, Miss Bourne," he said sharply, his voice at the level of a warning growl as he steered her through the crowd toward the refreshment anteroom. In the din of all the conversations, laughter, and music, it wasn't likely that anyone could hear their conversation. Even so, he didn't want to risk adding any more logs to the rumor pyres.

She bristled slightly, her gaze darting up to his, a stark, uncertain blue in a sea of white. "I have a good foot under me already."

"You've become presumptuous and have forgotten that our bargain is a means to an end. Which will *end*, indeed, when Daniel has married."

Yet, if that were true, then why had his thoughts lingered more on Briar than on the list of potential candidates she'd made?

"And, Temperance, don't forget."

"I haven't forgotten," he snapped, but realized with a degree of shame that Teense's potential nuptials weren't in the forefront of his mind. "My sole focus is on ensuring the contentment of my cousins."

And not on a kissing bargain that was only meant to serve as a diversion.

Yet, because he found himself constantly distracted by Briar, he decided to remedy it straightaway. He'd given the matter a good deal of thought, but his stomach still churned from the solution he had in mind. Even so, it had to be done, for both their sakes.

"As is mine," she said with a strained glance up at his

face. "Foolishly, I thought we were acquainted enough that we could tease each other good-naturedly."

"I am your mentor, and that is all."

He saw the instant the words struck her. She flinched reflexively, brow furrowed, eyes squinting to shield the blue of her irises with a crowd of lashes. And suddenly he wanted to take those words back and eat them, pretend they never existed. Which was absurd because he spoke the truth. They weren't friends. They were associates in this venture.

So, he pressed on. "As such, I have your third lesson. I saw on your card that you've met Lord Holt."

"Yes," she answered crisply, keeping well abreast of him as they passed through the corridor and headed toward the table lined with cups of pallid liquid. "Your aunt introduced us. Apparently, he has heard of the agency and is hoping to find a match."

A rich one from what Nicholas had heard. "And did you find him as handsome as most of the ladies do?"

"I suppose. Though it is a pity for him."

His brow furrowed in confusion. "Why is that?"

"Because of lesson number two, of course. He is handsome, ergo his wife will not be . . . well"—she blushed—"content."

"Yes, make sure you always remember that one." Nicholas felt a grin tug at his lips, but he subdued it and plucked two cups off the table, handing one to her as they moved to a corner. Then he glanced around them to ensure there was no one lingering within earshot before he spoke. "For lesson number three, I want you to flirt with Holt and see if he tries to kiss you."

"What?"

"I believe you heard me." He had a bad taste on his tongue, and the tart, lukewarm lemonade only made it worse. "This is a game men and women often play when they are seeking a mate."

"The Bourne Agency does not believe that love is a game of any sort."

"Perhaps not, but you will have clients who have experience with these types of manipulations, those who are innocently curious, and those who will use any means to procure a spouse. It is vital that you get a sense of which type you'll be dealing with, for I do not want my cousins married to the latter. And because of your own naive, romantic notions, you would not even think to look for such a trait."

"You underestimate me," she whispered, her shoulders stiff, her gaze fixed on the fragile cup locked in the grip of both hands.

He drained the last of the horrid beverage and continued without responding directly. "I saw Holt's name scribbled beside the waltz."

"And what of it?"

Nicholas tried to be nonchalant about the entire episode, but felt his jaw harden, the confines of his own irritation prickling like quills beneath his skin. "No doubt the young lord will mention something about the heat and offer to escort you to the terrace for air. He'll direct you to a spot, distant from the doors, and give you the reason that the quiet is necessary for conversation. But he won't be there to talk. Instead, he'll say something about the moonlight in your eyes and he'll sweep in and . . . kiss you."

"You cannot know this," she hissed, fury in every syllable, eyes flashing up to his.

"I do because all rakes think alike." His own gaze drifted to her tempting lips and he knew Holt wouldn't be able to resist.

"If that is true, then I've had more than enough experience in manipulation since meeting you."

"No. It must be someone else. Someone with whom you're not so familiar, as you are with me and my family." He looked away from her hard, wounded stare. "Though, you needn't worry that he will attempt anything more than a kiss. From what I've heard, he needs to marry an heiress to get himself out of debt, and he cannot risk your reputation. But still, be on your guard —no *immersing yourself in the experience*."

"It seems you've thought of everything." With alarming calmness, she stepped to the side and poured her lemonade into the urn of a palm tree. When she returned, she handed him her cup, her teeth bared in the taut semblance of a smile. "But what if I don't want to kiss him? As far as I am aware, I am still my own person."

"You are, indeed. You may decline, demure, storm away, or"—he swallowed —"submit if you choose. It matters not to me. You've proven to be too easily distracted by, what you perceive as, a friendship. It would be an unkindness to mislead you. As I said before, there is nothing between us other than an exchange of services—my tutelage for the eventual marriages of my cousins."

"Then allow me to assure you once more that I am never going to find myself in love with you—you arrogant buffoon. This entire arrangement is purely academic for me, *and that is all*."

Nicholas was glad she stormed off because, if she hadn't, he might have found himself doing something rash, like claiming the waltz for himself and showing her exactly what a rake would do.

BRIAR HAD never imagined a person could be furious when waltzing, and yet she was. Thoroughly. Her palms were damp and clenched, blood rushing in her ears, and all while Lord Holt smoothly swept her about the room.

She wished it was Nicholas instead, because she could easily envision wrapping her hands around his throat. Or perhaps she would do something even worse like . . . pouring a perfectly good cup of chocolate over his head.

And, the next time she had a cup on hand, perhaps she would.

Of all the nerve! Oh, he thought he was so clever that he could script Lord Holt's exact actions. Well, she could not wait to tell Nicholas that Holt had not once mentioned stealing her away from the protective eye of Mrs. Prescott, and the waltz was nearly fin—

"Would you care to join me on the terrace, Miss Bourne?" Holt asked, his smooth, drowsy cadence blending in with the intimate steps of the dance, his gaze shadowed by a thick fringe of minky lashes.

Briar's focus snapped to her partner.

Lord Asher Holt was a handsome devil, to be sure, but with his air of languid indifference it was impossible to believe him capable of careful calculation.

Even so, she barely had the chance to complete her nod before he deftly maneuvered her into a turn. Then they disappeared behind one of the potted palms and down a passageway that she didn't realize was there. And before she knew it, they'd emerged onto the terrace.

As Nicholas predicted, no one else was about. The others were still waiting for the waltz to end before heading in to dinner. And so, it seemed, the eleventh hour was nearly here.

Was Lord Holt planning to kiss her? Nervousness caused her stomach to tremble, the contents feeling like popping corn set near the fire.

"The night is rather warm even out of doors. Perhaps if we stand at the far corner we might capture a breeze," he said, his hand coasting over the small of her back as he guided her, every movement subtle, practiced, as if he'd done this countless times before.

It seemed that Nicholas had been right about this, too, and she hated him for it. She could well imagine drowning him in an entire vat of chocolate, maniacally laughing at his last sputtering breath as he slowly slipped beneath the froth.

She frowned at the scenario, disturbed. It wouldn't work—death by chocolate was too good for him.

"Is this spot agreeable?" Holt asked, his concentration on her expression, his own frown forming. "If you would rather return inside . . ."

"Not at all," she said quickly, tucking her annoyance away for the moment. "I appreciate the reprieve from the heat."

"Yes, I now have sympathy for every lamb roasted over a spit." He chuckled and slid a finger between his neck and cravat, revealing that he actually had a second one—black silk—beneath the snowy white.

Puzzled, she asked, "Why do you wear two cravats?"

"I don't normally, but the patronesses would refuse my admittance without the white one. And I wear the black as a matter of principle. You could say that I'm in a period of ante-mourning, and all too conscious of the debt that will be foisted upon me one day." An unrepentant smirk hooked one corner of his mouth. "In addition, the sight of it drives my father absolutely bonkers. So, of course, I can never be without it."

Assuming that he was teasing, at least in part, she smiled. "Well, then, you'll need to find a wealthy bride straightaway."

As luck would have it—she thanked her blue hair ribbon—the agency happened to have an applicant, a Miss Throckmeyer of Hampshire who had a fortune of £40,000. What a coup it would be to make such a match! But first, she would need Holt listed on their client registry.

"It isn't often that I find a woman who cuts so cleanly to the heart of the issue. I rather like that," he said.

"My uncle started the Bourne Matrimonial Agency to help every person we can. While necessity may dictate your need for an heiress, we'll ensure that you also find a bride who shares your interests, beliefs, and passions. Everyone deserves to feel that spark that only comes with their perfect counterpart."

"Not only pretty, but incomparably clever. I don't suppose you have a fortune lying around, do you?" Dark soulful eyes rimmed in black lashes focused solely on her, and his smirk transformed into a chemise-melting grin.

Holy handsomeness! Was there a woman alive who could resist such a rake?

"Paltry dowry, I'm afraid," she said with a high, tittering laugh that she'd never heard herself utter. She might even have been on the verge of swooning.

"Then we're in the same boat, aren't we?" He moved a step closer, setting his hand on the balustrade near hers. His gaze dipped to her mouth and then lifted to her eyes again. "Just the two of us, searching for the one that is out of reach, but so close we could almost taste them."

Oh my, he was awfully good at this. She was a bit lightheaded now, her heart beating faster, though from nerves more than anticipation. With Nicholas, she'd felt a degree of comfort having had the rules established ahead of time. But with Holt she was uncertain. The only thing she could cling to was what Nicholas had told her would happen.

"So tell me, what is the process at your uncle's business?"

"First, we will take your application and then cross check your responses with others we have on file . . ."

"Fascinating," Holt said, convincingly absorbed, sliding ever closer.

". . . then we'll arrange a meeting to see if you're compatible."

"Compatibility is very important."

Briar swallowed, watching as he glided his hand along the balustrade. He was going to reach for her, pull her closer, and press his lips against hers. And she was going to let him, she decided. In fact, she might even enjoy it.

She most certainly would enjoy telling Nicholas how superior Holt's kiss was—no matter what the results.

The final strains of the waltz drifted to them on a warm current of air, marking their time. It wouldn't be long before she was missed. Holt really needed to hurry this along.

She leaned forward in encouragement and he tilted his head, a question in his gaze.

Yes, she answered by way of rising up on her toes. But that put her at an awkward angle. To keep herself from tipping forward, she skimmed her hand over the railing and shuffled closer. The only problem was, something snagged her glove, causing her to twist. At the same time, the toe of her slipper caught on the edge of a stone. And the next thing she knew, she was falling.

Oh dear. Holt's eyes widened an instant before he caught her by the shoulders, and held her an inconvenient distance apart.

Briar had to take matters into her own hands. No longer attempting to play coy, she curled her fingers around his lapels and pressed her mouth to his. Hard.

She hadn't intended to be so aggressive, but momentum propelled her forward. And so there she was . . . taking advantage of Holt's mouth.

But his nose did not slide against hers. His lips were warm, but they did not taste like Nicholas. The scent of his skin did not remind her of a cozy autumn afternoon, or make her stomach clench sweetly.

While the flesh-to-flesh contact was pleasant, she did not have the sense that they were sharing the experience. This was just kissing for the sake of kissing. And while she didn't know precisely what that meant, she knew it was different.

Gradually, he eased her away, his expression chagrinned. "Miss Bourne, I apologize if I gave you the impression that I asked you to join me for any other reason than to discuss your uncle's matchmaking business."

"You didn't?"

"You are a tempting armful, but I'm not the kind of man who can be swept off his feet."

A tidal wave of embarrassment washed over her with sickening dread. "Do you mean to say that you weren't planning to kiss me?"

He chuckled. "Your lips are quite enticing and tasty, but I'm afraid I'm not one to mix business with pleasure. Complications and all that. Under the circumstances, perhaps it would be best if I did not fill out an application at your uncle's agency."

Briar was utterly mortified. And, to make matters worse, it was quite clear that her ribbon was not lucky at all.

Chapter 15

"She felt that half this folly must be drunkenness,
and therefore could hope that it might belong only
to the passing hour."

JANE AUSTEN, *Emma*

Over the next few days, Briar avoided Nicholas. Complete absence from his presence was the better alternative than being hanged for his murder.

Therefore, when she'd received an invitation from him to tour the museum with his aunt and cousins, she declined without even mentioning it to her sisters or uncle. Even when Temperance had invited her to tea, Briar refused. In fact, the only time she spent with her friend had been at the park for archery.

Sadly, Temperance, who tried harder than any person in the world, was so dreadful at hitting the target that she'd been asked by the head of the women's archery society to leave. Permanently.

Briar, in a show of solidarity, had refused to return as well. And whenever she found herself missing the activity, she blamed Nicholas for that, too.

Her occupation of finding him a bride, however, did not stop. In fact, she dove into it headfirst, compiling a list of the least alluring female clients in the agency's registry. Those with poor complexions, greasy hair, and missing teeth made the top of the list, along with those old enough to be his grandmother.

Then, after her pen-and-paper rant, she returned to genuinely perusing the applicants to find matches for Daniel and Temperance.

Walking into Ainsley's office on the off chance that they had any new clients, she found both her sisters present—Ainsley behind her desk and Jacinda in front of it, waving the *Post* as if it were a victory flag.

Jacinda turned with a smile, unsettling a lock of auburn hair, her turquoise eyes shining. "Briar, you are just in time to hear the news. You will never guess what has happened. Miss Throckmeyer—the very one I'd tried to match with Rydstrom—has eloped. And with her father's steward! Can you believe it?"

"I cannot." Briar pasted on a smile, but she wasn't at all happy. Miss Throckmeyer, of the £40,000 dowry, was the only chance Briar had of recovering from her terrace debacle with Lord Holt. She'd still hoped to secure him as a client, dangling Miss Throckmeyer's fortune like a carrot in front of a horse.

"What scandal! It couldn't be better news for us."

"Since Miss Throckmeyer was the only heiress we had left as a client"—Ainsley slid a pointed look toward Briar—"I don't see how this benefits us."

Before Jacinda could answer, Briar spoke up for herself. "There hasn't been a single mention of my blunder in the paper for over a week. And I've been making excellent progress with finding a match for Temperance."

Not to mention the half-dozen elderly women she had in mind for the Earl of Edgemont. But she would keep that to herself, along with her more earnest efforts for Daniel Prescott.

"I also saw that you acquired two new clients. Mrs. Teasdale and her son, Lancelot, which I sincerely hope is an endearment and not his actual name. That is, if the man exists at all." Ainsley lifted the two pages that had been left on a shelf in the closet—Briar's only office space. "Apparently, Mrs. Teasdale claims to have three properties and a fortune of twenty thousand pounds and yet has nothing better to do than sit in our parlor and knit. Well, I hate to be the one to tell you this, but Mrs. Teasdale is likely off her rocker."

Of course, any client Briar acquired wouldn't be good enough, no matter what. "She may be a bit eccentric, but I like her."

Jacinda came closer and patted Briar's shoulder. "Oh, don't mind Ainsley. She had another tête à tête with our handsome gaming hell neighbor. According to Mrs. Darden, our sister sent Mr. Sterling a written reprimand about the litter on the pavement outside his establishment."

"It is an eyesore. I had every right to complain."

"Instead of a written response, however, Mr. Sterling stormed across the street, barely dressed, and tore the missive in half, letting it fall to the steps."

Ainsley sat rigid in her chair, a slow flush climbing her neck above her sensible fichu. "Either Mrs. Darden or your sister has embellished the details. The truth is, Mr. Sterling was dressed, though without a cravat. I advised him that, if he should choose to approach our establishment again, he should be properly attired."

"To which he responded by removing his coat and slinging it over his shoulder before storming back across the street. And ever since, Ainsley has been acting as if her cup is full of pickle brine." An impish grin lifted Jacinda's cheeks as she turned her attention back to Briar and tapped her finger on the *Post*. "This scandal is truly the best thing that could have happened."

"Until someone realizes that Miss Throckmeyer was our client," Ainsley muttered.

"Our sister," Jacinda said with a sigh, hooking her arm through Briar's. "Such a storm cloud on a lovely day."

Against her will, a bubble of laughter rose in Briar and whatever irritation she felt toward Ainsley faded. At least for the time being. She would direct all of her ire toward Nicholas, who deserved it most.

"That was the only reason I popped by this morning. Crispin is at Tattersall's hoping to bid on an even-tempered mare for his sister. According to him, the Marquess of Knightswold will be introducing a few new thoroughbreds and nearly every gentleman in town will be there."

Briar perked up at this information, a plan forming in her mind. If the gentlemen were all at Tattersall's, then this might be the perfect day to visit Temperance. And with her friend's assistance, they could discuss this latest list and see which candidates might be best suited to Daniel. After all, Briar didn't need to run everything by Nicholas. All that mattered was that she upheld her end of the bargain. And, after the last lesson, she wasn't keen on receiving any more. "Then perhaps you could drop me off at Temperance's on the way?"

"I apologize, Miss Bourne, but Miss Prescott is next door with her mother. It seems that Lady Penrose's spaniel has a new litter of puppies."

Nicholas jolted to attention as Delham's monotone traveled from the foyer and into the study. His gaze swiveled to the open door.

The melody of Briar's airy voice reached him then, and without hesitation, he set the quill into the stand and left his desk with the speed of a bloodhound after a rabbit.

"Oh, bother. My sister's carriage has just trundled away."

"If you like, miss, I could send word next door."

"But I should hate to take Temperance away from new puppies, and I couldn't possibly invite myself over. I think perhaps I shall hail a cab and—"

"That won't be necessary," Nicholas cut in, striding into the foyer. "Delham, could you please send word to the kitchens to prepare a tray for Miss Bourne and bring it to my study?"

She jolted with a swift, startled glance before her attention snapped back to the butler, her shoulders straight, chin high. Clearly, she was still cross with him.

"I do not plan to linger," she said to Delham, smoothing her hands down pleats of pale yellow. But he paid no heed and bowed smartly before leaving them to stand alone.

Slowly, she turned to face Nicholas, her eyes the color of cornflower petals after a hard frost. She was breathtaking in her ire, eyes glinting, skin glowing in the soft buttery light sifting in through the transom window. And Nicholas nearly forgot that he was angry, too.

Then the swift reminder that she'd been on the terrace with Holt came back with full force.

"How is your hunt for spouses proceeding?" he asked, adopting a tone of nonchalance as he gestured for her to precede him into the study.

"Swimmingly. I found the perfect wife for you—a fishmonger's widow. She doesn't have any teeth and only four fingers on her right hand, but she is the only one I could find who matched your temperament."

In opposition to the dark mood that had beleaguered him these past few days, a grin tugged at the corner of his mouth as she stormed off ahead of him. "I meant for my cousins."

"I have a new list, though it is not as plentiful as the first."

"Considering the news this morning of Miss Throck-meyer's elopement, your *luck*— as you like to say—at the agency is bound to change." Normally one to avoid reading the society pages, he'd recently begun scanning them for any mention of the Bournes. Solely out of curiosity about the status of the agency, of course. He certainly wasn't trying to discover if Briar had attended any other events.

"Very true, and don't forget that I was well received at Almack's last week." The mocking lilt in her voice was clearly meant to goad him.

He pretended that his blood hadn't shot up twenty degrees and he wasn't fuming. "Is that so? And just how *well received* were you on the terrace? Did you happen to learn anything new?"

"A great many things, indeed," she said, eyes flashing fire now as she refused to take the seat he offered. "But you were wrong. For your information, Holt didn't kiss me."

Nicholas expelled a tight breath, days of frustration and foul temper slipping out of his lungs like steam under pressure. "Well, that's . . ."

"*I* kissed *him*."

". . . good." Abruptly the heat and annoyance returned. "You did *what*?"

She lifted her arms and removed the pins from her bonnet with cross, quick tugs, and when it was off, stabbed the pins through it again. "I believe you heard me. He hadn't intended to kiss me at all, but only to speak about an application. But you—you corruptor of thoughts—had me convinced otherwise. So I took matters into my own hands."

"You kissed him."

She issued a rueful laugh. "Oh yes, indeed. I think I even shocked him, taking him by the lapels the way I did. We nearly tumbled together to the stones."

Nicholas gritted his teeth. He tried to force the image from his mind, not wanting to think about her mouth on another man. Not wanting to think about her breath mingling with Holt's. Or her lips brushing back and forth in her *cup of chocolate* kiss.

That was *his* kiss. Not Holt's.

"And now," she continued, her voice rising above the low growl that rumbled in his throat, "after being so brazen, he wants nothing to do with the agency. Because of you, I lost a potential client. So your lessons, as you call them, are not improving my skills at all. You're no better at matchmaking than I am. And, just so you know, I am resoundingly angry at you!"

"Good. That makes two of us."

She stalked toward him, poking him in the chest with the brim of her hat. "Why did you really have me join Holt on the terrace?"

Before Nicholas knew what he was doing or saying, he took hold of her wrist, then took the hat and tossed it toward the desk. "Because I do despicable things and you need to understand that. I'm not kind or polite. I'm selfish and I have no intention of changing. And I never have foolishly romantic dreams about growing old with someone like in one of your scenarios."

"Well, I disagree." She huffed, her pulse thrashing beneath the pads of his fingers. "Obviously you once had such a dream or else you wouldn't have been married before. And just to spite you I'm going to find your bride before our bargain has concluded. Oh, and she will be clever, too. So much so that she'll lead you to the altar by your nose before you even know what's happened. She'll—"

Nicholas stopped her tirade with his mouth. He didn't want to hear any more. All he wanted was to silence her and release all this pent-up anger.

He plundered her mouth, claiming her lips in a rough, wet slide. She answered his onslaught by rising up on her toes. Gliding her free hand over his shoulder, her fingertips gripped his nape, tugging him closer. And he knew he wasn't the only one who needed this.

They punished each other with firm presses and little nips of teeth, growls vibrating in his throat and in hers. He wanted to feast on her anger, swallow it whole. He wanted everything she had. "Give me your tongue, damn it all."

She panted, her breath coasting over his lips. "You told me that I should learn to hold back."

"Not with me."

Never with me, he thought, opening her mouth with his and stealing inside the dewy heat. Her lips parted, her tongue shyly seeking his, a brush and retreat.

This was still new to her, he reminded himself, and gently coaxed her tongue back into his mouth, asking her to trust him. *You'll like this, I promise.* And yet, at the first tentative slide, he was the one who was lost in pleasure.

He gloried in the lush, slick coiling of flesh against flesh. She issued a soft, surprised mewl and gripped him tighter. Her spine bowed, the soft curves of her body pressing against his. Then she licked into his mouth as he was doing to hers, their kiss hungry, needy. She purred wantonly as if discovering something she enjoyed more than sipping chocolate. And he liked that thought more than he should.

Still he wanted more. He wanted to completely obliterate the memory of Holt from her mind. The younger lord may have been more handsome, but Nicholas had experience on his side. So he kissed her breathless, relishing the yield of her body against his.

Until she broke the kiss.

"Hands," she rasped.

And only then did he realize that while he held one

of her wrists, his other hand curled possessively over the curve of her hip, his fingertips flexing into soft muslin over her supple flesh.

He deliberated for an instant, thinking that he'd rather pull her closer and let her feel the effect she had on him than release her. And when he noted that her lips were temptingly plump, her eyes a dark wanton blue, he knew he could coax her back into their kiss.

Unfortunately, he also knew that the door was still open and there would be a servant coming in with a tea tray at any moment. Thus, with regret, he released her. But he was unable to step away before pressing his lips to hers once more, briefly. "There. That was your fourth lesson—an angry kiss. It is effective in letting off steam."

Her breaths matched his, pant for pant, her hand gradually sliding away from his nape. "I was sure I would be furious with you . . . all the days of my life. How did you even know . . . I would permit you to kiss me?" she asked as if mystified by her own response.

"I didn't," he said honestly. Knowing that wouldn't be enough of an explanation, he went on. "Men and women exhibit anger and desire in similar fashions. We crowd closer, either in an effort to intimidate or to claim. Our breath quickens, blood rushes hotter, cheeks flush, and eyes darken. Our sense of awareness heightens, too. Every subtle scent, or even a tilt of the head tells us if we should be wary of attack, or if we are about to engage in a far more pleasurable activity. I took a chance on the latter."

Then her softly hooded eyes sharpened. "Do not crow in triumph too quickly. I am still cross with you. Asking me to kiss another man was a betrayal of our bargain and of my trust. You likely don't know this, but my own mother allowed her heart to be broken by my father's betrayal. And while I may have a good many of her traits, I do not share that one. I will not tolerate another game of yours, Nicholas. Never do it again."

He inclined his head, in full agreement. His actions had been wrong in countless ways. "A most deserved scolding."

Apparently, she thought he was mocking her because she squared her shoulders. "Should I hide the way I feel? Act like a puppet in your control? Is that what you intended when we made our bargain?"

"No, love. Always tell me when I've done anything to offend you so that I do not repeat my error. I prefer to know your every thought, unfiltered."

He moved closer and cupped her face, losing himself in the cornflower blue striations in her eyes. She offered an imperceptible nod. They'd reached an understanding, then.

The pad of his thumb slowly swept over her lips and she shivered. Peculiarly, the vulnerable sensation tumbled through him as well, cascading down his limbs, and intensifying the unwelcome rise of guilt that now replaced the jealous fury, which had gone quiet.

He shouldn't have asked her to kiss Holt, or any other man for that matter.

Except for himself, of course. His conscience did not rear at him at all when her lips were on his own. In fact, he was tempted to keep them there for a while longer. Yet, before he could lower his head, the clink and rattle of dishes drifted in through the open door.

Looking over her shoulder, he straightened and dropped his hand. Then, for good measure, he moved behind his desk, and sank into his chair.

The maid entered the room and left the tea tray on the escritoire without any conversation aside from Briar thanking her. Then they were alone once more, which was exactly what he wanted. They still had unfinished business to discuss.

For the past few days, she hadn't responded to a single missive, but only returned them directly—tickets to the museum and Vauxhall Gardens included. Both respectable places to visit during an afternoon. He even took great care to gain permission from her uncle, who was willing to grant chaperonage to Aunt Lavinia.

"So, tell me, Miss Bourne, are you through punishing me by declining my invitations?"

"Punishing you?" A small puff of laughter escaped her. "I suppose I was in a way. And you still owe me recompense."

The tilted tips of her lashes winked in the sunlight and caught the corner of a sly grin. And suddenly he knew he was forgiven.

An inexplicable surge of warmth filled his chest, his heart pounding sure and steady. "What shall it be? Do you intend to commandeer my carriage again?"

Grinning, she fussed over the tray. "Tempting, but no. Splash of milk, no sugar?"

He nodded, surprised that she could have known. Then he remembered their tea on the terrace.

Throughout his life, he'd drunk thousands of cups, prepared by himself and by others, and yet he'd never noticed until this moment how intimate it was when someone else poured for him.

He watched as she removed her gloves and set them aside. Her arms were now bare from capped sleeve to delicately boned hands. Every movement was all ease and grace, the brush of fingertips over porcelain, the turn of her wrist. The noisy world beyond the window faded away beneath the soft whisper of steamy liquid filling the cup, the soundless stirring of the spoon, and the subtle aromas of tea and fresh linen. And all of it, he just realized, was disconcertingly, pleasingly homey.

After adding a nip of sugar to her own cup, she brought them both to the desk. Then taking the chair opposite his, she continued their conversation, ignorant of the peculiar thoughts running inside his mind.

"To make up for your horrid behavior, I want a wholly unrestricted conversation."

He took a sip of tea, puzzling over why it even tasted different, the flavor enhanced to a rich, earthy elixir, smooth on his palate and far too easy to swallow. Briar Bourne made an excellent cup of tea. "In my company, you are always free to speak on any topic."

"Then I want to know about your wife."

"Except for that one," he amended and set his cup down crisply in the saucer.

Across from him, she said nothing but sipped her tea with unnerving patience in her steady gaze.

Damn it all to hell. "Why would you want to know about her?"

"Because she is the one woman you decided to marry. And, I hope you can forgive me, if the memory is too painful, but I'm curious what it was that drew you to her and made you fall in love."

He swallowed down a wry laugh. "If your ultimate goal is to find a woman with her particular and most cunning characteristics in order to entice me into marriage, then you're wasting your time."

This, of course, did nothing to deter Briar. "How did you meet her?"

"She was a friend of my brother's wife and visited the house often after they married," he explained, swallowing down a rise of bitterness. "Not having reached my majority and under the guardianship of my brother after our father died, I lived there as well."

"So you saw her often and a companionship grew between you?" She paused seeming to mull this over. "Was she pretty?"

"Yes, and I was naive enough that I could not see beyond her raven hair and flashing violet eyes. A foolish young man, barely out of university, I did not even know there were women like her, so free and vivacious. And when Marceline wanted something, no obstacle was too great, no means of manipulation off limits."

Briar sighed, clearly misunderstanding, her eyes filled with flying Cupids and heart-shaped arrows. "Was she so in love that she was willing to do anything to have you?"

He looked toward the open window, wanting to avoid the memory that was still too close at hand, even after all these years. "You are partly right. She was willing to do anything, even to suffer the floundering attentions of a gangly younger brother in order to have a place in the earl's family."

In the earl's house. In the earl's bed . . .

"You speak as though you don't believe she loved you," Briar said, her tone listing downward. "Oh, Nicholas, that is a terrible burden to carry inside your heart. Don't you see? This is precisely the reason you should marry again. And I vow to find you someone who will leave you in no doubt of her affections."

He turned to tell her that it wasn't possible. That the years had changed him and he was no longer a foolish young man. But seeing the hopeful eagerness in her expression, he didn't have the heart to crush her dreams.

Chapter 16

"... certainly silly things do cease to be silly if they
are done by sensible people in an imprudent way."

JANE AUSTEN, *Emma*

Later that week, and sitting across from Mrs. Teasdale
in the parlor, Briar frowned at the *Post* folded in her
grasp.

"'Luckless titled gentleman of relatively good breeding
seeks wife—heiresses need only apply. Send all correspondence to the editor of this fine circular,'" she murmured
in disgust. "I cannot believe he took out an advertisement
for a wife."

She knew it was Lord Holt. After all, who else could it
have been? Abruptly Briar felt a renewed wash of shame
for having molested him on the terrace.

"Perhaps that's what you should do, dearie," Mrs.
Teasdale said amidst the ever-constant clicking of her
knitting needles. The new project was a long triangular
shape, with uneven rows and yarn the speckled white-
and-gray color of a dirty lamb.

She had become a constant figure at the agency, the first
patron to arrive each morning and the last to leave each
afternoon on the three days they were open. There were
some days when she was the only patron. Although, after
the news of Miss Throckmeyer's elopement had taken
Briar's blunder out of mainstream gossip, they did have a

small trickle of new clients. But what they needed was a flood.

Brooding over the paper and the loss of the client that never was, Briar propped her chin on her fist, slouching. If ever a moment called for a good slouch, then this was surely it. "We already have advertisements in two different circulars. Ainsley has even thought of pasting notices around the shops in town, to draw more people in."

"Mmm . . . I've seen them and they're a bit flat, to my way of thinking. They need to have a bit of spark."

At the mere mention of the word *spark*, gooseflesh scattered down her arms making the tiny hairs stand on end. That was precisely what she wanted—sparks for every one of her clients. She sat straight. "What do you mean, precisely?"

Mrs. Teasdale pointed to the paper with one of her needles. "Make folks think they're coming here to meet that one fated person. Not to be put on a list. Not everyone is patient enough for that. And besides, the Season's coming to an end, isn't it?"

Yes, it was already May. It was no secret that many people were scrambling to find a match before the Season was over. Much of society had already planned to travel to the seaside, or to their country estates, and away from the heat and stench of town. In fact, Briar usually spent a few weeks in north Hampshire at the Duchess of Holliford's country estate.

All the more reason to make haste. "You may be on to something, Mrs. Teasdale. It would have to be anonymous, of course. No direct mention of the agency."

She could just imagine Ainsley up in the house roof over something like this. But what a perfect idea, regardless.

Briar shot up from the chair and began to pace in the open area in front of the door, thinking of Temperance and Daniel. "I won't mention their physical descriptions at all because I believe a person who is serious would want to gain a sense of character first. I'll leave out a mention of dowry and income as well. Two thousand pounds is enough to bring in many an unscrupulous person."

"Sadly true. Brings to mind my fourth husband."

Briar was lost in thought, seeking the perfect phrasing, and the instant it came to her, tingles coursed down her limbs. "I've got it! 'Sensible maiden from an upstanding family seeks husband from the same. Gentleman preferred.' And then for him, 'Fine gentleman with a small country estate seeks steadfast bride. Debutantes preferred.'"

"I like that," Mrs. Teasdale said, tapping the needle against her chin and nodding. "Very good. I imagine, you could write a slew of them."

"If it works, that's precisely what I plan to do." It would take a bit more coin from her dowry, but she wouldn't need that anytime soon. She wasn't even remotely interested in looking for a husband until she'd made her mark on the matchmaking world.

Then, after Temperance and Daniel, Briar would take out an advertisement for every one of her clients. Except for Nicholas, of course, because he wasn't a client. He was . . . *hmm* . . . she wasn't entirely sure. The object of a challenge? A mere tutor?

No, to her, he was more than that.

After the lesson of the angry kiss, she felt as if they'd reached a deeper understanding. That fierce, stolen moment seemed to have unlocked a door between them. The barrier of tutor and pupil had given way to the beginnings of a friendship. After all, he wouldn't have revealed so much about his marriage to just anyone. She'd heard the pained edge in his tone when he'd spoken of his loss and her heart had twisted, feeling raw and tender toward him.

It had been on the tip of her tongue to ask more about

his life. Not just about the short duration of his marriage, but everything. What was he like as a child? What were his dreams of the future? Did he once have a dog, a fondness for sweets, a favorite color?

Frankly, she was surprised she hadn't leapt across his desk, a crazed look in her eyes, and said, "Tell me every thought you've ever had . . ."

And in that new, barrierless moment between them, she would have written down each detail on scraps of paper, stuffed them up her sleeves, down her chemise, rolled them up inside her gloves. Just to keep them with her.

Even now, she still felt greedy, needing to know all about him but not understanding the sense of urgency teeming through her. This new friendship of theirs was different than anything she'd ever experienced. And since she wanted to experience everything life had to offer, she never wanted it to end.

So perhaps while trying to find him someone irresistible, she should make sure that this woman could be her own friend as well. And then Briar could keep a small part of him with her always.

❧

THIS PAST week, Nicholas had found himself away from his townhouse in the afternoons, especially on the days when he knew Temperance was anticipating a visit from her friend. He didn't intentionally set out to avoid Briar but he knew it was better if he kept his distance.

After all, he didn't want her to imagine that he planned to repeat what had happened during their last encounter, or that he'd find a reason to pull her aside and kiss her each time he saw her. Because he wouldn't. He had far more control over his actions.

Besides, he was her tutor. Older. Wiser. A man of the world.

Men of the world did not spend their days thinking about clandestine kisses as if they'd been turned back into awkward, green pups fresh out of university.

Men of the world met with their solicitors and stewards, they caroused with old friends, visited clubs, spent evenings at Sterling's. And when they were at gaming hells, men of the world focused on the cards and the women whispering lewd promises in their ears. They did not catch themselves glancing out across the street to a matrimonial agency, interested in the light they saw burning in one of the windows, and wondering if it was hers.

Only a fool would do that.

Unfortunately today, his efforts of escape were foiled by Aunt Lavinia. She'd stopped him to discuss a letter she'd received from his mother, wanting to know when they might be retiring to the country. During their conversation, Viscount Eggleston and his lovely niece dropped off a parcel of freshly baked scones on their way out for new ribbons and handkerchiefs.

But that had not been enough for Aunt Lavinia. She'd invited them to stay for a visit and tour the garden, instead.

"After all," she'd said with a bright-eyed grin as she'd linked arms with the charming viscount, "the shops will be there tomorrow, but the blooms may well be spent today."

And that was how Nicholas had found himself seated beneath the ivy arbor on the terrace, determined not to think up different ways to lure Briar away for a moment or two.

"Your cousin seems miles away this afternoon, Temperance," Briar said with a certain wiliness in her tone. "Either that or he is glaring at the last scone because he is angry that Mrs. Darden refuses to give up her recipe."

Nicholas felt a smirk tug at the corner of his mouth, but resisted the urge to make a comment. It would not be wise to engage in playful banter. He might forget that both his cousins sat at the same table, while his aunt and her uncle observed them from a bench beneath a canopy of shade trees on the far side of the garden.

Temperance laughed. "For that, I might even wag a finger at my scone . . . if anything more than a crumb remained on my plate. But you are right. Nicholas does seem rather preoccupied. What do you think the cause could be, Daniel?"

"Nothing so dramatic," Daniel said, a glimpse of his former self in the grin on his face. "When we were in the country, his primary goal of existence was digging irrigation trenches on his land. Surely all he requires is a shovel in order to be content."

Nicholas focused on him, heartened to see the new changes that appeared every day, subtle but noteworthy. Daniel spent less time in his rooms. Even though he still preferred to stay home rather than attend a soiree, he joined the family for dinner and afternoon tea. And now, he was ribbing Nicholas.

It seemed that none of them were immune to Briar's effervescence. Surely this was a good development toward getting Daniel married by Season's end.

"Quite amusing," Nicholas said, a wry grin on his own lips as he glanced from one cousin to the next. Then his gaze settled on Briar. This afternoon she wore a frock in his favorite color—the exact shade of deep blue that her eyes turned when she'd been thoroughly kissed. "But Miss Bourne was correct. I am quite cross that this is the last scone."

He leaned forward to take it.

But suddenly he wasn't the only one reaching for the plate. The four of them shot forward, chairs sliding back, raking sharply on the stones. Surprised shouts of laughter followed. The playful slap of fingers. Then Briar sat back, lifting her prize above her head as if it were a trophy cup.

"See here. That's hardly fair. Mrs. Darden is your own cook, and I am your dearest friend."

"My sister is quite right. You likely have a dozen waiting for your return."

Briar grinned without shame. "Pitiful attempts. You'll have to work much harder if you want to make me feel guilty enough to rescind my prize. You forget, I have two older sisters who are quite skilled at that game. My lord, would you care to try?"

Nicholas eased down into his chair, fighting the impulse to eat the scone directly from her hand, nibbling her fingertips, licking every morsel. "Miss Bourne won it fairly."

"Thank yo—"

"If she can enjoy the flavor," he continued solemnly, "even though it is now tainted by the greed and selfishness of her actions, then who are we to deny her?"

He shrugged his shoulders, lifting his hands in innocence.

Briar lowered her scone. "Very well done. You are quite skilled at manipulation. It must be because you are so much older than the rest of us, and you've had more years of practice." Then, with a cheeky grin, she broke off a piece and popped it into her mouth. "Mmm . . . *greed and selfishness* . . . positively scrumptious."

Temperance threw her napkin at her friend, laughing. "You sound just like Nicholas when he ate the last three from the previous batch. Wholly unrepentant, the pair of you."

Nicholas didn't like the way that phrase rolled off his cousin's tongue. And he certainly didn't like the pleasurable jolt he felt hearing *the pair of you*. "Mind what you say, Teense, or I will not drive you to the opera tomorrow evening."

"Are you in earnest?" Temperance gasped. At his nod, she jumped up from her chair, nearly upending it onto the stones. "This will be splendid. Just splendid! Oh, but of course, you are inviting Briar as well, or else you would not have mentioned it in front of her."

"It would have been rude otherwise," he said, adopting a bored countenance as if he wasn't taken by surprise as well. He was fully aware of the faux pas should he not extend the invitation to all those present. So why did he bring up the opera if he'd been trying to stay away from Briar?

She eyed him shrewdly as if trying to figure him out, too. "I would love to accept. However, permission is for my uncle to grant."

Instinctively, Nicholas knew that would be her answer. Perhaps that was the reason he'd mentioned it now, instead of sending a written invitation. He'd learned already that those tended to return with refusals. And it was a matter of happenstance that her doting uncle was present.

"Then I will ask him this instant. Daniel, come with me in case he needs to be persuaded." Temperance rushed over to his chair, and after a few tugs on his coat, a patient, brotherly sigh, and the shriek of chair legs sliding back, they left.

Briar watched them go, shielding her eyes from the light with her free hand, then she turned back to him. "Are you going to make an excuse to leave the table as well?"

"Why would I do such a thing?"

She lifted her shoulders in a careless shrug. "It seems that you've been avoiding me these past few visits."

"Have I?"

"Mmm . . . the same way that I avoided you after that

evening at Almack's. I must have done something to bother you, or make you cross, but I cannot fathom what it could be. Unless . . . you're afraid that I will hound you with questions regarding the type of woman you would prefer. Or demand to know your favorite qualities and desired temperaments. I have an unending list."

"Of that, I have no doubt, but your matchmaking efforts do not frighten me." He chuckled.

Then his gaze caught on the bit of scone she pinched between her thumb and forefinger and brought to her lips, the tip of her tongue darting out to capture an errant crumb. He shifted in his chair, half of him wishing he could watch her nibble on the rest of it, and the other half ready to beg her to stop.

"Then it's as I feared. You still believe I am so susceptible to your charms that I have spent these many days pressing kisses into my pillow and whispering your name."

"At last, you admit it," he said on a hoarse breath, his mind conjuring that very thing. But in his scenario, it wasn't her pillow—it was his. And the sounds from her lips weren't whispers—they were wanton pleas.

She tilted her head, studying him closely, and likely noting his high color and the sheen of perspiration on his brow. "Are you coming down with a cold? Is that the reason you've enforced this unanticipated sabbatical from my lessons?"

"Perhaps I'm teaching you about anticipation."

"Are you saying you want me to think about you, Nicholas?" she teased, her voice whisper-soft, a slow grin curling her rose-petal lips. "That must mean you're thinking of me, whiling away the hours of your days— and for a man of your years those are too precious to waste. I must say, I'm quite flattered. But it would never work out between us."

Unable to help himself, he played along. "No?"

"I am already married to my calling as a matchmaker. You'll simply have to wait until I find your perfect counterpart." She broke the remainder of the scone in half and passed it to him. "And she's out there right now. Not a naive debutante who knows nothing of the world, but one who has sampled a bit of it, for you would want someone more likeminded, I'm sure. Someone who'll not only gift you with children—though seven might be a bit conservative—but will be your partner, sharing your likes and dislikes, introducing you to new things, surprising you."

"I'm not fond of surprises," he stated around a mouthful of buttery scone.

"With her it will be different. And since you're always so busy—running afternoon errands in town, digging trenches in the country—you'll need someone to help you relax."

"Endless holidays? Trips to the bank to clear out my accounts?"

"Not her. *She* won't have any grand notions of touring the continent and spending your fortune. All she wants is a honeymoon beside a lake, alone with you. And there, you'll discover that there is more to her than you could have anticipated."

"Like the fact that she has six toes on both of her hairy feet?"

She giggled, but then tsked at him. "Not all surprises are alarming. Perhaps you'll learn . . . oh, I don't know . . . that she is a remarkable fisherman."

"Not squeamish, hmm?"

"She always puts the small ones back," Briar said quietly, her cheeks softly flushing to pink. "She'll also have the forethought to prepare a picnic, complete with a blanket so that you can lounge in the sunlight, listening to birdsong and the buzz of dragonflies over the water, while she collects fish after fish."

His wry humor faded as he found himself oddly entranced by this scenario, and Briar's ability to create something he never would have imagined for himself. He drew in a breath, half expecting to catch the scent of the lake and the warm sweetness of sunbaked earth and cool grass.

Relaxing back into the chair, he swallowed down the last morsel. "And would this picnic contain any of Mrs. Darden's scones?"

Briar settled back into her chair as well, a sliver of sunlight stealing through the shade overhead to brush her lips as she smiled. "Perhaps I could convince her to share the recipe as a wedding gift to you."

"Now *that*, Miss Bourne, might be the *only* inducement for marriage."

Yet it wasn't just the scones that made the vision appealing. It was all of it. And worst of all, he could almost picture the woman on the blanket beside him.

Thankfully, before he could muse over it any longer, Temperance and Daniel returned, the former all smiles.

"Briar, your uncle has consented! We're all going to the opera."

Chapter 17

———

"... that first in anticipation, and then in reality, it became henceforth her prime object of interest ..."

JANE AUSTEN, *Emma*

"Miss Bourne, you look lovely this evening," Daniel Prescott said as he handed her down from the carriage, his face slowly saturating with red blotches above a high-necked cravat. "Of course, I did not mean to imply that it is *only* this evening but . . . that you are always . . ."

Stepping onto the pavement in front of the opera house, Briar smiled and quickly put him out of his misery. "Thank you, Mr. Prescott, and you look rather dashing yourself."

And so did Nicholas. He was rakishly handsome in his superfine black wool with brushed velvet lapels. With his hair swept away from his forehead, it drew attention to the sharp angles of his features and the bold slashes of dark brows.

As he waited to hand down his aunt, his gaze drifted to Briar. Those onyx irises darkened as they descended down her length of white satin, to the tips of her slippers, and back up to her fitted bodice and the flared sleeves perched on the very crests of her shoulders. She'd left her neck unadorned and her hair up in a twist with Mother's silver-and-pearl combs. If the warmth in his gaze was any indication, she believed she'd chosen wisely.

A rush of eager expectation filled every thrumming pulse. Her first night at the opera. Moonbeams were shooting out of her eyes and the tips of her fingers.

Temperance couldn't hold back another small clap, the happy sound muffled by her long milk-white gloves. And she looked breathtaking in a pale blue gown with gold netting, her eyes resembling topaz gems, faceted to capture every bit of light.

Even Uncle Ernest and Mrs. Prescott were dressed to the nines, the former handsome in storm-cloud gray and the latter in a lovely rich burgundy and looking ten years younger with the glow in her cheeks.

Once they were inside, Briar gasped at the splendor of the vast house. Beneath the domed ceiling, a tower of balconies was illuminated by chandeliers and flickering sconces. Rounded archways were adorned in gilded plaster moldings, and scores of society's elite were dressed in lush finery and glittering jewels. It was like standing inside a treasure chest.

"I feel that way, too," Temperance said from beside her, stepping away from the rest of the party. "Four Seasons and I'm still awestruck every time I attend the opera. This alone almost makes me want to beg Nicholas to fund a fifth."

"You won't need it. You'll be married by year's end. We just to need to find a handsome bachelor who holds a box here."

"Indeed, you make it sound so simple, as if I could point to the box with the best view of the stage and fall in love with the man who owns it."

"Love should be that easy. Close your eyes, point, and when you open them again, you'll see sparks." Briar pantomimed her words as she spoke, but felt the tip of her finger make contact with something hard and warm. She opened her eyes with a start, an apology on her lips, and saw Nicholas.

For an instant, the glimmer from a dozen sconces danced before her eyes.

He smirked down at the finger pressed to his chest. "Are you pretending to be a compass to find your way to where we're sitting?"

"No, Briar was looking for a husband," Temperance supplied helpfully.

Briar drew her hand back quickly. "For your cousin, of course."

"Is that the preferred method of matchmakers—point and seize? It seems rather primitive, if you ask me. I might have been able to manage this for her, if I'd have known it was socially acceptable. Very well, Teense. Point to your husband and I'll have him trussed up and waiting at the altar."

"Cousin, you are a true romantic," Temperance said dryly. "I should like to be wooed. No, I *deserve* to be wooed. And if said wooer happens to hold a box at the opera, then all the better."

Nicholas appeared to consider his cousin's request, glancing out toward the stacks of curtain-swathed, lamp-lit compartments. "I hadn't thought of this until now but an old friend, Lord Hulworth, holds the box next to mine. He is unmarried, but I do not know if he is looking for a wife."

"Did you say . . . Lord Hulworth?" Briar stammered, her expression caught between astonishment and hilarity.

"Yes. Are you acquainted?"

"No, but once upon a time, last year in fact,"—she gave a pointed look to Nicholas, hoping that he would remember—"I thought making his acquaintance would be the key to my becoming a matchmaker."

His brows gradually lifted. "Is that so? Had I known, I might have been able to assist you. He is a rather *elusive bachelor*, as I recall."

"Quite." Briar pressed her gloved fingertips to her mouth to suppress a laugh.

Temperance hummed thoughtfully. "You should arrange an introduction, cousin."

"Perhaps when he is next in town," he said without much conviction. Briar would have teasingly pressed the matter if the others had not joined them just as the musicians began to tune their instruments. The opera was about to begin.

Their party filed forth with Mrs. Prescott on Uncle Ernest's arm. Temperance snaked her arm through her brother's, leaving Briar to take Nicholas's. And she did, with an embarrassing lack of hesitation. However, before they'd made it to the stairs, Nicholas was hailed by a beautiful, dark-haired woman dressed in green organza.

"Lord Edgemont, what a pleasure to see you again," the woman said, smiling broadly.

Beneath her hand, Briar felt the solid muscle of Nicholas's forearm contract, tensing, and she wondered how he knew this woman. Observing him, she noted his outward ease and charm, his gaze settling with familiarity on the woman's face. And looking to the woman, she observed the same, along with the way her head was tilted and her eyes rested fondly on Nicholas.

The matchmaker in Briar might see this as an opportunity to learn more about how they were acquainted. However, a strange new part of Briar emerged, edgy and anxious to excuse herself and go on with the rest of their party.

But Nicholas laid a hand over hers, keeping her at his side.

"Lady Elston, you're looking well. May I present my cousin's friend, Miss Bourne."

"Ah, so this is the young woman I've heard so much about of late."

Briar had no idea what she could mean. What had she heard? The only thing that came to mind was her blunder from weeks ago, but surely that would not cause someone to gaze at her with such rapt fascination and—even more peculiarly—friendliness. It was as if she'd been eager to meet her for some time.

Uncertain, Briar stiffly curtsied. "It is a pleasure to make your acquaintance, Lady Elston."

"My dear, I wish we could have met at Almack's a fortnight ago, but I had been privileged to attend the Duchess of Holliford's dinner, where I'd learned that you had left a vacancy. An amusing coincidence, is it not? And that evening, Her Grace regaled us all with the many accomplishments of the Bourne sisters, you in particular. I must say, my curiosity mounted and I am so pleased to finally make your acquaintance."

"Thank you, my lady. I was honored to have been granted a voucher."

"Please, you must call me Elise," she said, reaching out to briefly press Briar's free hand, her gaze flitting warmly to Nicholas. "Edgemont never asks for favors, and considering he's an . . . acquaintance from many years ago, it was the least I could do."

With sudden clarity, Briar understood how Nicholas had made her evening at Almack's possible. But could he not have asked the favor from another person who wasn't quite so beautiful and showed such an obvious fondness for him as if they'd been—

She couldn't finish the thought. Another wave of strain trundled through her, tightening every joint in her skeleton, fixing every vertebra into a stiff line.

Elise lifted her hand to wave to someone out of Briar's line of sight. "Oh, my husband is beckoning me to his side, I must be off. I do hope we can chat more in the future, Miss Bourne."

"I should like that as well," Briar said, helplessly polite, her smile frozen. Then once left alone with Nicholas, she slid him a perturbed glance. *"Acquaintance?"*

"Yes, Miss Bourne. It should come as no surprise that I have enjoyed friendships with a variety of individuals."

She scoffed, ignoring the dark look he gave her in return. "Do you often enjoy these *friendships* with married women?"

Without answering, Nicholas led her toward the stairs, a muscle ticking along the hard ridge of his jaw. As they climbed, so did the palpable tension between them.

It was only after they traversed a series of corridors, lined by curtained alcoves, that he deigned to respond. "I don't see that it is any concern of yours."

"It is very much a concern of mine," she hissed under her breath, not wanting to be overheard by those in the boxes they passed. "If you are a philanderer, so ruled by baser impulse that you would think nothing of seducing another man's wife, then I would have to end our association immediately."

He glanced over his shoulder and then pulled her into an alcove. Before she could gasp, the curtains fell back in place behind them, immersing them in shadows, and he leaned in until his lips were near her temple, his hot breath fanning over the whorls of her ear. "Stop acting like a jealous harpy or you will incite rumors."

"Oh, now who's conjuring wild scenarios? Jealous, indeed. It just so happens that my family holds a firm abhorrence for adultery and it is something which I cannot abide." She huffed, unintentionally inhaling his scent—

that earthy essence of warm leather and autumn leaves. Drat. Why did he have to smell so good?

He crowded closer, the opening score of the opera growing louder on a rumble of drums. "We share that same sentiment, and it is only for that reason that I will tell you she was a young widow when we were acquainted. Many years ago."

"Well, perhaps I would prefer not to meet someone with whom you shared such an intimate acquaintance. Did you ever think of that?" By accident, her nose slid along the underside of his jaw, her lips near the top fold of his starched cravat. All at once she was fully aware of their close proximity, the rise and fall of his chest, not even an inch apart from her own.

"I never hid that part of my character from you. From the beginning, you knew who I was."

Briar huffed again, but not in indignation. She felt a sudden, aching need to draw in heaping lungfuls of him. How had she been able to withstand days without this scent? Air was so plain in comparison, like a brown homespun dress. A petal-less flower. An empty pod of chocolate. How had she lived most of her life without knowing how to fill her lungs properly?

"Yes. I've always known who you are," she whispered, shuffling closer, her nostrils flaring for another greedy breath. Lightheaded and lungs close to bursting, she looked up at him in the dim shadows, glad they'd reached an understanding.

Yet the tension remained between them, wrapping around them tightly, forbidding either of them from moving apart. So, she did the sensible thing and placed her hand on his waistcoat, splaying her fingertips over the hard plane of his chest as the heavy *whump-whump* of his heart met her palm. In response, his hand settled into the curve of her waist in strict violation of the rules. But she didn't say a word. Instead, she twined her arms around his neck, and felt his other hand snake around to the small of her back, hauling her flush.

"How long does a lesson in anticipation usually last?" she asked, burying her nose in his shirtfront, and thinking crazed thoughts like wishing she could coil herself around him like a corset he could never peel off.

"As long as it takes," he growled, his voice strained.

"Well, it seems that this one is taking quite a long time."

"Far too long."

"I was hoping you would say that," she said, barely breathing the words before his mouth descended on hers.

This was no tentative brush of the lips, but a hard, incinerating kiss designed to turn bones to liquid and melt her body like candlewax. She molded against him with a sigh, settling into the groove of his mouth, the nook of his nose.

Oh, she loved it here—*but no*, she reminded herself, *you cannot reveal how much you like his kisses.* Or how every cup of chocolate had gone bland since that second kiss. He'd done that to her—the chocolate thief.

She should be furious. But it was easy to forgive him now as he nudged her head back, easing her lips apart, delving deeper. His breath filled her mouth, hot and damp. Better than chocolate steam. Better than froth. His tongue moved in a slow, languorous slide against hers as if she was the food he'd been craving for days and he had no intention of leaving until he'd had his fill. Somehow, she'd become his chocolate, too.

He wasn't nearly close enough and she had to hold him tighter, her breasts crushed against the firm expanse of his chest. He nipped her bottom lip, tugging it into his mouth as if to reprimand her for being so bold. But then he hitched her high against him, his hand coasting down the curve of her bottom, lifting her.

He wasn't reprimanding her at all, but rewarding her, his tongue teaching her lewd, wondrous things. Her body yielded sweetly, hips arching, getting a better sense of him, and a much better sense of what drew men and women together.

Satin skimmed over warm wool.

Softness molded to hard planes and ridges.

She marveled at how wonderful it felt to tilt her hips and slide against him. So she did it again. *Kiss, tilt, and slide . . . Kiss, tilt, and slide . . . Mmm . . .*

But then he broke free, pressing his forehead to hers as he shook his head.

She nodded, but in disagreement. He couldn't stop now, not when it was just turning into the best kiss they'd shared. Trembling with need, she arched forward and whispered, *"More. Just a bit more,"* against his lips.

He growled, low and hungry, but then set her on her feet. His hands, however, lingered on her hips. He gripped her as if he wasn't sure how she was put together—splaying fingers to check the curve of her waist, gripping the flare of her hips, gliding thumbs along the angled bones, gripping again. Then after a staggered breath, he released her. Apparently, all of her parts were as they should be.

"Purely academic?" he asked, his voice hoarse.

She grinned in the dark. "What can I say? You are an exceptional tutor."

Chapter 18

"The introduction must be unpleasant, whenever
it takes place; and the sooner it could be over, the
better."

JANE AUSTEN, *Emma*

If Briar had known that the kiss at the opera was her only
reprieve from chaos for an entire week, she would have
done her best to keep Nicholas in that alcove. Perhaps
even tie him up with the tasseled curtain cords. *Hmm . . .
now there's an idea.*

Unfortunately, she didn't have time think up a scenario
for that. She'd become far too busy, never short of tasks.

The agency was suddenly a bustle of activity. Debutantes seemed in a frantic rush to find their matches
before retiring to their country estates for the summer.
From these new patrons, Briar received a few passing
comments, remarking on having seen her at Almack's
or at the opera on Lord Edgemont's arm. However, since
the memory of both those evenings tended to make her
blush—but for different reasons—she skillfully diverted
the topic of conversation, asking about their interests
and activities. From there, she kept her demeanor affable
and professional.

There was a great deal of interest in Lord Edgemont.
A bit too much for her tastes. So to every inquiry made,
Briar always responded with a shrug. "I'm afraid I'm not

well enough acquainted with his lordship to know the answer."

Yet, all the while, she wondered if perhaps the rumor of the challenge she'd accepted had somehow found its way to an eager ear, or two.

She sincerely hoped not. It would be much better if the cause were merely a sudden plague that struck the debutante population all at once, each one of them overcome with a case of spinster-itis. That would certainly be preferable to the possibility of Ainsley overhearing the rumor.

But Briar tucked her worry in her corset and kept to her work. She was filing more applications and serving more tea in the parlor than ever before. In fact, there were days when Mrs. Teasdale and her knitting did not have a place to sit. So, she'd taken it upon herself to wander in and out of the offices under the guise of tidying up when, in truth, she was eavesdropping. Uncle Ernest found her a nuisance, but Briar appreciated the inside information that she would provide about these new clients. And surprisingly, both Ainsley and Jacinda had warmed to her. There was even talk of inviting her to dinner, but Uncle Ernest quickly put an end to that.

Being so busy should have made Briar elated. The Bourne Matrimonial Agency had finally arrived!

Yet it couldn't have happened at a worse time. She had matches of her own to make.

She was struggling to find spare moments to go to the newspaper office. Not alone, of course. When she'd submitted her adverts last week, she had gone with Uncle Ernest, sharing part of her plan and begging him not to mention anything to Ainsley. Thankfully, he'd agreed.

After the adverts had run for a single day, Briar had received more than a dozen correspondences. But she wanted more, already planning a small gathering among the best candidates. There might be a dozen more letters waiting, yet now, Uncle Ernest was usually too exhausted at the end of the day to take her back.

In fact, they were all tired. Mrs. Darden was usually covered in a fine mist of flour from making so many scones. Ainsley hadn't time to harp on Mr. Sterling and seemed to be growing a bit testy because of it. Jacinda was yawning a great deal and looking a bit peaked. And Uncle Ernest, who'd actually been called upon to take applications instead of spending his day flirting and writing sonnets, seemed to be going through love-letter withdrawal. Just this morning, Briar had caught him staring distractedly at the empty salver on the edge of the desk and heard him sigh.

The day could not end soon enough.

HER HOPES were answered later that afternoon when Briar managed to convince Uncle Ernest to go for a quick jaunt about town. They stopped at the newspaper office.

Uncle Ernest, however, lingered at the flower cart across the street, where there were a handful of women to flirt with. This would surely lift his spirits.

As for Briar, she continued on and stepped through the door, the bell jingling overhead. The stuffy boxed room was lined with postings pinned to the paneled wall, along with rows of square shelves that reached from the floor to the low ceiling. A large burled desk took up far too much space in the middle of the room behind a half wall, bisected with a swinging gate.

Standing ahead of her was a tall man, and the matchmaker in her took note of his neatly trimmed dark blond hair, brown coat, and polished Hessians, a brushed John

Bull hat in his grasp. A gentleman by the look of him. Absently, she wondered if he might be married or interested in finding a bride. After all, the agency could use a few more gentlemen applicants to meet the recent demands of their female clients. But her plate was rather full at the moment, so she quashed the impulse to casually inquire.

"No letters since yesterday," the editor barked, the nub of a pencil clenched between his teeth. He never took his eyes off the stack of pages in front of him.

The man in the brown coat took a coin from his pocket and placed it on the desk. "I'd be obliged if you could run the advert another week."

"Can't. Pages are full up. I'd be glad to keep taking your coin, but after a month you're just wasting your time. Go on and buy the girl a new dog and be done with it."

Briar's heart went out to the gentleman who would go to so much trouble to find a lost dog in this city. He turned away from the desk. Seeing Briar behind him, he tipped his hat in an automatic gesture.

Then strangely, he stopped cold, his eyes widening. "Miss Bourne."

As far as Briar knew they'd never met. Yet there was something familiar about his handsome countenance, and in the shape and color of his brown eyes. They almost reminded her of Ainsley's . . .

All at once, tiny hairs on her arms stood on end, gooseflesh scattering over her limbs.

"Mr. Cartwright, your coin," the editor barked.

"Cartwright." All the breath left her body at once.

Of course, that was why he looked familiar. He was her father's son. But . . . he was much older than she'd ever thought. He had to have been at least six and twenty. Ainsley's age. Which could only mean that their father hadn't started another family after Briar was born—as she'd been led to believe—but had kept them from the very beginning of his marriage to Mother.

She wondered if Ainsley knew . . . But of course she must. Likely, everyone else in the family knew.

Briar felt a twinge of pain, wishing she would have known, too. Whenever she'd imagined meeting her half siblings, she'd always been warm and affable. Instead, she found herself silent and stunned, with so many thoughts rushing through her head that she could hardly take hold of one and examine it.

Mr. Cartwright—and she didn't even know his first name—removed his hat and placed it over his heart. "Forgive me. I never meant for us to meet like this."

"H-how did you recognize me?"

"I saw a miniature of you among my"—he cleared his throat, shifting from one foot to the other—"*our* father's things."

"Oh." That one final puff of air left her deflated. The miniature wasn't likely of her, but of Mother. As far as Briar knew, the only likeness Father possessed of her was from a dozen years ago.

In fact, she had been so young when Father had left that he'd seemed like a storybook figure. And when Mother had died, he'd been the villain. Since Briar never liked reading stories about villains, she'd kept that one closed inside her heart. But now part of the reality of the episode that had led to her mother's death stood in front of her, in flesh and bone.

For an instant, Briar was transported back in time, her mother going frighteningly pale as a letter fell from her grasp.

He gave them all his name, she'd said on a broken sob, *and they're living in our house as if we never existed.*

Alarmed, Briar had tried to catch her before she sank

to the floor in a boneless heap, but they'd both ended up tumbling together, legs and skirts twisting. *Who, Mother?*

Your father and his . . . no. This is all a bad dream, nothing more. I just need to lie down for a spell.

Yet, Mother had rarely left her bed after that. Until, gradually, she'd faded out of existence.

Behind her, Briar heard the bell chime above the door. Believing it was Uncle Ernest, she waited for him to come to her side and make conversation for her. To remove her from this awkward introduction.

But it wasn't her uncle after all.

"There you are, Briar," Temperance said, scuttling into the office and sidling up to her. "I knew that was your uncle's carriage out front, and I begged Nicholas to stop so that we could bid you a good day and perhaps even take you and your uncle to Berkeley Square for ices."

Still mute, Briar turned her head and witnessed the precise moment her friend's gaze collided with Mr. Cartwright. Temperance went utterly still. A wash of deep rose flooded her cheeks and her eyes glimmered as if a random ray of sunlight were caught in their amber depths. And Briar had a sinking feeling that she'd just witnessed the elusive spark.

No, please no, she first thought, but then felt inordinately guilty for it.

Coming out of her stupor, she had the semblance of mind to make an introduction. "Mr. Cartwright." It felt strange to say his name, as if the syllables were glued to her tongue and had to be pried off. "This is my friend, Miss—"

"It is a pleasure to make your acquaintance," Temperance interjected eagerly, even before the introductions were finished.

"Prescott."

Clearly too dazzled to make the connection, she held out her gloved hand, beaming.

He bowed over it. "John Cartwright, at your service."

John. Her brother's name was John. Briar knew nothing else about him. Then she recalled the lost dog and wondered if it belonged to his daughter. If she had a niece as well. "I happened to overhear that you are looking for a lost dog that belongs to your . . ."

"Sister," he supplied, chagrined.

She had a sister. Another sister. Though, how would she have known it? It wasn't as if Father had ever sent a note to tell her, or ever once bothered to inquire about her or her sisters. He hadn't been present for Mother's funeral, or for the years leading up to her death. He'd simply vanished from their lives like a carnival magician, only without the poof of smoke and scent of sulfur lingering in the air.

Michael Cartwright, Lord Frawley, left nothing of himself behind. Aside from his children.

Now as she looked at her half brother, she wanted to ask him how often he saw their father. Did they live in the same house? How many siblings were there in all?

But none of those questions were appropriate to ask under the circumstances.

Thankfully, Temperance filled in when Briar could not find the words to continue. At least, not the right words. "How kind of you to take such measures to find your sister's dog. My neighbor's spaniel recently had a litter of eight. And they are as adorable as you could imagine, with soft wavy fur and wet noses. Once they are weened, I'm sure Lady Penrose will be seeking homes for some. If you'd like, I could inquire. Oh, but I do not mean to sound dire when tragedy might very well be on your doorstep. It would be far better if you found your own dog. Alive, of course. And I very much hope that you do."

Then again, Temperance wasn't finding the right words either. If possible, the encounter had just turned even more awkward. Now they had the potential demise of a dog between them.

"Thank you, Miss Prescott. I should like nothing more than to continue our conversation, but I have an appointment at present. It was, indeed, a pleasure to make your acquaintance." John bowed once more. "And to you, Miss Bourne, I hope we can meet again. But if you are in like-mind with your sisters and would rather not, I understand."

It was worse than she thought. Not only did her sisters know about him, but they'd also made the decision for Briar not to meet him. As if she were a child.

Briar didn't hesitate before she nodded. He was her brother. They were already connected by blood, even if only now acquainted. "I should like to."

"Good. Until then," he said, settling his hat on his head and striding out of the office.

At the same moment, the bell above the door chimed and Nicholas appeared. The two men maneuvered past each other, one leaving and the other entering.

Then Nicholas's gaze locked on Briar, searching as if he could sense something altered about her. And there was. She was angry and hurt, and yet somehow, it felt like there was less of her now. As if the certainty of who she was had been subtracted from her overall person like counterweights from a scale.

Reflexively, her feet shifted on the floor, poised to go to him, knowing that if anyone could set her back to rights it was Nicholas. He was always so confident and secure, and she had the overwhelming urge to cross the short distance and find comfort in his arms.

But he came forward instead and stopped at her side. "Good day, Miss Bourne. Are you"—he paused, his brow drawn into furrows above the bridge of his nose, his voice low—"unwell or in need of assistance?"

She was oddly glad that he would ask, that he would let her decide whether or not she needed assistance, unlike her family. "I appreciate the offer, more than you can know, but I am well enough."

Then Temperance, who had moved over to the window to watch Mr. Cartwright walk past, swept back to them, her gloved hands pressed to her bosom. "He was the most handsome gentleman I've ever met. Ever so kind and cordial. Briar, please tell me that you are not in love with him."

"I am not. We only just met."

"Splendid!" She inhaled all the air in the room, then expelled it in a gusty sigh, her expression bright and eager. "Nicholas, you could have stopped him from leaving. After all, you promised to truss up the gentleman I pointed to and drag him to the altar. Well, I'm pointing."

Nicholas was still looking at Briar, his frown deepening. "Who did she just meet?"

"Mr. John Cartwright," Temperance supplied dreamily.

In the same instant, Briar said, "My brother."

NICHOLAS HAD taken everyone for ices in his open landau, the hazy sunlight beaming down on them. What had been a party of three with himself and his cousins now included Briar and her uncle. Yet after the news of Briar's unexpected encounter with her brother, she was not full of her usual cheer.

The curve of her lips might fool others into believing that the shock of her experience was over and she was eager—as she claimed—to enjoy the afternoon. But Nicholas knew her better.

He felt the absence of her vibrancy as if a pint of his

own blood had been withdrawn, drained into a leech's bowl. Though it wasn't as if she was always bubbly and full of sunshine—*that* would have annoyed him to no end—but she did have an innate talent for brightening a room. Her usual inclination was to put others at ease, instead of thinking about herself, and he wanted to do the same for her.

His first instinct had been to lavish her with sweets, knowing how fond she was of them. After ices, he'd gone to a confectionary shop, purchasing a parcel of comfits for her, and also for Temperance. That had earned a squeal of delight from his cousin, but only a polite grin from Briar and a murmured *thank you*. Her infectious smile remained absent, replaced by a still-life replica, her blue eyes lusterless and distant.

Now they were touring the park, ambling beneath a long stretch of shade trees. Time was turning toward twilight, well past the fashionable hour that brought crowds here, and the absence left their party with the illusion that they were walking the private grounds of an estate.

Nicholas had sent Adams up ahead to wait for them with the carriage. Daniel and Eggleston had found a common bond in poetry and had been discussing passages most of the afternoon, oblivious to the trio that lagged far behind and around the bend. Temperance, who was the most relieved that Briar was "not unsettled in the least" over meeting John Cartwright, stopped occasionally to pick flowers and sigh over them, too caught up in her new infatuation to realize her friend's light had been dimmed.

"You didn't have to ply me with sweets to cheer me," Briar said quietly, her unhurried steps in time with his on the path. "I told you I was not troubled by what occurred at the newspaper."

"Never doubted you."

She slid him a perturbed glance. "Do not do that to me—say things you clearly do not mean. I can hear your true thoughts in the tone of your voice."

"Then do not attempt to fool me either. I know better. Even though I'm only aware of the portion you've shared with me, regarding what you and your sisters experienced after your father left and your mother passed away, you still have every right to be bothered."

"But I am not," she insisted, enunciating each syllable. "The fact that my sisters *never* saw fit to discuss this with me is hardly a new development."

"Perhaps they were trying to protect you. To keep you from the pain they knew you would suffer."

"I'm certain *they* think so. But my family should have respected me enough to tell me the truth, allowing me to decide how I would feel instead of keeping me in the dark. And as for you"—she waved an angry hand in the air between them—"I certainly don't need you to pacify me with sweets as if I were a child."

"If I want to buy enough ices and comfits to fill the entire carriage—with the smallest chance that it might bring a genuine smile to those lips—then I will," he growled, without knowing why he was suddenly so irritated. This was not what he'd intended at all. He wanted to comfort her, not argue with her. Hang it all.

"Well, I'm far stronger than you think." She sniffed, a faint line of moisture gathering along the lower rim of her eyes.

He felt like a complete heel. Without conscious thought his hand reached out, closing around hers. The quick press of glove against glove, the turn of palm against palm, did little to assuage the sudden need he had to pull her into his arms. But this small act was all he could risk.

"I know that, love. You"—he took a step without minding the path and felt his foot sink—*"ah, horse shite."*

And it was still fresh, too. Steaming and a bit loose, likely from one of his own horses. He'd have to talk to the stablemaster about their diet.

Beside him, Briar hiccupped. Then she covered her mouth with her hands and started to giggle, her eyes wet but smiling. And he realized he would have stepped in a hundred piles just to hear that sound.

What an utter *nodcock* he was.

Stalking to the side of the path, he ripped a branch from the nearest shrub and made the best of it.

"I hope those aren't your lucky boots," she teased.

"I believe they are. Therefore, you owe me recompense." From the corner of his eye, he caught sight of a smirk toying with her lips.

"Because it was clearly *my* fault that you weren't paying attention to the path. Oh, very well, what shall it be?"

His mind turned quickly. Too quickly, perhaps, because he said the one thing that came to mind as the memory of their first encounter flashed before him. "Come with me to the coffee house one evening."

She gasped, hands splayed over her heart. "I could finally discover what gentlemen yearn for in potential brides. Oh, Nicholas! You'd be willing to do that? For me?"

Instinctively, he knew the offer would make her happy, but he hadn't bothered to think about how impossible it would be to take her there. "I spoke too soon. It would never work. You'd either have to dress the part of a trollop—"

"That had better not be another slight against the shade of my lips."

"—or a man. And no, I'm rather fond of your lips." *Very fond indeed,* he thought, his gaze brushing over them.

She blushed a pretty carnation pink and glanced down

to his mouth, returning the sentiment without words. And suddenly he couldn't resist temptation. With a hasty glance around to see that they were shielded by foliage, he dipped his head to steal a kiss.

But Briar took a step back, thwarting him with a hand between them. "That would be quite ruinous for both of our reputations. Besides, you owe me a lesson first. Perhaps after the coffee house?"

A pang of deprivation rolled through him, leaving him hungry, wanting. He didn't like it. "No one with half an eye would take you for a man. As I said, I spoke out of turn. It was a ludicrous idea. You could never conceal all those delightful parts of you."

She set her hands on her hips, showcasing a pair of them. "Nicholas, I truly do not like to be underestimated. As it happens, I already have a costume of gentleman's clothes. When I was younger, I had the part of a dandy in one of the plays my sisters and I used to put on for the Duchess of Holliford. And if I say that I can dress like a man . . ."

"Then I'll expect you to prove it to me," he challenged, earning another bright smile. Honestly, he was willing to do anything to keep her happy at this point.

"I wouldn't want anyone else to know, not even Temperance. So, I don't know how I'll arrange to be out alone."

The rakish side of him didn't have any trouble coming up with a plan. "If my aunt were to invite you to dinner one evening, would it be possible to come without your uncle, provided that I send a carriage?"

"I believe so. Uncle Ernest is much more trusting than my sisters. And he likes you, so that is in your favor."

"Then, after dinner, I could arrange to drive you home, giving the excuse to my aunt that I would drop you at your lodgings before I enjoy an evening at Sterling's. Since she is not so strict with these matters as your family, I'm certain she will make no fuss."

"Hmm . . . even so, we couldn't stay long without inciting some suspicion. Oh, but I would love to see what it's like inside a coffee house, hear all the things that men talk about, learn what they're really looking for in a wife . . ."

"I wouldn't get my hopes up in that regard if I were you."

She beamed at him. "Silly man. If you were me, then you would always find something for which to hope. And my sights are still set on finding the perfect bride for you. We've gained dozens of new applicants. So many that I haven't had time to pour over them all, but I'm sure there will be someone to tempt you."

He decided not to remind her how pointless her efforts were in that regard. "Any additional prospects for Daniel?"

"I do have two more names. The only problem I find is that they match his shy temperament. I fear, if left on their own after an introduction, not a single word will be spoken by either party. I wonder how he ever became betrothed in the first place, unless Miss Smithson had a rather exuberant nature and drew him out of his shell."

"Some might refer to her as bold," he said, fist clenching. "Keep to the shy girls if you can. I'll arrange for an introduction."

Beneath the brim of her bonnet, she eyed him with careful curiosity. "You ask after Daniel's matches far more than you do about Temperance's. Was his melancholy after his betrothed abandoned him severe enough to cause this . . . anxiousness I sense from you whenever we speak of him?"

Shame flooded Nicholas so swiftly that he almost couldn't swallow it down. He thought he'd been concealing his worry better. But lately, his need to help Daniel, to make amends for the suffering he'd caused, had started eating away at him more and more.

"It was," he said simply, without confessing his part. She nodded in thoughtful understanding, their gazes holding for a moment. He looked away first, to where Temperance stood near the stream, casting petals to the water one by one. "Do you plan to discourage her from Mr. Cartwright?"

"I could not do that to her. Never before has she expressed such an interest in a gentleman." Briar sighed, worry behind her eyes and in the tiny furrows on her brow. "Even so, I do not think they are likely to meet again, for illegitimate sons rarely travel in the same circles. I do, however, have other prospects for her. In fact, I have every hope of arranging an introduction to a handful of gentlemen on Friday at the agency, and ladies for Daniel as well."

He turned to her again. "If there is anything I can do, please let me know."

"Well . . ." she began, her eyes brightening, "if you could arrange for Cupid's arrow to strike, that would be lovely."

Then her lips tilted in a grin so beguiling, so dazzling that he felt struck by it. For a short-winded instant, the steady beating of his heart went out of kilter, stumbling awkwardly. And dimly, Nicholas wondered if the invisible archer had accidentally released a shot in his direction.

Chapter 19

"Ambition, as well as love, had probably been mortified."

JANE AUSTEN, *Emma*

Later that evening, Ainsley found Briar in the small library, bringing with her a weighted stillness that seemed to make the room too confining. Even before her sister spoke, Briar knew what the topic of conversation would be—John Cartwright.

After her initial mention of her half brother, Uncle Ernest had been quiet throughout the jaunt with Nicholas and his cousins, but also watchful. It did not take any leap of imagination to guess that he would speak to Ainsley first.

"I understand that you met Mr. Cartwright this afternoon," Ainsley said with a resigned exhale, not bothering to pretend she was here for reading.

Since Briar was still angry about being kept in the dark, she did not respond at first but continued to peruse her uncle's shelves, dragging her finger along the spines. She'd come here to find a book on cravats in order to complete her disguise for her outing with Nicholas next week, and she wasn't going to be distracted.

And yet, as she started to fume, she no longer saw the titles and could not keep silent. "He's much older than I would have thought. Is that the reason you never wanted to talk about Father's other children—because you didn't think I was ready to deal with the full scope of his betrayal?"

"Partly," Ainsley said after a minute. "But to tell you the truth, I don't think I wanted to confront it either. I still have anger left over from all that has happened and it wouldn't have been fair to talk to you about it."

Why not? Intuition warned her not to ask that question, advising her that she already knew the answer.

Even so, Briar couldn't subdue the impulse. She turned to face her sister. "Why not?"

She went still, waiting. Even the candle flames held steady, the candelabra on the chiffonier between them glowing in a harsh white-gold light.

Ainsley blinked, then averted her face toward a potted fern on a nearby pedestal. She moved toward it, beginning to pluck out the dead leaves as she spoke. "Because I prefer to deal with matters in my own way, without burdening anyone else."

"Hmm . . ." Briar murmured, believing that was only part of it. But she did not push further. It didn't seem now was the time to suggest sending an invitation to their half brother to get better acquainted either.

Instead, she decided to change the subject. "I've planned to host a gathering of potential matches for Temperance and her brother, here next week."

Ainsley did not look surprised by the news, but her mouth was set in a line of discontent. In Briar's opinion, her sister went far too many days with that same expression. If memory served, Ainsley had a stunning smile. It was a pity she was so miserly with it.

"Where did you find these potential matches, among our client list?"

"I put an advert in the *Post*," Briar answered, but suspected that Ainsley already knew this, too. Nothing got past her

She plucked at the poor fern more aggressively. "And did you bother to vet any of them?"

"No, I was hoping to fill the agency with cutpurses and murderers and introduce them all to my dearest friends." Briar rolled her eyes. Of course she had taken the proper precautions. "During the week, I took the liberty of filling out an application for each of them and set those papers on Jacinda's desk for investigation. When she did not find anything criminal, I decided to write invitations."

Actually, she hadn't yet sent the letters. She was still narrowing the lists down to the best prospects. However, she would mail them first thing in the morning and have everything settled.

"I wish you would have said something to me. I could have helped you find some other gentlemen from our client list for Miss Prescott to meet."

It was on the tip of Briar's tongue to say that she did not want Ainsley's help, but when she saw the hurt look in her sister's eyes, she swallowed it down. Her actions had already made that fact apparent. "I went through our list early this Season, and none of our clients appealed to Temperance."

Ainsley nodded stiffly, then took the mess of brown fronds—and a few green—to toss into the hearth. But Briar felt guilty for going behind her sister's back. She hadn't wanted to risk her sister taking over. And more than that, she admitted, she wanted to prove herself, and make her own contribution to the agency.

Still, it wasn't in her nature to leave matters in a state of discord between them. So she quickly thought up a solution. "I do have one problem, however. You see, Daniel is rather shy and wouldn't attend if he thought there was going to be a group of women here to meet him. So, after he escorts Temperance, I thought perhaps you might take him on a tour of the house, along with a handful of potential female applicants, arriving by invitation."

Her sister tilted her head, scrutinizing Briar. "And he will have no idea why he's really here?"

"No. But he is of a romantic nature and would likely prefer to meet his bride by happenstance," she said, parroting what Nicholas had told her in the beginning.

"Very well. But I cannot guarantee the results under such circumstances."

Briar knew Ainsley wouldn't embrace an idea that wasn't her own, but at least she was willing to help. That was good enough for now.

❦

WHEN THE day arrived, Temperance cajoled her brother into lingering for the event, bidding him to stay in the house in case she would prefer a quick escape. Ever the dutiful brother, Daniel agreed to accompany Ainsley on a tour of the house and their small garden, where—*coincidentally*—four young women were having tea.

In the parlor, Uncle Ernest was busy making the introductions, and Temperance looked positively lovely in her yellow-striped frock. The four gentlemen milling about the room were each a bit on the odd side. Then again, what could one expect from a gentleman who answered an advert for a bride? Though perhaps one of them would turn out to be a diamond in the rough.

Briar still had every hope that the day would be a smashing success.

Regrettably, those hopes were destined to meet a terrible end. Her first clue came when she sidled up to Temperance, who was valiantly attempting to chat with Lord Fortescue.

He had a tall wiry build and something of a restless nature, with the tendency to shift from one foot to the other while glancing around the room at all the other occupants. It was as if he expected a formulated attack at any given moment.

And when Temperance asked if his journey here was uneventful, *Lord Shifty*'s response was rather odd. "Are you always overly curious? I find that people with curious natures are those with the most to hide. Is there something you aren't telling us, Miss Prescott?"

"Since we have not been acquainted above thirty seconds, I suspect there are a great many things, my lord," Temperance said. She tried to feign a laugh but it came out in more of a whinny.

Briar used the moment as an excuse to extricate her friend. She patted her gently on the shoulder. "Dear me, it sounds as if Miss Prescott needs a spot of tea for her throat. Please excuse us, Lord *Shif*—Fortescue."

Stepping away from him, Temperance clenched her teeth together in a semblance of a polite smile and uttered, "Do not leave my side. At all."

Briar stifled a laugh, pressing her lips together. "Not for a single instant."

They encountered *Sweet William* next. Of course, that wasn't his real name but, after their encounter, Briar would never think of him any other way.

Mr. Dougherty was a round-faced, quiet man, nearly bald but with a forelock of wispy butter-colored hair. And only a few minutes into the conversation, he gazed adoringly up at Temperance—she was a good five or six inches taller—and said, "You remind me of my mother."

Temperance shot an alarmed glance to Briar, eyes wide as poached eggs. "Um . . . thank you, Mr. Dougherty?"

"She used to call me William," he said with a shy smile. "It would be fine if you did that as well."

"I don't think that would be appropriate, Mr.—Oh, very well, *William*."

And then poor, Sweet William burst out crying. Briar was quick to hand him a handkerchief as she linked arms with Temperance and they moved on to the next disaster.

Uncle Ernest was sitting with the robust Captain Cantrell in the chairs flanking the tray of lemonade and biscuits on the low table. The latter was speaking on the importance of keeping a sportsman on staff in order to stay in optimal health. Her uncle, who enjoyed meandering walks in the park and rarely lifted anything heavier than a lady's hand to kiss it, merely nodded.

Undeterred, the captain continued, clearly enjoying sporting *and* the sound of his own voice. He did, however, pause his conversation briefly to engage with Temperance, a neatly manicured blond brow arched in disdain. "That's your second biscuit, Miss Prescott."

Temperance turned a gimlet-eyed glare on *Captain Control* and popped the rest of the biscuit in her mouth. "Actually, it is my third."

Briar nearly applauded. Temperance even articulated every syllable and didn't lose a single crumb. *Brava!*

Uncle Ernest cleared his throat, his expression turning to stone. "Gentlemen in this house are always expected to act and speak with decorum."

Captain Control fixed a smile on his face that made him look as if he were in the midst of a stomach ailment. "Though, for such a large girl, you move with surprising grace."

Briar, who was seated nearest to him, stood up suddenly and *accidentally* spilled her lemonade on his lap.

Uncle Ernest pointed him toward the kitchens. With any luck, Mrs. Darden would throw the captain in the rubbish bin.

Their fourth gentleman was a bit of a rube, with dust

on his boots and the not so-faint aroma of pigs wafting from his clothes. He stood with thumbs tucked into the slitted pockets of his waistcoat. "You're not one of them bluestockin's, are you?"

Briar swallowed down a bubble of laughter at the enormous tragedy this entire afternoon had turned into, then offered him a sad shake of her head. "I'm afraid Miss Prescott is highly educated."

Apparently, that was enough information for *Lord Porcine*, for he offered a disdainful sniff and strode out of the parlor. Sweet William gave a tearful goodbye, promising to write Temperance. Lord Shifty skirted out of the room, pausing only to double-check the corridor before making his way to the foyer. Then, just as Uncle Ernest was about to close the door, another man entered.

With his five young children in tow.

Mr. Tittelwurst—sadly that was his actual name— quickly introduced himself, took one look at Temperance, and said, "You'll do."

Briar could not hold it in any longer. Her eyes began to water. She glanced at Temperance, who wore the same expression, and hiccupped.

Then they both burst into laughter.

Shortly thereafter, she learned that Daniel had chosen to linger alone in the library after enduring a quick introduction to the women in the garden.

"The advert-answering women were quite . . . eager," Ainsley told her from the doorway as they watched Daniel and Temperance's carriage trundle away.

Briar was afraid to ask. "How *eager*?"

"The words *ravening horde* come to mind."

Oh dear. Perhaps adverts were not the way to go after all.

Briar hoped that Nicholas was having better luck with the list of names she'd given him.

⸻

NICHOLAS STOOD in the foyer, skimming through the letters on the salver, when his cousins strode in. One look at Daniel's white complexion, crooked cravat, and disheveled hair, and Nicholas surmised that the afternoon at the agency had not gone to plan.

A sense of desperation rolled through him, guilt leaving a bitter taste on the back of his tongue and churning in the pit of his stomach. The Season was nearing a conclusion and, as of yet, none of the dinners Nicholas and Temperance had arranged, or even the few accidental encounters in the park, were working.

What more would it take to find Daniel a bride so that they could all forget the *Miss Smithson* episode for good?

"It is an utter madhouse over there." Daniel puffed as if he'd just escaped an angry mob. "I don't see how Miss Bourne can maintain her cheerful disposition, nor her sanity, when visited by such clients. Why, they're practically wild creatures, London's own form of cannibals."

"You're being dramatic. It couldn't have been that bad. After all, you weren't in the parlor with me," Temperance chimed in, rolling her eyes.

Daniel raked a hand through his hair. "No. I am understating the event out of deference to your maidenly ears. Believe me when I say I would have rather dealt with a dozen *Sweet William*s than the horror I faced. I'm covered in so much perfume and powder that I could open a shop. I need a change." And without waiting another moment, he sulked off toward his rooms.

Nicholas was caught between confusion and disappointment. *"Sweet William?"*

"A long story, one which I'll explain later." Teense waved her hand dismissively, peering over his shoulder to the mail in his grasp. "Oh, that one's for me, I'm sure."

Nicholas looked down at it and saw that it was from none other than Mr. John Cartwright. He frowned, his thoughts on Briar.

Temperance took it and turned it over, her countenance changing from merriment to wonder as she, too, saw the sender's name.

"It is from *him*." She wasted no time in breaking the red wax seal and opening it, consuming every word in a flash, grinning, and then reading it all over again. "A very good letter. Such a splendid, bold hand."

"*A very good letter?* There are no more than six lines."

"Some men make brevity an art," she all but sighed. "Indeed, a most excellent letter."

"And what does Mr. Cartwright want?"

"To whisk me off to the Mediterranean and feed me olives." She tucked the note behind her back when he reached out to snatch it, and grinned slyly. "He only wants an introduction to Lady Penrose, in case she would like to sell him one of her new puppies."

"Ah." He felt marginally better at this news. Still, he worried that the association had the potential to unsettle Briar's spirits, and wanted to shield her from the pain she'd experienced the other day. "Since Lady Penrose is my own neighbor, perhaps I should pen a note in response."

Teense tilted her head in puzzlement. "Whyever would you do that when you were not even introduced to him? He wrote the letter to me. Surely you cannot object to one simple exchange."

"No, I cannot. I was merely thinking that you would require a few moments to change for dinner this evening. Your friend is coming, is she not?"

Nicholas already knew the answer. He'd been anticipating this evening with Briar all week, turning into a clock *and* calendar watcher. But he was apprehensive about the trip to the coffee house later as well, uncertain that any costume could make her resemble a man.

"She is, but Briar has been here dozens of times. Tonight is hardly any different, and Mother has already approved the menu and table settings." She gave an absent shrug before gliding toward the staircase, the letter firmly in her grasp. "Therefore, I have plenty of time to send a missive to Mr. Cartwright."

Nicholas had a sinking suspicion that this would be only the first of many to come. But he would not be the one to tell Briar. Especially not tonight.

Chapter 20

"There is no charm equal to tenderness of heart."
JANE AUSTEN, *Emma*

As soon as she changed into her costume, Briar couldn't wait to take her trousers off. The wool scratched at tender skin usually accustomed to soft cambric and muslin. And they fit too snugly.

Her waist had narrowed from girlhood—when she'd last worn them—to womanhood and, when she'd made the alterations, she'd forgotten to account for the voluminous tails of the shirtwaist. Tucking in the folds caused a tight cinching over her midriff and against the rounder shape of her hips.

Of course, it mightn't have been so terrible if she hadn't gobbled up a large portion of steamed pudding at dinner tonight. Now, every brandy-soaked currant turned to the size of a stone at the bottom of her stomach.

Nerves had gotten the better of her appetite. Or perhaps it was the other way around. Apparently, it had seemed like a good plan to avoid thinking about disguising herself as a man by eating like a half-starved wolf in a sheep's pasture. And all because she wanted to learn their innermost thoughts.

Slouching on the red velvet bench—men were notorious slouchers, after all—Briar rubbed a hand over her waistcoat, feeling the small bulge of overindulgence. Her own little pudding infant. Giving it a pat, she giggled at the notion.

And that was how Nicholas found her.

He stalled briefly in the open carriage door, the lanterns illuminating the shadows beneath the brim of his hat, nose, and jaw. He said nothing as he slipped inside, shutting out the light. And he didn't utter a single syllable after he tapped on the roof and the carriage set off.

She sat up, bracing her hands on either side as Adams rounded a corner. "Aren't you going to tell me if I look convincing?"

Nicholas lit the lantern inside, keeping the flame low. But it was enough to illuminate his warm gaze, roving the length of her. "Quite fetching, Miss Bourne. Those trousers are so snug, you might as well be wearing nothing at all."

She blushed, suddenly aware of every woven stitch on her skin. Shifting, she made an attempt to look unaffected, even confident. "You're supposed to tell me that I look like a man, you cad."

A man dressed in everyday attire. But when his gaze drifted up to her breasts, and her nipples grew taut beneath her layers, she felt very much a woman in revealing clothes. Even though she'd bound her breasts in a strip of linen, the fitted waistcoat barely concealed the swells.

"That, I cannot do. A young dandy, perhaps, if the room is dark enough *and* if you do not speak. Though in truth, every delectable inch of you is feminine. But who tied your cravat?"

"I found a book on different knots in my uncle's library and I've been studying them."

Widening his legs, he leaned forward and tugged her to the edge of her seat across from him. Without a word, he began to untie her knot, deftly undressing her. Sure, it was only a cravat, but the action was so intimate that her stomach clenched sweetly at the mere thought of what it would be like if he kissed her while doing this.

She wet her lips, her tongue meeting the acrid flavor of the face paint she'd used to hide their color. Intent on his task, he didn't seem aware of the swift rousing of her imagination.

He bared her throat, the air warm and damp against her skin. He hesitated for an instant, keeping her exposed. Then his fingertip brushed the pulse that fluttered beneath her jaw, making her conscious of every rapid beat. The tender touch coasted downward in a slow simmering path along her neck, tracing the vulnerable niche, skimming inside.

"You are far too soft to be a man," he said, his voice hoarse, his eyes gleaming black and hungry.

A thrill raced through her as she recognized that look. "Am I?"

"Therefore"—he cleared his throat—"you'll need to wear your cravat higher to conceal your lack of an Adam's apple." Then without delay, he adroitly rearranged the folds until her bare flesh was completely covered.

A disappointed breath stuttered out of her. Of course she wasn't hoping to be ravished here in the carriage, but there was nothing wrong with sharing a small illicit moment, like the one they'd shared at the opera. Was there? "And I thought rakes would only be skilled at removing clothing, but you would make an exceptional valet."

"Not if I were your valet, love," he said darkly. The crook of his fingers grazed along her jaw to a finely angled patch of stubble she'd applied to give herself the appearance of side whiskers beneath her uncle's borrowed wig. "And what is this?"

"A whisker paste I concocted. It was inspired by the fine powder left behind on the work table after Mrs.

Darden had finished chopping walnuts. I combined them with a bit of egg white to make it stick."

"Yet another of your accomplishments—to see potential where others would only see rubbish." He smiled, the night turning his irises a deep, velvety cocoa as he pressed a brief kiss to her forehead.

"I have a hopeful nature," she said, closing her eyes to savor this moment, eagerness for the night to unfold swimming inside her heart. And it was all possible because of Nicholas.

In this—what she considered lesson six—she learned that rakes could be quite sweet. He listened to her and supported her endeavors. He treated her as if her own aspirations mattered to him as well. Precisely the qualities that one should seek in an ideal counterpart.

Briar couldn't have asked for a better tutor. Was there another man who would have gone to such lengths? She was certain there wasn't. Without a doubt, he would make a fine husband.

She truly ought to begin an earnest search for his potential bride, one of these days.

Just then, the carriage pulled to a stop in front of the coffee house.

Briar made a fuss of fitting her hat onto her wig, with her head turned so that Nicholas wouldn't see how nervous she was. "Remember, no coddling me or shielding me. I'm a man, after all."

"You'll do fine."

"And no words of encouragement either," she said, hoping he didn't hear the tremor in her voice. "Just a slap on the shoulder will do."

Nicholas just looked at her for a minute, the brim of his hat shielding his eyes so that she couldn't see what he was thinking. Then he reached out and put his hand on her shoulder, gave it a squeeze, and slipped out of the door.

Inside the coffee house, it was dark and crowded. A thick haze of smoke and the bitter scent of burnt coffee perfumed the air, and she could barely hear herself think over the low roar of conversation. It was absolutely perfect.

Nicholas shouldered his way through and found a place at one of the long tables. Briar followed close behind, bumping shoulders without the slightest wince, even though her arm might very well fall off before she made it to the table. She was a man, after all, capable and confident, not given to gasps and whimpers, not even when she took an elbow to the breast. But drat it all, that had hurt!

Sinking into the chair beside Nicholas, she noted the hard, unforgiving lines of his profile, the muscle ticking with agitation near the hinge of his jaw, belying his usual easy manner. He looked fierce and ready for a fight. She clenched her teeth, hoping that by some miracle she had a jaw muscle, too.

Nicholas lifted his hand for a serving wench. It wasn't until then that Briar suddenly remembered she'd forgotten her money. She'd left her reticule in a satchel in the carriage. Of course, the canary yellow silk bag would never have looked smart with this burgundy coat, she thought, as a rise of nerves nearly erupted in giggles.

He glanced at her sharply and laid two pennies on the table. The serving wench swiped them up summarily and left two dishes of coffee.

Briar wrinkled her nose at the foul-smelling brew. An entire penny for this? Since they were here, couldn't they at least have chocolate? But when she lifted her gaze to Nicholas, he must have known her question for he shook his head, the hint of a smirk tucked into the corner of his mouth. Reluctantly, she took a sip of coffee, and shuddered as it went down.

"And who is your friend, Edgemont?" The question came from a short gentleman with a booming voice, and a raised pint. He looked as if he'd had a few already, considering the way he raised his other hand to hold his hat to the crown of his head.

Nicholas greeted him with an offhand nod. "Roderick, this is Mr. Barret, steward of my cousin's estate, visiting London in the hopes of finding a wife."

Roderick sketched a bow with his pint, still holding firm to his hat, and making her wonder if there was an epidemic of hat thievery here. "Sir, what news have you from Tripoli?"

Briar fought the urge to look to Nicholas for a clue to what she should say in response. *Tripoli?* Instead she squared her shoulders. Then with a few coughs, as if she'd lived with a pipe between her teeth since infancy and it had worn away the lining of her throat, she adopted the bluster she'd used in the play. "News, sir? It is dry and hot."

The men around her chuckled and she felt a measure of relief.

Unfortunately, Roderick wasn't done with Mr. Barret.

"Are you referring to the weather or to your bride hunt?" he asked, earning a low rumble of laughter. "If it is the latter, perhaps Edgemont here can offer a fair bit of advice. Rumors abound that he could be married by year's end."

A great cheer rose through the hall and someone slopped a pint of ale in front of Nicholas, while others slapped him on the back.

Nicholas kept to his dish of coffee. "I can confirm that the rumors are wholly false."

"There are reports that you were seen at the opera, escorting a certain young woman who is the niece of an infamous matchmaker. Do you deny it?"

Beside him, Briar held her breath. The association was a bit too close for comfort for either of them. If anyone peered closely, she might very well be ruined.

Even so, part of her was squealing with glee on the inside. How wondrous was it that the agency was mentioned in the coffee house! She almost wished she could put up an advertisement or leave her card . . .

"It seems to me that Roderick has so much to say on the topic of matrimony that we all must wonder why he is not home with his wife," Nicholas quipped, gaining hearty laughs and comments about how Roderick should worry about satisfying his own.

Not short of the need for attention, apparently, Roderick altered the topic to politics, and it rolled through the crowd, picked up by supporters and naysayers.

Briar expelled a sigh of relief.

Now with the crisis over, she took in the room with the intention of memorizing every detail. In the far corner, three men were shouting lines of Shakespearean insults at each other in some sort of a game, proclaiming a merry "What ho!" every time they took a hearty swig of ale.

A few paces ahead, a man with a pencil nub behind his ear was reading poetry aloud from a pocket ledger, but only a few words were discernable by the time they reached her. Nevertheless, hearing *sunlight* and *beauty*, followed by *far sight* and *duty* gave her the impression that it was a love poem.

Next to him was a man whose fingers were as black as the charcoal in his grasp. He was angled away enough for her to see that he was drawing a sketch of a woman with lovely long hair and—*oh*—bare breasts as well.

She looked to Nicholas and he turned his head to meet her gaze. He had not shielded her as if she were too fragile for such an adventure. He had not changed his mind or decided to rush her out the door. Instead, he treated her like a fully-grown woman, one capable of making her own decisions and experiencing life's pleasures.

A swift rush of warmth and lightness filled her, too

great to be contained. She was sure her heart would burst at any moment. "It's all just as grand as I thought it would be. Maybe even more."

Nicholas offered a short nod and nudged the pint in front of her. "For you, Barret. You've earned it for surviving your first verbal fencing match in a coffee house."

Briar gripped the cup with both of her black-gloved hands. "Thank you, *Edgemont*."

Her upper lip tingled as it broke through the fragrant head of foam, and she hummed in delight as she took a long pull of the warm, yeasty brew, thinking that lesson seven might have been her favorite of all. Her tutor deserved an exceptional reward. And she couldn't wait to submit her payment.

Chapter 21

Nicholas checked over his shoulder one more time, nerves frayed, muscles coiled tighter than a spring.

The past half hour had been hell. With Briar disguised as a man, he'd been on constant guard, ready for accusations or attacks. Ready to defend her honor. Ready to fight for her if someone discovered her true identity. No matter what he had to do, he would have done it.

He let out a disbelieving breath when he realized they were not being followed. How could they not have seen her every blush, every luscious curve? Those men were all blind idiots. And one thing was for certain, Nicholas would never put himself through the agony of having her so vulnerable and exposed again. This was the last adventure for Miss Briar Bourne that he would be party to.

Intending to tell her that very thing, Nicholas climbed into the carriage after her. But he barely had time to close the door before Briar launched herself into his arms.

"That was the most excellent night of my life!"

He caught her reflexively. Her arms cinched around his neck, her cheek pressing to his, close enough for him to feel the faint scratch of walnut bits she'd cleverly used to give herself whiskers. But no matter the clothes, the wig, or the whiskers there was nothing remotely masculine about her. Not even the odors of tobacco smoke and bitter coffee rising from her gentleman's clothes. Her soft essence was there. And he breathed it in deeply, feeding her scent into his lungs, satisfying a craving he'd had all night. But it only left him wanting more.

He wasn't aware of moving, or of shifting her across his lap until he buried his nose in her cravat. Then, startled by his own actions, he lifted his head and pretended to brush a speck of lint from her shoulder. "What was your favor part? Roderick reciting horrendous poetry from the tabletop, or Beasley vomiting into his hat across from us?"

It was important to concentrate on something unsavory or else he might think about the enticing woman in his lap too much.

"All of it. Every moment." She tossed her head back and laughed, the bright, unreserved sound charging the air. "I spent an evening disguised as a *man*! Could have been discovered at any moment. The guards called. Me led away in irons. And yet, with you beside me, all my worries faded away. I was wholly immersed in a rush of excitement, and the utter freedom to do whatever I liked." Her soft breath puffed against his cheek, inviting him to turn his head. And when he did, she smoothed his hair back from his temples and smiled, her eyes bright and tender. "Quite a heady experience."

He was having one of those right this moment. She was so close. Close enough that he could taste her sweet breath on his tongue, and he wanted more of it, too.

Yet ever since their kiss at the opera, he knew it would be a mistake to indulge. Briar Bourne—whether swathed in satin or garbed in superfine wool—was exceedingly hard to resist. A damned terrifying realization.

His hands moved down to her waist, prepared to set her on the bench across from him.

"Wait," she whispered, holding fast to his shoulders. "Mustn't forget our bargain."

Later, Nicholas would wish that he had acted the gentleman and set her down, regardless of the enticing offer. Or that he'd told her that there was no need. That escaping the coffee house unscathed was all the payment he desired.

Instead, he held still, every nerve ending in his body thrumming in anticipation. Then she brushed her lips over his and, all at once, he was lost in the soft crush of her mouth, the languid slide from corner to corner.

"Oh, Nicholas, I've missed your kisses," she whispered against his lips, tasting him.

He groaned, willing his pulse to slow, to stay in control. "Continuing your academic study?"

"Well . . . I haven't been entirely honest with you about that."

His breath stalled, the twinge of an old wound starting to drum inside his ears. The thought entered his mind that she was going to tell him she'd been kissing other men. That this had all been a ruse to make a fool of him. He'd heard words like that before. And he was unable to stop a sudden rise of jealousy, fierce and possessive, his hands gripping tighter over her hips.

She lifted her head, cupping his jaw with her small hands, her gaze alarmingly serious.

"I'm actually rather fond of your kisses," she said with the sincerity of a convicted criminal offering a last confession. "I've been pretending otherwise, because I was afraid that, if you knew, you would stop. But it's been burning me up inside not to tell you."

As her confession took root, he was unable to form a response. Every stored breath rushed out of his lungs at once. He should have known better than to imagine the worst. This was Briar, not Marceline.

"And there's one more thing, too," she continued, leaning close to press whisper-soft kisses along his jaw, chin, cheek . . . "I've been fond of them from the very beginning. What I like especially is this spot right here, where my nose nestles into the nook beside yours. You have a rather exceptional nose, perfect for nuzzling."

He closed his eyes, feeling a rush of something other than jealousy, stronger than lust, and whatever it was terrified him with its intensity. So he did what he had to do.

Sliding a hand to the nape of her neck, fingertips nudging beneath the coarse wig, he kissed her. Deep. Driving away all thoughts and immersing himself in the slow, wet slide, the tangle of tongues. But it wasn't enough.

He needed to feel her without the disguise.

Ridding her of the wig, he didn't stop until he'd pulled the pins from her hair and let them fall to the carriage floor, loosening the tight coil. The silken locks cascaded through his fingers, warm and fragrant, her pleased sigh stealing inside his mouth. And he swallowed it down like a greedy addict, arousing the need for more, *more*.

He fitted his fingers to her scalp, massaging, burying his nose in her hair, breathing her in. She smelled good— here, and beneath her jaw, this little valley between her lips and chin—everywhere. He wanted to put her in a hookah and smoke her for hours, lounge back on silken pillows and take in long, languorous pulls.

Clearly, he was on the verge of insanity. And like a madman, he peeled off her coat with a jerk, then worked the knot of her cravat free, baring her throat so that he could press his nose against her flesh, inhale like it was his first breath. And his last.

"I think about kissing you more than I think about

chocolate, she said, panting another confession. "I think about the scent of your skin and the sharp bite of your whiskers. The intimate taste of your breath against my lips, filling my mouth, my lungs. The way I breathe your air and you breathe mine. And I think about all the people who've ever been kissed and how they must be feeling the same way, dying a little bit for every moment they aren't kissing."

"Then perhaps you shouldn't think on it," he said, his voice hoarse with desire. He hadn't had any spirits tonight, but he felt utterly drunk, supremely smashed, guzzling down every word, gorging on them.

"How can I not when you do such wondrous things with your lips? And your tongue . . ."

Her words drifted off as he opened his mouth over her rabbiting pulse, laving and suckling that tender spot.

"I'm jealous of every morsel that passes your lips. Oh bother, I think I said that aloud. Pretend you didn't hear the bit that makes me sound like I've escaped Bedlam."

He must have gone insane as well because he liked hearing it. "Say anything you like. Tell me everything."

Deftly, his fingers unfastened the row of her waistcoat buttons and nudged it off her shoulders.

"I suppose I should feel a rise of nervousness right now," she said on a raspy breath, her hooded gaze seeking his as her hands coasted up the seams of his lapels. "And yet, all I can think of is that it's hardly fair that I should have such an efficient valet, but you do not."

He grinned as she tugged at the knot of his cravat. "But I don't need a valet, love. You're the one changing back into your dress. I'm merely assisting."

Earlier, he'd told Adams to drive through the park, fully intending to step out to allow her privacy. But Briar surprised him with her kiss and now he was in no rush to leave.

"Such the good Samaritan, helping the wayward divest of their clothing," she teased. And before she could wrap her arms around his neck again, he drew out the tails of her shirtwaist and lifted it over her head.

In the dim yellow light, bleeding in through the shades of the carriage lanterns, he saw her bound in strips of white linen from ribs to breasts, milky swells straining above the edge with each rapid breath. He paused to savor the sight of her, quieting the urgency sprinting through him for just a moment.

She took the opportunity to lean in and kiss the underside of his jaw, sliding the silk free, nibbling her way down to the hollow niche beneath his Adam's apple. She rasped her tongue against his flesh. "Mmm . . . you taste of salt and heat. Do you taste like this everywhere?"

As if fully intending to find out, she shifted on his lap, wriggling, the curve of her hip grinding against his cock. He groaned again and pulled her closer. Rolling his hips, he was lost in a heady jolt of hedonistic pleasure. And still, he wanted more. With Briar, he wasn't certain he would ever get enough.

Hungry, he took her lips again, hard, tongues seeking, hands drifting over her ribs to cup her breasts. She pushed herself into his palms, arching back. He rasped the pads of his thumbs over the taut, eager buds, swallowing down her fevered whimpers, the back of his throat tingling with raw need. Tugging down the linen, he exposed her to the night air, pausing long enough to admire the creamy perfection, the pale pink centers, the ruched tips.

Then he closed his mouth over her flesh, her skin sublimely soft, supple, and . . . "You taste like a confection. Are you this sweet everywhere?"

She clutched his head as he sought the other velvety tip to verify his findings. "Tell me if it's true. Don't ever stop."

Never, he thought urging her closer, skimming his hand down her stomach, over the fall front of her ridiculously snug trousers. He settled over her core, the wool warm, damp, and inviting.

She gasped, and shyly tucked her face against his neck, but did not move away from him.

"Have you changed your mind already?"

"I should. Oh, Nicholas, I should . . ." she murmured, her hips hitching helplessly against his palm.

"Do you want me to stop?" While he waited for her decision, his fingertips wandered aimlessly over the contours of her sex, stroking, teasing.

She covered his hand with her own, pressing firmly against the heavy, frantic pulse between her thighs. "Not yet."

And what kind of man would he be to deny her?

Catching her lips, he nipped them closer on a rush of tenderness. She likely didn't know that she was teaching him how to please her. In turn, he showed her even more possibilities. Though it was a new experience for him to delve beneath the placard of a pair of trousers to find soft, feminine curls beyond the cutout that was designed for a man's member. But that thought quickly left his mind when he cupped her, his fingers meeting slick folds.

She gasped again, her head falling back on a wanton mewl as she parted her thighs for him. "Let's stay inside the carriage. Just the two of us. We'll live here, feasting on each other for days. Months. Years."

Yes, yes, it could work. He saw the scenario take shape as his fingertip nudged between her flesh, circling the tightly furled bud as his mouth dipped to sample her breast.

She held him there, hand at his nape, her nails digging deliciously into his scalp. "The rest of the world will disappear. Nothing exists outside these doors. We'll sleep on the benches, in each other's arms. And when we are hungry—*ah . . . Nicholas . . .*"

He nudged the tip of one finger inside, her body snug and drenched and clenching sweetly. The lush scent of her musk added to his addiction. His nostrils flared on an intoxicating breath, his pulse quickening, desire shuddering through him. He wanted to take his time, spending hours pleasuring her, hearing her wanton sighs. But when his name left her lips—knowing that *his* was the only name—suddenly he was too eager to feel her come apart.

He edged in deeper, knuckles wedging inside to the hilt. Observing every breath, every subtle shift, he rolled his palm against her. She held his wrist, desperate, frantic pleas spilling from her lips. He kissed his way back to her mouth, murmuring all the wicked things he wanted to do, where he wanted to taste her, how she would feel against his tongue, dissolving like meringue . . .

She came apart in a heady rush, shattering in his arms, her cries like music filling the carriage. At once, he was filled with a sense of primal satisfaction. And yet, the echoes of her ecstasy brought him to a jarring awareness of where they were and what he was doing.

Debauching a virgin inside his carriage.

She collapsed against him, panting, her head nestled into the crook of his shoulder. And his finger was still buried inside the tight clench, his cock pressed against the ripe curve of her hip.

Unable to help himself, he took his time before leaving, drawing out the last of her tremors, and imagining what he would be doing next if his conscience hadn't just got the better of him. But thoughts like those were dangerous.

Their kissing bargain had suddenly altered into something far more intense than he could have imagined in the beginning. Perhaps it was time to consider keeping his distance.

Yet since his exercises in restraint hadn't worked thus far, likely it would be best if he removed himself from London altogether. Even if it was the last thing he wanted to do.

"You're a very naughty valet, aren't you?"

He nipped the lobe of her ear. "Only with you, love. But now it's time to get you home, or else there won't be much of your innocence left."

BRIAR TWISTED sideways on the carriage bench, her back to Nicholas as he tucked the last of the pins—at least the ones they could locate—into her hair.

"There," he crooned, a finger trailing softly down the nape of her neck and setting off a series of pulse-thrumming tingles. He had very clever fingers. "Having never dressed a woman or styled her hair, I think I've done a fair job of it."

He'd insisted on setting her back to rights, stating his belief that she would turn shy if he left her alone in the carriage to dress herself. And he was likely correct. Even now, she could not stop blushing over the things that she'd said and done, and all the glorious, wondrous things she'd given him liberty to do.

"Then, perhaps, you would also make an excellent ladies' maid."

Leaning closer, his finger was replaced by his lips as he pressed kisses down her neck and along her shoulders. "I can well imagine hours in your bedchamber, dressing you, then undressing you, bathing you . . ."

She laughed. "I am old enough to bathe myself."

"Mmm . . . but where is the fun in that?"

He tugged her back against the solid wall of his chest,

folding his arms around her. And it was so easy with him that she didn't know why she'd felt shy at all. That was gone now, drifting away as she relaxed into him, the carriage ambling slowly toward home.

"And so that's what kissing leads to, hmm?"

"Some of the time," he said, his lips against her temple, his voice tunneling through her as the pad of his thumb made lazy sweeps against the underside of her breast. "There are lots of other things, too."

She closed her eyes, entranced by the rhythmic motions, half wishing they could do everything all over again, or even . . . try something new. She was positively wanton! But she loved every minute with Nicholas. With him she had the freedom to make mistakes, to get drunk—like she had that first day—to be completely, unabashedly herself. She didn't know the reason, but perhaps it was because he was always so unreserved. No topic was unapproachable. No question judged. Because of him she knew what it felt like to make her own decisions based on her own desires, and it was so lovely. She wanted to stay in this place for as long as she could.

But it was late, and she would have to do her best to sneak into the townhouse unnoticed. If not for that, and the list of tasks and responsibilities waiting for her, she might allow herself to dream. To fall in love . . . just a little.

It would be easy to fall for Nicholas, after all. Too easy, perhaps. In fact, if she were honest with herself, she might already be in love . . . just a little.

Or perhaps a lot.

Chapter 22

"What is right to be done cannot be done too soon."

JANE AUSTEN, *Emma*

Briar had known that it was only a matter of time before Ainsley found out about the challenge. It was one thing to find a bride for a wealthy earl. But a rake? Well, that was a different matter entirely, and one in which the eldest of the Bourne sisters would *never* approve.

Unfortunately, what had begun as a quiet brook of rumors, carrying in new applicants after the evening at the opera, was now a tidal wave of gawkers, more interested in hearing gossip than in becoming clients.

"What is Lord Edgemont looking for in a bride, precisely?" Miss Carrigan asked, following Ainsley down the hall.

In the process of carrying a tray to the parlor, Briar suddenly stopped, the cups and saucers clattering together. Ainsley stopped, too.

Turning slowly, her gaze flitted past Miss Carrigan and trained on Briar with an archer's accuracy.

"So it's true, then?"

Only four words, but they dropped like stones, weighted by disappointment. Apparently, Ainsley had heard the rumor before now, but must have given Briar the benefit of the doubt. Which made admitting it all the more difficult.

"It was a matter of upholding our family's honor," Briar said with a tense smile, not really believing her excuse. Especially when it was her own blunder that had tarnished it in the first place.

Ainsley crossed her arms, her dark brows lifted, mouth tight. "And? Any progress?"

Briar swallowed and adjusted her grip on the tray, which had suddenly become inordinately heavy. "Not exactly."

She highly doubted Ainsley would be thrilled to learn about the lessons. Or the fact that Briar might have accidentally begun falling in love with the object of the challenge. And that, every time she thought about finding a woman Nicholas couldn't resist, she felt a primal urge to club any potential candidates over the head with a candlestick. Which really did not bode well for the completion of her task, or for the future legendary status of the Bourne Matrimonial Agency.

Ainsley strode past her and stepped into the parlor. "If any debutante is here to fill out an application solely for Lord Edgemont, I'm sorry to say that he is not a client of ours, and as far as I am aware, not looking for a wife."

The flood of gawkers, Miss Carrigan included, left in a wave of disgruntled murmurs, leaving a sea of crumbs and empty teacups in their wake.

Ainsley walked back to her office and closed the door, without uttering another word.

Jacinda, a little late to the party and looking more peaked than ever, leaned against her doorframe. "What was all that about?"

"I've made a mess of things again," Briar said, setting the tray down on the demilune table nearest her.

Mrs. Teasdale stepped out of the parlor with her latest knitting mystery thrown over her shoulder like a royal train. "But you make a fine cup of tea, dear. Not everyone can."

Briar nodded, knowing that it was said with the best of intentions and trying not to feel defeated

"It'll all turn out in the—" Jacinda abruptly put a hand over her stomach, clutching the green muslin as a sheen of perspiration gathered on her face.

"I think you should sit down, or perhaps lie down. You look as though you might become ill."

Jacinda closed her eyes, resting her forehead against the plaster wall. "If the past four days have taught me anything, there is no *might*. Only *when*."

"Make your sister a cuppa with plenty of sugar."

"Jacinda doesn't like sugar," Briar said to Mrs. Teasdale, already pouring the strong brew into a fresh cup.

"That may be true," Mrs. Teasdale said, clucking her tongue fondly, "but the babe'll like it sweet, mark my words."

"*The ba*—" Briar and Jacinda said in unison, eyes wide.

Seconds later, Ainsley shot out of the connecting office, hands over her mouth, eyes glistening. "Is it true?"

Jacinda looked down slowly, the hand over her midriff no longer clenched but splayed protectively. "It is possible, I suppose. But Crispin and I have not been married very long at all."

As Jacinda blushed, her ears turning pink, Briar nipped off a chunk of sugar and stirred it into the tea. "Here. Try this."

"Why is everyone standing in the corridor? Is something amiss?" Uncle Ernest asked, coming out of his office and tucking a letter inside his coat pocket.

"We're watching Jacinda drink her tea," Mrs. Teasdale answered smugly, practically daring Uncle Ernest to ask another question, just so that she could state the obvious. They had not yet warmed to each other. But there was always hope. "Why it's as plain as the nose on a mayfly's face. Anyone could see that's what we're doing."

Then again, perhaps not.

Jacinda took several hearty gulps, waited a moment as it settled. Then she sighed, her mouth curling up at the corners. "I do like it sweet, after all. Briar, you brew a fine pot, indeed. But now, I beg that you will all excuse me, for I am going across town to see my husband."

Before she left, she pressed a quick kiss to everyone's cheek.

BY THE end of the day, after the Duke of Rydstrom had worn a hole in the rug outside his wife's bedchamber, the doctor confirmed the suspicion. A baby was due in the new year.

Briar was going to be an aunt! She heard the happy report just before she went with Uncle Ernest to the Duchess of Holliford's weekly dinner.

"Your mother would have been so proud to see her daughters grow into such fine, accomplished young women," Uncle Ernest said from inside the carriage, still wearing the same pleased smile he'd had since they learned of Jacinda's upcoming arrival. He patted Briar's hand. "You've each put so much of yourselves into our little endeavor. And what fine luck we've had . . ."

Briar could have argued that her own efforts had all failed thus far, but she kept that reminder to herself. She decided to use her failures to fuel her purpose. After all, she still had hope for Temperance, and Daniel, and she hadn't given up on Mrs. Teasdale and her son yet either.

But then there was Nicholas, she thought, conflicted. What was she going to do about him?

Each time she imagined introducing him to the other

half of his soul, the woman whom he would love for all
the days of his life, Briar did not feel an overwhelming
sense of rightness. There were no waves of pure joy rushing through her veins. Instead, she felt as if a volcano
rumbled inside her, scorching and sulfuric, acid climbing
up her throat.

The violence of her feelings alarmed her. How could
she commit to finding him a bride when every part of her
railed against it? When every part of her wanted him for
herself?

Oh dear. She gulped to soothe her suddenly dry throat.

"You've never once lost sight of your goal," Uncle
Ernest continued, unaware of how he'd just contradicted
the turbulent thoughts of his youngest niece, "to ensure
the happiness of others, when it was just out of reach for
her."

Briar knew from her mother's ordeal that choosing the
wrong man—a man who could not love her in return—
would only lead to misery.

She refused to let her own heart make the same mistake.

The only answer to her conundrum was to stop falling
for Nicholas. At once.

After all, to him, she was nothing more than the
matchmaker who was going to find spouses for his cousins, and their bargain was nothing more than a diversion.
He'd said as much. His rule from the beginning was not
to fall in love with him. He'd even told her that he was a
man who could never love her in return.

Therefore, she would tuck these dreamy thoughts of
him away. Immediately. In addition, she would limit her
contact with him, keeping him out of sight, the same way
she did with comfits to stop herself from devouring them
all. It was all a simple matter of self-control, really.

Briar nodded to herself firmly. And by the time they reached the duchess's townhouse, everything was settled in her mind.

Or at least she thought it was, until Uncle Ernest handed her down to the pavement. "Ah, I believe that's Edgemont's carriage coming up now. He must be joining us this evening."

Startled, Briar turned to see the familiar glossy black carriage with gold coronets on the corners, and her efforts quickly fell asunder. Her stomach fluttered. Her heart—not to be outdone by an inferior organ—kicked in a few additional beats and swelled to push out all the air from her lungs.

It was too soon. She hadn't even fully accepted the fact that she'd been falling in love with him, let alone had time to build up a good defense against those wayward emotions.

Knowing that her uncle would wait for Nicholas, she said, "I'll go on ahead and . . . um . . . escape this inclement weather."

With her gloved fingers, she fanned herself as if believing there would be a reprieve from the heat inside where there was no breeze at all. Thankfully, her uncle said nothing to contradict her.

She just needed a few moments to prepare herself. Once inside with her hostess, she hoped they would begin a perfectly mundane conversation that had absolutely nothing to do with matters of the heart.

But Briar was not so fortunate.

"How is your husband hunt proceeding, my dear?" the duchess asked, welcoming her with a fond smile.

"P-pardon, Your Grace?"

"For your friend, Miss Prescott."

"Oh, of course." Briar expelled a breath and gratefully accepted a glass of lemonade from a footman. "It is progressing, but slower than I had hoped. From what I understand, she toured the museum with a gentleman this week. Though she did not offer the particulars, she was quite pleased in her missive."

Briar was certain to hear more about the gentleman later, during a time when they could chat freely. And perhaps when her own thoughts weren't quite so muddled.

Then, as if her eyes were comprised of metal flecks and Nicholas was a powerful magnet, her gaze darted to the door just as he appeared. And worse, he looked terribly dashing and completely kissable. *Bother.*

"Splendid. And what of Mr. Prescott?"

"I had hoped for better results," Briar said distractedly. "In truth, I do not know if I have done anything productive, other than attempt to lessen his shyness."

"And what of Lord Edgemont? Were you able to entice him into becoming a client? I heard a rumor that you accepted a challenge of the sort." The duchess tsked, but there was a fond twinkle in her eyes as that very man came to her side.

Nicholas bussed the duchess's cheek with a kiss, then inclined his head to Briar, his dark gaze gleaming warmly, hinting at intimate knowledge. "Pray, do not let me interrupt. You were saying, Miss Bourne?"

All at once, Briar's thoughts were flooded with memories of their carriage encounter. She'd been wholly wanton, and must have told him *not* to stop at least a dozen times. And he, she thought in a rush of heated tingles, had deliciously obliged her.

Briar took a long swallow, attempting to cool her thoughts. After all, it was time to face the truth, not to reminisce. She would have the rest of her Nicholas-less life to do that.

Resolved, she squared her shoulders. "At first, I was

arrogant enough to believe that I could find him an irresistible bride. Someone with whom he could spend the rest of his life in contentment."

"And now?" the duchess asked.

"Well, during our brief acquaintance, he has never once indicated a desire for such a match. And unless he suddenly displays some miraculous change of heart, I fear my hands are tied. So the challenge will not be met."

There. She'd said it, confronting the unguarded fondness that had forced her hand, as well as the bitter agony of failure. She did this all without letting her voice dip a fraction in disappointment or releasing the forlorn sigh that was trapped inside her heart. In fact, she sounded rather worldly, even to her own ears. *And Jacinda thinks* she *is the better actress. Ha.*

If Briar's audience only knew, they would be applauding and throwing roses at her feet.

The duchess looked to him and clucked her tongue. "You are still unwilling to consider what it would be like to have a wife and family around you?"

Nicholas held Briar's gaze for a moment, his irises turning from rakish ebony to that velvety cocoa she'd grown so fond of recently. *Too fond,* she reminded herself.

Then he turned to the duchess. "I'm afraid Miss Bourne is correct. And if the most romantic of all matchmakers cannot convince me to take a wife, I'm afraid no one can."

And that was the most important lesson of all.

Chapter 23

"Her objections to Mr. Knightley's marrying did
not in the least subside. She could see nothing but
evil in it."

JANE AUSTEN, *Emma*

After dinner, his godmother's guests retired to the
music room.

Nicholas had a particular fondness for this room, and
the windows also had the benefit of the warm breeze
coming in through the garden rather than from the fetid
street.

The stench of town was not something he would miss
when he next journeyed to the country. Which, he'd come
to realize after his last encounter with Briar, needed to
happen sooner than he'd initially planned. He required a
break from the constant temptation she posed, and pref-
erably before he did something that would leave them
both altered forever.

In fact, he'd made the decision before coming here this
evening. He'd informed his aunt and cousins that they
would leave for the country next week.

Aunt Lavinia and Temperance had moaned their disappointment, but Daniel was relieved, offering up the
first genuine smile in days.

It did not surprise Nicholas that the last thought
brought his gaze to Briar. She was sitting at the piano

and playing a soft lullaby of a melody that entranced the party, sparse though it was with only eight in attendance. Even so, no one stirred in their seats, except with the lazy wave of a fan.

If he hadn't heard the tune before, he could almost believe she was composing it right this instant and just letting her fingertips glide aimlessly over the keys. The music of the matchmaker, of Cupid's arrows, and of summer nights.

As always, she was lovely, but somehow even more so with the light of the candelabra spilling over her face, her cheeks flushed, her eyes soft as they flitted to him. A smile touched her lips, almost wistful in design, the barest curl of rose-petal red. It made him curious to know what thoughts inspired this new, unfamiliar smile.

"She will make a young man quite happy one day," his godmother said from beside him, resting comfortably into the curve of the chintz sofa. "So accomplished. So amiable."

He murmured his agreement, but felt the flesh of his brow furrow as an image filled his head, of Briar with an anonymous *young man*—their hands clasped, her face tilting up to give this upstart a glimpse of this new wistful smile.

"I would have been pleased to welcome her into my own family," she continued, "but my nephew only had eyes for his Nelly, and he is happy. At least, I can be content in that. Though for Miss Bourne, I should like to see her married and opportunely settled."

"I'm certain, if it were her wish, she could pick from any number of her uncle's clients." His tone came out a little harsher than he intended, drawing a perturbed glance from Mrs. Fitzherbert for interrupting the music's spell.

His godmother shook her head and whispered behind

her fan. "No, indeed. Think of the scandal if *two* sisters were to marry their clients. It would be nothing short of monumental. Then again, you know a bit about scandals, don't you?"

He murmured his agreement, distracted by his own musings. With Briar rarely attending the typical marriage mart social events, she wasn't likely to meet her young man for a good while. He kept this thought to himself as he, too, eased back into the curve of the blue sofa, and watched the object of their conversation as she played the final notes.

After a round of applause, she stood, her uncle beaming with pride. He engaged her briefly in conversation, as a pair of servants stepped through the open doors, carrying trays of tea and coffee.

"That is why I plan to introduce her to Mr. Woodlyn, a handsome young cleric who has just moved into the parish near my country house. I'm sure they are well suited, and I cannot wait to introduce them when she comes to stay with me."

Suddenly, Nicholas did not find the sofa comfortable after all. He sat straighter. "I was not aware she was coming to stay with you. That is . . . Temperance made no mention of her friend being away from town."

"I only just spoke of it with her uncle at dinner. It is a custom of ours to have a prolonged visit in the summer. Unfortunately, neither of her sisters will be able to attend, as one will be staying at length in Sussex, while the other will remain with her uncle in town."

In that moment, Briar came near, her hand resting on the back of the bronze chair angled near him. "Uncle told me just now, Your Grace. I cannot thank you enough for inviting me."

"Tush. Holliford Park is your home as much as it is mine," she said fondly. "We should leave by midweek,

I think, for it has grown too hot and people are retiring to their country estates. Some are going sea bathing. Fortunately, Holliford Park has the advantage of a rather large pond that brings in the cool breeze. I'll have a small party, but not too many, for I enjoy equal parts company and solitude. Though I would be remiss if I did not extend an invitation to you, Lord Edgemont."

"I'm afraid I cannot attend. My aunt, cousins, and I are traveling to Blacklowe Manor to visit my mother and my brother's widow," he said, his gaze on Briar to see that her smile had fallen. "That is the reason I came this evening, to tell you both."

His godmother snapped her fan closed, tapping it on the edge of the cushion as if spurring a horse to a canter. "Why, Blacklowe Manor is only ten miles from Holliford Park. Perhaps you and your cousins might come for a picnic one afternoon."

"Perhaps," he said, without promise, ignoring the unwanted thrill that raced through him at the thought of her being such an easy distance away. Not even an hour on horseback. "But we are all likely to stop only briefly before departing for our own houses."

"Blacklowe Manor *is* your house. It has always been the primary residence of the Earls of Edgemont."

Not for him. As far as Nicholas was concerned, his brother was the last of the earls that would live there. "It is my mother's house more than anyone's. She holds an affection for it that I never had. Besides, I've always preferred my estate in Wiltshire. I've spent many a happy summer fishing in the lake."

His godmother nodded halfheartedly. "Hmm . . . yes, Broadmere is quite happily situated. Any young woman would be happy to be mistress there. But what of Miss Bourne? How is she to continue her matchmaking endeavors with all of you scattered about?" His godmother sighed. "Oh, I do wish our group had had the opportunity to celebrate one wedding before the end of the Season. I just learned this afternoon that Lord Aselton made an offer for Miss Baftig, who is still wet behind the ears and has very few accomplishments."

At the mention of Miss Baftig, the corners of Briar's lips tilted up ever-so-slightly. "A pity. I'd thought for a time that Miss Baftig would have been perfect for you, my lord."

The smile did not reach her eyes but he pretended not to notice and grinned at her jest. "Apparently not."

"But what I cannot understand," his godmother interjected again, "is what appealed to him so quickly. Rumor has it that they had not met above three times."

"A determined man will always seek what he desires most. When it matters, no obstacle will stop him." Nicholas shrugged. "Of course, that does not always mean he's making a sound decision."

He thought of his own hasty rush into marriage and the regret that had followed. Little did he know at the time, he was not truly the one making the decisions, but being led by the nose, instead.

"There is a lesson in that, I suppose." Briar tapped her finger against her lips thoughtfully.

His gaze followed and he was no longer thinking of Marceline at all, but of nudging Briar's finger aside, pressing his mouth to hers, then losing himself for hours in the soft cushion of rose-petal lips. "Indeed. There is most definitely a lesson there."

As if his thoughts were transparent, Briar blushed and slid him a glance. When their gazes connected he was transported to the carriage, feeling her body yield, arch, and shudder.

Let's stay inside the carriage. Just the two of us. We'll live here, feasting on each other for days. Months. Years . . .

But he was not in the carriage alone with Briar. He was in the music room, and inappropriately aroused. This wasn't even the first time he'd been in such a state in this very room in Briar's company, and the memory of that first kiss did nothing to cool his ardor.

So he thought of the one thing that always worked to dampen any and all desires—his inescapable wedding day, the blatant loathing in Marceline's eyes as he clumsily tried to secure the ring to her finger, the impatient tapping of her foot on the stones of the church floor, hissing, *Can you do nothing right, Nicholas* beneath her breath.

And that was all it took. He was, at once, recovered.

Even so, and as a matter of precaution against any further lapses, he rose and made his excuses to depart. His godmother patted him fondly and begged him to visit Holliford Park.

"I shall consider it," he lied, knowing that part of his reason for leaving London was to escape temptation. It would be folly to seek it out at Holliford Park.

She smiled, her eyes crinkling at the corners, and then looked to Briar. "Dear, if it wouldn't be too much trouble, could you walk him out on my behalf? I see that Mrs. Fitzherbert is preparing to leave as well and there is a matter I should like to discuss with her."

"Certainly, Your Grace." Briar rose and led the way out of the music room. Once they were in the empty corridor, she said, "I am glad to have a moment alone because there is something important I wanted to tell you."

He slowed his steps, his thoughts on their last encounter yet again. "Is this a conversation we should have in private?"

She shook her head, but the crests of her cheeks were tinged pink, and he knew they were both thinking of the carriage now.

"I just want you to know that I was sincere earlier . . . about giving up the challenge."

He frowned. "And why this sudden decision?"

"Lately, I've realized that I've become distracted by the lessons without ever putting them to their intended use." She drew in a breath and let it out slowly. "Therefore, you can rest assured that when you return to London you will not have to endure my futile and foolish attempts."

"I never thought you were foolish."

Briar's gaze flitted over his features, that new smile on her lips. "Then you are very kind, I shall add that quality to the unwritten list I've been making, the one that will never go on an application at the Bourne Matrimonial Agency." Then she looked away, her attention on the runner beneath their feet. "Besides, you already found your irresistible bride once. The odds aren't likely even I—born matchmaker that I am—could find another."

He didn't correct her. He was too perturbed by the self-mockery in her tone. Where was the self-assured Briar that he knew? The one who teased him incessantly on this topic? The one who'd conjured seven children and twenty-eight grandchildren for him? And a honeymoon by a lake?

"You're giving up without even discussing it with me?"

"Not entirely. I will honor my part of the bargain."

"And how do you intend to do that?" he asked, not disguising the irritation building within him, tightening his jaw, hammering away at the pulse in his throat.

She stopped near the stairs and laid her hand over his sleeve, her soft gaze imploring. "Please don't be cross with me. I know how much it means to you to ensure your cousins' happiness, and I won't rest until I find their perfect counterparts."

That wasn't why he was bothered. She just didn't understand.

Then again, he wasn't sure he did either. Yet he suspected there was something she wasn't telling him, so perhaps that was the crux of his irritation.

The darkened doorway of the parlor stood just behind her and he steered her through it, leaving the door ajar for the sconce light to illuminate her face. He needed to see what she wasn't saying aloud.

"There, now you can tell me what this is about. If you are feeling shy because of—"

"Not with you. Never with you," she said with a quick shake of her head, lifting her hand to his cheek. "And perhaps that is part of the reason."

"It needn't be."

Her quiet laugh was edged with exasperation more than humor. "I truly thought you would be pleased by my announcement, not question my every word. Which confuses me all the more because you are leaving as well."

"And I came here to tell you." When he felt her pull away, he covered her hand with his, keeping her there.

"It is better that we end the part that was our kissing bargain while it still rests very fondly between us. There is no need to continue, for it would turn our encounters awkward when I visit Temperance in the future. I would not wish that for us."

Us. He swallowed. "Awkwardness should never come between us."

She nodded once. "Because of you, I've learned more about making matches than I've dreamed. And more about myself, too. You taught me how to watch people more closely, taking account of the subtle nuances of posture to see what they are really saying. Lesson two about unattractive men . . . well, I suspect it may not be entirely true. In lesson three, I learned that not all rakes think alike, as I was told." She paused, her mouth tilting in a rueful smirk. "The results of which led to lesson four and how attraction can also feel like a desire to murder. Lesson five taught me that anticipation combined with jealousy should be handled with care or else it can overcome a person in unexpected places . . . like the opera."

He saw the memory of it glowing warmly in her eyes. Yes, that was one of his favorite lessons, too.

"In the next lesson, you proved that a person deserves to find someone who supports them in their endeavors, even if it is to dress up like a man in order to steal into a coffee house. Then, I learned more about myself, and also what happens inside of carriages when the shades are drawn."

"That's only seven," he said, reaching up to brush his fingertip over the flush of color on the apples of her cheeks. "I have not fulfilled my part of our bargain."

"Tonight, you offered two more. The first was one that you've been trying to teach me from the very beginning— that some men aren't inclined to change their minds, no matter how fervent the attempts are to persuade them otherwise. And the second was that a man will always seek what he wants, and nothing will stop him." She studied him, her gaze searching, imploring.

All at once, he was tongue-tied and uneasy, his thoughts scrambling to come up with another lesson. They couldn't leave it this way. He was supposed to give her one more. Leaving their bargain at nine felt too unfinished, too raw.

"No one else could have put me at ease or made me

feel so alive. I'll always cherish our brief . . . friendship," she said with a sigh, closing her eyes briefly. Then she slipped her hand free. Briefly, she rested it on his shoulder and, lifting up on her toes, she pressed a kiss to his cheek. "Goodbye, Nicholas."

Chapter 24

"With the fortitude of a devoted novitiate, she
had resolved at one-and-twenty to complete
the sacrifice, and retire from all the pleasures of
life . . ."

JANE AUSTEN, *Emma*

For the next fortnight, the sprawling brick manor of Holliford Park became something of a home to Briar once
again. Everything around her held memories—Ainsley
collecting flowers in the garden, Jacinda climbing the
ivy-shrouded trellis to free a kite, Briar floating aimlessly
in the rowboat on the lake.

As a girl, she'd painted watercolors of the green countryside, the rolling hills and clouds for hours on end.
She'd lain in the hammock, lazing the days away while
woodlarks warbled from the leafy boughs of the trees,
and dreaming of when she would finally reach the age of
one and twenty and become a woman of the world.

She didn't know why that age, in particular, had meant
so much to her younger self, but here she was, nonetheless.

Though, perhaps, she could consider herself a woman
of the world now. After all, she had appropriated a rake's
carriage and drunk a flask of his driver's whiskey. She'd
accepted an outrageous challenge from a strange woman
in a retiring room. Agreed to a kissing bargain with an
irredeemable rake. Entered a coffee house disguised as

a man. Enjoyed wicked things inside a carriage with the curtains drawn. And . . . she'd fallen in love.

All things a woman of the world would do. Her younger self likely would have been immensely pleased, if not a bit scandalized.

Current-day Briar, however, was not pleased or content in the least. She was restless.

She'd been unable to stay still for two solid minutes at a time until nightfall, only after she'd stirred herself into an exhausted sleep. But even then, her dreams kept her from feeling refreshed.

Since leaving London she'd been plagued by the same recurring image, of saying goodbye to Nicholas and watching him let her go. And when she awoke each morning, Nicholas was still on her mind.

She'd tried to stop falling in love with him. Unfortunately, falling in love was like catching a cold—once the symptoms began to present themselves, one was already stricken with the ailment. And she had none of Mrs. Darden's chicken broth to cure her.

So she did the next best thing. She'd immersed herself in matchmaking, of course.

From the very first night here, Mr. Woodlyn had been invited to supper. He came around for tea each afternoon as well. And sometimes, he simply stopped by to ask if anyone staying with the duchess would care for a quick jaunt down the lane in his curricle.

Since the duchess had mentioned her wish for Mr. Woodlyn to find a bride on several occasions, Briar felt it was her duty to secure one for him before she returned to London. And she already had the perfect candidate in mind: Temperance.

This time, Briar was taking her time in getting to know everything about Mr. Woodlyn, his family, and his interests.

Every day, she wrote to her friend to tell her about the handsome young man, describing his blond hair and tall frame in such detail as to arouse her friend's curiosity. Though, when Temperance's responses only showed halfhearted interest, Briar doubled her efforts, filling page after page of the insightful things he would say on occasion. And sometimes she would embellish these because, for a cleric, Mr. Woodlyn wasn't that inspiring.

Often, Briar had to pinch herself to pay attention and not let her thoughts drift to imagining what it would be like if she were here with Nicholas instead. There would be kissing, she was sure. Lots of kissing.

But not with Mr. Woodlyn. With him, she kept on her task. When she ran out of questions to ask about his life, she began to tell him about her wonderful friend, listing every single one of Temperance's fine qualities without the need for a single embellishment.

"Another letter for Miss Prescott, dear?" the duchess asked as Briar skipped down the stairs and laid the folded missive on the salver.

Immensely proud of her efforts and believing they would come to fruition, she beamed. "I've endeavored to write each day to keep her abreast of all the happenings at Holliford Park."

This time, to ensure she ensnared Temperance's interest, Briar wrote, "such a classically handsome cleric might even make some young woman a very fine husband one day."

That should do the trick.

"I did not realize it was such a thrilling place to be. Though, I suspect Mr. Woodlyn has something to do with that. I think I hear his curricle coming down the lane even now." The duchess went to the window and looked past the butler who was sweeping the stones beneath the wide portico. "Indeed, it is, and it appears as if he has brought flowers for someone."

Stepping up behind her, Briar peered over the top of her dove-gray coiffure to see Mr. Woodlyn holding a bouquet of drooping daisies in the hand where he held the reins. "I wonder why he would do such a thing when you already have flowers aplenty, both in the garden and in every room of the house."

After all, it wasn't as if he was courting anyone. There was no unattached woman here even close to his age other than . . .

Oh bother.

THE INSTANT the post came, Temperance dashed into the foyer, sliding on the hardwood floor and stopping just short of colliding with the milieu table. Eager, she scooped up the letters, shuffling each one behind the other before taking two from the stack.

If the past fortnight had taught Nicholas anything, he knew one was from Mr. Cartwright and the other from Briar. But he wasn't sure which one bothered him more.

Temperance's growing fondness for Briar's brother caused a contradiction of emotions within Nicholas. On one hand, he was thrilled to see his cousin's happiness. Yet, on the other hand, he was worried.

Temperance had confided in him that she had yet to mention this involvement to Briar and had even omitted using his name in her letters, citing the reason that she was waiting to tell her. Waiting for what, she did not say, but he had his suspicions that the relationship was now of a serious nature.

Nicholas didn't think it was possible for two people to fall in love merely from exchanging letters. At least he hoped not, for Briar's sake.

Though why he felt any pangs at all for Miss Bourne's spirits was a mystery to him. After all, as far as her letters to Temperance sounded, she was involved in a romance of her own.

Mr. Woodlyn featured very prominently in every . . . single . . . correspondence. In fact, he wondered if Briar ever spent a moment out of this young upstart's company.

Gritting his teeth at the thought, he absently shuffled through the stack of letters. Of course, he did not find one addressed to him from Briar.

No, indeed. She'd said her goodbye and clearly had meant it.

He should feel relieved. He was free of the burden of her company and wistful smiles, Free of the plague of her cornflower blue eyes and the way she hiccupped when she laughed. Free of her romantic scenarios, soft sighs, and *cup of chocolate* kisses.

Which she might very well be doling out to Mr. bloody Woodlyn . . .

"Will you stop your growling? You make it quite impossible to enjoy a good letter," Temperance said from where she sat on the stairs. She was always too eager to read her mail to even make it beyond the foyer.

"*Good letter*, hmm?" He wanted to kick himself as soon as the words came out. Could he be any more transparent?

She murmured a response, flipping the page over and reading the other side. Casually, he moved closer, resting his forearm on the curled handrail. At a glance, he saw that this letter was from Cartwright, the handwriting at a severe leftward slant. He knew this, of course, because Temperance had dreamily mentioned that Mr. Cartwright was left-handed. Apparently, that simple fact put him on par with Greek gods.

When she finished, she sighed and pressed it to her bosom, in no hurry to open the next letter. Hang it all.

"Ah, there you are, Nicholas. I've been looking for you." His mother strode in from the east wing, her grizzled hair set in a heavy twist at her crown, her dark eyes faintly creased at the corners, but not from smiling. He was sure she hadn't smiled once since his brother's death.

He spread his arms, preparing for an embrace he would not receive, but it was more of a jest between them now. "And so you have found me."

She arched a thin brow and lifted a letter. *Another letter, oh good.* His life seemed to be centered around them these past weeks.

"Mrs. Lake has returned from town. You remember her, do you not?"

"Yes. Her husband's hunting cabin was on the far side of the village." And James and Marceline used to go there during their supposed trips to the market. Nicholas had only learned of it after the accident, however.

"Precisely. Well, she has stopped there on her way to Northumberland, and has agreed to have dinner with us."

Nicholas felt that there was a catch coming next. His mother did not disappoint.

"She has a daughter, newly out. Lovely girl."

"I'm not interested in marriage."

"According to the rumors from town, you are considering it."

"Since when do you start listening to rumors?" Like the ones surrounding James and Marceline. The ones she'd completely dismissed.

When Nicholas had confronted her with the irrefutable knowledge he'd received on the day of the carriage accident, Mother had not shown the least ounce of shock. She'd known all along. Then she'd told him, for the sake of his brother's widow, never to mention it again. And that was what Nicholas had done.

He was an expert at that—hiding the truth. He was so

good in fact that he had yet to confess his own indiscretion to Daniel, and the reasons he'd sent Miss Smithson away. He wanted to explain everything to his cousin. The weight of guilt now pressed on him every single moment, growing heavier each day, and he ached to relieve himself of the burden.

But something else was also increasing— his fear that Daniel wouldn't forgive him. That too much time had passed and he'd lost his chance to make amends. And worst of all, that their relationship would be ruined.

Mother gave him a hard look, clearly not in the mood to reminisce. "Miss Lake is coming to dinner tomorrow evening. I'll likely invite them to stay until morning."

He inclined his head, ready to bid her to do as she wished and that it would change nothing. But then Temperance shot up from the stairs with a gasp and he could think of nothing else.

"Dear heavens! I think Briar is getting married!"

Chapter 25

"Every thing was to take its natural course,
however, neither impelled nor assisted. She would
not stir a step, nor drop a hint. No, she had had
enough of interference."

JANE AUSTEN, *Emma*

From the window, Briar watched the two carriages trundle down the lane toward the village. She wasn't feeling well enough for a church picnic. At least, that's what she told the duchess earlier this morning. But the truth was, she couldn't face Mr. Woodlyn quite yet—not after he'd declared his intentions yesterday.

Drat it all, but apparently, she was being courted.

She'd been so busy trying to match him with Temperance that she hadn't noticed the signs. And when he'd presented her with the flowers, and said all those unexpected things, she'd been so surprised that she hadn't known what to say.

The direct approach would have been ideal. However, considering that she still wanted Mr. Woodlyn to meet and possibly marry Temperance, the matter required a bit more finesse than utter, open-mouthed astonishment. Which was precisely what she'd offered at first.

Though, thankfully, she'd recovered with a polite "Thank you, Mr. Woodlyn," accepting an armful of drooping daisies.

Now, she did not know how to proceed.

Lost in thought, she walked the grounds, heading toward the summerhouse on the opposite side of the pond, glad that the duchess, the other guests, and most of the servants were off enjoying the village picnic. She needed to mull over this unfortunate blunder carefully. A bit of luck wouldn't hurt either.

Seeing a spent dandelion amidst the grasses near the embankment, she bent to pick it up, careful not to disturb the gossamer halo enshrouding the head. Oh, how she wished she could talk to Nicholas and learn his opinion on the matter. Then she closed her eyes and let out a breath.

Opening them again, she watched the seeds take flight in a tiny, haphazard flurry, scattering on the breeze. They drifted lazily toward the surface of the water, landing in a shaft of blinding, golden light.

Blinking to clear the spots from her eyes, she turned away, not seeing the figure approach until he was almost upon her.

And when she did, she startled and sputtered, *"Nicholas?"*

He cut through the grass with long, angry strides, twigs snapping beneath his boots, coattails flaring behind him. His face was set in a series of hard-slanted lines—the same expression he'd worn each night in her dreams.

"I hear congratulations are in order," he called out, his voice harsh and gravelly when it reached her. "It did not take you long to put those lessons to good use, suiting your own purpose."

Briar was still a bit dumbfounded and had yet to catch her breath. Blowing out the dandelion had apparently scrambled her wits. *"Congratulations?"*

He reached her in three more strides, ripping a crumpled paper from the pocket of his coat and holding it aloft. "In your letter to my cousin, you mention a certain *classically handsome young cleric*. Or have you already forgotten your intended? It seems your affections are rather transitory."

So he *had* been paying attention to her letters. Briar had hoped he would. Not for the purpose of misunderstanding, but with the wish that she might linger in his thoughts as well. Though, obviously, there was a matter of confusion as to the purpose of her writing about Mr. Woodlyn.

"Are you here to warn me against him?"

He crumpled the letter in his fist and shook it at her. "A fortnight is hardly enough time to make such a monumental decision. You cannot allow yourself to be swept away in a momentary infatuation."

She nodded thoughtfully and reached for the letter, peeling his fingers open one by one. Taking the paper in hand, she smoothed out the creases, carefully tucked it back into his pocket, and gave it a pat. "I think you are correct. Marriage is not an institution to be entered into with a foolish heart. As you've said, *some* sparks are blinding and fleeting. And yet, there are also those that flare to life, and are like stars that shine for eons."

"Romantic nonsense," he grumbled, his anger diffused to a mere bluster.

If only he could feel what was in her heart, then he would know the truth. But she could not tell him. He'd made a rule, after all.

Angling away, she bent to pick up another spent dandelion and blew on it softly. "Perhaps, but consider the source. I am a believer in luck, in wishes, and in far-fetched possibilities. I'd have thought you'd have known me better by now."

"I do. That is why I'm here."

She brushed past him, ambling alongside the pond,

smiling when he kept pace beside her. "How was your ride? You look rather windblown "

"I lost my hat along the way." He raked a rough hand through his hair, making it stand on end. "I cut through a field, and a low hanging branch knocked it free."

"And you didn't go back for it?"

"Clearly not." He swiped a fistful from the tall blades of grass and ripped them into pieces as they walked.

So testy, she thought, biting down on her lip to keep from laughing. Was he so driven to reach her that he might have knocked off his own head along the way?

A determined man will always seek what he desires most. When it matters, no obstacle will stop him.

She held her breath, remembering what he'd said a fortnight ago. Could it be possible that he came all this way to stop her from marrying Mr. Woodlyn? And perhaps because he felt more for her than a mere tutor would?

Turning her head, she scrutinized him, hair spiked, brow furrowed, mouth petulant. She laid a hand on his arm, and reached up to set him back to rights, standing close enough to feel their clothes brush, bodies press, to catch his familiar scent. She drew in a breath, her fingers combing through the thick strands, heat rising from his scalp. "I've missed you."

His eyes darkened, his nostrils flaring, but he said nothing. He kept his arms at his sides, a fierce tension emanating from him.

"And just so you know," she began, daring to draw closer still, to smooth away those furrows from his brow, "you're the only man who holds any claim over my *affect* —"

His mouth closed over hers at once. Hands stealing to her nape and her waist, he pulled her against him. And she went willingly, yielding.

It felt like decades since they'd kissed. Eons. The world had been broken apart and formed all over again. And now they were the only two people in existence.

He tore his mouth free on a growl. Pressing his cheek to hers, he went still as if he felt the continents shift beneath them, too, and needed to steady his footing. Waves of palpable indecision surrounded him as he held her, but he did not share his thoughts. He simply breathed her in, drawing in her scent as surely as she was drawing in his. Apparently, in this newly formed world, they were too primitive to form words.

Then he kissed her again, even hungrier this time, needy. His hands gripped her dress by the fistfuls, fitting her against him, letting her feel all the differences between their bodies.

This was a language of their own making, an unspoken communication. This felt like *I've missed you, too. Let's never wait this long again. Let's slide our bodies against each other like this. Isn't this nice?*

She murmured her agreement, nodding against his lips, clinging to him, desperate to be closer. Here, beside the primordial pond, they were brand-new and exploring the terrain of each other, reveling in the hard ridges that nestled perfectly into soft valleys, and supple hillocks yielding to firm, broad expanses. They fit together like they were created for each other.

Was this what it was always like between men and women?

But she already knew the answer. It wasn't.

This was something rare, something few people found. And she didn't know why he'd waited so long to teach her the most important lesson of all—*this is what it will always be like with us. Only with us.*

"Yes," she said on a sigh, breathing the word into

his mouth, feeling his tongue take hold of it, swallow it down. "More."

He growled again, tearing his mouth away long enough to look around them. Then taking her by the hand, he strode the short distance toward the summerhouse, not pausing until they were inside the sunlit room. The sweet scent of the lake and of sunbaked days was more concentrated here, blown in through the open windows, lingering in the walls and the painted wood floors beneath their feet.

Spinning in his arms, she launched herself at him and held tightly to his shoulders. She pressed a dozen unspoken *I love you*s to his lips, letting her kisses tell him everything she'd been holding inside. He grunted, staggering back a step from the force of her onslaught.

A sudden breeze blew harder and kicked the door closed behind them. They both startled but, seeing that they were alone, dove right back into kissing. And they were in a frenzy now. Mouths and tongues tangled together. Teeth scraped wantonly over lips and throats. Hands tugged at knots and buttons until garments sagged. Clothes were not permitted in this new world.

Nicholas shrugged out of his coat and waistcoat with hasty jerking motions, while she pulled the tails of his shirtfront free an instant before he whisked it overhead. And for a moment, she forgot her own name.

Her imagination had not done him justice. He was so hard and sculpted, so completely male, so . . . glorious. She could only stare—and touch—in wonder. Unable to hold back, her hands glided over the corded muscles of his shoulders, squeezing against firm flesh that would not give. She marveled at his form, her senses giddy with awareness.

"I . . . you . . ." Clearly, she was having language

troubles. She tried again, but not with a great deal more success. "Your nipples are darker than mine."

Those dusky discs drew taut beneath her fingertips, ruching like mushroom caps. He expelled a strained breath, his chest and abdomen muscles jolting to life, bunching beneath her hands. Fingers splayed, she roamed down the mat of crisp black hair that covered his broad chest and trailed in a thinner line down his flat abdomen, to form a *T*—the first written letter of the inhabitants of this new world. And further down, her curious, greedy gaze dipped to the heavy bulge filling the fall front of his fawn breeches.

Nicholas lifted her hands away and used them to pull her closer. He nuzzled her, pressing open-mouthed kisses down her neck, nipping her tender skin, tasting the susceptible niche, and sending shivers all the way to her toes.

"I think we should compare, don't you?" Of course, the moment he was able to speak, he said the most rakish thing, his voice husky and deep.

Reaching the edge of her sleeve, he tugged, drawing her dress down one shoulder and then the other. Then he slipped a finger beneath the tapes of her stays and chemise, and pressed his nose against her skin, breathing in as he glided over this newly exposed flesh, telling her that she smelled like sunlight and fresh linens and that he could never, *never* get enough.

She clutched him, fingers threading in his hair as his lips grazed a path along the ribbon border to the dip between her breasts. And then he licked her there.

Her entire body clenched, her nipples growing taut, their pale-pink peaks protruding through the cambric just above the gusseted cups of her stays. Reflexively, she pressed her legs together, and felt a responding kick of pleasure between her thighs and low in her stomach.

Then he did it again, slower this time, pressing his tongue flat and licking deep. Constricted by her sleeves, she arched toward him to get closer. He caught her by the waist, allowing her to bend without risk of falling as he nuzzled her garments out of his way, exposing her to the light.

A hot breath staggered out of him, fanning over her nipple, drawing it tighter still. She was aching now, might actually die if he didn't end the wondrous torment. But he seemed to know this and closed his mouth over the tip. She arched against him on a strangled sob, jolting with pleasure as he suckled the bud deep into his mouth.

A hungry groan rumbled in his throat as he walked her back toward the chaise longue. But before he laid her down, he lifted her dress away, freeing her arms. A few tugs, and her stays followed. Her chemise, next. And she was naked aside from her stockings and slippers.

He stopped, mouth open on a series of panting breaths as if the wind had been knocked out of him. He looked ready to devour every curve, valley, and swell. A garbled sound tore from his throat, telling her without words that he liked the look of her, too, but in that moment, he did not move. One hand lingered at the small of her back, and the other held suspended, hovering inches from her breast, as if he'd forgotten how to proceed.

Reaching up, she took his hand and molded it over her breast, the warmth coaxing her flesh to a new ripeness. This seemed to break him out of a trance.

All at once she was hauled against a wall of heated flesh, crisp dark curls teasing her breasts and midriff. Butter-soft leather met her thighs and pressed against her sex as he lowered her onto the tufted raw silk of the chaise. He didn't seem to have any trouble remembering now.

Arching up, she gripped his shoulders as he kissed her throat, her bare breasts, the underside of her jaw, her lips. He elicited tingles wherever he touched and grazed and kissed. And he was everywhere, mouth and hands molding over her contours, tasting every dip, exploring every mound, counting every rib. Briar was breathless and whimpering, eyes closed, and writhing with pleasure. Sensation merged together until she was one bundle of ecstasy that was likely to explode at any moment. And then she felt the gentle brush of his hand on her inner thigh.

She went still, her focus narrowing to the heat of his breath on her neck. To the sound of his low, reverent murmurs and illicit promises. And to the touch of his fingertips sifting through her curls. She held him tight, his firm back muscles bunching beneath her hands. And he hesitated long enough for her to feel the faintest tremble roll through him.

A rake bent on seduction would hardly tremble. But perhaps a man, who was just as overcome with need as she was, might.

Briar turned her head to meet his lips and kissed him with fervor, feeding him every ounce of love bottled inside her. She tasted the rawness of his groan as he caressed her slick, furled flesh. Helpless, wanton mewls tore from her throat. His movements weren't as practiced as they'd been in the carriage. These were more frantic, urgent, and answered the wild tremors racing through her. Her hips undulated, seeking. She wanted to shatter in his arms, to feel his finger push deep inside her like he'd done before.

He pulled back, instead, gripping her hip and breathing hard against her lips as if trying to gain control. But that was the last thing she wanted. She needed him to bare himself the same way she was doing.

So she soothed him with sure touches, skimming

down his shoulders and over his chest. This time, she followed the hair tapering downward and didn't pause at the waist of his breeches, but rolled the flat of her hand over the hard ridge she discovered there.

He hissed, arching reflexively, squeezing her waist. *"Briar."*

But he did not stop her. He let her explore him over the fabric, press her hand over the thick length of him, extending her arm to reach the taut mound at the base. His breaths quickened in labored rushes of heat against her temples as he endured her fascinated, untutored squeezes and caresses. Yet the instant she fumbled with the fastenings, he took hold of her wrists.

"There would be no going back from this," he said, his dark eyes imploring her to understand.

She smiled, lifting her head to press her lips to his. "I've known that for a while. I suppose you're a bit slower at understanding these things. But don't worry, I'm willing to provide lessons in exchange for—"

Nicholas didn't let her finish. Always interrupting her with a kiss, his lips curved in a grin, teeth nipping her bottom lip in reprimand. Still, somehow, it made the moment all the more tender, their gentle play, the ease they'd always shared, only enhanced.

He kissed her breathless again, endless long pulls, wet and tantalizing. The pleasure of light fingertip brushes against her nipples nearly made her forget her pursuit a moment ago. *Nearly.* But she remembered it soon enough and nothing would dissuade her from unfastening the placard, and sliding her hand inside to find him.

All of him.

And when she did, they both stopped breathing. Their gazes locked, mouths open, lips touching. His solid, heated flesh jolted and instinctively she gripped him, or tried to, her thumb unable to meet her finger. She watched the dark fan of his lashes lower, squeezing tight as if he were in pain.

"Tell me if I'm hurting you. How to please you."

He took several gulps of air before he spoke, his voice raw and shaky. "Every—everything you do"—another ragged breath—"pleases me."

She smiled at his admission, and slid her hand up, fascinated by the smoothness over the granite-like hardness, the heated blood rushing beneath her palm. His eyes were still closed, furrows on his brow, jaw clenched. He was enduring agony to satisfy her curiosity, and she felt another surge of love as she reluctantly released his prodigious flesh.

Then skimming her hands along the solid muscles of his back, she pulled him into an embrace, her open mouth coasting over his throat, tasting the salt of his sweat.

He kissed her temple softly, then lifted her higher on the chaise. Shifting, he gently prodded her thighs apart with his knees. She complied, surprised to feel her legs tremble as he settled between them. He soothed her with tender touches, making her forget all about silly trembling legs as his hands drifted over her, cupping her breasts, abrading the tips with the pad of his thumb. A gentle pinch arced through her, curling her toes as his hips moved in slow circles, thick flesh nudging against the heavy, liquid pulse.

"Briar," he said, his lips grazing hers, "lock your gaze on mine, and keep it there, hmm?"

She nodded and he lowered over her, the weight of him causing her breath to catch on a pleasurable gasp. Lifting her knees, instinctively she wanted to cradle him, to keep him there. Clearly pleased by this, a low, satisfied hum vibrated in his throat. Arm bent beside her head, he

trailed his fingertips through the loose locks of her unbound hair and his eyes turned to velvety cocoa.

He shifted again, pushing his flesh forward, seeking entrance, bit by bit, letting her adjust. Before this
moment, she'd assumed that her body was made to welcome his. After all, women and men had been doing this
successfully for a great number of years. But now, she
was getting the sense that this might not be as easy as
she'd thought.

Even at the first tender prodding, she felt her body
resist, clamping tight around the intruding flesh.

Seeking reassurance, she lifted her head and kissed
him again, eyelids lowering but still locked. Attuned to
her every feeling, his lips brushed hers in small sweeps,
replicating her kiss as if she were made of froth, the best
part of a cup of chocolate. And he pushed again, deeper,
enough to feel the sting of it. She sucked a breath from
his mouth and he took one from hers. He continued to
kiss her with those slow, methodical sweeps, keeping her
craving the firm pressure. And he wedged deeper still,
another sting, a faint burn.

He withdrew, marginally. The way his chest labored
for breath told her that this was not easy for him either.

But then he plunged inside, shunting deep, taking
her cry into his mouth. Her gaze turned watery and his
image blurred, her nails biting into his shoulders. Neither
of them moved. In fact, they weren't even breathing now,
but went still as statues.

At the thought, a gasping laugh bubbled out of her. "I
imagine . . . we look like . . . a pair of naughty statues at
the moment."

A choked sound left him, his body jolting inside her.
After he kissed away the tears clinging to her lashes, she
saw that his expression was part smile, part grimace, his
fingertips toying with the locks of her unbound hair.

"Very naughty statues, indeed." His nose nuzzled hers, pressing her into his nook, earning a sigh.

He kissed her slowly, teasing her mouth open with his tongue, licking inside bit by bit. She tried to press harder, to welcome his lips. But he eased back, keeping it light, nibbling relentlessly.

He was making her crave him again. And he was doing it while whispering shameful things and wicked promises until her entire body tingled with need, pulsing around him.

To assuage the low, thudding heaviness, she rolled her hips and pressed against his pubic bone. He rolled his hips, too, and deepened his kiss, making her gasp at both sensations, the languid, wet slide. This torment continued until they were no longer statues but bodies undulating together.

She didn't know how it happened, but all at once a frenzy started happening inside of her, out of time with his slow, measured movements. She was restless, ready to burst, clawing at his shoulders, wanting to arch, to scream. But he plodded onward, sweat gathering on his brow, keeping her coiled tight, and tighter still.

Then he lifted her hips higher, mouths inches apart but gazes still locked. His muscles flexed as he thrust forward, stretching her, stroking a place inside that made her jolt with a spear of pure ecstasy. She shuddered out an *Oh*.

He agreed. *Oh*, indeed. And then he did it again. And again. Until her eyes went blurry. Was she crying?

The answer came on a sob. The low, desperate sound tore out of her throat as he drove into her, his name tumbling from her lips on broken whimpers, her body clamping around him without any give. Without any release.

"Briar." Her name was a raw plea between clenched teeth, a last request from a dying man. Temple pressed to hers, he growled reprimands, telling her she was too wet, too tight, too perfect, and it was all too much.

"Let's stay here. *Forever*," she moaned, helpless as the first quakes finally claimed her. She broke wondrously, neck arched, and saw starlight behind her eyes, blinding and fierce.

Above her, Nicholas cursed, issuing a guttural shout as he drove deeper. His hips jerked hard, in and in and in, following the greedy pulls of her body until the very last tremor subsided.

∽᪅᪆∾

NICHOLAS WAS unable to move, his body sluggish, drugged. Briar made it even more difficult by fitting her leg over his waist, her soft hands trailing a constant caress over his shoulders, throat, arms, and chest. A man could grow accustomed to this.

But no, he'd better not think like that. It was far too dangerous.

He'd been raised with the firm belief that when a man took a woman's virginity, he married her. No matter what. But he had been down that road before and it only led to hell. He wouldn't do that to Briar.

Damn! He was a bloody fool. He hadn't been thinking clearly when he'd arrived.

Out of his mind with desperation to get here, he'd nearly killed himself in the process. But all he knew was that he'd needed to see her, and when he saw her, it wasn't enough. He had to kiss her, to hold her. And then that wasn't enough either. He had to have her. All of her.

At the thought, an awkward sense of panic staggered through him.

He realized he didn't know how to proceed from here.

Not only had he taken Briar's virginity, but he'd spent himself deep inside her as well. Where he was still, his cock happily twitching in the hot, tight clutch. What does a man do when he defiles a virgin but doesn't want to ruin her life with marriage to him? Let her marry someone else?

No. Definitely not. Every part of him railed against that solution.

Her eyes—a soft, unworldly blue—gradually drifted closed, a whisper on her lips. "I love you."

Nicholas stilled, his musings going silent. His lungs stalled midinhale, his heart midbeat.

"It is common to confuse affection with the notion of love in such moments. Do not worry. It will fade in time." He'd learned that lesson the hard way. And by telling her, he was only trying to protect her. After all, she had so much to learn. She was too idealistic and affectionate, too wonderful and selfless. Too soft and warm.

He felt his heart start up again as his gaze swept over her drowsy features, the fringe of golden lashes resting against her cheeks. He pressed a kiss to her temple, breathing her in.

A man really could get used to this.

She smiled drowsily, eyes still closed. "That may be true for some people, but you love me, too. You just haven't resigned yourself to it yet."

Nicholas could argue with her, explain that he had no heart to give . . . but even an irredeemable rake knew when faced with a losing battle.

Chapter 26

"... they say every body is in love once in their lives, and I shall have been let off easily."

JANE AUSTEN, *Emma*

"*I love you?* Did you honestly say that aloud?" Briar asked the reflection in the full-length mirror stand. She was thoroughly irritated at the woman who gazed dreamily back at her, her cheeks flushed, lips bee-stung and tilting softly at each corner.

She threw the toweling at the looking glass and stormed away, naked after a cool standing bath, and angrily jerked on fresh clothes. The duchess and the other guests would return from the picnic soon.

As for Nicholas, once she'd awoken from a cozy nap, snuggled up and limbs entwined with his on the chaise longue, she'd abruptly remembered what she'd said to him.

I love you . . . And Nicholas had listened to her with the equanimity of a priest hearing a confession. There was no rant from him about breaking the rules of their bargain. No argument about the possibility of marrying her for the sake of her honor or reputation. No reciprocation of her regard—either passionate or resigned. Though she'd imagined a brief scenario involving the former. It was lovely.

But no. Instead, he'd given her another lesson.

It is common to confuse affection with the notion of love in such moments.

Briar wasn't confused. She knew her own heart, and it had demanded that the truth was bared between them.

But you love me, too.

In response, he'd said nothing. Granted, he might have done, but she'd drifted off to sleep. However, when she'd awoken curled in his embrace, he had not acknowledged it. And while he was affectionate—his fingertips trailing down her bare arm, his hand covering hers where it rested above his heart—part of him had gone distant, contemplative. But whatever thoughts were turning inside his mind, he did not say them aloud. Clearly, he had far more control than she had.

"How should we proceed?" he'd asked, pressing a kiss to her forehead.

It was ingrained in her to remove awkwardness from any situation, and so she'd made a jest. "Since we are not naughty statues any longer, I suppose we should don our clothes."

"And after?"

She'd ducked beneath his scrutiny, pressing her forehead against his chest. The consequences of her actions were slowly creeping in, cooling her skin, and making her all-too-aware of her nudity, the slickness between her thighs. He, while still shirtless, had refastened his breeches and still wore his boots.

This had not been planned, on either of their parts.

Not only that, but there was a faint red smear discoloring one corner of the placard. Her blood. There was likely more of it in other places.

He'd been right—there was no going back from this.

"You shouldn't be here when the others return from the picnic. We'll discuss this the next time we meet, after we have clearer heads," she'd said, her tone calm and rather worldly. If she did say so herself.

He'd agreed with a "very well" and another kiss to her temple.

As he'd been after their illicit carriage encounter, he was soothing and attentive. He'd used his handkerchief to bathe away the brightly colored residue from between her thighs before helping her dress.

During this time, they'd spoken in short bursts of conversation, her telling him about how fine the weather had been these weeks, him telling her the same, but adding that he was worried about how little rain they'd had. He told her of the irrigation trenches on his estates, and she'd listened with genuine interest.

But they did not speak about the reason he'd ridden here in such haste, why he'd been angry about reading Mr. Woodlyn's name in the letter, what had happened between them, or what was to come. It was like a parlor game of *guess what I'm not saying.* And the person who spoke the answer was the one who lost.

Hearing the jangle of carriages now, Briar tucked the final pins in her hair and went down to greet the party. However, halfway down the stairs, she stopped, her heart rising to her throat.

Nicholas was here, and with the Duchess of Holliford.

Her Grace lifted her chin as a maid untied her lavender bonnet, keen eyes alighting on Briar. "My dear, look who we found in the village. Can you believe the luck? Lord Edgemont said he'd gone from Blacklowe Manor without a set course in mind, but I don't believe him, for he was too easy to persuade to join us."

Briar felt a blush creep to her cheeks, guessing that he'd been spotted in the village and then badgered into attending.

"I believe it was I who insisted, and rather rudely,"

Nicholas said, disproving her assumption, and stealing her breath all at once.

The duchess clucked her tongue at him, then smiled up to Briar. "The instant he met Mr. Woodlyn, Lord Edgemont stated that if he himself did not attend dinner, there would be an uneven number. And he refused to allow me to endure it."

Mr. Woodlyn! Drat, but Briar had forgotten all about him again.

Her gaze flitted to Nicholas and she saw his onyx eyes glimmer darkly. "How generous of you to think only of your godmother's happiness, my lord."

"I wouldn't say that was my sole reason. You and I were never able to finish our discussion."

"I don't know what you could mean," she said in a rush, gripping the railing and fighting the urge to press her hand against the pulse pounding at her throat. "Since it has been such a very long time since we've met, I'm sure I cannot remember the topic."

"Well, it must be regarding the matches for his cousins, dear. Unless"—the duchess turned to Nicholas—"*he* is thinking about becoming a client of the Bourne Matrimonial Agency. Are you, Edgemont?"

"Well, I do have questions regarding how one would *proceed.*" Arching a single brow, he boldly dropped the question—which she'd cleverly avoided earlier—directly into Briar's lap. Again.

She slid a panicked glance to the duchess, not wanting to have this conversation now, and wondering why he was doggedly pursuing it. "I'm certain I've answered all your questions."

"Perhaps," he said with a weighted pause. "But I seem to recall the mention of a certain *rule* that you have at the agency."

Ah, so that was it. She narrowed her eyes in keen understanding. All of this had to do with her declaration, which had clearly unsettled him. Did he truly imagine he could talk her out of loving him?

Silly man. "We have only one rule, and that is to never fall in love with the client. But I'm certain that will not be an issue."

Because she knew very well that he was never going to become a client.

"Good. I look forward to discussing it later."

Oh, indeed. She would make sure of it.

NICHOLAS UNDRESSED in the bathing chamber, situated at the end of the hall from his room at Hollifield Park. The duchess was kind enough to have her servants send up a few pails of hot water and a clean dressing gown from one of her footman to wear while he waited for his valet to arrive from Blacklowe Manor.

Just as he sank into the copper tub, he heard a faint scritch at the door and a familiar whisper of his name. Unbidden pleasure washed through him in a shiver. He knew he was tempting fate by being here, but they still had a matter to settle. "Enter."

Looking over her shoulder, Briar slipped through the door, and closed it quickly, pressing her back against it. Then she raised her eyebrows at him and grinned, keeping her voice hushed. "Am I interrupting?"

"Not if you plan to wash my back. I'll wash yours in return, *and* your front."

She tapped her finger to her lips, cheeks flushed. "Hmm . . . tempting. However, the others are all in their rooms resting, just down the hall. There's no telling if any one of them might stumble past and hear . . . splashing."

"Then lock the door," he said, already warming to the idea, the shallow level of the water doing nothing to conceal that fact. They could always have their discussion later. Much later.

"There is no key for this door. The duchess has always had a fear that someone might slip and fall in this room, so she doesn't allow it to be locked."

"Pity that. It leaves me at a disadvantage for our discussion."

"You at a disadvantage?" She arched her neck to peer over the side of the tub, eyes greedy as they roved over him, teeth digging into her bottom lip. "I cannot imagine that ever being the case."

"Come here, then."

She shook her head. "I can say what I planned to from this spot."

"Then at least pour that pitcher over my head. Just tuck that flannel beneath the door. It will keep the sound from traveling and be something of a deterrent from intruders."

"Oh, very well." And she did just that, coming to his side to lift the pitcher. "That was very clever of you to put the agency's one rule between us. I imagine it is your design to ensure that I am more careful in what I say when we are alone together."

He noticed that she did not say *what I feel* and he wondered if she was still under the misguided assumption that she really did love him. "I want only clarity between—"

She doused him with water, not letting him finish. "You have made your beliefs amply clear. And I want you to know that I have no intention of dragging a man kicking and screaming to the altar. I'm too aware of the damage a one-sided marriage can do. So you do not have to be afraid of my intentions or even what *you* are feeling toward me."

"I'm not *afra*—"

More water. Damn it all. How much did that pitcher hold?

Behind him, he heard her giggle, and a grin tugged at his mouth. She wanted to play, did she? Taking hold of the sides of the tub, he stood quickly, water sluicing down his body in rivulets. He turned, stepping one leg out.

Briar set the pitcher down on the floor and backed away, wagging her finger at him. "Now, Nicholas, I'm already dressed for dinner."

Then the other leg. The room wasn't overly large, so she couldn't get far. As he took a step toward her, she zagged to the side. He lunged. But he lost his footing.

The next thing he knew, he was lying flat on his arse, elbows hitting smartly on the floor, teeth jarring.

Briar rushed to his side, kneeling. Her soothing hands worried over him, even as she pressed her lips together and her eyes danced with suppressed laughter. "Oh, my love, are you hurt?"

My love. He felt a twinge in the center of his chest at the endearment and all other aches receded, though he refused to acknowledge it. "Only my pride."

Cupping his face, she kissed his damp temple, cheek, nose, lips, lingering briefly. "Can I help mend it?"

"I can think of a way," he said, nibbling against her lips until she sighed into his mouth. He eased her over his lap, lifting her skirts to straddle him, his fingertips gliding over her stockings to the softest skin imaginable. "And you won't wrinkle your dress too badly."

Bright curiosity lit her gaze as she perched her hands on his shoulders, followed by a shadow of trepidation. "And I won't hurt you?"

He chuckled, drawing her closer, his hands on her bare hips. "Quite the opposite."

"You aren't the least bit . . . tender?"

"Ah, right." He pulled back and looked at her, chagrinned. He was so hard and ready to bury himself in her snug heat that all other thoughts fled. "I'm a cad. I wasn't even thinking that it had only been a few hours. You're so small and sensitive to every touch, of course you will need time to recover."

Her delicate brow furrowed. "Am I so different from the other women?"

"Yes." In so many ways, but when he saw her frown, he knew it hadn't been the right thing to say. He clarified, swallowing first and feeling oddly shy. "I've never been with a virgin before, so everything was different and new and sublime."

"Surely your wife . . ."

He shook his head.

"Oh," she said on a breath, musing over this information for a moment as she glanced down at her hands, her fingers weaving through the damp hair on his chest. Then slowly she gave him a cheeky smile. "Did you say *sublime*?"

Chapter 27

⌒‿⌒

"My dear Emma, your own good sense could not
endure such a puppy when it came to the point."

JANE AUSTEN, *Emma*

The following day, Nicholas walked past the edge of the
garden, staring off at the lake where Dilar was currently
sitting in the rowboat, anchored near shore.

At breakfast, she'd asked his godmother for permission to take the boat on the lake, and of course it was
granted. He didn't believe there was a single person who
could ever refuse any request she might have.

It had been on the tip of his tongue to ask if she would
like him to row her, but Mr. Woodlyn had beaten him to it.

Woodlyn—who'd remained so late after dinner last
night that he'd forced an invitation to stay over. Woodlyn—
who'd already stolen every opportunity to *take a turn
with Miss Bourne*, willingness to *play chess should Miss
Bourne like the amusement*, and to *ask Miss Bourne's
opinion on* whatever thought crept into his hollowed-out
gourd of a skull.

Mr. bloody Woodlyn.

Though, this morning, it had turned out well enough,
because she'd refused Woodlyn, claiming that she had to
go out on her own because it was a *surprise*.

Curious, Nicholas ambled closer to the pond, continuing to watch her. Occasionally, she peered over the side,

her hands busily weaving a basket, of sorts, out of broad blades of grass.

"It would not be a terrible hardship for a man to pass the rest of his years in such company, I think," Woodlyn said, rounding the outside of the garden, apparently taking another tour around the lake. "Wouldn't you agree, Lord Edgemont?"

"Not a 'terrible hardship,' no."

"Did I hear correctly, that you are interested in asking Miss Bourne's uncle to find you a wife?"

Ambling near the mossy bank, Nicholas kept to the excuse he'd given his godmother. "I'm considering it."

"Though, it is a peculiarity that her uncle would allow her and her sisters the freedom to assist in such important matters. In small parishes such as these, the congregation typically turns to one like me to find them the ideal spouse."

"And if your wife wanted to assist you, just as Miss Bourne assists her uncle?" Nicholas asked, slyly raising his voice with the knowledge that sound traveled quite well over water.

He caught Briar's attention. She glanced up from her weaving and automatically smiled, the sight warming him.

Woodlyn chuckled. "It is the man's place to ensure the security and happiness of all who reside under his care, is it not?"

"And the woman's place . . . in your esteemed opinion?"

"Why, to do all those little things that women do—sketch pictures, embroider handkerchiefs, and whatnot."

Briar pursed her lips, flicking a frosty blue glance at the cleric, but kept her opinion out of the conversation.

Nicholas subdued a grin. "And is *whatnot* a euphemism for her own interests and pursuits?"

"What interests could a wife have other than seeing to the needs of her husband and children?" Woodlyn picked up a stick and trailed it absently through the tall grasses. Oblivious to his audience, he continued, gradually closing a noose around his own neck. "Certainly, a man who is courting a young woman provides allowances for a freer spirit, which one might have in their youth before true obligations are required of them. Even he may have a certain degree of wildness that needs tamed. But it is up to a man to rule himself, to take firm control and give up amusements when he is, at last, settled."

"Are you saying that a married man is not permitted a bit of fun, even with his own wife?"

"I have counseled a few young, newly married men, and I have advised them to temper their passions quickly and to strap on the yoke of life."

Nicholas shuddered. If this was the type of matchmaking provided by Woodlyn, he was surprised that anyone in the parish married at all. He made it all sound like nothing more than an obligation one performed—get married, have children, hate the rest of your life.

Actually, that sounded eerily similar to what Nicholas's own marriage might have been.

"After all, a married man does not keep a sporting gig and jaunt about the countryside. That is the pastime of a bachelor who is winnowing away the husk of youth."

"Don't you have such a gig?" Nicholas had heard all about it in many letters over the past two weeks. Pages and pages of it riding over the countryside, until he'd hoped that the wheels would fall off.

"I do, indeed. But I am ready"—Woodlyn glanced out across the water and waved when he saw Briar looking at him—"for a landau. And you, my lord? Are you equally ready to—"

"Strap on the yoke of life?" Nicholas was unable to say it without a smirk. "I'm a bit of a free spirit. I enjoy many amusements, which I want to enjoy for as long as

I am able. And, were I to marry, I should like someone to enjoy them along with me, and even invite me to enjoy some of hers."

"Hmm . . ." Woodlyn mulled this over, swiping the stick through the grass, so lost in his own thoughts that he missed the best surprise of all.

Briar extended her foot over one side of the boat, while she dipped her shallow basket into the reedy water on the other side. Then, after only a moment, came up with a pair of wriggling fish.

In that instant, the sun glinted off the surface of the water in a shower of sparks, blinding him. He recalled with perfect clarity the afternoon she'd shared her scone and told him of his perfect wife.

All she wants is a honeymoon beside a lake, alone with you. And there, you'll discover that there is more to her than you could have anticipated.

Perhaps you'll learn that . . . oh, I don't know . . . that she is a remarkable fisherman.

And Nicholas was suddenly wondering if Briar should add soothsayer to her list of accomplishments.

FROM BENEATH the stone arch of the side garden that afternoon, Briar watched Mr. Woodlyn's curricle hasten down the drive.

Not surprisingly, after overhearing his conversation with Nicholas, she no longer felt conflicted about his attentions. Nor did she worry about wounding his feelings and ruining Temperance's chance of marrying him. She wouldn't wish such a man on her worst enemy, let alone her dearest friend.

She growled, swiping a climbing jasmine off the vine, and tore its fragrant petals free, one by one. "Why am I such an abominable failure at matchmaking?"

"I wouldn't say that," Nicholas said, giving her a start as he came up beside her. "Mr. Woodlyn was quite smitten with you. I'm sure he would have made a very fine husband, and might have even let you out of the house every now and then."

His mouth curved in a grin that was a bit too pleased and too smug for her liking.

She narrowed her eyes and tossed the wrecked blossom to the ground. "For your information, he was never supposed to be smitten with *me*. I'd intended him for Temperance all along."

She relished the quick blink of shock that slackened his jaw.

"And the letters?"

"They were only meant to entice her," she admitted, though with a sudden rise of trepidation as she remembered that they had also brought Nicholas here.

He eyed her shrewdly.

She looked down at his cravat and reached up to dust a few crumbs from it. "It might have been in the back of my mind—the very back, darkest corner, mind you— to make you the ever-smallest bit jealous as well. Why are you covered in crumbs?" She gasped, lifting her gaze abruptly and wagging her finger at him. "You found the scones, didn't you?"

"I did, indeed." Unrepentant to the core, he had the nerve to lick his lips.

"They were supposed to be a surprise for later."

"Mmm . . ." He wagged a finger back at her, touching the tip of her nose. "But what I cannot fathom is how Mrs. Darden's scones could have traveled all this way and taste as if they were fresh out of the oven. Unless some little minx gave the recipe to my godmother's cook, when she refused to share it with mine."

She set her hands on her hips. "As a matter of fact, I

did not share the recipe. Mrs. Darden would never have approved. It is a family secret. She did, however, teach each of us girls how to make them ourselves, along with many other valuable skills."

"Like catching fish in baskets?"

"She taught me how to weave the basket, but using it to catch fish was something I learned on my . . ." She lost track of her thoughts as he crowded closer, skimming his finger over her lips and down her throat. She was suddenly breathless. ". . . on my own. Nicholas, you cannot kiss me here. Someone will see."

"Just one. Your lips are too tempting." He nibbled at the corners of her mouth, his hand at her nape, the other dipping to the small of her back, pulling her flush. "I simply can't resist."

Briar smiled and slid her arms around his neck. It wasn't a declaration of love, but it was the next best thing.

Chapter 28

"He owed it to her, to risk any thing that might be involved in an unwelcome interference, rather than her welfare . . ."

JANE AUSTEN, *Emma*

"We've come to steal you away for an outing," Temperance announced almost the second she stepped foot in Holliford Park manor the following morning. Enthusiasm fairly vibrated from her.

If her friend possessed a pair of wings, Briar would be embracing the tallest hummingbird imaginable.

The missive Briar had received yesterday afternoon was just as wild—a few lines announcing her plan to visit, and *a wonderful surprise* to follow, and to be prepared to depart at once.

"Can we not pause to bid everyone a good day, first?"

Temperance blushed and looked around to see that the Duchess of Holliford was framed in the archway of the sitting room, just off the foyer. "Forgive me, Your Grace. It's been such a long time since I've seen my dearest friend that I forgot myself."

"No need to apologize. Mrs. Fitzherbert and I greet each other in the same fashion," the duchess said, her mouth drawn into a tiny smirk, apparently pleased with her own jest.

Briar laughed at the vision that conjured—the two

older women giggling like schoolgirls while clutching their shawls, but then abruptly altering to austere expressions when another person might come into the room.

Daniel stepped into the open door next, greeting her with a shy smile and a bow before seeing the duchess and offering the same to her. "Your Grace."

Temperance, already over her embarrassment, tugged on Briar's arm. "Fetch your bonnet. And where is Nicholas? Ah, there you are, cousin."

He ambled toward them with a covered basket in hand, mouth moving suspiciously as he gave Briar an unrepentant look. "I came upon the rest of the scones, purely by accident and not rummaging about the larder at all. Assuming you planned to bring them along, I decided to do my part."

Daniel, recovering from his shyness, strode past her. "Are they Mrs. Darden's scones?"

"Even better," Nicholas said, rotating evasively as Daniel reached for the basket. If it wasn't for the compliment, Briar might have been quite cross. Instead, her heart kicked in a few additional beats, feeling quite too large for the cage of her ribs.

Temperance came up beside her. "I have the best news to share with you. Let's away so I can tell you all of it, hmm?"

"Very well, for if we do not leave this instant, I'm afraid there will be no scones left by the time we reach the carriage."

After bidding the duchess a good day, and her doing the same with a pleased smile on her lips, they left Holliford Park in an open carriage, sunlight peering down at them through a gradual gathering of clouds.

Temperance looked up at the sky with worry. "I hope it does not rain, for I want today to be perfect."

"And am I ever going to learn our destination, or is

that part of the grand surprise?" Briar asked, watching Nicholas and Daniel on the opposite bench, each with a hand on the lip of the basket.

Temperance turned, angling toward her. "Before we get into all that, you must tell me about your gentleman. Your Mr. Woodlyn."

"Well . . ." She exchanged a wry look with Nicholas. "It was all a terrible misunderstanding, I'm afraid. He portrayed himself as a much different person at first, but after your cousin arrived, I was able to see his true nature."

"It's rather fortunate then that Nicholas read your every correspondence," Temperance said, a sly glance darting between the two of them. "When he snatched the last letter out of my hand and left without a word, I never imagined that we would learn he'd ridden all the way to Holliford Park, and even more shockingly, that he'd decided to stay. I thought, perhaps, his horse had gone lame."

"You make a very good point," Briar said, feeling a bit daring as she sent a grin across the carriage. "I never inquired, my lord. Why did you remain at Holliford Park?"

His lips quirked back. "Perhaps I enjoy the pond."

"There is a pond at Blacklowe Manor," Temperance supplied.

"Ah yes, but there isn't a summerhouse, and I'm rather fond of those."

Briar turned away from the warmth in his gaze and tilted her face up to the sky so that anyone would think her cheeks were pinkened by the sun. Of course, the sky chose that precise moment to darken, lavender-tinged clouds crowding closer together.

"Come now, cousin, you could build one of those, if you truly wish, so that is not an answer."

"If I were Nicholas," Daniel said, sneaking a hand into

the basket, "I'd stay wherever I could find these scones and never leave."

Nicholas did not respond, but turned his gaze heavenward as well, a contemplative frown on his lips. "How much further to our destination, Teense?"

"Not far, for the place is only five miles from Holliford Park."

A cold shiver skirted down Briar's limbs at the mention of the distance. The cottage where she grew up, where she had lived with Mother, was only five miles from the duchess's residence. Though, surely that was a coincidence.

She shrugged off the sensation, blaming it on the cool breeze here beneath the shade of elms on either side of the road.

It was a familiar setting. The village was just to their left, houses and old stone buildings with thatched roofs, nestled up to a narrow cobblestone lane that led to the square. With her sisters, she'd taken this path many times in her youth, but not once after Mother died. They'd gone to live with Uncle Ernest, and his estate was nearly twelve miles in the opposite direction. Even when they were invited to visit Holliford Park, they never found reason to return. It had been too painful.

"And now for my news," Temperance said after they'd chatted for a while. Drawing in a steadying breath, she shook out her hands as if her short gloves were making them hot. Then, after a moment, she laid them in her lap, her expression earnest and excited. "I've been exchanging letters with John Cartwright."

If Briar had been suddenly bounced out of the carriage and run over by it, the sensation would have made less of an impact. "You have?"

"When you said you were not bothered at all by our

introduction, I gave myself over to the fullness of the feelings I had the instant we met. And when he wrote to me that first exceptional note, I knew he'd felt something, too. From that point, and from each correspondence since, my affections have only grown. He has confessed the same to me. I've already told Daniel."

"In great, unending detail," Daniel said, rolling his eyes.

"And Mother knows, too. In fact, that is where we are headed today. It's rather serendipitous that he should have a house here, *and* to be visiting north Hampshire precisely when we are."

"Temperance," Nicholas said, his voice low with warning as he sat forward, looking from his cousin to Briar, his surprise and displeasure apparent. "You should have mentioned this beforehand."

His cousin disagreed with a shake of her head. "You couldn't be more wrong. Briar understands these things better than most. And I didn't want to tell her because she would have felt obligated to arrange for harp music and rose petals. Isn't that right?"

Laughing, Temperance clasped her hand. Briar nodded but looked down to shield her expression beneath the brim of her hat. She wasn't certain she could fix a smile on her face. Too frozen with shock, any movement at all might break her.

There was so much news coming at her all at once that she hardly knew how to process it.

Then before she could even begin, the driver turned down another lane, passing a familiar obelisk with the letter *C* cut into the pitted stone. *C* for *Cartwright*.

Unspeakable dread filled Briar. She had traced that letter hundreds of times. When she was young, and still Briar Bourne-Cartwright, she'd thought of the marker as a wishing stone. If she held her breath, ran around it, and traced every *C* with her finger, it would surely work to bring Father home and make Mother well again.

But he never came. Not for his wife. Not for his legitimate children. And so, years later, Briar and her sisters had abandoned his name, like he had abandoned them.

"Briar," Nicholas said quietly, his low tone so tender that she felt the first prickle of tears.

Without looking at him, she shook her head in silent communication. *Not now, when I'm so close to falling apart.*

Temperance did not seem to notice her distress. Understandably, she was caught up in the thrill of meeting someone she was fond of. Briar could not fault her for that.

"Oh, I think we are here. Is that he? Daniel, move your enormous head out of the way."

"Miss Bourne, are you unwell?" Daniel asked.

Gathering the last bit of strength, she flashed a glance up to him and hoped that a smile touched her lips. "Perfectly hale. A bit too much sun, perhaps."

No sooner had she uttered the last syllable than the rain began, proclaiming her a liar. It was a small scattering at first. The droplets warm on her chilled skin. They beaded up on her forearms, magnifying the sparse golden hair. She almost wished she could disappear into one of the tiny domes.

The driver spurred the horses, jostling the party—and Temperance with a gleeful giggle—as they drove the final stretch to the cottage where Mother had died.

Briar still couldn't look up. It would be like seeing Mother's eyes drift closed for the last time. To see her skin change from glowing cream to the ashen gray of death, like the façade. To hear her mournful sighs slowly give way to that awful, wet, and wheezing final breath.

It stood to reason that someone in her father's family would live here, she supposed. But in the back of her mind, she'd always thought of it as a crypt more than a house. Memories died here. So did her childhood.

The carriage came to a halt, the horses shifting nervously as if they sensed it, too. Nicholas called for the driver to help raise the top panel. Daniel was quick to leap down, and took Temperance by the waist, helping her without waiting for the step.

"Miss Bourne," Daniel said, his hand appearing in her line of sight, which was still limited to her lap.

"I have her," Nicholas answered, his boots shifting into view. He laid a hand on her shoulder and leaned down to whisper, "Can you hold on another minute while I put up the hood?"

She nodded and took comfort in the rocking of the carriage beneath his feet, the jerk of movement as he freed the corner fastenings. Then at once, she was enshrouded in shadow, listening to the rain patter against the leather hood and the sound of Nicholas's breaths.

He shuffled past her and leapt to the ground, turning with his arms extended. She lifted her face, needing the contact of his gaze.

"I . . . I'm not certain I can," she rasped, her throat raw from holding back years of pain. Anguish that she wasn't aware could ache this much after so long of being buried deep. But that was the problem, she supposed. She'd never had an outlet for all the hurt. They never talked about Mother or Father or their half siblings, or anything really. And oh, how she wished they would have done. If she'd had the chance to release the pain, she might have filled up the void with her own strength instead. Yet she didn't have any right now.

"It'll be fine. I'll be by your side all the while. I'll never leave you for an instant," he promised.

Briar told herself she could do this, and that she didn't need to be shielded, protected, or kept in the dark any longer. But she couldn't move.

Her gaze flitted past him to see Mr. Cartwright holding an umbrella over Temperance's head as he escorted her inside. The door was open wide enough for her to glimpse the banister she used to slide down whenever Ainsley wasn't watching. Jacinda's name was probably still carved into the bottom stair tread. Mrs. Darden had once tripped over Briar's doll and spilled an entire pot of tea on the round Persian rug.

So many memories.

"I wasn't expecting this either, but I know you're strong enough to sit in the parlor and get to know your brother for one afternoon."

She stuttered out a breath. "The last time I was in that parlor, my mother's casket was there."

Nicholas drew her exhalent in on a hiss, then let it out with an oath. "This was your home? I didn't . . . *Damn.* I'm taking you back. No, wait, Blacklowe Manor would be closer."

She nodded, willing to go anywhere. It didn't matter. "But don't tell them. Just say that I'm . . . suddenly unwell. I don't want to spoil Temperance's day. Even though I know it will disappoint her."

He was only gone for a minute.

Then he was beside her, crooning softly as the first sob took hold, his arm a comforting brace around her shoulders. Pulling her onto his lap, he never stopped holding her, all the way to Blacklowe Manor.

Chapter 29

"Nothing hastily done; nothing incomplete. True affection only could have prompted it."

JANE AUSTEN, *Emma*

They made it to Blacklowe Manor, but it wasn't a journey Nicholas would care to repeat anytime soon. The roads weren't prepared to take so much rain at once, and it made travel treacherous on occasion.

On their dash inside, the paving stones were slick enough that Nicholas just lifted Briar into his arms until they were safely inside. The housekeeper was there to fuss over her immediately, whisking her away to a guest chamber before Nicholas could help with her knotted bonnet ribbon.

Pushing a wet hank of hair from his forehead, he stared after Briar's retreating figure. He wished he'd had more time alone with her. She'd cried only briefly, until the driving rain had drawn her attention and nervous glances out the window as water sluiced over the sides, forging deep, wheel-eating runnels into the road.

"Not far now," he'd said whenever they hit a rut, and he'd tighten his hold, hoping to reassure her. "Though there's time enough to talk about what is pressing on your mind."

And on your heart, too, he'd thought, wanting to alleviate the pain he'd glimpsed.

She'd offered a watery laugh. "From our previous conversations, I believe you know that I speak on every topic, regardless of whether you want me to or not."

Did she think that she could fool him?

He'd chided her softly without a word, but by pressing a kiss to the top of her head and expelling a sigh, willing to be patient.

"It is a common enough story," she'd said after a moment. "Our father was unfaithful. He abandoned us. My mother died. And until today, I didn't know how raw I still felt inside. You see, my family never talked about it. At least, not with me in the room."

"Then I suppose it's lucky that you are here with me, instead, *and* it just so happens that I have a pair of ears. I'm willing to lend them to you for as long as you like."

She'd shaken her head at first and then, issuing a shaky breath, she'd wobbled a nod. "Might I also have the use of your shoulder and your arms around me?"

You can have any part of me you like, he'd thought, but had not spoken the words aloud.

Instead, he'd simply pulled her close and listened. And even after their journey, he still yearned to hear more, to learn everything about her childhood, her life, the dreams that she'd lost, the hopes she still had. To climb inside her head and hear every thought. To be inside her lungs and feel every breath. Inside her heart for every beat.

Looking down at the empty hall now, he didn't like that she was so far away from him. He wanted to be at her side in case she needed his arms around her, his shoulder to cry upon, his lips to soothe away her tears.

He hated the futility of these urges. They made him feel restless, desperate.

A cold shudder raked through him like claws underneath his skin. After his marriage, he'd vowed to neve become that needy man again, to beg for affection, to exist on the smallest shreds of attention. But now . . .

The butler handed Nicholas a flannel and he angrily swiped it through his hair. "Where is my mother?"

"Lord Edgemont," Bartrand said, helping him off with his coat. "I'm afraid that her ladyship and the Countess Edgemont left with Mrs. Lake and her daughter early this morning to the Lakes' hunting lodge."

Which meant that Nicholas and Briar were essentially alone. And unless the rain let up soon, they would be stranded for the night. Unchaperoned. They needed to leave as quickly as possible, and before anyone was the wiser.

Or else the only way to save her reputation would be marriage. Society's strictures would demand it

He'd been led to the altar before for such a reason.

Nicholas strode to his chamber for a change of clothes, waiting for the usual dose of bitter cynicism to roil violently in his gut.

Strangely, it did not come. Though, perhaps he'd grown so jaded that not even this prospect affected him, or even left a bad taste on his tongue. Then again, perhaps after assisting Briar for these many weeks and being bombarded by the subject of matrimony, he'd built up a tolerance. It was possible, he supposed. Or perhaps after taking her virginity, he'd already resigned himself to the idea.

Still, those thoughts did not hit the target soundly, but were just shy of the blackened center ring.

Nicholas feared that the true reason was more complicated. That, perhaps, something else—or someone else, rather—had altered his opinion. Had made the idea of marriage not so terrible.

But then reality and experience intruded and his blood

turned to an icy flood in his veins. Marriage was only for the needy and naive, for desperate fools and romantics who believed in perfect counterparts and eternal love.

In other words, not a man who knew better. Not a man like him.

After donning fresh clothes, Nicholas found Briar in the gallery, her hands clasped behind her back as she studied his wedding portrait—the only one still in existence. Mother hadn't permitted him to destroy this one. So it hung here, serving as a reminder, lest he ever forget.

Briar's gaze did not leave the mismatched couple as he approached and stopped beside her. "She was lovely."

He'd once thought so, too, but then he'd glimpsed underneath her disguise. Even so, as a young man, it hadn't mattered that Marceline was cold and often cruel, barely able to tolerate him. He'd only wanted her to be his, and his alone.

"I wasn't a good husband," he said, needing Briar to understand, to strip away whatever naive vision she saw whenever she looked at him with that soft wistful expression. "I was young and awkward, too clumsy, not sure of myself at all. The combination made me"—he cleared his throat—"pathetic."

Briar laid a hand on his arm. "We are all uncertain at times. I'm sure she understood and loved you all the more for it."

He shook his head, biting down a bitter laugh as he stared at Marceline's pitiless violet eyes. "Ours was not a love match. As I mentioned before, I was not her first lover. Only I wasn't aware of it at the time she stole into my chamber late one night and kissed me while I was asleep. And when I awoke to find her beneath the coverlet, she permitted my advances. *Endured* my hastened, inept attentions. Then, weeks afterward, she claimed that she was with child. We married by special license."

"And was she?"

He could hear the sound of his teeth grinding together, the creak of bone on bone. "My brother's child—another fact I learned later."

Briar stepped in front of him, forcing his attention to her soft wistful expression, to the welcome and understanding he saw in her eyes. "You know about betrayal as well, then."

He nodded and took her hand, pressing their palms together, fingers catching. "According to what she'd confessed the morning of the accident, she and my brother had planned my wedding from the start. You see, Mother had handpicked James's wife, Catharine, but he'd always loved Marceline. So in turn, Marceline spent years acting as Catharine's friend, doting on her, sharing confidences, making it impossible for her to see the truth. Then, when Marceline discovered she was with child, James came up with a plan to keep her near him and watch his child grow."

Briar gasped, her wispy brows threaded. "That's despicable. To use you. To toy with your affections. Your own brother."

"Yes, well, we all have our sordid tales. The things that were once raw but now are covered in calluses."

"No wonder you abhor the very idea of marriage." She launched herself at him, her arms wrapping tightly around his waist, vibrating with fury. On *his* behalf.

A startled puff of air left his lungs, the void giving way to a sudden conflagration of joy and wonder that left him shaken.

"I hate what you suffered," she hissed, vehement. "Absolutely despise it! I want to take away every single one of those days for you. If I were a surgeon, I would cut it out of your memory and burn it so that it was nothing more than ash."

"You're rather violent. Remind me to keep sharp knives out of your reach," he said, attempting to make light of it. To ignore the firestorm burning inside him, hotter than a thousand sparks, more intense than a thousand stars. He held her with equal ferocity, lips pressed to her temple, heart thudding in swift, panicked beats.

"And the courtesans you mentioned once . . ." She lifted her gaze to his. "You sought them out because of how Marceline had made you feel?"

He didn't intend to respond, but felt an involuntary nod when she took his face in her hands. Then she rose up on her toes and began to scatter kisses all over him.

"You could have been clumsy with me. We could have learned together. I would have loved all your awkward fumbling, because you would have been mine. All mine. And I wouldn't have shared you."

He growled in response, capturing her mouth in a fierce kiss. Reprimanding her for saying those tender things. For wanting the gawky, callow young man he'd once been. For making him wish to go back in time to make that possible. But she deserved so much more than *him*. She deserved everything he wasn't capable of giving her.

He broke free, pressing his forehead to hers, gripping her hips, letting her feel his hard, unrelenting need. "I have to deliver you to the housekeeper. She is the only one who can act as chaperone."

"Let me love you first." She smiled, not playing fair as she nibbled her way along his jaw. "Show me how to please you without wrinkling my dress."

Her adept little fingers started flicking open his waistcoat buttons. And he, pathetic fool that he was, didn't stop her. Instead, he took her by the hand and hauled her through the nearest door—a small sewing room with a quilt stand by the windows, where beads of water scattered prisms of sunlight into the room.

The rain had stopped. The garden below already appeared dry, soaking up the shower like a sponge. The roads would be clear soon.

She giggled when he pulled her eagerly to him. "A hedonist to your very core."

"Yes, and had we more time, I would take you to bed, tie you up, and do terrible, wicked things to you."

A tremor quaked through her as she panted into his mouth, pausing her attempts to pull his shirtwaist free. "Can we not still pretend?"

"Now who is the hedonist?"

"I suppose I am. I just want to feel you all the time." Her hand slipped inside, splaying over his abdomen, drifting up and over, everywhere she could reach. Then she lifted the linen shirt and pressed her face against him, inhaling deeply. "Your skin has so many different, glorious textures . . . and your scent makes my pulse race. Part of me wishes I could make clothes out of you, just so I could wear you next to my skin all day long."

"Disturbing notion," he lied. The truth was, he wanted to do the same to her. Clearly, they were both mad as hatters.

She pressed frantic kisses over his flesh, drifting down to the waist of his trousers, nipping his hair with her teeth, robbing him of breath. "Well, we are in a sewing room. I could make quick work of you, stitch you into my chemise."

He couldn't respond. All at once, he was overwhelmed by that terrifying sense of desperation. He wanted to be rid of it, wanted to spit it out, but it wouldn't come. It clawed up his throat, strangling him, a tight knot lodging there.

Tenderly, he took her face in his hands and brought her mouth to his, hoping that she could untangle him. Then, not so tenderly, he kissed her, delving deep, shuddering with the violence of these feelings. He would die if he couldn't get this out of him. He knew nothing about untying knots.

The way she clung to him, greedy whimpers rising from her lips, told him that she understood. *I'll untie it for you. I can feel it now. We're so close, just don't stop.*

He turned, pressing her back to the door. Gripping the lush curve of her bottom, he bunched her skirts up and out of the way, lifting her against him. And her sweet moan filled his mouth as she arched into his hand.

She was wet, his fingers drenched. He pulled them into his mouth and closed his eyes, tasting her nectar on his tongue, wanting more, wanting to take his time, to feast on her for days. But the knot of this *thing* inside him wouldn't wait. It was only growing larger, immense. He was afraid it would be trapped in his throat, in his chest, until his last breath.

Freeing his cock, he positioned the thick head at her swollen slit. Trembling from the rawness that tore through him, he drove into her slick, tight heat and swallowed her gasp. *Yes, love. Yes.*

Fully impaled, he went still, savoring the sweet clench surrounding him. He was already so close to losing himself.

"Never stop. Promise me," she ordered, nipping his bottom lip. Her eyes were blue-glazed with passion, hooded, her hips hitching in tiny spasms, urging him onward.

But he couldn't promise—he still couldn't speak. The knot was even bigger now, wedging deeper with every new thrust, every frenzied kiss.

He was choking on it, neck arched, close to surrender.

"Briar," was all he could say. And so he said it over and over again until she understood everything. She answered him by crying out his name in return.

Her body convulsed, gripping violently. And he was barely able to wrench his flesh out of her, and spill in thick pulses against her thigh.

❧

HE HELD her against him stiffly, his arm an unbreakable band around her waist. When his breath rushed out in a guttural groan, punctuated by her name, it sounded like a declaration.

A pledge.

Smiling, Briar let her head fall against his shoulder, her body thrumming where they were just connected a minute ago. "I don't like it when you leave me."

She knew she sounded insane, but she couldn't seem to help it. More than anything, she wished to keep part of him next to her. Locked inside her. Always.

He kissed her temple, rasping the tails of his shirt against her inner thigh. "I can't take the risk of spilling my seed inside you again, not like the first time."

"I hadn't even thought about that. I just assumed that you . . . being a rake and all . . . Oh, I don't know," she murmured with a blush, feeling woefully green.

He set her down carefully, his gaze not meeting hers. Then taking a step back, he folded the end of his shirttail in on itself before tucking it in his trousers. "That was a mistake. I should have taken better care."

A mistake. Ouch. That pinched her heart a bit. She splayed her fingers over it like a shield.

Then as another realization settled in, her hand drifted down to cover her flat midriff. A spike of worry lanced through her. "And if I'm carrying your child?"

He glanced down, then quickly looked away. "We'll face it *if* or when we must."

So he would marry her, but under duress. "Like an unpleasant chore. How lovely. Essentially, marriage to me would be like emptying a chamber pot every day for the rest of your life."

"That's not what I meant, Briar. You deserve more than what we can have together, more than these elicit tuppings. You should be wooed with tender care, not thrust up against a door."

"But this was exactly what I asked for, if you'll recall. Sometimes I feel wild inside, and I like that I can become unleashed with you. No one else understands that part of me. I've been sheltered, and protected, and treated like a porcelain doll for most of my life . . ."

"Which is precisely what I should have done."

She huffed, her hands on her hips. "Then why didn't you?"

"I don't know." Tension radiated from him. He stared at her intently as if he were about to spill out every secret he'd ever had. Then something akin to fear glanced over his expression. His pupils turned to tiny dots, a splatter of ink. He looked away and shrugged. "Because I'm selfish."

She felt that *something* still lingering in the air between them, raw and close to unfurling. She moved closer and took his hand, a slight tremor rushing from him into her. "Or, perhaps, because you love me, too."

"Briar," he warned.

"Nicholas, this is love. I'm sure of it." She lifted his hand and placed it over her heart. "Do you feel that? My heart lurches every time you are near. My skin aches when we are not touching. And you may be right that these are only symptoms brought on by pleasure. But that does not explain why I long for your happiness, and to hear your wicked laugh, to see your dark eyes turn soft and velvety whenever you look at me, to watch your hair change to gray over time."

"This is the reason I made that rule in the first place." He pulled his hand away and stalked to the window.

She followed, and leaned against the other side. "I know you've been hurt, but you can trust me with your heart. I'll take special care of it . . . if you'd let me."

"And who would take care of yours, London's most irredeemable rake?" He laughed without humor and shook his head. "No. I won't allow it."

She rolled her eyes. Honestly. Did the man know nothing about love? She couldn't simply stop because he decreed it. "Oh, very well. Then you'll have to give it back. But first put it in a box, stuffed with rose petals and wrapped in silk ribbons. The return of a heart should be done with a bit of fanfare, don't you think?"

The corner of his mouth quirked. Reaching out, he tugged her into his embrace with a resigned sigh. "Whatever am I going to do with you?"

She burrowed closer, fitting perfectly. "I can think of five scenarios off the top of my head—three are rather scandalous. Would you like to hear them?"

Chapter 30

"You look as if you would not do such a thing again."

JANE AUSTEN, *Emma*

Before Nicholas could be tempted by any more of Briar's scenarios, he sent for a carriage.

"A curricle, really?" She slid him a wry glance as they stepped out into the sunlight beaming down from the pools of brilliant blue, breaking through the clouds. "Could you have chosen a more open or snug vehicle?"

He gave her little waist a playful squeeze as he lifted her onto the seat. "Strange, but I thought you were rather fond of jaunts through the countryside. Or is my company not as good as Mr. Woodlyn's?"

"I think you know the answer. But if you are trying to ensure that my reputation is secure, I think you're forgetting one small thing."

He cleared his throat and raised his brows. *Small?*

Her cheeks colored bright pink. "Not that, of course. I meant the fact that we left Temperance and Daniel in a closed landau."

"Which currently has a broken wheel after our mad dash, and I did not want to wait for it to be repaired." He swung up into the seat beside her and released the break. Before they set off for Holliford Park, he curled her arm in the crook of his.

"But where is Daniel going to sit? Surely not on the boot" She glanced over her shoulder to the small platform, no larger than a satchel.

"He'll learn to hold on, I imagine."

"You seem surer of him now. When you first spoke of finding him a bride, I did not have the impression that you had faith in his abilities."

"When it comes to his choosing a wife, I don't. I still need you."

She turned her head and cupped a hand over her ear. "I'm sorry, but could you repeat that last part?"

"I still need—" He stopped the instant he saw her cheeky grin. "Minx."

Clearly, she was determined to bring him to his knees. He feared that she could accomplish that with the barest nudge of her finger, then down he would go. Straight off a cliff.

He was fairly certain he wouldn't survive the fall. Not with Briar.

At least with Marceline, he'd had bitterness and dark, seething hatred to see him through. But every part of Briar was light and laughter. Uninhibited joy and hope. All that was sweet and good in the world. She was everything.

When he gazed down at her head resting on his shoulder, he was overcome by a fierce need to keep her here beside him, right where she belonged. He could not imagine a happier place to stay for all the days of his life. He felt a pleasant tremor roll through him, marveling at how appealing the notion was.

"Briar," he said, weighing his words carefully, "why did you first decide to accept that challenge to find me a bride, knowing that I was a rake?"

She stared off in the distance, thoughtful. "Because of something the woman had said, about how much you loved your family and you were loyal to a fault. I knew that a man like that, even a rakish one, could never be wholly irredeemable."

Then she grinned up at him and he was caught by a sensation of falling—stomach lifting, suspended, heart in his throat as if the horses had got away from him and they were tumbling over a precipice and into an abyss.

All at once, he knew what the *thing* was that had been choking him, lodged in his throat, wanting to get out. And he also realized it was already too late to guard himself against it.

He'd flouted his own rules, heeded none of his own warnings, and found himself terrifyingly, exhilaratingly in love with her.

Soft cornflower blue peered up at him fondly, unblinking, and without the smallest degree of surprise. *You're a bit slow, my love,* her gaze seemed to say just before she settled against him once more.

He was in love. There was something else in him as well, something fragile and new and trembling. Hope.

He'd never been particularly content with his life, and yet he'd never yearned for more either. Actually, he'd never thought it was possible. But then Briar swept in—with her romantic scenarios, her *cup of chocolate* kisses, her bubbly laugh and dark humor—and showed him what it might be like to be happy. Truly happy.

Briar Bourne had managed the impossible, it seemed. She'd made the idea of marriage . . . well . . . enticing.

On a deep breath, he pressed a kiss to the top of her head.

"Besides," she continued, unaware of the earth-shattering transformation that had come over him, "I have it under good authority that rakes can reform if they choose to. In fact, the only thing I would deem completely unforgivable is an act of betrayal against one's own family. But I'm sure you and I share that belief."

He murmured in agreement, a sudden chill stealing through to the marrow of his bones, robbing him of that warm, new contentment. *Completely unforgivable.*

"Though, the instant the woman said your name, I knew that Temperance's most beloved cousin would never be capable of doing something like that. You love them far too much to hurt them."

Nicholas didn't deserve her good opinion, not with the mistakes he'd made. And now they festered like a boil beneath the skin.

At first, he'd wanted to ignore the pain his betrayal had caused, spending months in the country with Daniel, digging trenches and pretending that everything was as it should be. Then, as the melancholy lingered, Nicholas had tried to cover up his guilt by hiring a matchmaker to find a replacement bride.

But he should have known that such a wound would only grow larger, spreading beneath the skin until everything near it was left raw and infected.

He could lose Briar over this. He could lose everyone he cared about. And yet, he knew there was no way to move forward without owning up to the pain he'd caused. There could be no secrets between them, nothing dark and festering.

The only way to treat an injury of this magnitude—he reasoned—was to lance it cleanly, drain the poison, and pray that it healed.

He needed to tell Daniel the truth, without further delay. Then he would tell Briar, and hope that, by some miracle, she could forgive him.

❧

BRIAR DID not ask Nicholas to linger at Holliford Park. For most of the drive back, he'd seemed restless and pre-occupied.

His conversation had turned laconic, as if he were weighing every word carefully, which wasn't like him. His usual manner was to say whatever he was thinking, no matter how shocking. Needless to say, this alteration caused a ripple of unease to skate through her.

Yet she managed to shrug it off, preferring to assume that this shift was due to nothing too dire, but likely stemmed from the rutted state of the roads and an eagerness to fetch his cousins. So she urged him to depart and promised to explain his absence to the duchess.

She squeezed his arm one last time and through a great feat of self-restraint—which she would reward herself for later with a ginger comfit—she resisted the urge to kiss his cheek.

Inside, she briefly explained the morning and early afternoon hours to the duchess. As Nicholas had said to Daniel, Briar kept to the claim that she'd felt unwell, and drove on to Blacklowe Manor in the rain, where they waited for it to stop.

In turn, the duchess eyed her shrewdly, taking in her wrinkled dress. "You know how fond I am of you and your sisters, my dear. But you are in my charge. To have you return, unchaperoned, when you were alone with a gentleman—whose own reputation has been called into question on more than one occasion—does not look well upon me, or you. Pray, where are his cousins?"

"They are at my father's cottage," Briar said and went on to explain Temperance's surprise for the day.

Before she even finished, the duchess was at her side, patting her fondly. "No wonder you were ill, my dear. Had I known that your friend shared an acquaintance with that young man, I could have forewarned you. I'd heard Mr. Cartwright had taken up residence there a few months ago—as well as keeping a house in Cheapside—

but I did not want to mention it. Truth be told, I never thought you would be acquainted. Oh, and to think I had the most distressing few moments when I saw you drive up, alone, with my godson, I thought for certain you were ruined and nothing would ever be right again."

Briar felt herself grow pale, warmth leeching from her cheeks. "I was under the impression that you were rather fond of him."

"I am, my dear, but so are you." Her lips curved in a knowing smile, her penciled brows arching. "I'm sure I'm not the only one who has seen your heart in your eyes these past few days. And he is only a man, after all. If he were alone with you for any length of time, how could he resist such a temptation? But now that I know he has behaved with such honor toward you, I have great hope that I was right all along."

"Right?"

"About him being ready to marry again, of course. A rakish gentleman, bent on gadding about town without care for his own reputation, let alone another's, is only thinking about satisfying his own pleasures," she said, dropping her voice to a scandalized whisper and glancing over her shoulder to be sure they were still alone in the parlor. "And a woman does not catch a husband by giving her favors too early."

Briar shivered, chilled to the marrow. This was another lesson she'd never considered. She'd only been following the demands of her heart, certain of the return of her affections. Now she was filled with sudden doubt.

Nicholas had told her not to fall in love and that he had no intention of marrying again. He'd made himself quite clear on numerous occasions. But Briar hadn't listened.

Suddenly, she wondered if she'd started to believe in one of her far-fetched scenarios.

"I never set out to catch a husband," Briar said dimly, now questioning if Nicholas truly felt anything for her at all.

"Only time will tell," the duchess said with another fond pat as she bustled out of the room. "Oh, and I believe a letter arrived for you, my dear."

Thoughts adrift, Briar moved to the table in the foyer, dimly searching through the small stack. Two for Mrs. Fitzherbert, and two for Briar—one from Uncle Ernest, and the other Genevieve Price.

The challenge. Briar knew she'd be hearing from her at some point, but she never would have expected it to be so soon.

Dear Miss Bourne,

I learned you were visiting Holliford Park. Since I am passing through the nearby village on the morrow, I should like to meet and discuss our matter of business. Twelve o'clock at the Red Fawn Inn.

Looking forward to the best of news.

Your friend,
GP

"I HAVE something to confess," Nicholas said when Daniel joined him in the study, shortly after their return. There was no point in waiting a moment more, after all. It had already been too long. He crossed the room to hand his cousin a glass of whisky. "But here, you're going to need this."

Daniel took it and saluted him, a wry grin on his lips.

"I have a sense of what you're going to tell me, and I think it has to do with Miss Bourne. But if you're worried that I've formed an attachment to her, let me put your mind at ease. I've known for a while that she's in love with you and, I believe, *you* hold a certain regard for her as well."

An icy wave of dread washed over him again, like clockwork that operated solely on the mention of Briar.

. . . the only thing completely unforgivable is an act of betrayal against one's own family.

Nicholas trudged back to the escritoire where his own glass waited and he downed the contents, hissing a breath between his teeth. Then he poured another. *Pot-valiance*, and he was never more in need of it than now.

"This isn't about Miss Bourne. It is about Miss Smithson."

"My Miss Smithson—Genevieve?"

Nicholas took another drink and turned to see that Daniel had gone deathly pale. Instinctively, he hesitated out of a need to shield him. But what good had that done so far? None. This terrible truth had to be spoken

The best course of action was to proceed without delay, like removing a splinter from a finger. Or, in this case, a knife from his cousin's back.

A shudder of self-revulsion rolled through him. "I am sorry to tell you, but I am the one who forced her out of your company. I am the one responsible for ending your betrothal."

Daniel shook his head, generously choosing to believe his own cousin wouldn't be capable of such a betrayal. Which made this all the more difficult. "But in the letter, she stated that it was her family. *They* would not permit the match. I know, for I've read it a thousand times."

"That was part of the agreement I made with her father. I paid off all his debts in exchange for his willingness to find her another husband, without delay."

At the time, Nicholas assumed he was protecting Daniel, for his own good. Since then, however, he'd come to a different understanding. By acting behind Daniel's back, he'd treated him as if he were incapable of dealing with the facts and making his own decisions. This was a realization he may not have learned if it wasn't for Briar. She'd taught him that when you truly loved someone, you did not keep them from experiencing life. Not even the hard lessons and bitter truths.

Nicholas only hoped that there would be forgiveness in love as well.

Suddenly, Daniel collapsed onto the leather hassock, his glass crashing to the floor. "But you knew how much I loved her, how much I needed her. She was the very air I breathed."

"Yes, I knew." Nicholas felt cold with regret and the fear of what was to come. "I never once questioned your feelings, only hers. You see, that day we encountered Miss Smithson on the lane was not actually the first time I met her. I had been acquainted with her in London. Intimately acquainted."

He watched as that sank in, color gradually suffusing Daniel's cheeks even as he shook his head again in firm denial.

"We met at a masquerade and did not even exchange names," Nicholas said, the words tasting of bile on the back of his tongue.

"Not Genevieve. She was too pure. She was . . ." Daniel swallowed, his gaze a hardened amber that was suddenly full of stark clarity. "Were you going to marry her, then? And I got in your way?"

He swallowed and said simply, "No."

"Is that who you truly are—a scoundrel who takes his pleasure by whatever means he chooses?"

"It wasn't like that," Nicholas said, bristling with

denial. And yet, he couldn't defend his actions, not after what he'd done.

Daniel stood, glass crunching beneath his boot, hands fisted. Anger and betrayal marked his usually soft countenance in harsh, slanting lines. "Until now, I thought those were only exaggerated rumors. I thought the man I knew, the man I'd once looked up to, could never be so despicable. But I see that I was deceived in this as well and I am ashamed that we share blood."

Panicked by the finality of the statement, Nicholas stepped forward and grasped Daniel's arm as he turned to leave. "We are like brothers. Our bond is stronger than mere blood."

"Not anymore." Daniel shrugged free and said exactly what Nicholas had feared all along. "You and I are no longer family."

Chapter 31

"She had talked her into love; but alas! She was not so easily to be talked out of it."

JANE AUSTEN, *Emma*

Briar walked into the village with one of the maids the following day. The duchess offered them the use of a carriage, but Briar felt that she'd taken advantage of her hospitality too much.

Lost in thought, she kicked a stone on the path with the toe of her half boot, while beside her, the young maid chattered about the housekeeper needing silver polish, the cook needing eggs, Her Grace wanting blue thread to finish a pillow slip—not pale blue or dark blue but the one in between . . .

Briar sighed, barely listening, uncertainty still plaguing her.

Last night, Nicholas had sent a missive. And, of course, given her current state of mind, she took careful note of every word that had been written. And every word that had not.

Miss Bourne,

I regret I cannot return to Holliford Park this evening, due to a family matter that has arisen.

Nicholas

"Cannot return." Deciphered to: *I am capable of re-turning, after all I possess several horses and carriages, I'd just rather not see you again this evening. When we were together earlier, your moony-eyed gazes made me uncomfortable.*

"A family matter": *Since I have no plans of adding you to the family, now or in the future, I do not want your interference or your opinions.*

"Nicholas": *Here is my signature. I'm sending no fond wishes, affection, or warmest regards. Honestly, Briar, did you expect anything else?*

And yet, she had. She'd even hoped for another missive this morning. But none had come.

Briar didn't like the dark turn her scenarios had taken. They were usually a source of comfort, a moment of brightness in her day. Doubt, it seemed, had gotten the better of her.

She hoped that, by the time her meeting with Miss Price concluded, she would feel more like herself. She was ready to put the unsuccessful challenge behind her, and to think about starting afresh for next Season. After all, whatever else was between her and Nicholas, he still wanted her to find a wife for Daniel.

Once they reached the village, Briar told the maid that she'd meet her back at the Red Fawn. By the clock in the square, it was quarter of twelve, giving her time to see if the inn had any cups of chocolate.

Coincidentally, Genevieve Price was already inside. Dressed in crimson from her feathered hat to her hem, she sat at a small round table nearest the door. Then she smiled, that peculiar thin-lipped grin, her green eyes glinting. "Miss Bourne, I see we're both eager."

"Good day, Miss Price. I hope your journey here was pleasant," Briar said, politeness ingrained in her. She did not particularly like this woman. Even so, she appreciated having met her, if only because this woman's challenge had spurred her toward a new understanding of herself.

Briar had become a different person since accepting their bargain. Not necessarily one who made better choices, but one who was worldly. And could one put a price on newfound experience? Well, in her case, it had cost ten kisses, her heart, soul, and chastity. *A bargain really,* she thought wryly.

"It was, thank you," she said with a quick gesture to the other chair. "I've taken the liberty of ordering tea just now. Perhaps before it arrives we might settle our business."

Right to it then. Briar sat down and adjusted her cream-colored skirts. "I'm afraid I was unable to find a bride for Lord Edgemont."

"Were you not? Such a pity." She tsked, absently tugging on the wrist of her red glove, fingers stretching like claws. "Though to tell you the truth, I knew the task was close to impossible. Edgemont was forever proclaiming he would never marry. But he was a bit too smug about it, if you ask me. He didn't know what it was like to be in the trenches of the marriage mart. So . . . I thought, why not put him there? And that, my dear, is where you came in."

Feeling her brow pucker, Briar looked across the table, wanting to understand. "You never expected me to succeed?"

The tea arrived and so her answer was delayed for a moment. During which, Genevieve Price withdrew a silver flask from her reticule and poured a liberal amount of amber liquor in her teacup.

"Not really. More than anything, I wanted him to be beleaguered by debutantes until he was ready to run mad through the streets of London. But from what I've heard, you've done excellent work keeping him in the midst of the warfare, so good on you," she said, taking a sip, and without adding any tea to her cup.

By rote, Briar poured her own, but was in no mood for tea. A faint memory seemed to twitch at the back of her mind. "I'd been under the impression that you'd chosen Lord Edgemont's name at random, a rogue whom many knew by reputation."

"No, indeed. I was quite attached to the family at one time, before I was married and when I was just a debutante with a small dowry, doing whatever I could to marry well. As each of us must do."

Mismatched pieces began to merge together. "Your maiden name wouldn't be . . . *Smithson*, would it?"

Her smile curled slowly. "Yes."

"You were Mr. Prescott's betrothed." Briar was suddenly outraged on Daniel's behalf, but what she couldn't understand was . . . "First you abandon Mr. Prescott to marry someone else and then you challenge me to *beleaguer* Lord Edgemont. What do you have against that family?"

"Are you certain you wish to know?" she asked, her green gaze watching Briar with the same excitement as a cat spotting a mouse, and she did not wait for a response. "It was Edgemont who stopped me from marrying Daniel. And the reason is because . . . well, I'm sure you can guess. After all, you were there, outside Sterling's the morning after, when Edgemont was bidding me adieu. Of course, I did not know at the time that his attentions were so fickle. Some men are so easily distracted."

Briar recalled every part of that first meeting with perfect clarity. The woman in the crimson cloak. Nicholas's hands roaming over her body as if acquainted with every inch. And now, she learned that the same woman had been Daniel's betrothed?

Briar went cold. He'd betrayed his own cousin for an illicit encounter?

"You had an understanding with *Nic*—with Lord Edgemont?" she asked, her voice cracking with disbelief. Or rather, with wanting to disbelieve.

Miss Smithson, Genevieve Price, or whoever she was, nodded.

It was even worse than Briar thought. He wasn't redeemable at all. Instead, he was the exact type of man who would seduce a woman with his charm, leading her to believe he was interested in more, only to abandon her in the end. Just like her father.

"That's part of who he is, you know. He pretends to have this big heart and love for his family, wanting to protect them. But the truth of the matter is, he only wants to satisfy his own insatiable appetite. He is a rake, after all. So take care, Miss Bourne, for I've heard tales that he's been doting on you lately."

Sick to her stomach and sick at heart, Briar stood on trembling legs, unable to hear any more. This was already too much. "I'm afraid I . . . I must be going."

"Oh dear. I see that my warning has come too late," her companion said with mock alarm.

Briar turned and walked toward the door, but stumbled against a chair. She couldn't see past the wetness in her eyes. But hands—familiar hands that she would know anywhere—clasped her shoulders, righting her. Nicholas's scent filled her nostrils and his face blurred before her. "Let me go."

"I cannot," he answered softly. "Not when you're clearly—"

"Why, Edgemont," Genevieve Price said, her voice curling into a sneer, "serendipity smiles on us once more."

"Yes, I believe the two of you are quite well acquainted," Briar said, holding back a sob.

Nicholas's hold tightened reflexively. "It isn't what you think."

"Don't underestimate my ability to see things clearly. I'm no longer as unworldly as I once was. Though it is unfortunate that it should have taken me so long to figure out the reason you were desperate to find Daniel a bride. Apparently, you needed to clear your own conscience," she said, wishing there was more force behind her words. But they were all broken and wet. Even so, complete and utter loathing gave her the strength to shrug free. She swiped angrily at her tears, knowing that he didn't deserve them. "I was a fool to imagine a life with a man like you. Please move out of my way."

"Briar." His voice was low and raw, barely a rasp, clearly strained by guilt. "I have things I need to tell you, but not here. Come away with me and let me explain."

She shook her head, unwilling to hear anything he had to say. He could confess and make excuses to someone else, to someone more gullible than she, if such a person existed.

When he did not move, Briar—who had never been rude or violent to anyone in her life—put both hands on his chest and shoved. He did not budge, but she felt as if she'd made her point.

Then, skirting sideways between the chair and the wall, she rushed out the door.

NICHOLAS WAS numb with panic, his limbs leaden as he watched Briar's retreating figure.

Behind him, Genevieve clapped her hands. "My dear Edgemont, what a wonderful show. Why, this is even better than I imagined."

At Holliford Park a short while ago, his godmother had

informed him that Briar had already gone into the village to meet someone on a matter of business, offhandedly remarking that a letter had come from Genevieve Price.

At the mention of the name, Nicholas's blood had turned to ice.

It didn't take him long to come to the conclusion that Genevieve had been the very person who'd challenged Briar in the first place. But none of that mattered. All he knew was that he had to get to the village, to explain everything before it was too late.

Briar could find the good in anything, he told himself. Surely she would understand what was truly in his heart, and that he'd never intended to hurt anyone. She would take one look at him and see that he was, in fact, redeemable.

Nicholas held on to this one last shred of hope as he'd ordered Adams to push the horses to their limit.

Yet it had all been for naught.

Years of mistakes and roguish behavior had caught up with him, looming like the dark shadow of Death, a razor-edged scythe catching the light. But Nicholas wasn't about to give up.

Shielding his eyes, he staggered onto the pavement, ignoring Genevieve's laughter. He found Briar next to his black carriage, talking to Adams.

"Miss Bourne, are you all right?"

She shook her head, swiping at the wetness on her cheeks. "I am not, actually, and I need to leave immediately. Can you aid me?"

Nicholas didn't give Adams the chance to answer. He stormed up, imploring her to listen even as she held up a hand to ward him off. "Briar, let me explain. Then, I'm sure you'll understand."

"I know very well what you're going to tell me, but

it will make no difference. I finally see you for the man you really are." Those once-warm cornflower blue eyes turned frosty and distant.

"No. I'm not like that anymore. Can't you see that you've changed me?" He crowded closer, but only to watch her recoil from him. A wave of sheer desperation burned in his throat and veins, churning his stomach. He had to make her understand. "From the beginning—that very first day—you breathed life and effervescence into my soul, chasing away all the bitterness that once hardened me."

She closed her eyes, a breeze catching her shuddered breath. "If I could travel back to that day, I would choose never to meet you. I want nothing more to do with you, Lord Edgemont."

No, this wasn't happening. He refused to believe it was over.

"My lord, let me take Miss Bourne away from here," Adams said, coming down from the perch and bringing Nicholas's attention to the villagers that were gathering, gawking at the spectacle.

But he didn't care if they all saw him making a fool of himself. This was too damned important. He was losing everything that mattered. "Briar I . . . I need you."

Not swayed by the bald agony in his voice, she took Adams's hand and stepped into the landau. In the velvet interior, she stared straight ahead, unblinking.

Nicholas raked a hand through his hair, feeling everything slipping away, even his grip on sanity. "Yes, appropriate my carriage like you did that first day. Plague me with your warm smiles again. Badger my ears with the sound of your sweet laughter for the rest of my life."

The sounds of laughter from the crowd came instead, but he paid no heed.

"Do you want to bring me to my knees? Then here I am," he said, dropping like a felled tree, arms open, begging, pleading.

But still, she did not look at him.

"Damn it, Briar. Will you just . . . just marry me?"

Chapter 32

"... and it is over—and may never—can never,
as a first meeting, occur again, and therefore you
need not think about it."

JANE AUSTEN, *Emma*

London
Three days later

Briar returned home to the Bourne Matrimonial Agency,
greeted by the pale marble foyer, as cold and lifeless as
her dim-witted heart. How could she have been so wrong
about him?

Ainsley and Uncle Ernest were there, too, anxiously
hovering over her, asking questions she just couldn't
answer. Because if she said, "Yes, Lord Edgemont asked
me to marry him," that would lead to, "No, I did not
accept," which would lead to the question *why* and the
answer to that she couldn't say aloud. The words were
simply too horrendous to utter.

Because he'd betrayed his own family in order to
slake his lust. He was a rake who caused women to fall
in love with him, only to abandon them.

The worst of all crimes.

She would rather have fallen for a murderer. And not
just a duel-at-dawn murderer either, but an ax-wielding
one who spent spare time chopping the heads off puppies.

She shuddered at the dark scenario. No, better not make it puppies. That would be insupportable. Geese instead. She'd been attacked by a goose as a girl and wasn't disturbed at all by the thought of them being slaughtered. At least not today.

"Another shiver. She does that occasionally," the duchess said, her voice threaded with worry, and speaking of Briar as if she weren't standing there. "She's barely said a word in the past three days, then mutters such terrible anguished cries in her sleep. Most of the words I cannot decipher, but I did hear her call out for her mother countless times. It breaks my heart."

"Do you know what happened?" Ainsley asked, wrapping a shawl around Briar's shoulders and chafing her arms.

"Other than the proposal I wrote you about, no. Ever since she came back from visiting the village, she's been like this. Mind you, when my maid came in and told me the news, I was elated at first. So happy that my godson had decided to settle down once more." She hesitated and sighed. "But when I saw Briar, I knew something dire was wrong. I was even more certain of it when my godson stormed into Holliford Park, wild-eyed and demanding the chance to explain. Though what he'd wanted to say, I do not know, for I shooed him out the door and told him he could not return until I knew what was what."

"And?" Uncle Ernest asked impatiently, pressing the back of his warm hand to Briar's forehead and then to her cheek, his face lined with worry.

"I still do not know. Though I will tell you that he followed us to every inn."

"Terrorizing my sister? I'll scratch out his eyes if he steps—"

"No, my dear. I'm sure you needn't worry on that account. These past days, he has always kept his distance, but said he'd needed to be close at hand in case she wanted to talk to him or rail at him. Though, mostly, he stayed equally quiet, and looking more wretched than I have ever witnessed before. Whatever happened, he is clearly heartsick about it. I shouldn't be surprised if his carriage is outside on the street right this instant."

Uncle Ernest stalked to the door, then slammed it closed. "If the earl has a black carriage with red wheels, it's there."

"Briar?" Ainsley crooned, her brow rumpled with worry as she tucked the stray strands of hair away from Briar's forehead. "If you want him gone, all you have to do is tell me, and I'll . . . I don't know . . . I'll ask Mr. Sterling to get rid of him."

Another dark scenario took shape. Briar could see Reed Sterling, former boxing champion, ripping Nicholas out of his carriage and pummeling him with his fists. She felt sick, bile rising up her throat. Whatever else she thought of him, she didn't want to see him hurt.

"No." The word tore out of her, nasally and broken. It must have unlocked something within her because a wrenching sob followed. She covered her face with her hands and collapsed in her sister's arms.

LATER THAT night, when Ainsley had finally left her bed-chamber for a moment, Briar took the red leather volume of *Emma* and held it tightly. "Mother, I fell in love, and it's just as awful as I feared it would be. Now I know why you didn't survive it."

Chapter 33

"Respect would be added to affection."

JANE AUSTEN, *Emma*

Adams drove Nicholas home late that night, claiming he couldn't stand the stench rising from the carriage. The blackguard even helped him inside his townhouse and up to his chamber.

"I'm going to fire you if you don't take me back this instant," Nicholas slurred, drunk from lack of sleep, and possibly from too much whisky. Adams's fault. He'd given Nicholas his flask, likely wanting him to drink himself into a stupor just so he would pass out.

"Fire me tomorrow, my lord. You're too tired today."

Nicholas tipped forward and landed in a heap on his bed.

And that was the last thing he remembered until there was daylight streaming in through his windows.

The bitter scent of coffee wafted over from the bedside table, making his stomach roil.

"You look like hell," Daniel said from the doorway, appearing as though he'd slept a few days in his clothes, too.

"Isn't that right where I belong?" Nicholas winced, catching the scent of his own breath, whisky and bile coating his tongue, about five layers thick by the feel of it. And the pulpy mass of his brain was trying to push its way out of his temples by way of a battering ram.

"Yes, though hell might be an improvement from where you are."

'l'rue. Nicholas couldn't deny it. But he would suffer this agony a hundred times over if he could see Briar once and tell her that he loved her, and that she wasn't wrong.

He'd been a coward by not admitting it when he'd had the chance. And if he could just go back to the beginning, he would change everything. Absolutely everything.

"I came to finish our discussion," Daniel said.

"I wasn't aware that there was anything left to discuss. After I told you what I'd done, you said we were no longer family. And rightfully so."

"Then you know how hard it is for me to stand here."

Nicholas nodded. He swung his legs over the side of the bed. Disgustingly enough, he was still wearing his boots and they were covered in filth that he could not even name. "Is there anything I can do to earn your forgiveness?"

Daniel scrubbed a hand over his unshaven jaw, squinting at him. "You don't sound like yourself. Where is your famous arrogance? Your certainty about every choice you make? Barking orders, threatening to tie me to a column in the ballroom?"

"Lost somewhere in one of the rooms at Blacklowe Manor, I think." Nicholas tried to stand up, but his balance was off, his head spinning. He gestured to the bureau. "Hand me a knife from the top drawer. I'm cutting off these boots."

"Don't be an idiot. You'll cut yourself and bleed to death and then I won't be able to torture you for the rest of your life. Therefore, I'll assist you."

"Thank you," Nicholas said, humbled. "But be warned. I cannot identify the source of the putrescence on the outside or on the inside."

Daniel swore and covered his nose when he drew near.

"You smell worse than a scavenger cart. At least have the wherewithal to suffer in dignity."

"I'm afraid I lost that, too."

Daniel turned his back, took hold of the boot, and yanked hard, stumbling forward when it slipped free. He tossed it to the side and wiped his hands on his trousers. "Blacklowe Manor—where everything is lost and nothing is found."

"If I had a flagon of ale, I would toast that statement."

The second boot came off, after more of a fight, and Daniel collapsed on the chair opposite the bed. He leaned his head back against the wall. "I want to know what made you do it. Forget about your pious redemption right now. I want to know what drove you to send my fiancée away without having the decency to tell me in the first place."

"I suppose I owe you that much, and more," Nicholas said, resigned. "Very well. For months, Miss Smithson flirted shamelessly, trying to seduce me."

Daniel swallowed. "She was passionate and playful. Her exuberance was one of the things that drew me to her."

"I never had a moment's peace when she was there. I had to lock myself in my study."

"You didn't."

"I did," he said, embarrassed. "I knew I had to do something or else you were going to marry her. And if you did, I think she would have found a way to . . ." He hissed at his own memory and muttered under his breath, "just like Marceline.

"Anyway, I didn't want that life for you," he continued. "I didn't want you to become dark and bitter like me, so I went to her father. I believed I was saving you from a horrible fate, when I was actually trying to save myself from reliving one." He drew in a breath, hefted himself up, and staggered over to the washbasin. "And it was all my own doing. If I hadn't left the masquerade with her that night—"

"You needn't repeat it." Daniel stood, too, and moved to the door. He paused there, considering, his hand gripping the frame. "Tell me one more thing. Do you believe she would have gone through with it—our marriage, I mean?"

"Do you truly wish me to answer that?"

"I believe you just did."

Nicholas stared down into the bowl, loathing the watery reflection glaring back at him. When he looked at the doorway, Daniel was gone.

"I'm NOT going through this again, Briar. Up. Up. Time to join the rest of us in daily misery," Ainsley said, hands on her hips as she stood at Briar's bedside. Her voice might have sounded forceful, but the worry lines beside her eyes betrayed her.

Briar drew in a deep breath and stared up at the rose-colored canopy. It was strange. She didn't even know how she was breathing. Or why. Every bit of air burned down her throat, raw and ragged, stuttering in and out like a broken bellows. "I thought I was stronger. I thought love would never hurt me."

"Ah. Is that what happened? You fell in love."

"With the wrong sort, just like Mother," she wheezed, tears gathering in her throat. Her heart was shredded into red strips of flesh that would never be mended. "And now I know it will break me, too."

She couldn't imagine living like this, with part of her wanting to be with Nicholas and the other abhorring what he did.

Ainsley took her hand and placed it between her own.

"It wasn't that long ago that you were determined to prove that you weren't like Mother."

"Now I see that you were right all along."

"That *I* was right?"

Briar's head listed to the side and she stared at her sister. "When you look at me, I know you think of her."

Ainsley blanched. "You resemble her, yes. And you have some of her mannerisms, but then we all do. But you're not her, Briar. You've always been stronger, more hopeful. Where you always see a ray of light in a cloudy sky, she only saw rain."

Stronger? Now that was a surprise, indeed, and likely the last thing Briar ever thought she would hear from her sister.

"But for your sake," Ainsley continued, solemn, "I wish she was still here. You were so young when she fell ill and never had the chance to really know her—*that* is what I think of sometimes when I look at you. And I worry that I have not honored her wish that I look after you."

"She asked you to . . ." Briar let her words drift off in disbelief. "I always thought you were protective because you believed I was incapable."

Ainsley heaved out a watery sigh and sank down onto the bed beside her. Hand in hand, they stared up at the canopy. "Do you want to know the real reason I never wanted you to be a matchmaker?"

"Yes," she said quietly, holding her breath.

"It wasn't because I underestimated you. It's quite the opposite. Actually, I was afraid."

"Of what, *me*?"

"In a way. You're accomplished at everything you do. I knew you would also be good at this. Better than me. And this—the agency—is all I have. All I'm good at. I can manage accounts, ask questions, take down information, and sort through names. I don't play any instrument. You know I can't sing or draw. I barely speak French, let alone all the languages that Jacinda knows. I don't devise new ways of catching fish on a whim. I don't even have much of an imagination. Compared to my sisters—especially the youngest one—I'm rather boring. So you could say that I kept you from becoming a matchmaker because I've always been jealous."

Briar blew out a disbelieving breath. "You sound like Mother. That's the type of thing she always said. But I don't believe that is the real reason. You're too strong and confident for jealousy. Capable of meeting challenges head on. I've always wanted to be like you."

"Strange how we both see each other the same way, isn't it?" Ainsley squeezed her hand and they shared a look. A new understanding. "We'll switch roles, then. You'll take my office and I'll have a good cry in bed and cup after cup of chocolate."

Briar rolled her head toward the bedside table where three tall cups of chocolate sat, untouched. "I don't want them. I told Ginny, but Mrs. Darden keeps sending more."

"They're not from Mrs. Darden."

"Then who?" An uncanny suspicion rolled over her, starting with a quick shiver along her instep. "You don't mean they're from . . ."

Ainsley nodded. "Edgemont is rather persistent."

"Is he making a nuisance of himself by sending messengers all around town and to our door, collecting chocolate from the coffee houses?"

"No. He's here."

Briar sat up, her head spinning, heart pinching. "Here?"

"Apparently, he's earned Mrs. Teasdale's favor. But Mrs. Darden is glowering at him for taking over her kitchen to make your chocolate."

"*He*'s making the chocolate?"

"He won't budge either. It doesn't make any sense, but he says that he's trying to make the froth just right."

"Bother," she growled. "You'd better help me dress."

A quarter hour later, Briar arrived on the scene of a tragedy. The bittersweet scent of burnt chocolate hung in the air. Dirty dishes were piled on every surface, and dark brown splatters covered the table, the floors, even the windowpanes. And there was Nicholas, hunched over the stove.

"What have you done to Mrs. Darden's kitchen?"

He whipped around, then staggered in place, his hair standing on end. His face was pale and drawn with dark smudges along his nose and cheek. Even his clothes were in disorder, muddy from ingredients. His coat hung on a peg by the back door, and he stood before her in his ruined waistcoat and shirt, his sleeves rolled up to reveal more spatters intermingling with the crisp dark hair on his forearms.

"You're out of bed," he breathed. His gaze, red-rimmed from exhaustion, turned warm and eager. "Feeling better?"

"No, irritated." She huffed.

Actually, it hurt to see him. She ached all over, her skin prickling. Her heart lurched out of rhythm as jolts of sensation scattered down her limbs, telling her to rush into his arms. And worse, the last words he'd spoken played like a melody stuck inside her head. One that she couldn't be rid of if she tried.

Can't you see that you've changed me?

From the beginning—that very first day—you breathed life and effervescence into my soul . . .

I need you.

Still she refused to go to him or to believe that what he'd said was anything other than a charming rogue's manipulation.

Instead, she took hold of the back of a wooden chair,

a shield between them. "What are you doing here, aside from making a horrendous mess?"

"Did you try the last one? I think I'm getting closer to—"

"No, and you're not," she interrupted. Angry, she swiped a hand through the air. "Look around. You've created a disaster."

He wavered on his feet but didn't take his eyes from hers for an instant. "But you always see possibility amidst chaos. That's one of the things I love about you."

She gasped, her lungs burning from the charred air. A similar sound came from Mrs. Darden. At a glance, Briar saw her press her hands to her bosom and tears gather, clearly swept away in the moment and forgetting about everything Nicholas had ruined.

The old Briar might have done the same. But she'd changed. This small admission was not enough to make her forget what he'd done.

"I'm not that person any longer. My eyes have been opened to what is real, and you cannot undo what has been done. No one can go back to the beginning and start again," she said, turning her back on him and leaving the kitchen.

Chapter 34

"Harriet was one of those, who, having once begun, would be always in love."

JANE AUSTEN, *Emma*

Briar went down to the kitchen the following morning, prepared to help Mrs. Darden set matters to rights. But when she arrived, she was surprised to find the room immaculate. Even more so than ever before. Sunlight gleamed through sparkling clear windowpanes and off the surface of the copper pots and faucet fixtures. The stone tile floor looked glossy and new.

She hardly knew if she was standing in the same house. "What happened in here?"

"He stayed here all night cleaning up, refused to leave even a speck behind," Mrs. Darden crooned, hugging an earthenware bowl to her generous bosom and beaming.

"*Nic*—Lord Edgemont did all this? By himself?"

"Indeed. What a dear. Didn't want you to see a disaster, so he worked himself into exhaustion. Practically had to prop him up to get him out the door early this morning."

She eyed Mrs. Darden coolly. "Don't tell me you've warmed to him, too."

"Can't a woman appreciate a man who knows how to take care of a mess?"

"Some messes are just too large to fix," Briar huffed, and went about making a tray to take upstairs. After all, it was important to carry on with her life as it was. She couldn't sit around feeling sorry for herself for the rest of her days. And besides, she had no doubt that a certain someone would be there with her knitting.

Briar looked forward to the distraction. Though, when she went into the parlor, Mrs. Teasdale wasn't the only person she found. Daniel was there, too.

Briar nearly dropped the tray. "Mr. Prescott. But what are you doing in London? I would have thought . . ."

He came forward to assist her. "That I would want to be as far away from my cousin as possible?"

Mutely, she nodded.

"Is there someplace we can talk?" He glanced uncertainly at Mrs. Teasdale, sitting on the sofa.

"Don't mind me, for my attention is on my knitting. Won't hear a word," she said, click-clacking away. "This is as good a place as any, the way I see it. After all, it's Miss Bourne's office."

Briar opened her mouth to argue, then the strangest thing occurred to her. With fresh eyes, she looked around at the cozy little parlor with the rose silk wallpaper, a landscape painting of a boat on a lake, and the furniture she'd arranged for ease of conversation. And she realized something important. This *was* her office. It had been from the very first day.

All along, she'd felt excluded and left to do a job that meant nothing. Only now, she realized that what she provided was just as important as taking applications, vetting clients, and making matches. She put people at ease with friendly conversation and, perhaps, she even gave them hope. And a monkey, no matter how well trained, could not do that. No, indeed.

"If it is amenable to you," she said, standing a bit taller as she gestured to one of the tufted armchairs. After he placed the tray on the low table and they settled in, she poured for him, this new awareness brimming inside her.

Peculiarly, she felt a sense of peace for the first time in days.

She handed a cup to Daniel. "I apologize for leaving Hampshire without bidding farewell, or without explaining my sudden illness the day we drove to . . . Mr. Cartwright's residence."

Daniel nodded, his expression solemn. "Under both circumstances, your absence was perfectly reasonable. My regret is that you had to suffer at all."

"We all have our trials, dear," Mrs. Teasdale said with a tsk to her yarn. In the silence that followed, she looked up. "Well, go on. I was only giving a little encouragement. Not listening to a word."

Daniel shifted uncomfortably. "Yes, well. You see, I came here to tell you that I plan to leave in a matter of days, but I wanted you to know that I hope we are able to meet as friends in the future."

"Of course. I can think of no reason it would be otherwise."

"You are all kindness, especially when the matter that ended my betrothal was the very thing that finished yours as well."

Briar sucked in a breath, her hands trembling as she set down her cup. "Your cousin and I were not engaged."

"My apologies. With the way Nicholas has been moping around and muttering strange things about starting from the beginning, from the day you met, I thought surely . . ." He shook his head, confusion marking his brow in furrows. "Well, perhaps I have misunderstood. I've just never seen him this way."

"I marvel at your ability to speak with such compassion. Had the same been done to me, I don't think I could ever forgive him."

He looked down at his cup, thoughtful. "I am disappointed. He showed me little respect by withholding the simple fact that he'd been acquainted with Miss Smithson before I met her. Then he showed me even less by offering her father a fortune to marry her off to someone else, without even discussing it with me. He'd always been of a nature to protect me, but this time he went too far."

Briar's heart stalled, blood rushing in her ears. "Did you say he knew her *before* you met?"

It seemed to take an eternity for Daniel to speak. He stared back at her with his head tilted in scrutiny and then suddenly his brows shot up and his face grew pale. "I think I understand now. Miss Bourne, let me assure you that Nicholas would sooner cut off his right arm than to . . ." He stopped and averted his gaze, clearing his throat. "I did not know Miss Smithson when she was in London."

"Oh," Briar breathed, realizing that she'd misunderstood that part. Tears gathered in her throat, threatening to spill.

Yet, before she was too swayed by this information, she reminded herself that it did not alter what Nicholas had done. He'd still acted without conscience or concern about who he may have been hurting.

"I am ever so sorry for what you endured," she said to Daniel.

"Miss Smithson was unlike anyone else and I was captivated by her vivacity." He glanced sideways at Mrs. Teasdale as if expecting a comment, but to her credit, she didn't break her knitting stride. "I was so caught up in her spirited attentions, reveling in my good fortune, that I ignored every flirtation she cast in Nicholas's direction. And I ignored every warning from him, too. I turned a blind eye to how uncomfortable she made him, how many times he would leave a room when she entered. I even made excuses for her."

Briar shivered, the images forming in her mind. Hearing Daniel's account, she couldn't help but compare this with what Nicholas had gone through with Marceline. How both his wife and brother had deceived him.

Then Briar thought of how Genevieve Price had left London and had ended up in Daniel's path. Of all the men she might have encountered, it was uncanny that she should have formed an attachment to Nicholas's cousin. And perhaps a bit too convenient.

I was just a debutante with a small dowry, doing whatever I could to marry well.

And yet, Daniel's annuity was more on the conservative side, which made Briar doubt that he had been her true target for marriage.

"Sounds to me that lad had good reason to break the betrothal," Mrs. Teasdale interjected.

"Mrs. Teasdale, please," Briar chided, even when the same thought had run through her mind. "It was still Mr. Prescott's decision to make. Not only that, but he wasn't given the opportunity to truly confront the situation."

Briar knew what it was like to be underestimated and made to feel as if you're incapable of making your own choices. And yet, after her talk with Ainsley, she'd come to realize that there are often reasons for family to think they are acting with your best interests in mind.

Then it occurred to Briar that she'd done something similar to Daniel. *Oh dear.*

"I'm afraid I have a confession as well," she said, abashed. "I've been secretly trying to find you a match these past weeks."

He grinned shyly. "I've known all along. My mother is not the best at keeping secrets."

"I hope you know that I meant no disrespect."

"Easily forgiven."

Mrs. Teasdale gave an irritated sigh, lowering her knitting to her lap. "That's all well and good, but what about your cousin?"

But before Daniel could respond, they were interrupted.

"Forgive me, I don't mean to intrude," a gentleman said, appearing in the parlor doorway, looking down at a card in his hand.

The instant she saw him, Briar felt her jaw go slack and heard Mrs. Teasdale make an inarticulate sound of appreciation, her knitting needles dropping to the rug in a brief pit-a-pat. The stranger was a tall handsome man with wavy hair the color of caramels and strong, elegant features.

Lifting a pair of remarkable gray eyes, he scanned the room. "Oh, Mr. Prescott, perhaps you might be of assistance."

"What are you doing here? Interested in matchmaking all of a sudden?" Daniel asked with the wry amusement that one usually reserved for close acquaintances.

"Well, not exactly," he said then, looking to Briar and Mrs. Teasdale, who were both likely fish-faced. "I seem to have come to the wrong address. Edgemont sent me this card and, well, perhaps you can make out your cousin's abominable handwriting."

Daniel stood and took the card, but paused to make the introductions. "Brandon Stredwick, Lord Hulworth, might I present Miss Bourne and her friend Mrs. Teasdale."

Hulworth? Briar stood as another tumble of shock fell through her. Nicholas had sent Lord Hulworth here? First the chocolate and now this . . . but what could be his reason?

. . . Nicholas has been moping around and muttering strange things about starting from the beginning, from the day you met . . .

Briar's heart quickened.

"Miss Bourne, a pleasure." He bowed, then turned and bent to pick up the fallen knitting needles and offered them. "Mrs. Teasdale."

She gave him a saucy wink. "How do you feel about the number five, Lord Hulworth?"

"I suppose I like it as much as any other number." His broad mouth quirked in a wary sort of grin and then he returned his attention to Daniel. "Again, I apologize for the intrusion, but I don't believe I've got the correct address and I can't make out what the card says at the bottom."

Daniel chuckled and lifted a plate from the low table. "You're in the right place. The message at the bottom says to 'try the scones.'"

"How odd. That's precisely what I thought it said." With a shrug, he took the offered pastry, then a bite, and in the next moment he looked at it with wonder.

The magic of Mrs. Darden's scones.

"Brandon?" a lilting voice called from the corridor. "Brother, where have you gone?"

At once Daniel stood straighter, turning to face the door, his cheeks abruptly ruddy.

Then the voice's owner appeared. She was a lovely young woman with porcelain skin, glossy black hair, and eyes a pale, clear blue that lit with recognition on Daniel. And then came a stunning smile. "Mr. Prescott, surely that is not you, for you have grown ancient since we last met."

"Meg." Her name came out on a strangled breath and then Daniel stumbled over a correction. "Miss Stredwick, you haven't altered one bit."

She set her hands on her hips, arching a winged brow in indignation. "A fine thing to say. When we last met, I was still in braids."

"And climbing a tree, if I recall."

"Well, you climbed it first. I wanted to show you that girls are just as good at climb—"

"Meg, you are in a room of strangers to whom you should be introduced," Lord Hulworth said with fond exasperation as he made the introductions, then added, "I see that I have clearly wasted a fortune on finishing school."

By the dazed look in Daniel's eyes, it was clear he did not agree. And if Briar wasn't mistaken, she might have just witnessed a rather substantial spark.

BRIAR SPENT the morning in the parlor with her new acquaintances. By the time Lord Hulworth had sampled his third scone, London's most elusive bachelor seemed to warm to the idea of filling out an application.

And it was all because of Nicholas.

Late in the afternoon she went out to the small garden— once the scene of her infamous blunder—and sat beneath an arbor, heavy with overblown roses, the sound of bees thick in the warm, breezeless air.

But her thoughts and feelings were too scattered to enjoy the scenery.

The ones lingering in her mind were indignant, railing against a man who would go behind his cousin's back instead of allowing him to decide his own future, and warning her that he was a rake. *The wrong sort.* Yet the others—the ones in her heart—clutched their bosoms and sighed about a man who would make chocolate all day, clean all night, and even send his friend to her doorstep in the hopes that she might make a match for him. Just as she'd proclaimed that first day they'd met.

He was going back to the beginning. How could she not love that?

Yet, before she could form a complete, thoughtful answer, Temperance arrived.

She flew down the garden path and smothered Briar in an embrace. "Had I known that Mr. Cartwright was living in the same house where you . . ." Her voice broke and she sniffled. Drawing back, she revealed eyes that were wet and filled with tea-colored remorse. "I'm so very sorry. If I'd told you where we were going, you never would have endured that pain."

"There is no need to apologize. How could you have known, when not even I knew until that very moment?" Briar soothed her friend's worries.

"And yet, if I'd have been forthcoming with my growing fondness for your half brother, you still might have been spared."

Briar looked down at her hands, having given the matter much thought in the past few days. "Your growing fondness had nothing to do with it. I very much wanted to get better acquainted with Mr. Cartwright. I still do, in fact. But when I saw the house, a pain that I unknowingly buried suddenly came forth in a rather unexpected and dramatic fashion. I feel like a ninny, thinking back on it. But it was your cousin"—Briar's heart quickened again, her heart lodging in her throat—"who helped me by letting me pour out every bit of it until it was all said."

She swallowed and drew in a steadying breath, the rest of the memory warming her.

Last night, she'd spoken with Ainsley about their half siblings, expressing a desire to invite them here for tea one afternoon. Her sister—while still holding on to her own reservations—had agreed to send an invitation when Mr. Cartwright was next in town.

"Besides," Briar continued, smiling at her friend, "part of me is glad you did not tell me. For I was able to see your happiness untainted by my own confused feelings on the matter. And if I had confessed that to you, then you might never have begun exchanging letters with him, and the spark I saw between you would have faded out of existence."

"I did feel something the instant I saw him. It was as if I had known him for all the years of my life and he was only now returning into my company. Does that sound strange to you?"

"To me? Do you forget who you're talking to?" Briar laughed quietly, but felt a wistful sigh pinch her heart. A day ago, her answer would have been much different, dire even. Yet, today, she felt more like herself—but a newer, wiser version. "If I have learned one thing, it is that nothing is guaranteed. You must seize happiness when it is upon you, and hold fast."

A sob escaped Temperance, her eyes brimming again, her mouth spread in a broad smile. "I was hoping you would say something like that. Oh, I just knew you would understand. But what about your own happiness?"

Briar shook her head, her thoughts still preoccupied with everything she'd learned. She hadn't come to a firm conclusion on what she would say to Nicholas.

"Do you think you can ever forgive my cousin?"

"It is not my place to forgive him. It is your brother's."

"But for Nicholas to betray Daniel in such a way . . ." Temperance expelled a long drawn-out sigh.

"Surely *you* can forgive your cousin," Briar prodded. "You've said yourself that he has always been selfless with his affection and caring toward you. I've never seen a man who loves and dotes on his family more."

It was true and she'd seen it firsthand. He was loyal to them as well, if not a bit misguided. He certainly would never turn his back on them

"Oh, I hated her from the very first day," Temperance admitted, suddenly smiling. "So did mother. It was almost a relief when she was gone. If not for Daniel's melancholy, I would have dusted the entire episode from my hands."

"Then why were you being so hard on your cousin just now?"

"I was only attempting to show you support. After all, you're the one who's making him grovel."

Briar scoffed. *"Grovel."*

"I cannot fathom what else you'd call it." Temperance eyed her knowingly. "I mean, he followed your carriage all the way from Hampshire, waited in front of the agency for nearly a day, came here to make you chocolate because he knows it's your favorite. He *made* it himself, Briar, when he could have hired a servant to buy it and bring it here, instead."

"See here, how do you know all this?"

"Adams told me on the way," she said with a half shrug. "But I already knew something was between you from the beginning. After all, you're not the only one who can spot a spark."

"I thought I'd hid my feelings rather well." At least until he'd come to Holliford Park, then she was all over him like ants on a secret stash of comfits.

Temperance shook her head as if she were talking to a dimwit. "Not you, silly. Nicholas. I've seen the change in him all along. Whenever you were near, his eyes turned all soft and dark."

Briar swallowed, trying not to think about how much she loved it when he looked at her that way. "They're always dark."

"I also knew because he asked you to marry him," Temperance said quietly. "He's never done that before. Not even the first time."

"That wasn't a proposal. That was a moment of panic," Briar said, indignant.

"Because he was afraid of losing you. He couldn't imagine his life without you."

"Now you're just putting words in his mouth. He always went out of his way to tell me that he would never marry. I was the one who filled my head with romantic scenarios, not him."

Aside from that brief slip of the tongue in the kitchen, he'd never once told her he loved her. And yet, the thoughts in her brain that had been shaking fisted hands a moment ago weren't so indignant any longer. In fact, they had defected to her heart.

"Then why didn't you give him an answer?"

"I did."

Temperance shook her head, adamant. "Adams told me, and he was there for the whole thing."

"Well, 'no' was implied, then." There hadn't been any point in answering when she knew he wasn't sincere.

"Hmm . . . I don't think he understood. Perhaps that's all the two of you need, just to settle things once and for all. Simply meet with him and give him your answer."

"Are you going to badger me about this?" Briar crossed her arms.

Temperance grinned. "Until the end of your days."

Chapter 35

"It is such a happiness when good people get together—and they always do."

JANE AUSTEN, *Emma*

Today was the day.

Briar's fingers fumbled with the clasp of her cloak as she gave the red leather book a cursory glance. "I don't know why I'm so nervous. I know he wasn't serious and he isn't even likely to renew his addresses. And if he does so out of some perceived obligation, all I have to do is say *no*, and then leave. We'll part amicably, the way that Uncle Ernest does with his . . . *friends*."

Mother did not agree this time. She knew it would be difficult.

"Yes. I know that, too." Briar rubbed the place over her heart where it pinched uncomfortably. "I cannot imagine why his missive said for us to meet at dawn, unless he means to have it all over and done before anyone is aware."

She squeezed her eyes shut, trying to stop the dark scenarios that filled her head. "He's sending Adams with the carriage, but I didn't dare tell Ainsley or Uncle Ernest. So, I'm simply sneaking out, like before. And when I return, no one will be the wiser."

That was for the best. After this morning, she'd be able

to forge ahead with the rest of her life. And in time—a long, *long* time in the future—she'd be able to look back on this and sigh with fond remembrance.

At the door, she looked over her shoulder. "Wish me luck."

Briar was certain she would need it.

She crept quietly downstairs and slipped outside, careful to leave the door on the latch. A filmy layer of fog greeted her in the gray light, but nothing to keep her from seeing Adams perched atop the carriage.

He tipped his hat to her. "Morning, Miss Bourne."

"And to you, Mr. Adams," she said, but was surprised that he didn't come down to help her inside. However, in the next instant, she learned the reason.

Nicholas came out of the carriage, his tall frame unfolding before her, and her heart lurched. His expression gave nothing away, his dark eyes searching. "I thought we could have our conversation in the carriage, if that is agreeable to you."

She wobbled a nod, and reached out to put her hand in his. She was relieved she was wearing gloves because she didn't think she would be able to take having one last touch of skin on skin.

Inside, she settled her skirts and carefully avoided looking at the man across from her. But it was rather difficult when he picked up a parcel from beside him and held it in his lap. It was covered in brown paper and tied with silk ribbons in an array of vibrant colors—red, blue, green, and violet.

Suddenly, she recalled the jest she'd made to him about returning her heart in a box wrapped in silk ribbons and filled with rose petals.

The organ beneath her breast twisted feebly.

"Perhaps this wasn't a good idea, after all. Whatever

we have to say could surely be said in a letter." Yet, just as she started to reach for the door, the carriage jolted into motion.

"I'm afraid you're wrong. What I have to say cannot be said in a letter."

That's right, she forgot he had abominable handwriting. So she supposed it was better this way.

"Very well, then. I'm listening." She sat up straighter, keeping her eyes on the box as if it were a coiled serpent ready to strike at any moment.

He thrummed his fingers hollowly against the sides, taunting her. "You seem rather curious about what I'm holding."

"Not at all."

He chuckled warmly. "Coward."

Her gaze flashed up to his, meeting the velvety cocoa of his irises. "You have always been one to speak your thoughts and wishes plainly. So I imagined that, should you like me to know what is inside, you would tell me."

"Valid point." He thrummed his fingers again. "Inside are some of my most prized possessions. Would you like to see them?"

"Only if you want to—"

He put the box on her lap. "Open it, Briar. We haven't much time. Adams isn't going to drive around all morning."

Apparently, Nicholas was just as eager to get this over with.

She swallowed down a sudden bubble of sadness, tasting the flavor of what might have been. Hands still trembling like before, she pulled on the ribbons, untying each of them before unfolding the paper. Then, lifting the lid of the box, she found it full of rose petals and that bubble of sadness rose up her throat once more, threatening to come forth on a sob.

But on closer inspection, she noticed there was something intermingled with the fragrant dark red, and she delved her hand in to see what it was. Her gloves. The ones with the ink stain.

Perplexed, she looked up at him, only to have him nod toward the box. "There's more. Keep digging."

And she did. She pulled out a blue ribbon, which she'd apparently left behind after her night at Almack's. Several hairpins, the reminder of losing them inside this carriage causing her to blush. The tip of an arrow, from when her shot had gone astray. And one embroidered stocking. "You kept this for me, all this time?"

He shook his head, a smirk curled into the corner of his mouth. "Not for you. As I said, those are *my* prized possessions."

"Nicholas, you know very well that they are mine."

"No, indeed. I recall finding each one of those objects after some of the happiest moments of my life. Except for the blue ribbon. You can keep that one." He reached for the box.

She tugged it back, a laugh slipping past the sob still waiting to come out. "I'm keeping them all. They were my moments, too."

"Tell you what, I'll give you each one of those items in exchange for lessons."

She eyed him, affronted. "Do you think I'm still in need of lessons?"

"No. But I am," he said, his gaze earnest, tender. "I want to continue my studies with the most exceptional tutor an unlearned man could ever know. You see, you've been giving me lessons all along. You've been teaching me how to fall in love, how love should truly be. I never understood it before I met you."

Stunned into stillness, she let him take the box from her and set it down. "Are you saying that you . . ."

"Love you," he finished for her. Then, just in case he wasn't perfectly clear, he said it again. "I never stood a chance, you know. How could I resist falling in love with a carriage appropriator, creator of *cup of chocolate* kisses, born matchmaker, secret scone baker, and fish catcher? And now, I cannot imagine a life without you. I had a glimpse of it these past few days and I couldn't bear it. That's why I need the lessons."

"I think you're doing remarkably well on your own," she said, breathless and smiling.

"Do you?" He took her hands, threading his fingers with hers. "I was hoping that each object in that box would provide payment for a decade's worth of lessons. The hairpins alone would give me fifty years, add in the stocking and the—*oof!*"

She launched herself across the carriage at him, scattering kisses all over his face, and taking special care to nuzzle the nook of his nose. "Yes, I'll be your tutor. I'll teach you how to fall in love, and how to be loved in return every single day. I'll be the best tutor you've ever had. It will cause a scandal, of course—with you coming to the agency all the time for your lessons. But I'm willing to live with it."

He drew back, his expression serious. "Briar, you know that I'm asking you to marry me."

"Marry you? I couldn't possibly. I'm already married to my work as a matchmaker. In addition to that, I've just acquired a new position as tutor to an irredeemable rake. I'll be quite busy for the next few decades."

"If that's how you want it, then reach into my pocket and throw the special license out the window," he said as he began to nibble on her throat, ignoring her gasp. "I'll just hold on to my grandmother's ring. And, of course, we'll have to drop by the church to tell Temperance to stop scattering rose petals on the steps. We'll send the harpist home. Your sister and uncle were due to arrive as well. The wedding breakfast will go to waste . . ."

She cupped his face, staring down at him in wonder. "You arranged all that?"

His shy nod was so sweet her heart nearly burst from too much love. "I wanted to save you from needing to invent a perfect scenario."

Nicholas was the only one who understood her wild heart. And she knew with utter certainty that he would cherish and protect it, the same way she would his. All the days of their lives. "I think I'm still in need of lessons from *you*."

"Tell you what," he began, his momentary shyness giving way to his rakish grin, "for every kiss you give me, I'll give you something in return."

"*Hmm* . . . a most irresistible proposal."

And so she kissed him.

Epilogue

"He had made his fortune, bought his house, and obtained his wife; and was beginning a new period of existence, with every probability of greater happiness than in any yet passed through."

JANE AUSTEN, *Emma*

Four years later

Nicholas glanced to the rosewood clock in his study and frowned, expecting Briar home by now. "Any sign of her, Delham?"

"Nothing yet, my lord," the butler said, his usual monotone strained with concern. "Wait a moment . . . yes. I believe I see her ladyship's carriage now."

It never failed. Whenever Nicholas heard those words, his lungs expanded on a heady rush of joy, his heart drumming faster. He usually met her at the door or even on the pavement, anticipation always getting the better of him, but today, he had to keep to his chair.

Everything had to be perfect.

Picking up the paper, he got into position, but found an errant rose petal on his desk. Damn, he'd missed one. Snatching it from the blotter, he tucked it into his waistcoat pocket. And just in time.

"Good evening, Delham."

Briar's soft voice reached Nicholas and an automatic grin tugged at his mouth as he posed again, rustling the paper.

"And to you as well, my lady. The children are with Mrs. Cartwright," Delham said, uncharacteristically verbose, before clearing his throat. "Pleasant day at the agency?"

Hold it together, man. Don't give us away, Nicholas thought. While the butler possessed the countenance of a gargoyle, he was pure pudding inside, especially when it came to Briar.

"It was an exceptionally good day," she said brightly. "Is my husband in his study?"

No sooner had she asked the question, then Nicholas heard the hastened patter of her slippers over the stone floor.

"I'm home, my love," she said, skirting around his desk in a rustle of blue and pressing a velvety kiss to his cheek. "Did you not hear?"

Nicholas drew in a pleased breath, filling his lungs with her scent. It took every ounce of control to keep the paper in place and not turn his head and take the kiss he'd been craving since she left this morning.

Feigning absorption in the latest news, he turned the page, his grip tightening, his knuckles white-edged. "Good day at the agency?"

"Hmm . . . strange. Delham asked me the same thing."

"I don't see what's odd about that." Nicholas clenched his jaw. *Hang it all, Delham, she's on to us!* He lowered a corner of the paper and watched her discreet attempts of searching the desk. "What are you looking for?"

She closed the last drawer, a frown tucked into the corners of her mouth. "Oh, nothing. I just thought you'd have a flower for me. You usually do when I come home with the news that I've made another match."

"Have you? Well, that's capital." He folded the paper and set it aside before pulling her onto his lap, his pulse thrumming contentedly.

She sighed, absently plucking at his waistcoat buttons. "And you really don't have a flower for me?"

"If you'd like one, I'll pick a rose from the garden right this instant."

"No, it's fine. I suppose I shouldn't expect one every time I make a match, not even if today happened to be my one hundredth success."

"I thought it was one hundred last time."

"No."

He shrugged, trying like hell not to grin, but she was so pretty when she pouted. "Well, that's a milestone, isn't it? You definitely deserve a flower for that. Perhaps even two."

"You gave me an entire bouquet of roses when it was fifty."

"Did I?"

"Nicholas, you know you did. And I'm certain you could not forget what we did with the petals," she said in a whisper, her cheeks tinged pink.

"Ah yes. And the silk ribbons." He lifted her hand and pressed a kiss to the inside of her wrist, her fluttering pulse meeting his lips at the shared memory. "Perhaps we can try that again this evening. Do you want to be tied up, love? While I do all sorts of wicked things . . ."

Her breath caught and she swayed for a moment, the curves of her body molding against him.

Then she pulled her hand free and stood up, smoothing her skirts. "No. I think I'll just drive over to my brother's house and pick up the children. Temperance will surely be excited about my achievement."

"I'm afraid she'll be disappointed because I gave her leave to keep them overnight."

On the opposite side of the desk, Briar stopped, pivoting on her heels as twin spheres of cornflower blue narrowed in thorough scrutiny. "Whyever would you do that?"

"Because Henry asked if he could, and you know how fond he is of his cousin," he said offhandedly. "Why, he and George are like brothers. And since Tecnse doesn't yet have a girl of her own, she loves to dote on little Heloise."

To his own ears, the excuse sounded believable and he thought he might have fooled her. But then, the unmistakable strain of a violin being tuned drifted in through the window. He tensed. The string quartet should have already finished with that by now.

"What was that noise?"

"I don't know what you mean."

But he could see by the knowing glint in her eyes that she was on to him. Clasping her hands, she left the study. "Delham, did you hear something?"

Nicholas followed and caught sight of color rising to his butler's cheeks.

"*Hear*, did you say? I'm afraid I'm deaf as a turnip, my lady."

Pathetic, Nicholas thought, rolling his eyes to the ceiling as Delham slinked out of the foyer.

Briar turned, a knowing grin on her lips as she poked him in the center of his chest. "You do have a surprise for me, don't you?"

Only thousands of rose petals poised to rain down on her over the terrace, a candlelit dinner, dancing, and whatever else her heart desired.

He smiled. "Well it isn't every day when London's finest matchmaker can claim one hundred matches."

"What is it? No, don't tell me. I just want to bask in this moment and say that I could not possibly love you more." She launched herself into his arms and he spun her in a circle, getting drunk on the sound of her laugh. Then, when he set her on her feet, her expression turned playfully serious. "Though, I should be cross with you for teasing me."

"Is that so?"

She nodded, her warm gaze resting on his mouth. "You owe me recompense."

His blood quickened. This was one of their favorite games. "Shall I settle up now, or after your surprise?"

Briar grinned and took him by the hand, leading him toward the stairs. "Yes, Nicholas."

Ainsley Bourne loves running the business side of the Bourne Matrimonial Agency from their St. James's townhouse. She does *not* like the unsavory, scandalous things that occur at the gaming hell and boxing club across the street. And she absolutely *loathes* Reed Sterling, the huge, handsome former prizefighter who owns it.

She thinks he's a devilish brute. He thinks she's an uptight spinster. Neither is willing to admit their constant arguments simmer with unrequited attraction.

Let the games begin . . .

The Rogue to Ruin

The final Misadventures in Matchmaking novel
Coming Summer 2019!

And be sure to grab Jacinda and Crispin's story . . .

How to Forget a Duke

Available now!

*Next month, don't miss these exciting
new love stories only from
Avon Books*

Governess Gone Rogue by Laura Lee Gurhke
James St. Clair, the Earl of Kenyon, knows his
wild young sons need a tutor, a man tough
enough to make his hellions toe the line, and
James is determined to find one. Miss Amanda
Leighton knows she has all the qualifications to
be a tutor. And while female tutors are unheard
of, Amanda isn't about to lose the chance at her
dream job. If Lord Kenyon insists on hiring a
man, then she has only one option . . .

Moonlight Scandals by Jennifer L. Armentrout
Even a ghost hunter like Rosie Herpin couldn't
have foreseen the fateful meeting between two
mourners that has brought her so intimately
close to the notorious Devlin de Vincent.
Everyone in New Orleans knows he's heir to a
dark family curse that both frightens and
enthralls. To the locals, Devlin is the devil.
To Rosie, he's a man who's stoking her wildest
fantasies.

Discover great authors, exclusive offers,
and more at hc.com.

REL 0119